Terror filled the outlaw One Ear's eyes and he shuddered at the looming wrath looking down at him. "The name of your general?" Gath demanded. "The castle you attack?"

"Nobody knows!" One Ear pleaded.

"Your tribe? The location of your war camp?"

One Ear's face lost all color. "Don't ask me that!"

The Barbarian tightened his grip on One Ear's face, and the jaw bones shifted in their sockets, threatening to break.

"All right!" mumbled the outlaw. "It's to the east, ten, twelve days' ride, in Barma High Country."

"The castle?"

"Let me go and I'll tell you."

Gath let go of the face and One Ear opened his mouth to speak, but shrieked in pain instead. Flames burst from the red spot on his brow, and his skull split apart under his flesh, tearing it open. Killing him instantly.

Gath pushed away, rising, and stared in horror. The outlaw's own dark magic had silenced him.

also by James Silke
published by Tor Books

FRANK FRAZETTA'S DEATH DEALER BOOK 1:
Prisoner of the Horned Helmet

FRANK FRAZETTA'S DEATH DEALER BOOK 2:
Lord of Destruction

FRANK FRAZETTA'S DEATH DEALER BOOK 3:
Tooth and Claw

FRANK FRAZETTA'S DEATH DEALER

BOOK 4
PLAGUE OF KNIVES

JAMES SILKE

TOR
fantasy

A TOM DOHERTY ASSOCIATES BOOK
NEW YORK

PLAGUE OF KNIVES

Copyright © 1990 by James R. Silke

Artwork and Death Dealer character copyright © 1990 by Frank Frazetta

A Tor Book
Published by Tom Doherty Associates, Inc.
49 West 24th Street
New York, N.Y. 10010

Cover art by Frank Frazetta

ISBN: 0-812-50332-5

First edition: June 1990

Printed in the United States of America

0 9 8 7 6 5 4 3 2 1

For my wife, Lyn, who knows
what it takes to hold center stage
and give your dreams away.
                              —James Silke

One

THE HAMMER

He rode out of a stand of pines, and slowly cut a dark path through the blanket of snow with a precision and pace born of inevitability, like blood passing through a vein on its way to an open wound. Dead ahead, a plume of red-orange flame rose off the white mountainside, a burning house wagon.

Except for his bald, oval head, fur robes covered him, and he sat his horse with the motionless sobriety of a monument posed on a pedestal, carrying his forty-two years the way time carries history. His smooth, hairless, almost shiny flesh was a pale walnut, his features level and flat, a mask of indifference. But the pale gold eyes behind the slits moved furtively. Hunting. Observing. Measuring.

Reining up on a spread of bald earth ten strides short of the blazing wagon, he watched it burn, like a man enchanted by a troupe of dancers.

Red and orange flames spread down the spokes of its garish pink wheels, scurried along empty traces, climbed the yellow and vermilion sideboards. The vehicle's gaudy paint bubbled and smoked, and the fire reached the baskets and bundles heaped on the roof. They crackled and came apart, sending flames twenty feet into the air, bright red and orange tongues licking the gray winter sky.

The rider's expression did not change, except for the warm light caressing it.

A side of the wagon fell away, and the body of a man came with it, crashed lifelessly to the ground. A dagger stuck in his back, dark against the blaze of his shiny yellow blouse.

Within the wagon, a line of masks, hanging on the interior wall, stared through the smoke and flames. Clown masks wearing comic and tragic faces. Feather boas, bangles and beads hung beside them. Tambourines, a huge drum and racks of costumes crowded the floor. The drum exploded. The flames soared, contorting the masks into grotesque expressions, and the wagon collapsed amid sheets of sparks and flaming debris.

The rider waited for the flames to die down, then walked his mount through the rivulets of melting snow and smoking rubble.

Beyond the wreckage, the remnant of a camp lay scattered over the exposed earth. Three bodies occupied it. One was alive, a thin man with long rubbery limbs, wearing the bright red tights and jerkin of an actor. Heaving with grief, the performer squatted beside what appeared to be his two dead comrades, a small brown bear wearing a bright red collar with a yellow ruffle, and a chubby but pretty girl. Her flower-print skirt had been pushed up over her naked hips, and dirty handprints marked her thighs.

Unobserved, the rider walked his mount closer to the scene of slaughter and reined up, his expression suddenly betraying mild interest.

Black-handled daggers stood erect in the chests of both the animal and girl. Markers left by their murderers.

The rider glanced around warily, listening.

The Great Barma Range rose in all directions, its white peaks glistening in the sunshine above the treeline. The mountains stretched from the Great Forest Basin, nearly a moon's ride to the west, to the northern border of the Kitzakk Empire, three days' ride to the east. Savage tribes and outlaw bands roamed this land, but there was no sound, except for the wind singing in the tops of the pines and the flutter of the dying flames, no sign of danger, except for trails left by the killers' horses in the snow. He dismounted, looped the reins around the pommel of his saddle, and faced the actor, confident that his furs and masklike face hid his identity.

The performer looked up, blinking. Wrinkles plowed the high forehead of his once handsome head. Yellow stained his once dashing mustache. Surprise showed in his moist eyes, and he nodded in somber greeting. Then his head dropped and he continued to weep.

Squatting beside the dead girl, the rider ran a fingertip along the cherublike beauty of her pallid face. Then he covered her nakedness, removed the knife from her fat breast and wiped it clean on her skirt. Studying it, he turned his back on the older man, dipped a finger into the neck of his tunic and withdrew a ring strung on a silver chain. He held it up to the dagger. The handle of the weapon and the stone in the ring were black onyx, and each was carved in the shape of a young voluptuous girl. A naked savage writhing in total abandon.

His masklike face moved slightly, forming the subtlest of smiles. He had no idea who the figure represented, if anyone, but the touch of the knife, like that of the ring, stirred his blood with sensual hunger, a sensation long denied him.

He returned the ring to its hiding place and, standing, turned to the actor.

"Who were they?" The entertainer looked up, shocked by the sound of the rider's soft, low voice. "Tell me, old man! Quickly. I have no time to waste."

"I . . . I don't know. They, they just rode up and attacked us. For no reason."

"Soldiers? Outlaws? Priests?"

"Outlaws, I suppose. They were filthy, and their eyes were wild. As if their minds were gone."

"Why did they spare you?"

"They didn't. I was in the trees gathering wood. They struck my friends down and rode off before I could return. They never saw me."

"What did they take?"

"Nothing," he looked down at the dead girl, "except their pleasure with my Thalma, and the horses." He looked back. "But those were afterthoughts. All they really wanted was to kill us. Just like the others."

"Others?" The rider squatted, his eye slits white with curiosity.

"Yes," the actor said bitterly. "These are dark days for

the likes of us. Terrible. There was a troupe of twenty players murdered at Upper Crow, and others at Leege and on the road to Covilla. And now,'' he paused as if unable to continue, then added quietly, ''the black daggers are everywhere! Not only cutting down minstrels and traveling shows, but anyone who can dance a jig and bang a tambourine. It's like a plague, as if the demons wanted to destroy all the stories, all the songs.''

''Demons? Sorcery?''

''What else could it be?''

The rider held up the black-handled dagger, displaying its voluptuous handle, and the old performer nodded.

''Yes. The daggers are part of it. The assassins always leave them behind, so everyone will know it was them. They're proud of what they do. The filth!''

''You're going after them?''

The old man looked at the girl, tears again welling in his eyes, and shook his head. ''I'm too old to play the avenging hero. I'll bury her and her bear, then retire. The open road is meaningless to me now. There's a castle, a sanctuary for aging minstrels, five days north. I'll hole up there until they drive me out. Then I'll do what we all do, I guess.'' He smiled fatalistically at the rider. ''But it won't be pretty, sir. Dying is the poorest scene my kind play. There will be no parade, no pomp and glory for me, like there will be for you.''

''You know me?''

''Oh yes, General. You're not easily forgotten.''

''I fear you are mistaken.'' The rider stood with deliberate casualness. ''Surely we have never met.''

''No, not face-to-face. But I saw you enter Harchacka after the siege. You were riding an elephant all covered with bright silks and gold, parading your troops through the city before you set it to the torch.''

''Harchacka!'' Caution tightened the rider's mouth.

''Yes! I was there.'' The performer stood unevenly. ''I was one of the three hundred inhabitants you spared. And I'll always be grateful to you for that, sir. Always. I've offered prayers a thousand times in the name of Izzam Ghapp.''

The rider's masklike face suddenly became animated, frowning.

"Oh!" the old actor gasped. "Forgive me." A shudder ran through him and he clasped his hands together in front of his chest. "I'm sorry. I wasn't thinking. I shouldn't have said your name aloud." He glanced around at the empty hillside. "An important man like you, riding alone this far from Kitzakk territory, surely doesn't want to be recognized. I'll not say your name again. I'll forget we met."

Ghapp nodded casually. "Thank you, that would be wise." He scuffed the ground with the heel of his boot, testing its hardness. "I'll help you bury your friends. The ground is frozen, and I have a pickaxe in my saddlebags."

"Oh, no, sir. That wouldn't be right, you being a general and all, and I've got my own pickaxe, if it hasn't burned."

Izzam Ghapp nodded agreement. The actor grinned timidly and turned toward the smoking rubble, presenting his back to the general. With one stride, Ghapp reached him, drawing his long thin knife, and caught him by the chin. Setting his feet wide, Ghapp yanked the older man back and drove the blade under his left shoulder blade. It was a sure, swift death stroke, one he had learned long ago as a child. But the knife hit the shoulder blade and sheared across it, missing the heart.

The entertainer screamed and thrashed. Scowling with chagrin, Ghapp kicked the actor's legs from under him. The old man fell, his face meeting the ground, and rolled over on his back among the flaming embers, stunned. His hair and blouse bristled with flames, and his eyes opened wide, accompanied by a howl of pain.

Ghapp dropped on him, driving the knife into his flaming chest, this time on target. The man gasped, went limp and Ghapp leapt to his feet, backed out of the embers, knife in hand.

Color stained his round cheeks. Excitement animated them. The murder was a simple act of duty and necessity: he had been ordered by the high priest in the Temple of Dreams to travel alone and keep his presence secret no matter what the cost. Nevertheless, the act released long-dormant instincts and pleasures which for the moment drove off his troubles, destroyed his mask.

In a last convulsion, the old actor twisted fitfully, trying to avoid the flames, and fell over on his face, one leg shuddering and mouth agape. His clothing burned brightly. His charred hair smoked, the black stink rising in lazy spires.

Izzam's cheeks lost their color, and he took a step back, dropping his knife.

Something writhed within the smoke, something tormented and beautiful. Then he saw what it was. His ghosts. They crawled from the bloody gaping mouth of the dead man, fled through the flames, floated and convulsed in the smoke. The ghosts of screaming girls and women trapped in the cities he had put to the torch. Beautiful, panic-stricken, crazed women. They ran wildly along the ramparts, down the alleys and through the corridors of blazing castles, their long tresses flaming behind them. Others lay crumpled in the narrow, walled streets, their lovely breasts stitched with arrows. Still more struggled under fallen towers, their fair bodies crushed but alive. Screaming. Pleading for pity. But there was none. The loveliest women lay stretched over wine barrels, naked, with sweaty soldiers convulsing and grunting above them, their armor and chain mail gouging thighs and bellies. Mouths agape and screaming, eyes wild with terror and pain, the ghosts all screamed his name over and over, as if the castles and cities themselves howled for mercy. The ghosts of his yesterdays.

Only a few years earlier, he had relished cries of torment. They were the heralds of victory. Now they haunted him. Filled him with emotions he detested, emotions no soldier could tolerate. Pity. Compassion. Mercy.

Izzam Ghapp turned away. It was their fault. His ghosts had made him hesitate, made him miss the actor's heart just as they had made him hesitate as a general, made him indecisive, made him lose his command to younger generals, while he, the Hammer of the Kitzakk Horde, its legendary Siegemaster, rotted in the military academy of Tamaal, talking of old campaigns, using words instead of catapults and siege towers, words that only made his ghosts stronger.

He leapt onto his horse and kicked the animal into a trot, grateful for the feel of movement. Eager, desperate to rid himself of his memories. When he reached his destination, he would gratefully accept whatever task his new employer offered him, even if it was no more than a puny tribal feud. Action was his only cure now. Bloodshed. Battle. War.

Two
PINWHEEL CROSSING

Billbarr tied the reins of the wagon around the brake handle, stood on the seat of the driver's box and jumped off the wagon, doing a somersault in the air. Fleka, sitting in the driver's box, and the huge black bear, snoozing in the cage roped to the open bed, took no notice. They had seen his acrobatics all too often.

Shrugging off his disappointment, the boy climbed back beside the girl and squatted on the seat. Spikes of chestnut hair, as thick and straight as nails, bristled from his large head, and a simple brown tunic covered his slight but muscular body of fourteen summers' growth. Fashioning an artfully cheery smile on his boyish face, he inched closer and his knee touched her arm.

She still paid no attention to him. Her elbows rested on her bare knees, and her hands, each finger sporting a brightly painted wooden ring, gripped her freckled cheeks, as if she felt her head might fall off. Her annoyed eyes, outlined with a thick line of kohl, stared under straw-colored bangs at a log inn standing in the sun on a spread of snow-covered ground, separating the roads to the villages of Coin and Weaver.

On the floorboards between the boy and girl, covered by a tattered gray blanket, sat the horned helmet, the headpiece of living metal that belonged to the Death Dealer, to Gath of Baal, their traveling companion. The boy glanced at it, then spoke.

"Stop worrying! He'll be right back."

"What good will that do?" she complained. "You heard what those people said yesterday. This bukko we're looking for, this supposedly brilliant stage manager and his wagons, they haven't been seen in these parts for over a year. The last anyone heard of them, they were headed for someplace over a moon away from here."

"The Barma Mountains."

"Yes, the Barma Mountains! At the other end of the world! We'll never find them there. But you know him, he's going to try." She sank back against the backboard and folded her arms under her small breasts, so that the freckled slopes swelled above the low, red-trimmed collar of her tunic, making them appear twice their size. "He lied to us, Billbarr. He doesn't care about us. All he wants to do is find his old girlfriend and this bukko, Brown John." She frowned at the boy, making her plain face plainer. "You can forget about showing off your fancy dancing bear."

"Fleka," Billbarr pleaded, "stop talking like that. It's just going to take longer than we thought. Besides, the bear can't even dance a jig yet."

"Well, I can." She glared back at the inn, tightening the fringed scarlet sash that belted her pale yellow tunic. "When's he coming out of there, anyway?"

"He just went in," the boy said, exasperated, "and he'll come out when he's found out what he wants to know." He jumped down again, not bothering to show off this time. He kicked through a bank of snow, then stopped, shouted back at her. "I'll be right back."

She glared at him. "You're going to leave me alone again? That's all you do, isn't it?"

"I'm just going to read the marker over there." He pointed across the clearing. "I'll be back in a minute. Just don't touch the helmet, remember?"

"I remember," she mumbled, and scooted a little farther from the headpiece.

Leaping from dry spot to dry spot, Billbarr dashed across Pinwheel Crossing, a large open spread of ground with roads heading off into deep forest in all directions. Reaching the far side, he pushed through a snowdrift to a marker nailed to a stake. It stood directly below a massive rock promontory, thrusting up out of a dense stand of pines, overlooking the crossing. He brushed the snow off the letters carved in the wood, then read them, a smile of magnificent delight instantly growing to proportions too large for his cheeks. Then he dashed back the way he came, doing cartwheels and flips, and climbed into the driver's box, taking the smile with him.

"Guess what?" he exclaimed, then continued, not waiting for Fleka's reply. "That marker, it's all about him! About Gath! That's where he stood." He pointed at the promontory. "On that rock! Three years ago! It happened right here, Fleka. The tribes from all around here, the Barhacha, Kaven, Wowell, Cytherian, Grillard, all of them, from every part of the Great Forest Basin, marched down these roads and gathered in this crossing. All of them! Right here, where we sit now, and they cheered him! Cheered our Gath! Calling him Lord of the Forest, the Dark One, the Death Dealer." The boy shook with excitement. "This is where he formed the Barbarian tribes into an army! Tribes that had never even considered joining together before! Then led them up Amber Road and through the Narrows, the very pass we arrived by. And when they reached the desert, he and his army defeated the entire Kitzakk Horde. They burned the Kitzakk capital, Fleka! Bahaara! The same city where he found you—and me, too. At least that's where we first became friends."

"What are you blabbing about now?"

"He's a champion, Fleka. Gath is famous here. And this bukko, Brown John. He's famous too! He was part of it. The king!"

"Billbarr," she groaned, "I'm tired of your lies."

"It's true!" he blurted. "The words are carved in the marker. And the inn, look!" He pointed at the inn's sign. "It's named after him, the Lord of the Forest. That's what

they called him when he lived in the Shades, the forest where
we caught the bear. And you don't get an inn named after
you unless you're famous.''

"But it doesn't make any sense, Billbarr," Fleka said
firmly. "And neither do the other things you've told me about
him. If he's so famous and important, what was he doing
running with bounty hunters, trying to catch that cat girl in
a godforsaken place like the Daangall? And why'd he take up
with the likes of us, with slaves?''

"We're not slaves anymore! He set us free.''

"Did he?'' she asked cynically.

"Yes, he did,'' the boy said, his tone suddenly wise. "He
hasn't laid a hand on you, Fleka. Not a finger. And that's
why you're upset.''

"That's right,'' she muttered bitterly. "Take his part, just
like you always do.''

"I'm not taking his part. I, well, it's just that we aren't
slaves.''

"I do all the cooking and washing, and I do it when he
wants it done. What do you call that?''

"Yes, I know. But he provides the meat and wine, and he
brought you clothes, a tambourine, beads, everything you
asked for. And I help! I take care of the bear and wagon, and
we all stand guard.''

She made no reply, folding her thin legs under her, and
fondled the jade and agate beads dangling from her scrawny
neck. Then she shook her head. "It still makes no sense. A
man like him, as strong as he is! He could be rich. If he
wanted to, he could own three castles and a dozen villages,
even his own army. But instead, he's chasing after a tribe of
traveling players, trying to find this fancy wench he's so crazy
about. And he'll never find her. Never.''

Billbarr sat silent until she looked at him, then said quietly,
"I think, Fleka, that Gath can find whatever he wants to
find.''

She started to argue, but held her tongue as a figure
emerged from the inn, passed behind the horses and wagon
teams tied to the front railing, and stepped into the sun. Gath
of Baal. A dark fur wrap covered his broad shoulders. Knife-

cut black hair tossed on a breeze beside the blunt features of his handsome head. Belts for sword, dagger and satchels crisscrossed his square hips. His booted feet parted the snow with loose, easy strides as he approached the wagon and mounted the black stallion tethered to a wheel.

"Which road do we take?" Billbarr asked.

"Guess," Fleka said bitterly.

Ignoring her, the Barbarian said, "Amber Road, to the north, then east on Silk Road."

"To the Barma Mountains?" the boy said, anticipating the man.

Gath of Baal nodded. "The innkeeper said the same thing. The last anyone's seen of Brown John and the Grillard wagons, they were headed that way."

"But those mountains are weeks away," Fleka moaned. "And these Grillards haven't returned to their village for the winter, something they've never done before. You said it yourself. They could be dead, and if they're not, somebody could be killing them right now!"

Ignoring her outburst, Gath said to Billbarr, "We'll ride as long as we can see the road, then camp in the forest." He untied a satchel from his saddle horn, tossed it to Fleka. "You better skin the meat while there's still light."

Fleka, nodding reluctantly, caught the satchel with both hands and sat back, her face in a frump. Gath turned his horse north, prodded it, and Billbarr flicked the reins of the wagon. The huge draft horse lowered its head and pulled, yanking the wagon free of the mud, and started after the Barbarian.

Billbarr gave Fleka a reassuring smile, and she deliberately ignored it. Then, as was her style, she pulled her tunic a little lower over her breasts, knowing that would delight the boy and let him know she wasn't as mad as she acted. Grinning, the boy sat back, the reins firm in his small hands, and put his eyes on the Barbarian's huge back.

It seemed to Billbarr that his large friend was now sculpted, not only from mountains and night shadows, but from indomitable resolve, the kind of resolve with which the wolf and lion survive the long winter. The kind by which a great adventure so often begins.

Three
DALS, KRAMS AND SCALING LADDERS

Izzam Ghapp walked his horse through the narrow pass into the hidden valley and smiled. His destination finally lay before him.

Dark muddy roads cut across the valley's flat, snow-white floor, heading like the spokes of a twisted wheel toward a palisade wall defending a large camp spread in front of a tier of rock ledges. There, black tents billowed on the breeze, their undulating bodies dark and forbidding in the late-day sunshine. The tents of the outlaw Jani, the shadow people whom some believed were the chosen assassins of the Lord of Death.

A horn sounded, blown by the lookout in the camp's signal tower. Instantly, bearded Jani warriors in black furs and bright steel armor rode out of the gate, the hooves of their thick-chested horses clattering on the log road that bisected the camp.

Eager for the rattle and scream of combat, even if it meant commanding these simpleminded, foul-smelling, savage outlaws, and catering to their goddess, a woman old and wrinkled as time itself, Izzam Ghapp rode on, his mask in place, moving as serenely as a shadow cast by a passing cloud.

Annoyed by his imperturbable calm, the sentries circled him, and the red spots on their foreheads began to glow and smoke as they shouted curses, threatened him with spears.

Betraying no annoyance, the Kitzakk answered their abusive questions by displaying the black ring with the voluptuous goddess carved in it. Seeing it, the guards fell silent and backed their horses away, allowing him to pass.

Ghapp tucked the ring back in place, walked his horse through the puzzled bandits and rode through the gate into the Jani camp.

Plank trails led off the log road, reaching across the muddy yard to raised, wooden platforms. There hammers clanged against sparking anvils as blacksmiths shaped sharp-edged weapons. The racket of saws, axes and mallets filled the center of the yard, where bare-chested woodsmen tramped indifferently through the mud, building wagons and trimming logs into lumber.

One of the mounted guards galloped past Ghapp, hailed an old hag wearing dark rags, and reined up beside her, speaking hurriedly. The old woman promptly motioned at Ghapp to join her.

The general dismounted and tethered his horse to a railing as she started up a footpath toward a log building standing on the highest ridge. As he followed her, Ghapp's quick eyes assessed the camp.

Stacks of spear, pole-axe and sword blades rested on the floors of the blacksmiths' sheds, along with heaps of shovels, pickaxes and barrels of sturdy nails. The weapons appeared to be superbly crafted. The reason was evident. The blacksmiths were not Jani savages, but pale-skinned Oollaar tribesmen, craftsmen of uncommon skill from the high country of Paillitt. Shackles bound their legs and Jani overseers watched them carefully, using long black whips to instruct them in proper work habits.

Liking what he saw, Izzam Ghapp smiled, then suddenly stopped.

On platforms at the far side of the rock ledge, a group of enslaved carpenters, belonging to a tribe he did not recognize, constructed large shields mounted on wheels. The shields were wicker and bound with rattan. A little farther off, more carpenters chiseled points on thick, straight tree trunks, transforming them into battering rams, while others constructed scaling ladders of sturdy bamboo. In the opposite direction, fletchers were hard at work, enslaved Tammbal natives whose homes were twice as far away as his own. They sat cross-legged on mats, tying goose feathers to reed shafts, carving bows from yew wood, making arrowheads. Krams, incendiary arrowheads named after the god of fire which had small cagelike tips to hold burning embers, and dals, crescent-shaped rope cutters.

The Jani were not just preparing for a war, but Izzam Ghapp's kind of war. A siege.

He hurried after the hag, questions raging through his mind. Who and what did they intend to attack? And why? What was the prize?

At the top of the footpath, the old woman waited in front a large wicker cage covered with a dirty blanket. She bowed, with what he thought was a smile moving among her wrinkles, then suddenly pulled the blanket away. Ghapp's masklike face turned cold with horror.

Three men shared the small prison, or rather three creatures which had once been men. One sat with his head slumped against the bars. It was three sizes too big for his body, too heavy for him to lift, and the flesh on his bald head was split, as if his brains were trying to spill through the seams. Another crouched and shook the bars like an ape. Fur grew from the tops of his shoulders and cheeks, and the sores on his legs smoked. The third, a handsome lad with aristocratic bones, sat motionless, staring at nothing. He had no mouth, was starving to death.

The Siegemaster turned sharply on the crone, his eyes demanding explanation. Half-bowing, she hurriedly backed up to the recessed entranceway of the sprawling log house.

Guards in plain leather tunics and steel armor stood at attention beside the entrance, eyes and bodies alert, massive fists holding finely crafted vermilion crossbows. Workmanlike soldiers with brains as single-minded as a castle wall. Disciplined. Or were they enslaved by some magic? Red spots also glowed on their foreheads.

The old woman bowed again, indicating the door. "Please enter, my lord. She awaits you. I will take your coat."

"First, old woman, tell me how your antique goddess is called, here in these mountains?"

"She is the Dagger Queen, more than that I dare not say. Please." She motioned anxiously at his coat. "You were expected many days ago."

Frowning warily, Ghapp removed his fur and handed it to the crone, then entered the covered entryway and faced a low circular door of dark wood.

Its handles were black onyx, crudely carved with the same youthful, voluptuous body of the black bitch who graced the ring and dagger. He took hold of the handle with one hand, and a cold sweat broke out on his palm. He jerked his hand away, but his fingers did not release the handle. He shook and twisted them, but they would not let go. Instead, his grip tightened slowly, and his hand pushed the door open, as his legs, no more obedient than his hand, propelled him inside.

Four
THE DAGGER QUEEN

Smoky shadows, scented with jasmine, musk and sandalwood, greeted him, and his hand let go of the handle, the door thumped closed behind him. The subtle perfumes stirred a long absent ardor in his groin, drawing him along a dirt-floored passageway toward the orange glow of a fire, streaming through a partially opened door at the far end.

Constructed of thick oak timbers, and banded together with silver bars inlaid with amber and jade stones, the circular door shimmered with seductive invitation.

Reaching it, he pushed the door wider, stepped through the round aperture into a circular room.

Flames blazed in a fireplace at its center, casting flickering light over figures mounted in altars recessed in the curving wall. Sculptures of black stone depicting naked couples embracing sensually, each statue demonstrating a different act of carnal worship. A sanctuary for sacrificial offerings of voluptuous pleasure to the Jani's decrepit goddess of lust, the Black Veshta.

He advanced around the fire to another circular door on the opposite side of the room. A smaller altar glowed above it.

It held a doll of a man. A man of medium height with a bald, oval head and no eyebrows. An exact miniature statue of himself. Or was it? There was something different about the doll. Then he saw what it was. Confidence emanated from the tiny figure, the confidence of a ruthless, decisive warrior. The doll was not the image of who he now was, but of who he had been. The Hammer of the Kitzakk Horde.

Shaken, Ghapp took a loose step back and the door swung open in invitation. Beyond it waited a room undulating with hazy golden light coming from dangling oil lamps of brass and gold. Plumes of jasmine, myrrh and sandalwood floated out, swirling past his face, and the last fragment of his will drifted off with them. He entered.

Polished granite formed the ceiling and floor, and ebony screens stood in front of the irregular walls of a cave carved from the rock cliffs. A massive golden dome, set in the ceiling directly above a circular bed, reflected a dazzling spill of jewel-like light over a girl sprawled over the scarlet silk sheet covering the bed.

She lay on her stomach, feet in the air and elbows supporting her. A sealskin robe hid her body, except for bare feet and a head of yellow hair combed in pomaded spikes to form a perfect pyramid. Without bothering to turn and look at Ghapp, she dipped a tiny brush in a clay pot of orchid paint, held out a finger and applied the paint to her long nail, as she spoke in a tart, husky voice.

"Don't stand there trembling, General! Come over here."

She extended a thin arm to the side of the bed, set the tiny brush and clay pot on the floor.

Izzam Ghapp took a step toward the bed and stopped short, transfixed.

Her arm was trim and strong and sensual, more audaciously and tantalizingly nude than any arm had a right to be. She sat up leisurely, accidentally offering him a glimpse of her flat, brown belly. In the gold light, her flesh was a warm walnut, smooth and unblemished. The perfect invitation to the throne of her womanhood, hiding somewhere within the black fur.

Seeing he had not moved, she stood abruptly. "You insect! I did not bring you here to ogle me. Have you never seen a queen before? Or did you expect some idiot savage with her brain between her legs whom you could intimidate!" She stepped forward, studying him, and a mocking smile crept into the tawny flesh of her heart-shaped face. "You did, didn't you? You're exactly what your high priest said you were, aren't you, General Ghapp? A mockery of the man you once were. Impotent in bed as well as in war. You were hoping to find a woman who would be no contest for you. You thought the Black Veshta would be a wrinkled old bag of bones who would break at your touch!"

"Forgive me," he pleaded. "But I was told you were three hundred years old."

"I am," she purred. "But my body is seventeen, General, and will always be seventeen."

Laughing like a flirty girl, she stepped close to him, her eyes bold. Vivid white and pearly gray, they stared over brazen orchid cheeks. Hostile, quarrelsome and playful all at once. Doorways to a mind more cunning and ruthless than a roomful of ambitious generals.

Short and sleek in her dark-skinned robe, she had to look up to meet his eyes. That made her frown. "You're too tall. I don't like men I have to look up at. But that can be changed."

"Changed?" His masklike face twitched with caution.

"Yes," she said with tyrannical casualness. "But that is the least of our problems." She turned away, then looked back over a slick, black shoulder. "You will call me Tiyy, nothing else. I have many names, Niobe, Jamene, the Nymph Queen of Pyram and others. But these days I am known simply as Tiyy, the Dagger Queen of the Jani outlaws. And, except when I am in my quarters here, I dress like one of them. Surprise is essential to my plans." She took another step away, again glanced back. "I trust no one knows you're in the Barma High Country?"

He bowed stiffly. "Only one man, now dead."

"Excellent. Now relax. Even though I find your impotence repulsive, I know it is not your fault. You are simply another victim of her sorcery."

"Sorcery?"

"The White Veshta, the Goddess of Light." Her black-lidded, sloped almond eyes grew fractious. "Your misery is her fault. I knew it as soon as I heard the symptoms. She has twisted your senses, General. Corrupted them."

"But how can this be? I have never been to one of her temples, never seen one."

"It makes no difference," she said crossly. "You can never tell where she might work her arts, at fairs and carnivals, even at campfires and on street corners. Her spells are cast in all kinds of ridiculous ways, which I do not comprehend or wish to. But that is of no importance now." She sat on the edge of the bed and folded her naked legs under her like a sassy girl. "Your priest said you were eager to be the man you once were, to once more command an army worthy of your unusual skills, and that if I found you worthy, and agreed to exorcise your corruption, you would not falter at my price. Is this true?"

Ghapp bowed. "Yes, your holiness."

"Stop bowing," she snapped. "And spare me those ridiculous titles. He also said he told you that you would receive an unusual gift for your bravery, is that right?"

"Yes."

"Well, General," she said, rising and smiling like a tavern bawd. "I am that gift."

She parted her robe and the slick, heavy fur piled at her feet, like a black pedestal. A scanty halter of silver chain mail embraced her small breasts, hard untamed balls straining against the delicate metal, more holding it up than being held. A slim, triangular breechclout of the same material covered her womanhood, held in place by a thin silver chain circling swelling hips slightly wider than her narrow shoulders. The metal glistened like jewelry against the dark walnut sheen of her tight, voluptuous nudity. Not five feet tall or fully grown, she was a temptress, a vixen spitfire not yet out of her teens, a spoiled child who obviously delighted in enslaving full-grown men.

Smiling, she sidled close, delighting in the dazzle that shone in Ghapp's eyes, measuring him, allowing her heat to envelop him. She smelled of midnight orchids, young men and power.

"Now, General," she said simply, "I will show you what I expect of you, then you can judge if my offer is fair. Come."

She led him to an ebony screen, with a hide map of the Great Barma Range stretched on it. Red arrows were drawn alongside the lines indicating the location of the main roads, all heading north toward a black dot. She pointed at it.

"Here, General, is the legendary castle, Whitetree, which guards Jade Pass, the route by which the wealth of the northern empires departs and enters. The castle is garrisoned by the finest bowmen ever to draw a bow, the White Archers. The legendary defenders of the White Veshta." Her eyes met his. "The truth is, they have never defended anything more than her name, not in three hundred years. But the legends say that one day they will guard her living flesh, and that time is at hand." She pointed at the extremities of the map.

"I have sent Jani assassins to the farthest corners of the land, from the Great Forest Basin to the borders of your beloved Kitzakk Empire, and instructed them to execute every traveling player and minstrel they come across." She smiled malevolently. "I have created a plague of knives, General. A contagion of death that will drive every minstrel, acrobat and dancing girl before it. It will herd them along these roads," she indicated the arrows, "until they enter Whitetree, and the girl, who stole the jewels of the Goddess of Light from me, will be among them."

Ghapp's questioning eyes followed her as she stepped back to the bed.

"I know this to be true, because I have seen it," she answered, not bothering to look at him, "in the flights of vultures and the blood of the jackal. I do not know why or precisely when, but the White Veshta *will* enter Whitetree with the performers."

"But why would these entertainers all go to one place?"

"The castle is a sanctuary for traveling players," she replied, facing him. "And every ninth year there is a great festival held there, a festival which, with songs and dancing and dramatizations, celebrates the resurrection of the White Veshta." She sat down, grinning impishly. "She never truly appears, of course, an actress always performs the part. But this year, General, she will appear in the flesh." Her eyes suddenly moved like dark feral animals. "And when she does, you will lay siege to Whitetree, trap her within the castle's walls, then bring it down around her. Destroy her, and all the gaudy, madcap fools who spread her dreams! Everyone who serves her, down to the last dancing bear and tambourine!"

Excitement pushed Ghapp toward her. "If that is all you ask," his tone rang with anticipation, "it is a small price to pay for what you offer. The challenge alone would be reward enough."

She waited until he reached her, then glared petulantly. "Don't interrupt! I have only mentioned the easier obstacles. This girl has a champion."

"Champion?" His tone became guarded.

"Yes," she said, sprawling restlessly on the bed. "A man you Kitzakks know only too well, the one who destroyed your desert armies and drove you from the sands." She smiled tauntingly over a perfect shoulder at his shocked face. "Yes, the Death Dealer, General, and it will take far more than an army to defeat him." She lay over on her back. "That is why you, Izzam Ghapp, must give yourself, body and soul, to my master, the Lord of Death."

"I have already given my blood oath to the high priest in his secret altar."

"I know that!" She sat up. "But if you are to be exorcised, if you are to become the essential ingredient in the fetish that will guarantee the defeat of Whitetree, then much more is required than a mere oath."

Her threatening tone sent a chill up his spine.

Enjoying his show of fear, she coiled her legs under her. "Did you see those creatures in the cage outside? They were my first experiments, my first attempts at regenerating a man's spirit, and linking his Kaa to my own." Her voice dropped an octave. "I offered them the same reward, General, and they accepted eagerly. But their Kaas were weak, and my magic imperfect."

"And now?" he asked, suddenly cold.

"It depends completely on the man. On whether he has the strength, the will, the character to hold on to his own nature while the magic enhances it."

He wiped his face with the back of his hand. "Then there are still risks?"

"There are always risks," she said, peevish cruelty suddenly glistening behind her eyes. "Even for me. Three years ago the Death Dealer and this girl destroyed my castle, Pyram, and with it my laboratories! My priests! And nearly all of my sacred black wine, the elixir with which I corrupt nature, confound earth, wind, fire and air. The black wine is my covenant with the Master of Darkness, my power, and the Death Dealer stole its source, the jewels of the Goddess of Light. I can produce no more. Do you know what that means? No, you could not. It means that I had to use my own powers to enslave these Jani outlaws. And I will have to drain my body again in order to provide even the most ordinary demons needed for the siege. That will leave me weakened, General, make me vulnerable. Not my life, that is immortal, but my flesh. I can now be blemished. Scarred. Disfigured. But to once more possess the jewels, Izzam Ghapp, I will willingly risk even that, my perfection." She stood and ran a warm hand around his cold, wet neck. "So you see, we must both take risks . . . in order to earn our rewards."

He shivered, and she chuckled. "You hesitate."

"I did not know of the risk. The priest made no mention of it."

"He is no fool, General. He knows you have lost your courage, and he had to make sure you came to me."

"You trapped me."

"I need you," she said simply. "And I knew that once you had traveled all this way, it would be too great a waste to turn back."

"No!" he blurted, shaking his head. "I can't take the risk. It's too great."

She laughed at him as if he were nothing more than a shamefaced, smitten boy, and wrapped her arms around him, pressed her scarlet lips against his mouth. He shuddered, trying to squirm from her grasp, and she nipped his earlobe. He moaned and trembled. His hands hovered at his sides, as if they had no will at all. Suddenly they took hold of her naked back and roughly hauled her against his chest, his lips ravaging her open mouth. She gasped with pleasure, and her heat swirled around him, growing hotter. He pulled away, his chest heaving for breath, and his eyes widened in a confusion of horror and desire.

Embers glowed behind her orchid cheeks. They broke into flames, then spread like wildfire throughout her body, transforming her into a voluptuous sheath of perfect flesh, laced with molten fire.

His mind told him to run. His body refused. She pressed her nudity against him, kissed his dry, parted lips, and her heat overwhelmed him. He dizzied, dropped to the floor. The cold stone revived him slightly, and he saw her crouch over him. She removed the onyx ring strung around his neck, lifted his hand, and slid it on his finger.

"Now, Siegemaster," she whispered, "I am your promised bride."

"Yes," he muttered. "Yes, yes."

Five

THE DAGGER

Tiyy parted her sealskin robe, removed her chain mail halter and breechclout and placed their precisely measured weight on top of a short column standing against one wall. Stepping back, she waited, a beautifully malignant, black opulence against the white purity of her laboratory, an underground cell hidden beneath her bedroom.

It was a poor, impoverished substitute for the obsidian temple of thaumaturgy in Pyram the Death Dealer had demolished, but its magic had proven muscular, if primitive. Hopefully, not too primitive. Time was short. Izzam Ghapp was her last chance.

White candles stood in irregular clusters on the white floor, like tiny acolytes flaming with zealous passion. Their golden light played over the white walls and ceiling, danced on the greenish glass of flasks, retorts, tubes and bottles arranged on the worktable, gathered in a smoky haze that swirled around the bare legs of the general. With his wrists manacled to short chains, he dangled from iron rings set in a blood-spattered wall at the opposite side of the room, unconscious, as limp and silent as his belts and leather armor piled at his feet.

The pedestal trembled as the weight of her metallic garments tipped a delicate counterbalance, and began to sink slowly into the floor. Simultaneously, a panel of the wall slid back, revealing a secret altar to her lord, the Master of Darkness. A black saurian skull the size of a human head, set upright on an onyx pedestal, the jaws spread wide in unholy invitation.

Tiyy picked up a candle, passed the flaming tip between the jaws, and flames crackled to life in the hollow of the skull. She set the candle down, again waited.

Fire boiled in the brain cavity, filling it, and the empty eye sockets glowed with red-hot brightness, as if alive. Slowly a smoking tongue of red stone protruded from the mouth. The stench of burning stone permeated the room.

Hearing Ghapp's boots shift slightly as his strength began to return, Tiyy stepped to her worktable, opened a shiny black box. Inside, stone vials of black wine, Nagraa, waited. Scarlet string knotted at the narrow necks secured their leaden stoppers. She removed a vial, untied its cord, lifted the tiny vessel to her breasts with one hand and picked up a candle with the other, then crossed to the Siegemaster.

His head lifted slowly. His eyes had the shine of hard lacquer. His feet found a perch on the floor, and he stood uncertainly. She passed the candle over his battle-scarred body, smiled.

"Your scars recommend you, General. That is encouraging."

He did not reply. His eyes opened onto an inner emptiness. Body and soul had surrendered, awaited her cruel touch.

The nymph queen set the candle on the floor, raised the stone vial to his eyes. "Watch, General. Witness the power of the black wine. Understand why I must have the jewels."

She removed the leaden stopper and a shaft of black light shot out the mouth, lanced the Siegemaster's shoulder, staggering him, searing his flesh. It hit the wall, exploding into a flashing maze of darting needles that ricocheted around the room, bouncing off walls, breaking bottles, overturning flasks, then streaked toward the startled man. His chained arms shielded his face, and the needles of light stung his forearms, set their hair smoking, then swept past them, pierced his open mouth and cheeks. He spun away, ducking and twisting, and the dark glowing spears struck again, lacerating his chest. He flailed, banging his chains, then dizzied and slumped unconscious.

Tiyy, taking no notice as the streaks of black light passed harmlessly through her body, replaced the stopper and looked at Izzam Ghapp with rising satisfaction. He had not cried out.

She raised her left hand, palm exposed, and the streaking black light flew at it, disappeared within her flesh. Returning to her worktable, she opened a pinewood box and removed a harp string, a tiny tub of crimson rouge and a piece cut from the skin of a tambourine, totems of a vestment and instruments sacred to the Goddess of Light. Then she removed scrapings of limestone and tree leaves, taken from Whitetree, and three pubic hairs and a vial of urine stolen from the castle's high priest. Totems of contagious magic. She placed the items in the fire of the dark altar, and they crackled in its intense heat as her dark master's fire corrupted them, transformed, confounded and redirected their purposes.

The eyes of the saurian skull grew brighter. Suddenly their pitiless hot glare reached across the room, struck the cheeks of Izzam Ghapp. He jerked back to consciousness, instantly spellbound by a new terror.

The nymph queen held a dagger with a black handle carved in her image, which she had taken from the pinewood box. She placed it on the red tongue protruding from the saurian skull. The tongue drew back into the skull cavity, and the corrupting flames embraced the blade. It smoked, began to glow with red heat, then white.

A sheen of sweat broke out all over Tiyy's agitated body. She shrugged off her robe and stood naked in front of the altar, its hot glance stroking her with an orange glow. Once more, her body became a vessel of flames.

The smoking tongue emerged from the skull, presenting the dagger. Her fire-filled fingers picked it up by the dark handle, held it to her face. The steel had been transformed into a needle-sharp blade of shimmering black light, an instrument of thaumaturgical surgery.

Her scarlet lips kissed the glowing tip, then she turned and faced the Siegemaster. Her heat cast a red glare over floor, ceiling, walls and man. He flinched as she crossed to him, and her heat turned his perspiration to steam. He gasped for breath, tried to speak but could not. She held the dagger before his blood-streaked eyes.

"This is the blade," she said with ceremonial calm, "that will cut the sacred light out of the White Veshta's heart, remove her jewels. This means, General, it can also remove her light from your heart."

His flesh turned chalky. He fought wildly against his chains. Then, his eyes fixed on the dagger, he turned cold, moving no more than melting ice.

Tiyy placed the point of the dagger against his chest, above his heart. A trickle of blood showed under the sharp tip, and her eyes narrowed. Clutching the dagger with both hands, she thrust, the weight of her body driving the blade into his chest.

He screamed. Flesh and muscle sizzled and flamed around the wound.

Wrenching violently, Tiyy turned the blade in the wound, then ripped it free. A gush of blood chased it out and splattered across her back as she turned. Dropping the dagger, she snatched up the vial of black wine. Forcing his head back with one hand, and removing the leaden stopper with her teeth, she poured the contents down his throat. A howl of thundering pain erupted from his spread lips, accompanied by bars of black light as thick as saplings. His body doubled up, and he heaved repeatedly, vomiting black smoke. Then he sank in place, supported by the manacles.

Tiyy edged back, trembling and wide-eyed, and dropped the vial, hugging herself. Would he survive? Turn into another deformed pet?

Izzam Ghapp jerked. His head flew back. His lips convulsed spasmodically. Ripples ran across his bald scalp, then his head began to swell. Tiyy whimpered and staggered back. His cheeks ballooned. An ear puffed up. The dome of his skull welled larger and a vein erupted under its flesh, ran in a dark forked pattern across it.

She cringed, certain his skull would explode.

He stood with a jerk. His spine convulsed, slamming him against the wall. He bellowed in rage, coughing up puffs of smoke. Suddenly he shrank, then again and again. Tears of blood showed along the forked vein in his skull, then his skull deflated. Slowly he hauled himself erect, staring blindly at nothing, glazed eyes the size of pinpoints.

The wound in his chest spread apart, as if it had lips, and blood trickled out, sizzling and steaming. Then a flash of white light shot forth, the exorcised spell of the White Veshta.

Tiyy leapt forward, caught the stinging impact of white light on the curve of a hard breast, trapped it there with her hands.

Ghapp's eyes cleared. He blinked, looked into her eyes, and a smile lifted the corners of her mouth. There was no anger in his eyes, no indignation, no threatened, or even offended, male pride. No emotion except unbridled lust.

Tiyy laughed girlishly and looked down at her hands, holding her breast. A white glow glimmered between her fingers, trying to escape. She squeezed tighter and the glow dimmed, turning darker, then black. She removed her hands and held the dark glow up on a palm. It billowed, then faded, leaving a chip of diamond on her palm. It flashed brilliantly.

She placed it in a black jar, along with many similar chips, then released the Siegemaster.

He now stood five inches shorter, exactly her size. His arms were three inches longer than before, there was a dark forked vein running across his scalp, and the look in his eyes said he was not only the man he had been but much more.

He reached for her, as if she were a citadel of flesh to be broken into, ravaged, plundered, and she lifted a hand. He withdrew his arms, obedient, despite his frustration.

She carefully ran her fingers over the place where the dagger had stabbed him. There was no wound, no evidence there ever had been one. The fetish was at work, clearly made visible by the presence of a triangle of red dots glowing on his forehead. The sign of the Dagger Queen. His mark of authority over her army.

"You are mine now," she whispered, gathering his hands at her breasts. "She will never touch you again. You are the Hammer again, General Izzam Ghapp. My Siegemaster. Once more you will break into stone and flesh, and breathe fire, eat the living, sleep on the dead. No city, no castle, no wall, no woman can withstand you . . . not even I.''

His fingers curved over her breasts and she held them away. "Not yet. The magic needs time to root, and you have an army to raise, and discipline, train . . . siege weapons to build.''

"Your troops will obey me?'' he asked, more curious than concerned.

"Every word. Pick your own commanders, reorganize each unit, do whatever you think must be done. No one will argue. And there are tribes, outlaw bands, queens and warlords eager to join us for a share of Whitetree's booty. Your army can be whatever size you require.''

"I must see the castle. Measure it.''

"You will,'' she said. "But first your impatience must feed the fetish, make it grow strong. In two, three weeks I will meet you there.''

His expression said he did not care to wait. "What will the fetish do?''

"It will assure victory, General, make certain that you and your army will break into Whitetree, and tear it down.''

"And the White Veshta?''

"I will deal with her,'' she replied. "She's just a girl, of no more than twenty summers. She belongs to a tribe of traveling players called the Grillards, but no longer dwells in their camp in the Valley of Miracles. She was called Robin Lakehair, but has obviously changed her name. I have hunted her for three years, and there has been no sign of her, no word.''

"She hides?''

"Yes. But she can hide no longer, not from me. I can see her aura, and I leave for Whitetree within the hour to watch for her arrival.''

"You are certain she will be there?''

"Yes. A close friend of hers will betray her, take her to Whitetree for the festival. This I have also seen.''

"A woman?''

"Of course not. A man.''

Six
PRATFALL

Brown John's short, bandy-legged body carried fifty-six years of growth, including a noticeable paunch and eyes that blurred everything less than an arm's length away, making his passage through the deep snow difficult. Nevertheless, he moved with cumbersome haste, his knees cutting a deep path across the white mountainside, his cheeks sporting a rosy bloom in the cool moonlight.

Being the *bukko*, stage manager and leader of a troupe of traveling players, as well as the sometimes King of the Barbarians, he was accustomed to making hard decisions. Now the most difficult, and easily most daring, decision of his life swelled inside him, inflated by chance and adventure. Feeling as buoyant as a soap bubble, his mind naturally turned to thoughts of brown-skinned girls with very little to wear. This had the inevitable result. He began to whistle "The Women of Boo Bah Ben."

He passed through a stand of pines, climbed a spread of boulders and stopped on the crest of the hill, puffing and pleased with himself. All around him rose the awesome snow-covered peaks of the Barma High Country, but he barely noticed.

A hundred strides down the hill, the footpath joined Log Trail. Not six hundred strides beyond that, orange squares of light flickered between leafy limbs of tall cedars, the windows of the tavern at Jade Crossing. The Willing Virgin. There Doll Harl, the essential player in his bold plot, awaited him.

Confident in his gifts of garrulous persuasion, the *bukko* strode on. The long winter had hammered his hungry players unmercifully. His women had had to whore and his men steal, instead of singing for their supper. But this would soon end, and the certainty of it made his smile inviolate. He was about to shake the world upside down, then put it right side up again, and in the doing of it, cast his name among the legends, add it to the lyrics sung around the campfires.

Suddenly he stopped short.

A moving darkness, coming from the direction of Jade Crossing, filled the road. A darkness of bulk and size that glittered metallically. A darkness of demonic proportions which moved with wild resolve, as invincible as a storm.

Excitement lifted the old man's tangled white eyebrows. Only one man in all the world could make an entrance like this. His friend Gath of Baal. The Death Dealer. The man with whom the *bukko* had defeated the Kitzakk Horde, and helped Robin Lakehair steal the sacred jewels of the Goddess of Light from the Nymph Queen of Pyram. Now, after more than three long years' absence, Gath was unexpectedly returning precisely when Brown John needed him most. The old man raised his hands to his mouth to shout out in welcome, and held still. Silent.

Three riders, wearing black furs and leather armor, emerged from the shadows on galloping black horses. Cursing, they veered sharply into the trees, avoiding the revealing spill of moonlight, then regained the trail, where shadows concealed their passage, and rode on.

Brown's eyebrows closed over his eyes. How many times had he thought he had seen Gath in looming night shadows? How many times had his hopes soared only to be thrown down? Too many. He was forever allowing his theatrical nature to get the better of him, seeing only the things he wished to see. Gath was not coming back. He had to face that. The days of high adventure and raucous laughter they had shared would not come again. Besides, he did not need Gath's help. Not now.

The stage had set itself. It was the Year of the Tambourine, the time of the Festival of Resurrection at Whitetree, and he held magic in his hands.

He took three strides down the hill and paused again.

Who were the riders? Why did they wish to hide their movements? Would they stay on Log Trail, or would they turn off and head for the clearing where the *bukko*'s wagons were camped? Were they friends or enemies? The glint of metal indicated they were armed, but that was natural in these parts. Or was it? He had seen no swords or spears, so what did they carry? Could it have been black-handled daggers? Could the three riders be carriers of the plague? Assassins?

Panicking, he ran back up the hill, fought through the deep drift, and reached the trees. Puffing and breaking out in a cold sweat, he plunged recklessly through the shadows. Branches cut his cheek. Thorny leaves scratched his throat and shins. Breaking free of the trees, he stopped short at the edge of the clearing.

There was no one about. The only movements were the campfires' dancing flames and the garish slashes of light they cast across the sides of the five faded Grillard wagons.

The *bukko* sighed with relief, turned to once more set off for the Willing Virgin, and the door of Robin Lakehair's wagon, parked at the side of the clearing, slammed open.

Jakar's trim figure emerged and stood in the flood of candlelight spilling from the wagon. Behind him, his wife, her red-gold hair shimmering in the smoky yellow light, stared with teary eyes at the angry back of her aristocratic young husband.

Brown slid back into the trees, listened.

Jakar sagged against the doorjamb, the smoky light silhouetting the clean lines of his darkly handsome face, and his cultured voice spoke in a low, calculated tone.

"I'm sorry I lost my temper. But you should not have given the doe away. You haven't had more than one meal a day in over three weeks, and I killed and butchered it for you! Not for a wagonload of grubby children. And you knew that!"

"I know," Robin Lakehair said, her tone filled with regret. "But they looked so thin . . . and I did save some meat for us."

"Yes, and let me eat all of it before I found out what you'd done."

He looked at her, his gaze steady and accusing. When she spoke, her voice held enough self-pity for two skits and a monologue.

"You're not happy, are you, Jakar?"

"That's got nothing to do with it."

"Yes it does. Because it's me you're not happy with. Admit it! You think I'm a terrible housekeeper."

"You are a terrible housekeeper," he said quietly.

"That's not fair!" she blurted. "I try."

"Try!" He nodded at the interior of the wagon. "Look at that mess! Is that trying? Your costumes are all over the place."

"I was trying a new combination, and didn't have time to put things away. Besides," she added, the inevitable anger entering her voice, "Brown John asked me to. He's planning some special kind of performance, something that will feed us all, and wants me to make a costume for it. That's . . . that's why I didn't think the doe was so important."

"Don't blame it on Brown." Jakar dropped lightly to the ground. "He doesn't throw your blanket on the floor every morning. Good God, I must pick it up ten times a day."

Robin's face gathered in a frump and she turned her back on him, holding one arm tight against her side by the elbow.

Neither said anything for a long cold moment, and the *bukko* frowned sadly. The young couple had been married for nearly two and a half years, joyously and romantically married. But there had been no child, and Jakar blamed himself. At first he had taken it lightly, defying with humor whatever deities ruled his seed. But when Robin remained barren, he had turned melancholy, then silent, bitter. Ever since winter set in, he interpreted everything Robin did or said as an indication of her lack of respect for him, and of her declining love. She had pleaded with him, tried in every way to convince him of her continuing devotion. But he would not be convinced, and his stubbornness wore her down, until all she could fight back with was her own bitterness.

Brown could see it now, as she moved to the open door.

The swells of her maturing breasts surged angrily above the square-cut collar of her faded tunic. Her small fists hung threateningly at her sides. But neither her all too human anger nor her sadness dispelled her magic. She carried the jewels of the goddess within her, carried the unbounded gift of dreams and, to the *bukko*, those dreams looked all the more compelling when graced by the reality of life's rags and patches.

"All right," she said tartly to Jakar's back. "I'll put my blanket away. Where do you want it? At the end of the bed?"

"That's up to you," he said, not turning.

"All right," she said again. "Suppose I throw it over my shoulders, like Zena and Dorain, and go down to the crossing . . . lie down for any man willing to pay three aves for his fun. Maybe that will make you happy?"

Brown John groaned quietly as Jakar turned slowly to face her, saying nothing. She folded her arms under her breasts, and cocked a hip as only she could. But tears leaked from her eyes, revealing her true feelings, and she sagged against the doorjamb, covering her head with her bare arms, and began to sob.

"I'm sorry. I didn't mean that. I know you'd never want that."

The *bukko* rose quietly to leave, and a figure bolted out of the shadows between two wagons on the opposite side of the camp. A short, bearded man clothed in furs and armor. Something glittered in one hand. A dagger.

"Look out!" Brown screamed, drawing his sword and lunging toward the couple.

Jakar turned, bending at the knees slightly, and the hurtling attacker struck at him. Jakar's forearm came up, deflecting the blow, and the assassin's body hit him, drove him backward.

Robin screamed, dashed back into the wagon.

The racing *bukko* more heard than saw members of his troupe pile out of their wagons. His eyes held on a second assassin, dashing toward the fight from his right.

Robin reemerged, a small sword in hand, and jumped to the ground.

"Nooo!" screamed Brown.

Robin looked up, saw Brown, then saw the second attacker closing on her, and froze.

The assassin's mouth frothed. His eyes were wild and glazed, impervious to danger. Drugged with murder.

Brown John drove his disobedient body toward a spot between Robin and the second attacker. He felt like he was swimming in thick soup. The knife in his hand hung as heavily and awkwardly as a shovel. But he closed the distance, drove a foot hard against the ground, launched himself at the man's driving legs. There was a resounding pop and pain cut into his calf, as if someone had kicked him, and his leg gave out under him. He ran face first into the muddy ground and slid for what seemed a hundred yards, watching in horror as the assassin raced past.

Nearing Robin, the assassin raised his dagger, but a heavy arrow drilled his chest, brought him to a shuddering stop. A second arrow knocked him backward, and he sat down hard. Ignoring the arrows and glaring at Robin, he lurched onto his knees and crawled for her.

She raised the sword again and Bone and Dirken, the *bukko's* sons, stepped in front of her, bows in hand. Taking aim, Bone put a swift, booted foot in the assassin's face, driving him through the air. The killer hit the ground and rolled to a stop.

A few feet away, Jakar rose slowly. Beneath him, the first assassin lay on his back. His hands trembled weakly as they tried to reach his dagger, standing upright in his chest. It had a black handle carved in the image of a wanton savage goddess.

Robin raced into Jakar's arms, sobbing with relief.

The *bukko* and his Grillards gathered at the scene of the fight, their eyes scanning the shadows. Silent. Wary. No more assassins appeared.

Sighing with relief, Brown rubbed the hard, throbbing knot swelling in his calf, and realized no one had been anywhere near enough to kick him. A tendon had torn itself away from the bone under the strain of his effort. His assailant was age. Hiding his embarrassment, he studied the sprawled assassins.

The first attacker lay in a shawl of his own blood, dead, his stiff hands clutching his dagger. Blackish smoke smelling of burnt stone drifted from the red spot on his forehead. The second lay perfectly still, shaking, as if he were doing everything in his power to stand up and finish the job he had come to do. Then his red dot began to smoke, and he got down to dying like it was the serious work it was. Suddenly he fell slack against the muddy snow, dead.

"All right," Brown barked at the troupe, "you've seen enough. Back to your wagons." The Grillards began to drift toward their wagons and he turned to Bone and Dirken. "Double the guard, then search these fiends and bury them. Deep." His sons moved off, picking men, and Brown spoke quietly to Robin and Jakar. "You two stay out of sight in your wagon, until I call you."

They nodded and Jakar helped Robin up the steps into the wagon, closing the door behind them. The *bukko* glanced at his Grillards, climbing back into their wagons, then back at the site of his less than spectacular heroics.

All that remained was a muddy smear in the snow, a smear made by a man who was obviously too fat and too old to play heroes. Brown scowled with humiliation. Nevertheless, he placed the details of the sorry event in the library of his mind, recalling each moment: the sight of his driving knees, the loud pop, his miserly gasp of pain, and the wet splat as he hit the mud. He felt as if he had slid forever, but it had been no more than ten feet. A pittance, dramatically speaking. Plus there was no gash of blood on the snow, nothing to recommend it, not even the flash of his naked buttocks in the firelight. It had been a perfectly ordinary pratfall.

A clown's routine. A novice fool's.

Seven

THE PLOT

When the bodies had been dragged away, and the camp again slept quietly under the sheltering trees, Brown John sat on the steps to Robin's wagon, one of the assassins' daggers in his hands. The smell of burning stone, the scent of the Master of Darkness, hung faintly on the cold night air.

He thumbed the black figurine, then rapped it against the wagon door. Robin and Jakar emerged, and she sat beside Brown; Jakar dropped to the ground. Frowning unhappily, Brown handed Jakar the dagger.

The young man examined it and nodded. "It's the same design as those we saw in Leege and Apple Tree. And they had the same smoking red dots on their foreheads."

"The plague!" Robin murmured.

Brown nodded and Jakar asked, "You think this is the work of the nymph queen, don't you?"

Brown shrugged. "Hard to say, given the world for what it is. But if it is the black bitch, she's getting awfully close."

"Too damn close," Jakar snarled.

"Yes," Brown said thoughtfully, taking the dagger back. "But it was clear they did not come here looking for Robin. They attacked the instant someone showed himself. Wildly. Blindly. They didn't care who they killed."

"Maybe," Jakar said coldly. "But Robin's the one that black bitch wants."

"That, Jakar, we have all been more than aware of for better than three years, and saying it over and over again does not help."

"Moving the wagons will," Jakar said defiantly.

Brown shook his head tiredly. "No. Going further into hiding will change nothing. If we keep running away, we'll only feed our fears and shame, weaken ourselves. The final result, I'm afraid, will be far more tragic than our mere deaths."

Robin and Jakar shared a confused glance, and Jakar said, "What are you talking about, bukko? What are you up to now?"

"It's simple enough," Brown said with an air of inevitability. "I've been wrong, right from the start. I can see that now. We should never have gone into hiding." He smiled apologetically at Robin. "I admit it openly. Changing your name, all of it, was dead wrong."

"You've gone daft, old man," Jakar said softly. "Tiyy would have found her within a month."

"That's true, Brown, isn't it?" Robin asked.

"Perhaps, child," the *bukko* replied. "But for three years I've watched you gradually lose what small power you had over the jewels to begin with. One moment you light up mountains, the next you can't even manage a flash."

"I know," she said. "I try, but—"

"It's not your fault, lass," Brown said profoundly. "It's mine. We should have done it the other way around, revealed you immediately." They looked at him, their eyes startled. "Think about it. If I had displayed you as you deserve to be displayed, devotees would certainly have come forth, and the rest would have followed. A priesthood, a college of priestesses, cathedrals, total control of your powers and all the rest. Even if Tiyy and her henchmen had found you, under those circumstances I sincerely doubt they would have had the power to harm you."

"You don't know that," Jakar said, scowling.

"Please, Jakar," Robin pleaded. "Let him finish. It's me Brown's talking about, my life. If he's found a way I can control the jewels, I want to know everything about it."

Grunting, Jakar gave them his back. Robin stared at him, her eyes pained, then turned to Brown. He glanced at Jakar, then lowered his voice.

"I can't be certain, just as Jakar says, lass. But the jewels were created to be seen, to inspire, and we've hidden them. That's why they're slowly dying. I'm sure of it."

"Isn't it a little late for this, bukko," Jakar said, turning on Brown.

Brown John paused deliberately. "I respect your concern for Robin's safety, Jakar, more than you might think. But I also respect my own sincere beliefs, and can no longer ask her to play the coward."

"Why you old bouse bag," Jakar snarled. "Are you calling her a coward? After all she's been through? You'd have been no part of stealing those jewels if it wasn't for her bravery."

"Jakar, please," Robin begged, rising and blocking him from the *bukko*. "Don't get mad! And don't say that. It's not true! Brown played a great part, just as you and Cobra and Gath did."

"All right, all right," Jakar said, avoiding his wife's eyes. "I'll stay out of it. You make your own decision, you don't want mine anyway." He looked back at her, his eyes hard and cold. "But understand what he's asking. He wants you to show yourself, not just here and now, but on every stage and street corner he can find, anyplace he can find a crowd to pay to watch you."

Robin's cheeks flushed. "That's not fair, Jakar. Brown never did anything just for silver or fame, and you know it."

"We'll see," Jakar said, his eyes on the *bukko*. "We'll see."

He turned, strode into the shadows and disappeared. Brown and Robin looked after him a moment, then Brown spoke.

"He's right in one way. I do want you to perform, and on a stage." He turned to her. "But it's the grandest stage in all the world, and the part, Robin, is the greatest one you will ever play—yourself."

"You're my bukko," she said submissively, "but are you absolutely sure this is the time?"

"I'm sure," he said.

A pause separated them, then she smiled. "Then I'll play it, Brown. I couldn't refuse that. Who can I be but myself?" She hesitated, then added, "But are you really absolutely sure? I mean, we were always going to wait for Gath to return before we did anything like this.''

"I know. That's my biggest mistake. I thought Gath was essential, and I was wrong. The Death Dealer, axes, horned helmets, armor, battles, war, have nothing to do with the White Veshta.'' He took her hands in his. "It's not Gath's job to give you to the world, it's mine.''

"Yes,'' she agreed softly, ''it is.'' Then her eyes brightened. "So, now that's all settled, where's this marvelous stage, and what do I wear?''

"Whitetree,'' he replied soberly, ''and you will wear shooting stars.''

"Whitetree!'' she gasped, her eyes revealing that she understood all the word meant. "Oh, Brown, it is the Year of the Tambourine, isn't it?'' He gave a nod and she added, "But Brown, shooting stars! I can't.''

"You can, child, you can. I have discovered there is a library in Whitetree entirely devoted to your divinity, a library filled with scrolls and tablets, each one detailing the spells, incantations, rituals and scriptures pertaining to your powers. Your entire theology is there. All I have to do is find the right formula.''

"Oh, Brown,'' she crooned, helpless with excitement. "Are you sure? Do we dare?''

"We dare,'' he said with finality. "The world has a right to you, and I will not deny it any longer.''

"Ohhh, Brown, you are going to take care of everything, aren't you?''

"Everything,'' he agreed, rising stiffly. "I'm off to the Willing Virgin now, to make the final arrangements with Doll Harl.''

"Doll Harl!'' Robin exclaimed. "What part has she to play in this?''

"An essential one. She has been charged with providing the dancing girls and actresses for the performances to be staged at the festival, and she holds great influence with those who will cast the part of the goddess. Without her help, we won't get an audition.''

"Will she give it?''

"That is what I am about to make certain of."

"But even if she doesn't, will it matter? I mean, I don't have to have a big stage, not really . . . do I?"

"On the contrary, lass. The stage, the timing, the presentation and the audience are all essential. You are a deity, and you must start thinking like one. You are never going to play second tambourine to anyone again."

Eight

THE WILLING VIRGIN

Doll Harl was redheaded, five feet tall and one hundred and seventy pounds of pink abundance, most of which consisted of hips, breasts and cheeks painted apple-red. Although sitting absolutely still behind the Willing Virgin's only secluded table, she jiggled like pudding, threatening to spill over the low collar of a fuchsia blouse, and between the split seams of a tasseled skirt, featuring violet rosebuds on a field of black. With her shiny, black eyes on the *bukko*, sitting opposite her, she held a frothy mug in hands wearing more rings than fingers, and said, "I need a girl."

Brown John smiled his boyish smile. "Then your problem is solved. I've got *the* girl."

"Ha!" Doll chuckled mockingly. "You've always had *the* girl. You even saw something in me once. But this is different, Brown." Her husky voice lowered. "This sugarhole is going to have to dance for men! Full-grown men. Blooded aristocrats as jaded as roosters on a chicken farm." She emptied her mug, shoved it aside. "I need a girl soft enough to make mushy twelve-year-olds fall in love, and still have the sass and spice to knock a regiment over with her hips. A girl,

Brown, both angel and harlot. A girl who can turn the world upside down. Make lechers court her with poetry, and give a eunuch an erection.''

Brown John laughed easily. ''You arrange the audition, Doll, I'll provide the girl.''

She shook her head tiredly. ''You don't get it, do you, old friend? I'm dead serious. I can't let these priests down. They're my bread and butter, and they're counting on me to deliver a lass with real class and style, not some silly old man's idea of class and style.'' She shook her head again. ''I can't use your tart, Brown.''

He smiled an absolutely-sure-of-himself smile. ''You're not going to listen, is that it?''

''We're talking, aren't we?'' She leaned close and winked. ''I know you're up to something, you old cockroach, or your wagons wouldn't be this far from home this time of year. You're putting the pieces of some mad plot in place, right? So go ahead, talk to me, Brown. Tell me your lies. I may even believe you.''

He glanced across the empty tables at the handfull of soldiers drinking with sleepy whores in the opposite corner, then looked her in the eye. ''All right, Doll, I'll say it straight. You need a bukko to stage the resurrection for the festival, you're in a position to influence those who'll pick him, and I want the job.''

A crafty smile jumped her cheeks. ''So, you've grown up after all? You're finally looking out for yourself. It's about time, friend, and smart. The festival's going to be big. The biggest. They've expanded the stage, built thunder and smoke engines, even brought in fire eaters from Valatti. This year the bukko can put fifty drums and a hundred tambourines on stage just by asking.'' She winked. ''Yes, friend, you could really make a name for yourself.''

''Then you'll put my name in, use your influence?''

''I'd love to,'' she said, her tone warm. ''The festival just might be your last change to do something big, something special, something that will live past your days. But I'm not sure you'd be able to put up with the problems. The priests make all the essential decisions. You'd just be carrying out their orders.''

"They hire the dancers, set the stage, select the costumes?''

"No, you'd do most of that. But nothing gets on stage without their approval, and they're all over the place whenever a pretty face is involved.''

"Then I've got what they want.''

"The tart?'' He nodded and Doll shook her head. "Not interested, friend.''

He leaned close, breathing in the scents of cinnamon and musk lifting off her red cheeks. "You were when you saw her perform at Clear Pond.''

Her eyes sharpened. "That was over three years ago.''

"Yes, and she's filled out nicely. Perfectly, you might say.''

Interest flashed behind her dark eyes. "You're talking about the lead dragonfly? The one that did the fancy somersaults and dives? The redhead? The natural one?''

"Yes, the natural one.'' Now he smiled. "Robin Lakehair.''

She turned her head slightly, watched him out of the corners of her eyes. "But they, the redheads, were all killed by that demon filth.''

"Not Robin.'' Brown returned to his whisper. "I hid her just before that last, tragic performance. I've kept her hidden ever since.''

"Hmmm. She did have a certain class, style.''

"She's got more now.''

"Full-grown, is she?''

"She's made an art out of it.''

Doll laughed. "You're hiding something, Brown. What is it, a husband?''

"She has one, but no one will notice.''

"You'll hide him?''

"That's the plot.''

"You old cockroach, you *are* up to something.''

"Yes, I am,'' he said, great importance ringing in his tone, and looked carefully around the room, back at Doll. "What I'm going to tell you, Doll, must be kept to yourself.'' She leaned closer, biting, and he added, "The lass, Robin Lake-hair, has come into the possession of a treasure of extraordinary diamonds, jewels that radiate a blinding white light, a transcendent light of exploding sparks and shooting stars. Diamonds, Doll, that have merged with her flesh, vanished within her beautiful body. You don't know they're there until she dances."

Doll lifted an eyebrow. "You mean she lights up? Flashes?"

"Yes. She flashes. She sparks, she radiates, she makes whatever kind of light she feels like making. She can fill all of midnight with shooting stars if you ask her to."

Doll gave a nod. "That's a nice touch, Brown. Different. Just so she doesn't overdo it and frighten people."

He stared at her, dismayed. "You haven't the faintest idea of what I'm telling you, do you?"

"Hey," she said lightly, "don't get excited. So she has a few tricks, that won't bother anyone. Every girl does whatever she can to look her best."

"They aren't tricks," he said, jaws clenched. "What I am telling you, Doll, is that she wears the jewels of the Goddess of Light."

"I see." She chuckled ironically. "Then she'd be perfectly cast, wouldn't she? Providing the priests see it your way."

"Damn it!" he snarled. "I'm serious."

"You are, aren't you, you old lecher?" She grinned. "Well, that's fine, Brown. Be a fanatic. You're entitled at your age. But keep it to yourself, or you'll make people nervous."

"Don't lecture me, Doll. I know how to talk to priests." He paused, then added, "It's just that I wanted you to know."

"Why? Even when I was kid of seventeen, you knew better than to try and seduce me with this kind of nonsense." She put a hand on his. "Relax. Enjoy this foolishness if it makes you happy. But don't bring it into my bed. I'm done with dreams and dreamers. I take the world for what it is, and I take all I can get."

Brown John sat back, a sudden emptiness filling him, and nodded. "You're right, Doll, I'm letting myself get carried

away. But there is one thing. I'd like to take a look at the
castle's library when we get there.''

"Let's worry about first things first. If they cast her, that
won't be a problem.''

"Then the audition is set?''

"If the redhead looks and acts anything like she did at
Clear Pond, I'll see to it. But I can't guarantee the part or
the job as bukko. That's up to the priests.''

"I'm not asking for guarantees, Doll,'' he said, unable to
hide a sigh of relief. "Thank you.''

She set her elbows on the table, put her playful eyes on
his. "Now, will you relax? I thought maybe we'd take a ride
in that big wagon of yours, like the old days. But the way
you've been acting, I get the feeling you might fall out of the
saddle.''

He chuckled. "Haven't changed, have you?''

"Oh, yes,'' she said with enthusiasm, "I've changed a lot.
And so have you, Brown, so have you.''

Nine

WHITETREE

The Jani outlaw walked his mount carefully through the oak
and pine forest. Snow dappled the ground, and more floated
down through the spreading branches, settling on his fur hood
and the bright vermilion body of the loaded crossbow held
in his right hand. A sticky yellow substance covered the tip
of the steel bolt. A snowflake fell on it, sizzled, and disappeared in a puff of steam.

He reined up short of the edge of the trees, and sat still in the quiet as another outlaw, vermilion crossbow in hand, appeared two hundred strides off. Scouts.

Beyond the tree line, snowflakes filled the air with a blinding whiteness, landing somewhere far below on the floor of a valley nestled in the Barma High Country.

A hundred strides up the mountain, on a barren ridge overlooking the valley, the Dagger Queen's bodyguards sat motionless and silent. All cradling vermilion crossbows in their thick arms, their alert eyes watched the shadowed forest, guarding a small group of riders on the ridge.

Aillya, the nymph queen's body servant, three mercenary officers, commanders of General Izzam Ghapp's engineers, sappers and attack regiments, General Ghapp and the Dagger Queen.

Wrapped in snow-flecked black furs, Tiyy and her general waited at the front of the others, their eyes on the whiteness hiding the valley. He sat proudly erect on a beautifully saddled stallion, while her black and white spotted pony had a blanket for a saddle. She wore rawhide boots and a hooded sealskin coat, her bare legs showing below the knee. They waited in silence.

Within her shadowed hood, Tiyy's heated smile trembled with rash impatience.

The days of eight and nights of ten had been counted, the offerings of incense and incantations had been made. The fetish had rooted in Izzam Ghapp, and he had reorganized her army, employed mercenary commanders, instilled fear and discipline in her troops, started work on a dozen siege engines, recruited mercenaries and enlisted the troops of the booty-hungry warlords and queens of the Azaabii, Corran, Kleyytil, Lorraiil and Umoori. More warriors rode into her war camp every day. Her army was nearly ready. The fetish was at play, but his sacred corruption was not complete, still uncertain.

Would the ensorcelled black wine channel his truant nature and confound him? Would Izzam Ghapp, before day's end, wear the enslaving leash of lust she had so artfully crafted for him?

Not until the curtain of snow fell away to reveal the castle would she know.

The sound of a cracking twig came out of the forest. Turning sharply toward it, she gripped the handle of the tiny vermilion crossbow sheathed at her forearm. One of her bodyguards rode into the trees and a fox dashed into the clearing, dove over the ridge out of sight. The outlaw returned to his position and the nymph sighed with relief, but kept her hand on the weapon.

For the last weeks she had camped in the forest above the ridge, and patiently watched the castle as troupes of entertainers poured into it. She had seen no sign of the White Veshta or her champion. But now, with her impatience growing with each heartbeat, she thought she saw the Death Dealer in every shadow, heard him in every sound. Only her confidence in the weapon's poisoned dart, and in those in her bodyguards' crossbows, quelled her fear. The carefully concocted poison would finally subdue the Dark One, destroy the White Veshta's influence over the horned helmet, make the living metal behave as she had designed it to behave. Make the Death Dealer its prisoner, and if he disobeyed it, his executioner.

Hearing Ghapp shift with sudden tension in his saddle, she turned anxiously toward the concealing snowfall.

The light behind the gray cloud cover grew steadily brighter, then the blinding whiteness glowed intensely and a shaft of sun speared through the thinning snow, fell across their horses.

Ghapp jabbed his heels into his horse's ribs. The animal bolted forward, and he reined up hard just short of the precipice, pushing his hood back to see better.

Forcing herself not to hurry, Tiyy walked her stallion up beside him as flashing bars of sunlight dashed down through the thinning snowflakes. Suddenly the whiteness fell away like an effervescent veil, and Ghapp stood abruptly in his stirrups, the three red dots on his forehead glowing hotly.

A pure white castle commanded the white valley, standing as regal and natural and invincible as the towering white mountains surrounding it, as relentless as the icy river rushing beside it. A castle of white stone chiseled from an outcropping of limestone, rising seven hundred feet off the valley floor. Spires of smoke rose out of its courtyards and chimneys, passing through the gnarled, twisted limbs of huge lime trees standing at the top of each tower. The trees, with trunks as thick as five men, had rooted in the rock hundreds of years earlier, producing the castle's name.

Whitetree. A castle completely carved, chiseled and sculpted from white rock. The home of the White Archers.

The citadel crouched like a beast made of massive boulders, with its head, a separate fortified outpost, rising off the valley floor to the south. Beyond it, the neck, a stone bridge, passed over the river. A lowered drawbridge joined the neck to an entrance passageway between the gate towers. Beyond the gate, walls and towers, rising out of the natural cliffs, angled around the lower yards, the main portion of the castle. A wall, linking towers at the eastern and western ends, separated the lower yards from a higher shelf of rock, the Sacred Close, a large, flat, open courtyard. At its north end, a Curtain Wall, a raw cliff with ramparts sculpted from its crest, defended the Stronghold, at the heights of the rock. It consisted of thick walls joined by guard towers and two massive square towers.

A river ran south along the western face of the castle, following the natural incline of the valley floor. On the opposite face a moat defended the walls. Beyond it, bogs and marshes made any approach from that direction nearly impossible. Jagged piles of impassable rock guarded the narrow northern slope, and the gate towers, bridge, river and Outpost defended the southern approach.

Snow cover concealed the roads and trails passing across the valley to the citadel, but in the distance a deep cut in the shoulders of the mountains marked the location of Jade Pass, the vital artery of commerce from which Whitetree had grown rich.

Directly below the ridge, a band of travelers had appeared on the distant valley floor, cutting paths through the snow to reveal the location of Jade Road. Bits of bright color showed on their clothing, and a garishly painted house wagon accompanied them. Itinerant performers. The guards at the Outpost let them enter without questions or inspecting them.

"As you see, General," Tiyy said, smiling behind her feral eyes, "the Jani knives have done splendid work."

"Yes," he mumbled absently.

She made herself wait a moment, then said, "Well, have you seen enough?"

Ghapp turned slowly toward her, the effort making the forked vein on his skull stand up and throb. The triangle of red dots smoked. His eyes were wild places, dark pits leading to a brutal mind, a savage hunger.

Tiyy's breathing quickened. The fetish was channeled. His passions had been confounded and leashed, and she held the leash.

"What is it?" she asked. "Does something disturb you about the castle?"

With the same slow effort, he looked back at the castle, and the forked vein grew red against his brown skull. "I must look closer. From this distance, the castle's extraordinary construction betrays no weaknesses. It is impossible to tell which walls and towers are vulnerable. The white rock hides everything. If masons had built it, I could easily see where they had placed their strongpoints and attempted to shore up their weaknesses. But they did not. The builders adapted their design to the natural stone. To find the weak points, I must walk the ramparts, climb the towers. If the walls cannot be breached, then I must determine the depth of the river and moat, and of the supporting rock itself. If it merely rests on the valley floor, that could aid us. But if it goes deep into the earth, then—"

"What difference would that make?"

"It would mean our sappers would have to cut through solid limestone. It could take months."

"We do not have months. If you give the White Veshta time, there is no telling what allies might come to her aid."

"Then I must enter. There is no other way."

"Impossible," she said loosely. "You could be seen. Identified. And if she and the Barbarian enter while you're inside the walls, the horned helmet would sense your presence and come after you."

He said nothing, his hunger shaking him. Suddenly he dismounted, and defiantly looked into her eyes. "I must enter." The thoughts ranging behind his eyes violated every part of her.

Tiyy ran the tip of her tongue slowly between her lips. "Your cold, calculating manner appears to have deserted you, General." He remained silent, plumes of black smoke snarling from the triangle of red dots. Deliberately provoking him, she shook her head. "Send your commanders. I cannot risk your life on a mere inspection tour."

Beads of sweat ran down his cheeks as he shook his head. "Only I know what to look for."

A moment passed, then she said, "All right. Your passion is very convincing. Go."

He threw off his fur and began to undress, shouting at one of the soldiers to do the same. The pair, hurrying against the biting cold, dressed in each other's clothes. Then Tiyy removed a long-eared cap from her saddlebags, handed it to Ghapp.

"Leave it on at all times," she commanded. "The red dots tend to act up under certain conditions, and that makes people suspicious."

"You knew, didn't you?" he said. "You planned this?"

"Yes," she said flatly. "I had to know if the fetish was accurately channeled. Now, all that remains is for the imitative magic to be made flesh. When it is, the sympathetic contagion will spread into stone, tower and wall. But that will not happen until you have determined how you will destroy Whitetree." She nodded at the crone. "Take Aillya with you. For forty-three years she was body servant, whore and scullery maid in Whitetree. She knows every alleyway and passage, every tunnel and shadow."

The crone dismounted, and bowed to Ghapp.

Slipping on the cap, he faced Aillya. "There is only one gate?"

"I have never seen another, Lord General," the crone replied, "but I have heard rumors of a secret postern gate."

"How many wells?"

"Two," she replied. "One in the lower yards for the commonfolk, a larger one in the Stronghold, for the White Archers."

"And dungeons?"

"Many, both under the lower yards and the Stronghold. Horrible tunnels, pits and cells, even passageways to the underworld, some say. They go deep, where there is no light or air. No one has used them for a hundred years, many are blocked up."

"Blocked?"

"By rubble, cave-ins, water."

Liking that, Ghapp turned to Tiyy. Every thought and sensation within him now played vividly in his expression, rang in his words. "I will return to the forest camp, meet you in your tent, as soon as I can."

"No," she said, "you will take your time. You will examine every foot of the castle's body, invade every intimate part, until you cannot resist it a moment longer. Then we will meet."

He hesitated, then asked, "The fetish, it is complete?"

"Nearly. A few details must be added, then you will see it."

Ghapp bowed and hurried down the ridge, into the trees, with Aillya hurrying after him. The old woman paused at the line of trees and glanced back over a bent shoulder. The nymph queen nodded and the hag vanished behind the trunks. Moments passed, then the pair appeared far below, crossing the snow-covered foothills. Reaching the valley floor, they drew a dark line across the whiteness to Jade Road, joined more travelers there, and moved up the road and into Whitetree.

Seeing them enter, Tiyy gasped audibly, suddenly consumed with desire. Startled by the unexpected demands being made by her body, she clutched her furs tightly to her breasts and gasped for air. Had she made the fetish too strong? No. She was supposed to be out of control.

Jumping off her horse, she dropped her coat and, standing

on it, began to undress, her hands ripping feverishly at her clothing.

Ten
INFECTIOUS IMITATION

Tiyy felt naked. She wore a colorless felt cloak, a heavy homespun tunic, boots and ragged leg wrappings from her ankles to her thighs. Bundled against the cold like an impoverished tart, any interested male would have to spend a week removing her rags before finding anything that looked remotely like a girl. Nevertheless, her unwashed disguise did not alter the sensation. She always felt naked on the hunt. It was the savage in her.

Leaping puddles and skirting the deep mud at the center of Jade Road, she hurried toward the entrance to Whitetree. Alone. Unencumbered by the pressures of royal responsibilities and expectations, by the rituals and requisites of maintaining her fatal glamour, she felt suddenly free. The sensation combined with the rampant passion inside her to create the kindest cosmetic a girl can wear. She glowed from every pore.

Her spiked hair sprouted in wild disarray and she smelled of hair and dirt and strong cinnamon, the preferred scent of tavern bawds. For the rest of the day, she could be the truant nymph her lithe, restless body said she was. Daring. Bold. Shameless.

Her sacred duty now waited in the castle, only there could the imitative magic be made flesh, and it waited in the common, vulgar form perfectly suited to her animal heat, in the form of a man.

Approaching the outpost, she slowed.

The branches of the lime tree growing out of the center of the circular fortification reached well beyond its thirty-foot walls. Three ropes dangled from them, weighted by three heads impaled by sharp hooks. Two of the heads had red dots on their temples. Jani assassins.

A tremor of fear shot through her, but she cast it aside and marched toward the group of White Archers in front of the open doors. The pristine white tunics covering their armor were crisscrossed with belts bearing quivers of arrows, sheathed swords and daggers. Drinking and conversing, they blocked the entrance. Stopping behind them, she tapped one on the shoulder, by way of asking them to step aside.

They glanced at her over their mugs. Tall, muscular, lithe, their fair blond hair was cut short, like a brush. Rings of gold and precious stones glittered on their ears. It was the only light in their faces.

One, wearing an exceptionally long sword in a brilliant red scabbard, turned to her with effortless dignity.

"Good morning," she said gaily. "It is still morning, isn't it? I slept late."

Not bothering to reply, Redsword searched her with a shameless hand, as if needing confirmation that her breast was firm. Tiyy slapped his hand away, and he scowled at her insolence. Cowering, she snatched up his hand and put it back where it had been. That put a smile on his face, drew chuckles from his friends.

The large man hooked a blunt thumb under her chin and put his face close to hers. Recently shaved, he smelled of bath powders, roses and wine.

"What are you hiding, wench?" he asked in a brazen tone.

"Nothing you cannot find, sir," she replied in kind.

The other archers laughed, and Redsword grinned. "A pretty thing like you could get in a lot of trouble in there," he nodded at the castle. "We've let all kinds of riffraff in for the festival."

"I'll be all right," she said brightly.

"I don't think so," Redsword said slowly. "Have you been here before?"

"No. I was too young to come to the festival last time!"

"Then you'll need a guide. It's a big place and you can get lost fast. I'll show you around."

"Thank you," she said, stepping aside, "but it's not necessary."

"Oh, yes it is, tart. I don't want you to miss a thing." He took her by the elbow and led her between his friends into the castle outpost, the archers' laughter following them in.

They passed through a tunnel big enough for a large wagon, then under a rusted portcullis, and out the rear door onto the bridge. Wide enough for two wagons, it provided a playground for a fast-footed bunch of dirty children bundled in rags.

The bridge took them to the drawbridge and Tiyy felt the heat of a hundred fires sweep out of the gates, along with a din of happy music and boisterous activity. She hurried across the drawbridge, and they passed under a massive portcullis, then through the tunnel between the looming gate towers into the maze of moving bodies, colorful wagons and campfires that filled the lower yard, the Market Court.

The snow had been cleared and stood in melting heaps beside grilled drains at the corners of the yard. Food stalls and wandering vendors were everywhere. Acrobats, jugglers, performing animals and dancing girls worked the staircases rising to the wall walks, the tops of barrels and the roofs of the wagons. They sang, twirled and banged their tambourines and drums, as merchants shouted over the music, hawking everything from green apples to their own wives. Tent brothels billowed in every corner. Mendicants, snake charmers and peddlers, soldiers, shoppers and an occasional goat or pig flowed in all directions. Eating. Drinking. Babbling. Laughing. Honking.

Tiyy hugged Redsword, squealing. "It's incredible. I've never seen anything like it!"

"You can gawk later," he said, dragging her through the crowd toward a ramp on the far side of the yard. The ramp rose up to a gate, passing through the wall sealing off the Sacred Close. More White Archers stood on the ramp, watching the fun.

Tiyy, stumbling after Redsword, looked about frantically, saw a merchant selling apples and yanked to a stop, pointing at him. "Oh, please," she pleaded. "I haven't eaten all day. Please. Please."

"All right," Redsword said, dropping her hand. As he approached the apple stand, drawing a coin pouch from his belt, Tiyy dashed into the crowd. She slipped one way then the other through the massed bodies, leapt a small fire and scurried into shadows cast by a colorful house wagon parked below the eastern wall. Panting, she glanced back the way she came. No one followed her. Sighing, she sagged back against the wagon.

A group of entertainers in bright tattered clothing sat beside a fire watching her. She lifted a finger to her lips, asking them for silence, and they grinned with understanding. She climbed the roof of the wagon and peered over the baskets and bundles tied on top.

Redsword stood in the middle of the throng where she had left him, glaring furiously from side to side, green apple in hand. Suddenly he threw the apple down and shoved his way through the crowd, heading toward his friends on the ramp.

Tiyy did not smile. She dropped to the ground, dashed to the nearest staircase and ran up the steps, taking three at a time.

Hours passed as she searched the ramparts, towers, alleys and courtyards, and the sun climbed into the middle of the sky. Then, from the heights of the western wall, she caught sight of Ghapp and Aillya far below in the Water Court, a smaller, slightly raised yard overlooking the Market Court. The old woman sat tiredly on the rim of a huge circular well, as older women and scullery maids drew water from it, filling pitchers and jars. The general squatted in the shade cast by a cluster of huge lime trees, inspecting a wide crack in the rock ground.

Tiyy raced into the nearest tower, descended four flights of stairs, and dashed into the Water Court. Women still moved to and from the cistern, but Ghapp and the crone were gone. The nymph raced to the spot where she last saw him. The crack was all of four inches wide. Leading away from it, wet bootprints headed across the yard to a tunnel-like passageway at the north end.

Tiyy raced across the yard, plunged into the stone passage, emerged at the far end, and stopped short, frowning with frustration.

She faced a rubble of snow-covered rocks, ancient fallen archways, crumbled buildings, broken staircases and towers. The ruins spread in an irregular pile for four or five hundred paces along the base of the western wall. Plumes of smoke rose behind heaped stones where camps had been laid. Children scampered over rocks and through the muddy snow, firing snowballs at each other. Here and there, dark holes opened into the ground where broken ramps and staircases descended to abandoned tunnels and chambers. Sooty smoke billowed out of them, reeking of fatty meats and porridge.

Scrambling up a half-fallen wall, Tiyy looked over the area. In the distance, the backs of Aillya and Ghapp bobbed into view, then the old woman led him down into one of the hole-like openings. Tiyy jumped off the wall and raced along a muddy trail that turned and twisted through the rubble. Rounding a corner, she slipped in a muddy puddle, jumped up and ran full tilt into Redsword.

He grabbed a fistful of her hair, yanked her to him, her eyes only inches from his snarling lip. His cheeks glowed hotly. His lids fell loosely over drugged eyes. Squirming, she tried to pull away and he shoved her into the arms of two White Archers standing behind him. All three men held beautifully crafted composite bows of bone and alder.

"Bitch!" Redsword growled.

Taking hold of the collar of her cape, he yanked it, ripping it away and throwing her to the ground. Tiyy more bounced than jumped back up, handfuls of mud in each hand, and flung them wildly. The dark mud caught Redsword's face with a wet splat, blinding him as he reached for her. He tripped, falling hard, as Tiyy scrambled over a sprawl of rocks.

She heard the archers curse and rush after her, but she did not look back. Dashing through a crowd of children, she

turned down a narrow trail between huge slabs of broken
wall, pulled to a stop over a hole in the ground. Firelight
glowed in the shadows below. She dropped through the hole,
landing in a stack of hay being eaten by goats. Driving
through the animals, she fled past a fire tended by goatherds
and plunged down a narrow dirt ramp into darkness.

Coming to a stop with her back against a wooden wall,
she waited. No sound alerted her. Slowly her unholy eyes
adjusted to the beloved darkness until she could see as clearly
as she could in sunlight. She looked around. She stood in a
large room walled with rough-hewn logs. Heaps of dry straw
covered the floor. In the far corner, a stairwell opened in the
floor, descending to more darkness. She started for it and
stopped short, hearing heavy male breathing. The sounds
came closer. Then torchlight filled the room, coming from
both ends, and torches appeared, held by Redsword at one
end, and his two friends at the other.

Tiyy held still.

Chuckling darkly, the archers placed their torches in brackets on the wall, and orange firelight did bright but unpleasant
things to the snarl on the young queen's suddenly feral face.

Rape was not repugnant to her. It was a natural act aroused
by the passions and hungers she deliberately, and so skillfully, aroused in men. But to be raped by White Archers
would destroy all her carefully laid plans. Ruin her carefully
crafted fetish. Reverse it. Give Whitetree power over her
body, instead of giving her power over the body of the castle.

She fingered the tiny crossbow on her forearm. It would
drop one of them, but she would not be able to reload fast
enough to stop the others. She could emit the dark vapors
which flowed from the palms of her hands on command and
snuff out their torches, but that would reveal her identity,
endanger the siege. Her only recourse was her cunning and
wit.

She scurried one way, then the other, trying to keep the
archers at bay. They took only casual notice. Holding positions that cut off any escape to the ruins above, they strung
their bows, nocked their arrows and took aim.

"There's no need for that," Tiyy said saucily. "I'll undress."

They laughed and Redsword drew and fired quickly, his bowstring twanging in the quiet.

Tiyy dashed aside and the arrow thudded into the log wall beside her. She gasped and another plunged between her thighs, pinning her tunic to the wall. She growled and yanked free, tearing her clothing.

Redsword smiled.

Snarling, the nymph dashed and twisted and ducked to no avail. With incredible accuracy, the arrows plucked at sleeve and collar and hem, pinning her to the wall. Repeatedly wrenching free, her clothing was shredded, reduced to rags. Then the shafts pinned her in place, her arms and legs spread wide. Panting, she watched in terror as shaft after shaft snatched away her belts, bits of rag, a lock of hair. An arrow nicked her waist, then her throat, and blood spidered down over her dark firm breast. She heaved and growled like a trapped animal, but the arrows kept coming, stripping away everything but her loincloth, scraps of her tattered leggings, sheathed crossbow, boots and a hot moist glow.

The archers lowered their bows and started for her, then stopped, their eyes on the tiny crossbow. Then they chuckled with sullen confidence, obviously aroused by her helpless, belligerent beauty, and began to undress.

Her body heaving with exhaustion, Tiyy took a loose step sideways, and tripped on a protruding shaft. Staggering, she crushed aside a forest of shafts, then fell on the soft straw, rolling onto her back.

"That's it, bitch," Redsword said. "Now you've got the idea."

Laughing darkly, the naked archers advanced on her, one holding a torch. Tiyy let them come, undulating sensuously as the archer holding the torch passed its hot light over her body. Suddenly she rolled upright, heaving an armful of straw over the torch. The flames incinerated it. The archer dropped the torch and burning straw flew everywhere, igniting the straw on the floor. Flames shot across the room, raced between the naked legs of the archers. They jumped and dodged, snarling, as Tiyy, grabbing the torch, jumped to her feet and dashed down the stairwell into the darkness below.

Finding heaps of straw and refuse in a narrow passageway, she threw the torch on it, and flames crackled and soared, licking at the naked legs of the archers as they descended the stairs. She watched them retreat, then raced down the narrow, steeply descending passageway, her escape hidden by a wall of flame.

She came to a room with several exits. From one came a cool breeze that stirred her alerted senses. Trusting her instincts, she dashed into it and descended deeper and deeper into Whitetree's underworld. She passed through deep puddles, and along walls slick with slime, down angled tunnels too shallow to stand upright in. Moisture dripped from the ceiling on her bare back. Crouching, she half-crawled through a tunnel and entered a long low-ceilinged room. The glow of a fire flickered at one end. She hurried to it, came to a barred doorway and smiled with dark heat.

Her instincts had served her faithfully once again.

Beyond the bars, Izzam Ghapp and the crone crouched beside a fire on the floor of the adjacent room. The old woman sagged tiredly, her shivering, wrinkled hands held up to the flames. The Siegemaster appeared oblivious to the wet cold. Sweat drained along his arms, dripped from his forehead, as if a fever possessed him. Kneeling over a three-foot-wide fissure in the stone floor, he cupped his hands, dipped them into the water filling the fissure, and sipped. Then he ran his tongue over his lips, tasting the water carefully, and smiled with triumph.

"I'm right," he whispered to the old woman. "It's river water."

"I thought so," she said, wheezing for breath. "It tasted the same under the Stronghold."

He turned to her. "And the fissures, how wide were they under the Stronghold?"

"Wide enough to bathe in, some of them. Two even had bridges over them."

Ghapp smiled, dipped his hands back into the water, drank again.

Tiyy moved to the doorway and pressed her naked flesh against the bars so that the light from the adjacent room caressed it. "Does it tell you what you wish to know, General?"

Ghapp looked up with startled eyes, his hands spilling water over his knees. Behind him, the crone rose abruptly, shocked by her queen's appearance.

"I'm all right, woman," Tiyy said. "Leave us! Your work is finished here."

Bowing repeatedly, the crone stumbled backwards to an arched staircase in the far wall, and vanished into it.

Ghapp appeared unable to move. "Why?" he murmured. "How?"

"Come to me," she whispered, her tone throaty. "Hurry! We have only a little time. They hunt me."

He stood abruptly and rushed to her, drawn like water drained by a whirlpool. Questions crowded his eyes.

"There is no time for words." She reached through the bars, grabbed a shoulder and a handful of his hair, and pulled his head down to hers. Their lips brushed, then stabbed at each other. Their breath mingled hotly and his arms came through the bars like heavy clubs, took hold of her body, pulled it against his own. The bars stopped him and he pulled back.

"The bars," he gasped.

"Forget them," she breathed. Heat showed on her face. Flames sputtered under her dark cheeks, outlining blotches of mud. "Take me," she breathed. "Feed your hunger."

His hands came back through the bars, hesitated. "This is madness."

"No," she breathed, and kissed him roughly. "We are the fetish, Izzam Ghapp. Our bodies and the castle are joined in the same cup of darkness. What I feel, what I do, the castle will feel and do. It cannot resist. Our fetish is too powerful. What you do to me, you will also do to the castle." She put a leg through the bars, locked her knee behind his. "Break into me, Izzam Ghapp. Now!"

The sound of a rock splashing in a puddle echoed through the rooms. They held still, listening. Another rock fell.

"Someone's coming," he whispered.

"Then hurry," she breathed, running her hands inside his tunic, loosening his belt. "Hurry!"

He helped, threw the belt aside, hauled off his tunic and she thrust her belly against the bars, touching his. He grabbed for her and a torch appeared behind her, held by a dark, lumbering figure. Ghapp pulled back and Tiyy turned, snarling.

The figure emerged. Redsword, torch and sword in hand. He snickered, rolled his shoulders and started for her. Tiyy let him come, as Ghapp stared helplessly through the bars. Suddenly she drew her tiny crossbow, thrust out her arm, fired.

Redsword ducked. Too late. The tiny dart stung him in the cheek, and he flinched, touched his cheek. Then he laughed, again strode for her. His second step had no leg in it, and he fell facedown, dropping both sword and torch. Gagging and convulsing, he clutched his belly and heaved dryly. Suddenly his cheek smoked around the tiny dart, and little flames erupted. His meaty hands groped at the dart and the flames spewed between his fingers, spread to his eye socket. His hand flew away, melting like wax, and his mouth opened wide to scream. But flames burst forth instead, then from his nostrils and ears.

Redsword convulsed, the flames died and his flesh and bones melted to a bubbling puddle. The tiny dart floated on top. The nymph picked it up, reloaded and cocked her weapon, then holstered it, making certain the tip of the dart dipped into the vial of poisonous paste secured to the bottom. Then she turned to Ghapp.

The interior of her body still flamed. Her breath came in wanton heaves. She pressed herself back against the bars, her eyes meeting his, and he lost control. His hands plunged between the bars and hauled her off the ground, roughly pulling her against his hips, taking her. She moaned with pleasure. Her hands tangled in his hair. Their mouths fed on each other. Gasping, their joined bodies slammed against the bars. Sweat broke out down her back and on her cheeks. She arched, screamed in ecstasy, shuddering again and again.

Then she sagged lifelessly, slipping through his arms, and folded up on the ground like a gutted rag doll.

Ghapp staggered back, soaking wet and weak, and stared at her. She rose onto her elbows, a satisfied smile playing across her face, then spoke with a certainty of knowledge normally reserved for libraries.

"The castle is ours now, Izzam Ghapp. It will fall to dust, screaming, just as I did."

They dressed quickly, she in his cloak, then each found their way back to the surface, met at the main gate and hurried across the bridge, through the Outpost. Leaving it, they passed a string of five house wagons, the once brightly painted but now faded vehicles of a tribe of traveling performers. But the nymph took little notice.

Eleven

ONE EAR

Gath turned the stallion off Silk Road, and it galloped through tall pines, following a muddy trail in the snow. Shafts of sunlight shot through the gaps between the thick trunks, warming the cold morning air. Beyond the trees, clouds drifted through the valley, billowing balls of ivory and peach in the morning light. In the distance, thrusting peaks rose out of their illusory bulk, a world resting in the sky. The beginning of the Great Barma Range.

Reaching a spread of concealing elderberry bushes, the Barbarian plunged the horse between them, and reined up in a clearing, sheltered by leafy boughs. Billbarr and Fleka, still wrapped in their night blankets, stood beside a small campfire, knives in hand and eyes startled. The huge black bear ambled freely just beyond the wagon.

"Outlaws!" Gath barked. "Crossing the bridge at Blue-water."

"More knives?" Billbarr gasped.

"Not the plague again!" Fleka groaned.

"I don't know," Gath said sharply. "Run the bear off and get in the trees. Stay there until I come back."

He swung the horse around and it bounded back the way he came, the blade of the axe slung across his back flashing as he swept through the swaths of bright sunlight. Making Silk Road, he headed west at a run, then slowed the horse to a walk as it rounded a turn, and Bluewater came into view.

The camp consisted of a sunny clearing, a spread of sandy beach siding a pond formed by a turn in the river, the Marl, and a log bridge over the river. The high forest, common to Checket Territory, walled the road, the clearing and the river. Hide tents, belonging to the Checket tribe, occupied the clearing, along with several wagons and campfires belonging to travelers. They and the local natives stood silently where he had seen them moments earlier, huddled together before the largest tent, the tavern. Frightened and saddened, they looked across the road at two shadowed bodies dangling by ropes from a tree limb, hanged by the neck.

The outlaws, nine roughs wearing dirty furs and assorted bits of armor and weapons, had crossed the bridge and teth-ered their horses to trees about ten strides from the hanging bodies. Now they sat on the beds of needles, sheltered by the trees, and drank from steaming cups of hot cider served to them by two Checket tavern wenches, short, wide-boned, middle-aged women with skin as fair and firm as young girls. The wenches kept their heads turned away from the gruesome sight, but the outlaws watched the sway and turn of the stiff bodies with amused eyes, pointing and making jokes.

Gath walked his horse down the middle of the road and reined up opposite the hanging bodies. The outlaws stopped talking and put their eyes on him. The wenches hurried back across the road, joining the huddled group. They also stared at him, whispering nervously. He took no notice and looked at the hanging bodies, his eyes hard, alert.

They had been murdered, and in a manner designed to entertain dark minds jaded with pain. They had been hanged from separate ropes, but together, their bodies bound face-to-face, like lovers, so they could watch each other die. A skinny rubber man wearing the pink hose and jerkin of an acrobat, and a young woman weighing over three hundred pounds, wearing the bright yellow tunic, pink circles on her cheeks and dyed yellow hair of a performing fat lady. A bright yellow loop earring fell below one ear, and a black-handled knife protruded from her shoulder, put there as a marker. Their contorted faces said they died of strangulation.

The Barbarian's eyes did not change. His body did not react. He glanced across the road at the wagons parked among the tents. One, a single-hitch buggy with a short bed, was painted yellow and heaped with cages filled with cooing doves. They had ribbons tied around their feathered necks. Performing doves.

He walked his horse across the road and past the huddled group, reined up beside the yellow wagon. From his saddle, he reached into the bed, and one by one picked up the cages, broke them open, set the birds free. No complaint or sound of any kind came from the huddled bodies. But one of the outlaws, a thick brute, his face all but hidden by his shaggy hair and beard, stood abruptly, as if annoyed.

Gath ignored him, removed a blanket from the driver's box, and crossed back to the swaying bodies. Standing in his stirrups, he cut them down. Dismounting, he removed the black-handled knife from the woman's back, wiped it off on her tunic and tucked it under his belt. Then he covered the bodies with the blanket and faced the outlaws.

The brutes shifted in place, two rising behind the one already standing, as if accused. The shaggy-haired one, apparently the leader, waved them back into place and, advancing like the strutting savage he was, moved to Gath. He stuck his thumbs under his wide leather sword belt, and looked the Barbarian up and down. Only his small blue eyes and broken nose showed through his hair and beard, except where his

hair was tied back to display his ears. Only one looked like
an ear. The other was scar tissue, his badge of brutality. He
scratched it as he spoke.

"Large, aren't you, stranger? I could use a man your size,
and that axe on your back as well." He smiled sluggishly.
"You belong to somebody, or are you, maybe, looking for
work? If you are, I can give you, and a hundred men like
you, all you can handle."

"The pay?" Gath asked.

"Booty!" One Ear replied, grinning proudly. "Booty from
the richest castle you or I will ever see. And women! Not
your ordinary frightened widows, but fine women. Beauties
gathered from every village and city in these parts."

"I've heard of no war in these hills," Gath said.

One Ear laughed. "It hasn't started yet, stranger. But you'll
hear of it when it does, believe me. A smart man would join
up now, 'fore the ranks are filled."

"The name of your general? The castle?"

The brute shook his head. "No questions, stranger. You'll
find out soon enough."

"I'd rather know now."

One Ear shook his head again, grinning vapidly.

Gath's eyes held One Ear's until his grin lost its humor,
then he said, "Get yourself a shovel, and help me bury these
two."

One Ear's small blue eyes grew smaller, knotting in the
meat of his pimpled face. "What'd you say?"

"I said get a shovel, and get your men over here. I need a
burial detail."

"Are you telling me or asking me, stranger?" One Ear
said, turning his head slightly to show Gath his missing ear.

"I'm telling you," Gath said, his husky voice now quiet
and low. "And when you're finished, I'll let you name your
general, the castle."

One Ear's thumbs came out from under his belt, and his
hands dropped beside the grips of his sword and dagger. A
thread of smoke rose out of the matted hair hiding his forehead and he scratched at it, pushing the hair aside to reveal
a glowing red dot, the source of the fumes.

The Barbarian's eyes glanced at the dot, then met One Ear's eyes again. "Your tattoo seems to be acting up."

"That's none of your business."

Gath shook his head and unslung his axe. One Ear's hand closed on the hilt of his sword and Gath kicked his legs out from under him. The outlaw hit the ground with a grunt, rolled onto his knees, sword in hand. The Barbarian swung his axe, hit his sword arm with the flat of the axe blade, driving the sword ten feet off.

The other outlaws, having jumped to their feet, drew their weapons and Gath shouted, "This is personal!"

He drove his axe upright in the ground, showing them he had no intention of killing their leader. The outlaws held their places as One Ear, holding his numb arm with his good one, struggled to his feet. Gath turned on him.

"Who made the mark on your forehead?"

One Ear replied by drawing his dagger. The Barbarian moved for him, stepped inside the striking dagger, blocked the blow with a forearm, and put his fist in One Ear's gut, just under his circular brass breastplate. The outlaw doubled up, and Gath drove a fist into his forehead, knocking him over onto his back. Dropping to his knees, straddling the outlaw, Gath hit him in the head again, aggravating the demon mark, and smoke spewed forth in black, angry complaint.

The huddled group gasped and the outlaws stared in shock, lowering their weapons.

One Ear, writhing under Gath, grabbed his forehead with both hands, and smoke swirled between his dirty fingers. The Barbarian drove his arms aside, took hold of his face with a big hand and squeezed his jaw.

"Who made the sign?" Gath demanded. "What kind of demon spawn are you? Who do you serve?"

"I don't know," One Ear muttered. "Nobody does."

Gath hit him again. Flames flickered from the red spot in complaint, and the outlaw's face contorted with blind rage. He clawed at Gath's face, bucked, tried to bite the Barbarian's leg. Grabbing his face again, Gath slammed his head against

the ground and leaned close. Terror filled the outlaw's eyes
and he shuddered at the looming wrath looking down at him.

"The name of your general?" Gath demanded. "The castle you attack?"

"Nobody knows!" One Ear pleaded.

"Your tribe? The location of your war camp?"

One Ear's face lost all color. "Don't ask me that."

"Name it!" Gath growled. "Tell me where!"

"I dare not," the outlaw gasped.

The Barbarian tightened his grip on his face, and the jaw-
bones shifted in their sockets, threatening to break.

"All right!" mumbled the outlaw. "It's to the east, ten,
twelve days' ride, in Barma High Country."

"The castle?"

"Let go and I'll tell you."

Gath let go of his face and One Ear opened his mouth to
speak, but shrieked in pain instead. Flames burst from the
red spot, and his skull split apart under his flesh, tearing it
open. Killing him instantly.

Gath pushed away, rising, and stared in horror. The dark
image ruling the outlaw had silenced him. He turned away,
then looked back. A speck of bright yellow showed through
One Ear's tangled hair. Kneeling, Gath pushed the hair aside,
found a yellow loop earring dangling from his good ear. It
matched the fat lady's.

Gath saw to the burial of the two traveling players, then
returned to his forest camp. Billbarr and Fleka came down
from their hiding places. She helped the boy find his bear,
then they led it back into its cage on the wagon and sat down
facing the Barbarian.

Gath, having removed his horned helmet from his saddlebags, sat down facing the fire. He drew the dagger he had
removed from the fat woman from his belt, studied it. The
handle was carved in the shape of a nude, wanton, savage
nymph.

"Another marker, huh?" Fleka muttered bitterly, staring
at the dagger. "That figures. Just when I decide to join a
troupe of players, this plague breaks out." She put her eyes

on Gath. "Are we going to keep heading for those mountains, or use our heads and get out of here?"

"Not now," Billbarr whispered to her, and turned to Gath. "Was it the . . . the ones we saw yesterday? The fat lady and rubber man?"

Gath nodded and Fleka whimpered, tears welling in her eyes as she turned away. "I suppose they killed all their birds too?"

"No," Gath said quietly. "They again share the sky with the wind."

She looked over a shoulder at him, moved by his unexpected tone and manner of speech, and Billbarr nodded at the dagger. "Who is it?" he asked, referring to the figure on the handle.

"I don't know," Gath replied.

He set the dagger on the ground in front of him. Then, grasping the horned helmet in both hands, he lowered it over his head, and picked the dagger back up. A moment passed, then a tremor shook his body and his fist clenched the dagger, burying the voluptuous handle within his grip.

Billbarr and Fleka shared a wary glance, and the Barbarian removed the helmet, set it back beside him. Billbarr looked from Gath to the dark figure on the handle of the dagger, then back at Gath. "You . . . you know her now, don't you?"

"Yes," Gath said, his whisper low and brutal. "She is called Tiyy. She made the horned helmet."

The boy shivered and the color left his cheeks. Fleka put an arm around him, holding him close, and they looked at Gath.

The Barbarian thumbed the dagger handle, then looked off through the trees at the beckoning mountains beyond the clouds.

Twelve
PATCHES

Robin Lakehair squatted on the floor of Brown John's house wagon, sewing a black patch to the hem of his tunic. The *bukko* stood on a stool, holding the garment in a shaft of sunlight so she could see. The lilt of music, laughter and activity coming from the Water Court outside spilled through the window with the sunshine but failed to alter the sober mood in the wagon.

Symmetrical black patches now covered Brown John's brown garment. Unlike the frayed, haphazardly arranged bone- and umber-colored patches, which Robin had removed on their arrival at Whitetree nine days earlier, each perfectly cut patch was piped with violet silk and placed in a sedate arrangement. Starting with small ones at the collar, they gradually grew larger as they descended to the hem. The effect was grave. Dignified.

Leaning back and tilting her head, Robin surveyed her work and frowned. Along with his new black boots and soft velvet cap, the patches made the *bukko* look like some pompous ass she had been trying to avoid all her life. She shook her head as she spoke.

"I still don't like them, Brown."

"Child," the *bukko* said, his tone lofty enough for an eagle's nest, "we can no longer be shy. We are the essential players in life's great plot now. This is Whitetree, Robin." He spread his arms, taking in the entire wagon and the castle outside. "The Citadel of Endless Dreams, the stage upon which you, the glory of all glories, will create illusions that will fill the theaters of our minds, and of our children's, our children's children's.''

"Brown, please," she pleaded, tying off the last thread. "Don't get so excited. I haven't got the part yet, and I'm not sure I even want it anymore."

"You want it, butterfly," he chided her. "This castle is the asylum for both the dream and the dreamer. It's your holy ground. It would be a sacrilege for us to hide here. And," he looked down at himself approvingly, "when you are dealing with aristocrats, you must look at least as well off as they are or they don't respect you. Now, how does it look?''

"Well, the patches are black," she said, and bit off the thread. "When are we going to see the priests?"

"Your audition is the day after tomorrow, just like I told you yesterday and the day before. So start preparing yourself. I want you bathed, your hair trimmed and your tunic dyed a brilliant yellow, to go with the new baubles I'm going to purchase from the Issbaaks." He chuckled with glee, twisting and turning to look at himself. "Their designs are incredible, a mix of gorgeous pinks and oranges."

Robin scooted back and tilted her head skeptically. "Well, I sure hope my costume doesn't look like yours. With all that black and your new boots, you look like you're selling fear instead of laughter."

"Nonsense," he said, fluffing his tunic. "The darks will contrast beautifully with your sacred light."

"What light?" she said, a rush of shame coloring her cheeks.

He frowned at her, his white eyebrows arcing dramatically. "I told you, I do not want to hear that tone in your voice again."

"But nothing's happened, Brown. I've tried, but I can't raise a glimmer. In fact it's gotten worse. Ever since we came through the gate, I've felt empty." She sagged back against the edge of his bed and looked at the floor. "I think the jewels are dead, Brown. I don't even feel the aura anymore. I feel naked all the time."

"That's enough of that," he snapped, and jumped off the stool. Hitting the floor, his knee gave and he grunted with pain. Grabbing his bad leg, he sat down heavily on the floor. "Damn! It just won't heal."

"Are you all right?" she asked, concerned.

"No, I'm not all right."

"I'll wrap it," she said, sitting forward.

"No you won't," he growled. "You'll sit there and listen to me. Because this is the last time I'm going to say it. Stop worrying about the jewels. Once you have the part, I'll have access to the castle, and when I find the right formula you'll be fine. Now stop talking about it." He rubbed his calf hard. "Damn! I've really done it this time. I've got to calm down, and stop bouncing around all the time."

"That's what's bothering you, isn't it?" she asked quietly. "That's why you're making all these changes. You're not in control of things here. Not even a little bit."

"No, but I will be," he said grimly. "We've just got to be patient."

She smiled wanly, drew her knees up, hugging them, and looked off at the dust drifting in the streaming sunlight. "I don't know, Brown. I'm beginning to think this is all a bad idea. Something . . . something is wrong here. This castle is spooky."

"Spooky?"

"Yes." She looked at him. "I feel like something is crawling on me all the time."

"You're just not used to castle life, child. That's the grime, the lice."

"Oh, Brown, stop it. That's not what I mean."

"Don't be too sure," he said belligerently. "You haven't bathed since you moved in with me, and the river's right out there waiting for you. I'm surprised you didn't jump in the day we arrived."

"That's just it, Brown, the river frightens me." She looked out the window at a plume of snarling smoke and shivered. "Everything frightens me. There's something wrong here, Brown. Something evil."

He chuckled. "You're making things up now, butterfly. You just miss Jakar, that's all."

"I suppose that's part of it." Her eyes found his. "Is he

all right, Brown? Does he mind living with the other men? Is he eating well? Does . . . does he miss me?''

"He misses you, just like you miss him. But it has to be this way. Besides, he needs time to himself to think things over. He's lost his sense of humor, for months now. He takes himself far too seriously. It's a trait of the Kavens. But it will pass."

"Are you sure?''

"I'm sure."

She smiled warmly. "Thank you, Brown. If I didn't have you to talk to, I don't know what I'd do. Here," she took hold of his boot, "give me that." He put his foot in her lap and she removed his boot, then picked a roll of cloth off his bed and began to wrap his sore calf. A moment passed before she spoke.

"Brown, there really is something wrong here in White-tree, something nasty. The men look at the women in a way that isn't nice. I know it's a festival, and I'm no naive child anymore. I know what goes on. But it's not joyous like it is in other places. And some of the women have been hurt, you know, some of the harlots."

"You're talking about the White Archers." She nodded and he added, "Well, that's how aristocrats get sometimes. This castle hasn't been threatened for a hundred years, and they're bored. They haven't anything to do but spend their money, drink and chase women. But they're not bad men, not really. You'll get used to them."

"I don't want to get used to them," she said flatly. She knotted the wrap in place, slipped his boot back on, then put her eyes on his. "I've made up my mind, Brown. I wasn't sure, but now that I've thought about it, I am. I want to leave here, before something terrible happens." He chuckled and she stopped him. "Don't, Brown. Trust me. Just this once."

"I do trust you," he said gruffly, then stood. "If I didn't, we wouldn't be here." He put his weight on his bad leg, testing it. "Earthshaking events are about to occur, and we, you and I, Robin, are going to do the shaking." He glared back at her. "Just because you are suddenly confronted by a few ugly truths of this world, you can't let them blind you to your duty.''

"I know my duty," she said angrily, rising behind her words. "But this castle is hurting us. It's too grand. It's making you act differently. Big and important . . . and pretentious!" He scowled at her. "It's true. And you want me to act the same way, and I can't. I . . . I don't feel right about it."

"I'll decide what's right," he snapped. "I'm the bukko, remember?"

"Yes," she said tiredly, "but—"

He took hold of her by the shoulders, stopping her. "Yes, and you are the future." His tone rang with grave portent. "I see things coming, Robin. A time when there will be only masterless men and women, when the only barriers will be those imposed by the limits of our imagination."

She turned out of his grip, sat on the bed and scolded him with her eyes. "You're repeating yourself. That's what you said about Gath when you first sent me to him."

He flushed with embarrassment, turned and moved to the window. When he had composed himself, he nodded. "You're right, I did. But now I'm saying it again." He turned to her. "Three years ago, I thought it was Gath my visions foretold of. But it wasn't. It is you, child. It's you who will drive the nightmare from the children's sleep, and fill their minds with soaring dreams worthy of the dreaming. Not Gath of Baal. You! So stop thinking about him. Your destinies aren't linked. Not anymore!"

"Brown," she said quietly, "don't do this. You're making this all up, just to feed your pride."

All boyishness left his face, suddenly dangerous. "Robin," he whispered, "we're going to stay right here until you get the part. Then we're going to stage the resurrection and perform it. When all that has happened, we'll discuss leaving. Not before."

"No, Brown. I won't stay. I want to go back to Jakar and live normally."

"Forget about living normally! You weren't made for one man! You were made for the world. You have shooting stars within you, Robin Lakehair. I know this, even if you do not. You are the answer to every question. If you do not make magic, then none will be made.''

She stared at him, shame and rage and fear flooding her body. The door burst open, and Doll Harl stuck her head in.

''So there you are, you old reprobate! I've been looking all over for you. The audition time's been changed. The priests are waiting for her in the Vestry now.''

''Now?''

''All right, be fussy. Not now, in twenty minutes.''

''But Robin must bathe. Her hair is a mess. She—''

''It'll have to wait. This is the only chance you'll get.''

The finality in her tone made the *bukko* look at Robin, his eyes suddenly helpless, pleading. She stood uneasily, her fingers fumbling with her hair, her face still defiant. He hesitated, then whispered, ''Please, Robin. Do this for me.''

Thirteen

THE STAGE

The two acolytes stood just inside the gate through Link Wall, joining Round Tower on the western side of the castle, and Moat Tower on the eastern. Their white-gloved hands were folded before them in perpetual prayer to the White Veshta, and they wore white sacking belted with white ropes. Hidden in the shadows of their hoods, their faces were dark voids as serene, mysterious and threatening as the vast, almost empty courtyard spreading beyond the gate, the Sacred Close.

When Doll Harl, Brown John and Robin Lakehair reached them, the acolytes dipped their heads in silent greeting, then turned and started across the polished white stones.

Robin shivered slightly. Brown took her hand, and they followed the acolytes, the *bukko* thrilling to the natural amphitheater.

The floor of the Close sloped gently toward the northwest corner, providing the perfect angle for an audience viewing the stage under construction there. Beyond the stage, the jagged, sheer face of the looming Curtain Wall, stretching the full width of the Close and sealing off the Stronghold at the upper, north end of the castle, provided the perfect backdrop.

As they neared the stage, the *bukko* puffed up proudly, as if he were already its master.

Built of wood, it stood on a scaffolding nearly seventy strides wide and three stories tall, and consisted of three sections, the two side sections angling slightly toward the larger center section. A black castle formed the left section, a forest the center and a white castle the right.

Carpenters swarmed over the structure, making final repairs on the wings, balconies, stairways and towers, and raising pennants of the White Archers over the white castle, and black flags featuring death's-heads over the black castle. Painters added the last touches to three already colorful house wagons standing in the fictional forest, and sweepers swept up. Above the center stage, a huge saurian skull, its jaws spread wide, took up the second and third stories. Jagged red teeth, as tall as full-grown men, sprouted behind blood-red gums. A tongue covered with a bright red carpet protruded from the mouth, forming a ramp that led into the shadowed skull cavity. A figurative ramp to the underworld, to the realm of the Master of Darkness.

Reaching the stage, the group paused, eyes bright with excitement as they stared up at the dramatic structure.

"It's incredible," Robin gasped.

"Yes it is," Brown replied. "It is easily the largest stage in the world, and it stands here all year round."

"They never tear it down?" Robin asked, amazed.

"Never!" Brown said and pointed at the red tongue. "There, you see that tongue, that is where I am going to have you make your entrance. Bound in black ropes, and with flames burning behind you. You will emerge from the breath of the Lord of Death in a cloud of smoke.''

"Smoke? Flames?''

"Yes, real flames. And thunder, the crack of lightning!''

"Oh, Brown, I can't believe it. I didn't know. I thought you were just making it all up.''

"That's not all,'' he said with a ring of piety, and pointed at wheels set in wooden grooves at the base of the huge skull. "You see there, those wheels will roll the entire second story forward, right at the audience.''

"The whole upper story?''

He nodded. "That's when I make my entrance. As it rolls forward, the fire and smoke engines will shoot flames and black smoke out into the crowd, blinding them for a moment, terrifying them. Then I, in the black costume of the Lord of Death, will come forth from the mouth of the underworld!''

"You're going to take the dark part?''

"Yes,'' he said with a show of reluctance. "I don't think anyone else really understands it.''

She nodded only mild agreement. But the *bukko* took no notice. Smiling broadly, he stuffed his thumbs under his belt. "I'm going to do this right, Robin, do it as it deserves to be done. Nothing will be spared. At one point, I will have three hundred performers on these boards.''

"All at once?''

"All at once. And that does not count the musicians behind the scenes, or the people working the engines, the costumes, the props.''

"We won't do them ourselves?'' she said, delight widening her eyes.

He shook his head. "No, child, this castle is full of experts. You'll even have someone to do your hair and makeup, and a girl with nothing else to do but keep your dressing room in order.''

"Oh, Brown, my dressing room?'' Her words danced. "Really? Can we see it?''

"Not now!'' Doll said sharply. "You've wasted too much time already. They're getting impatient. Come on.''

She hurried across the face of the stage toward the two

acolytes waiting at the north end, and they turned, vanishing around the corner of the stage. As they followed Doll, the *bukko* put an arm around Robin and spoke hurriedly.

"You'll see everything as soon as we have more time, child. And you will be even more amazed than you are now. Any doubts you had will vanish completely. There is even a thunder barrel, and underground rooms and tunnels for traps and secret entrances, and a whole room full of counterpoises and pulleys and wheels for the ascensions and flying sequences."

"Flying?"

"Yes, some special acrobats, fliers, have been hired for the abduction and resurrection scenes. And the carpenters here are magicians. They've made a mechanical ass and ox which bow to the Veshta during the adoration sequence, and dummies whose arms and heads fall off, spout blood during the massacre of the jugglers."

"But flying?" Robin gasped. "You can't really mean fly?"

"Yes, fly, but that is nothing." He patted her shoulder. "Wait until you see the shooting stars."

"Oh, Brown," she said, shamefaced. "I'm sorry I gave you so much trouble. I'll try not to do it again."

He laughed warmly, and they rounded the corner of the stage.

Doll and the acolytes stood in front of a solid gold door, the entrance to the Vestry. The door stood in an arched stone opening at the base of the Curtain Wall, thus providing two entrances into the Stronghold. From the raw color of the stone around the door, it was apparent that it was a recent addition, the contemporary owners of the castle, having no fear of attack, being more concerned with access to the Close than defense of the Stronghold.

One of the acolytes pulled a cord hanging from a hole in the face of the door, and a bell rang gently somewhere beyond it. As they waited in silence, Robin glanced back at the stage and shook her head in amazement.

"I just never knew, Brown. I never could have even imagined it."

He leaned close to her ear, whispered, "They don't know

it, but they built the whole thing just for you." He grinned. "How's that make you feel?"

"Frightened," she whispered. "Really frightened."

The gold door swung open. The trio followed the acolytes into the dark narrow passage beyond, and the door swung closed behind them, as if it had made the decision itself.

Fourteen

PRIESTS OF LIGHT

Iptur, the High Priest of the Goddess of Light, wore a smile so pious and benign it could have shamed a rose into blushing. But when he laid that smile over Robin, standing barefoot on a circular white stone pedestal facing his throne chair, it covered her like a boy's shameless fingers, betraying his assiduous dedication to his own divine eroticism. His cavernous blue eyes studied each eyelash, turn of lip and curve of thigh with religious intensity.

Dagan, the Celestial Clerk, sat on Iptur's right, and Surim, the Great Scribe, on his left, their raised chairs forming a semicircle around the pedestal, supporting the trembling girl. Being novices in comparison to the high priest, Dagan's and Surim's sublime attention focused on less subtle aspects of Robin's attractions, her breasts and hips.

Tall, white, flaming candles standing at intervals against the darkly draped wall of the Vestry behind the masters of Whitetree revealed that each of them sat in precisely the same manner, and wore the same vestments, white velvet and leather robes bearing patterns of concentric circles. In addition, Iptur wore a white leather skullcap with long pendant ears that tickled his wrinkled throat.

Moments of sacred study passed, then Iptur folded his bony hands against his chest, as if he were extremely fond of himself, and tilted his narrow head so that his massive forehead and waves of thick gray hair glistened in the bright candlelight. Using a voice as melodious as a temple gong, he said, "Perhaps, child, you would remove your cloak?"

"Of course," Robin said nervously, bowing for the fourth time since entering the small circular room, and quickly lowered her cloak to the floor, bending at the knees so as not to let it drop and make an unseemly sound. Then she stood pertly, fists on hips as the light invaded every tear in her poor tunic, illuminated every embarrassing stain and dirty fingernail.

Brown John, standing at the back of the small room, shifted nervously and cast a wary glance at Doll Harl, standing beside him. She ignored him. Shifting again, he glanced at the two acolytes standing beside a large wooden wheel set in the wall, then at the guard at the door, a common soldier in leather armor as burnished by time and battle as his ruddy face. He did not appear to be afraid to speak in the presence of the priests, as everyone else was. But neither did he appear to have any interest in speaking, or in Robin, the priests or anything, except his own sardonic grin. This, according to the *bukko*'s theatrical way of thinking, set the soldier apart from the others and made him unique. But none of these rambling thoughts did the *bukko* any good. The audition was going badly. He could sense it, and there was nothing he could do if they did not let him talk.

A moment passed and Iptur raised a finger, barely. The acolytes cranked the wooden wheel and Robin's pedestal shook, staggering her slightly, and began to rotate slowly. She made three full revolutions and Iptur raised a hand. The pedestal came to a stop.

"Hmmmm," Iptur said, admiring Robin's smile. Then he folded his hands like religious relics. "Would her bukko please step forward."

Sighing with relief, Brown John stepped into the glare of candlelight and bowed for the third time himself.

Iptur deigned to look at him. "Welcome, bukko. It pleases

us to greet you to Whitetree. The name Brown John frequently appears on our scrolls alongside the most famous troubadours in the land.'' Brown's mouth dropped open and the priest smiled. ''That this surprises you is understandable. Few people know of what we do here, and even fewer understand. It is the holy duty of the Priests of Light, since our beloved goddess is the benefactor of all entertainers, to chronicle the lives and maintain accurate records of those who serve her with diligence and adoration. Particularly those, as is your case, who serve her with enlightenment.''

Brown puffed up, his cheeks burning with sudden exaltation.

''It also pleases us, bukko,'' Iptur continued, ''to find you are a man of keen perception.'' He nodded at Robin. ''This child is indeed lovely. Her left elbow and her earlobes are truly remarkable works of the goddess's divine art, to say nothing of her more obvious charms.'' Suddenly his smile fell to the floor and his tone rang with indignation. ''But to present her to us in this manner, robed in dirt and tatters, is a serious insult, not only to the sacred role you presume to ask us to consider her for, but to ourselves.''

Dagan and Surim muttered grave agreement and Brown John's face colored.

Iptur let him suffer, then said, ''Prior to your appearance here, I had given serious consideration to appointing the girl and yourself to the posts you seek, basing my considerations on our records of your notable feats and Dame Harl's lavish claims. In addition, since we have decided Whitetree should have its own bukko, a permanent master of its stage, a master who would see to it that performances take place throughout the entire year, and since your name headed the list of candidates, I intended to offer you that post as well. Make you the king of bukkos.'' His face sagged with an expression of grave betrayal. ''I was counting on you, sir. But now, you commit this sacrilege! Bring me this,'' he wagged a bony hand at Robin, ''this perfectly beautiful lass dressed in rags, and I have lost all confidence in you.''

Brown's knees went weak. His bruised calf throbbed all

the way up into his buttocks. "I . . . I beg your forgiveness,
my lords, I—"

"Silence," Dagan snarled suddenly. "Here you only speak
when asked to."

Brown John, biting his tongue, bowed again. Iptur shook
his head slowly, allowing time to pass in silence. Then he
looked at Robin, and his dedication to his own stimulation
lifted his sagging cheeks a good two inches. "You have
spoiled her," he said to Brown John without looking at him.
"Hidden her charms. If it was not for my own keen perception, she would have been dismissed immediately." He turned
on the *bukko*. "What do you have to say for yourself?
Speak!"

"It was a misunderstanding, my lord," Brown blurted.
"Not on your parts, of course, only my own. I thought the
audition was still two days off. If . . . if you could allow me
a little more time, I assure you that I can present her in a
more than satisfactory way, a manner that will not only
delight but honor you."

"Words," scoffed Dagan, rattling his heavy coin purse
nervously. "Nothing but words."

"You had time," Surim said, arranging the folds of his
vestments to hide the dusty stains of a man who socialized
with scrolls and tablets more than people. "You had time."

"Lord Surim is correct," Iptur said with finality. He waved
Brown back into position and put his wet eyes on Doll.
"Speak, Dame Harl. Do you have another girl?"

"Not another girl, my lord," Doll said, bowing slightly,
"but a suggestion."

"Make it."

"A bath, my lords. Let me wash this lovely child, and
remove every trace of grime and artifice, and then display
her to you."

"Without rouge?" Surim asked it, his face shocked.
"Without her hair styled and combed?"

"Yes," Doll said firmly. "In fact, I suggest you audition
every candidate in this manner, without their bukko's tricks
and artifice, and without their own. With nothing to recommend them except your own immaculate judgment."

Iptur smiled a smile Brown had not seen him use up to this moment. "Unpainted?"

"Yes, my lord," Doll returned the same smile. "Unadorned."

Iptur's smile spread like a contagion to Dagan and Surim. The three priests shared a nod, and Iptur turned toward the soldier at the door. "Sergeant Roundell, conduct the two ladies up to the baths and see that Dame Harl is provided with soaps, unguents, towels, whatever she requires."

The guard swung the door open. Doll helped Robin off the dais, and they hurried out, the guard closing the door behind them.

Iptur, Dagan and Surim stood. The high priest motioned at Brown, instructing him to follow them, then descended the dais supporting the throne chairs, seemingly floated to a small wooden door in the shadows of the Vestry, and removed a key from his robes. Unlocking the shallow door, he opened it, stooped slightly and passed into the shallow stone passage beyond. Oil lamps set in brackets lit the way.

Reaching the door, Brown John hesitated and the two acolytes motioned him to enter. He did, and the acolytes, remaining behind in the Vestry, closed and bolted the door behind him.

Fifteen

SOAP BUBBLES

Brown followed the priests down the passage, through a twisting, underground tunnel, then up a steep incline and through a door into a small room. Black carpet covered the walls, ceiling and sunken floor. An oil lamp hung from the

ceiling, casting faint light over three black divans heaped with
black pillows. They faced a wall hung with heavy black
drapes. Pull ropes hung to one side. The air was warm and
moist, laden with exotic perfumes. Black Narcissus. Throat
of the Lily. Sigh of Jasmine.

Iptur, Dagan and Surim, their footsteps muffled by the thick
velvet, descended the stairs to the sunken floor and lay down
on the divans, their backs propped up by the plush cushions.
Without turning, Iptur said quietly, "Make yourself comfortable, bukko. If she is anything like you think she is, the
appointment is still yours."

His boyish smile bouncing, Brown sat down on the raised
bench behind the divans, reminding himself to remain re-
spectfully silent no matter what might occur. Then, growing
moist from the dank heat, he removed his cloak, loosened
his tunic and waited.

Moments passed. The priests talked quietly, then looked
up as the sardonic soldier entered and nodded to Iptur.

"Thank you, Sergeant Roundell," the high priest said quietly. "You may proceed."

Sergeant Roundell went to the lamp, and warm light
washed over his thinning, brownish-gold hair, pale blue eyes.
All but hidden amid smile lines, they carried the wary squint
common to killers of men. Seeing the *bukko* staring at him,
the soldier looked directly at him and measured Brown with
no other emotion than curiosity, then doused the lamp.

In the darkness, the *bukko* heard the soldier descend to the
sunken floor, then the velvet curtains parted slowly and silently, revealing a wall of black metallic gauze, penetrated
by thousands of tiny holes. Steam, filled with undulating light,
seeped through the mesh and wafted into the darkness, followed by effervescent laughter and the trickle and splash of
water.

Brown John, leaning forward, focused his rising curiosity
on vague forms moving beyond the atomized mist, and realized that the gauzelike metal wall was almost as transparent
as a silk veil. Then his mouth dropped open.

Within the vaporous light, clusters of succulent, naked female forms lounged and frolicked in frothy bubbles, dipping

into and floating on a large oval pool of steaming water. They lathered their breasts and bellies, preened and combed their luxuriant locks of blond, brunette and red hair. Their movements, some indolent and others spirited, seemed to have no purpose or direction, as if their bodies had no reason to exist other than to provide playgrounds for the beads and rivulets of glittering water which romped and trickled over their heaping portions of quivering flesh.

Brown John sighed, enervated by the sublime lassitude of the vision. It seemed illusionary, too perfect to be real. But the belts of perfumed air and the totally unselfconscious laughter on the young vibrant faces told him this was no theatrical act.

The women had no idea they were being observed. From the opposite side, the metallic gauze wall, with light from the bath hall's many oil lamps flooding over it, undoubtedly appeared solid.

Delighting in the spectacle, Brown dissected it with the practiced eye of a *bukko*.

Each girl appeared to be perfect example of the qualities of beauty her tribe was known for. The Issbaaks, from the Sea of Peace, were tall and strong. The Dowats and Checkets, from the Great Forest Basin, were squat and voluptuous. The local Barma tribeswomen were thin and angular. The Azails and Chooodaats, from the eastern mountains of the Kitzakk Empire, had raven hair that hung to the backs of their knees. The Tirs were all redheads and tattooed. The Kellits were no taller than eleven-year-olds and wore agate, ivory and jasper earrings. The Jallalibads were all breasts and hips, and braided their yellow hair.

When Brown caught his breath, he found Iptur looking over a shoulder at him. Brown leaned toward him and the high priest whispered, "Those gathered there," he pointed at a group of more reserved women at the left end of the pool, "are the regimental wives. Being married to a White Archer gives them position and importance, but diminishes their sense of humor. The rest are the regimental courtesans." His hand swept the breadth of the pool. "Unfortunately, our supply is dangerously low."

Brown found that difficult to accept, even though the priest sounded quite matter-of-fact, as if discussing loaves of bread.

"This is true," Iptur assured him. "One of the duties of the castle bukko will be to select and buy women for the Hall of Beds, as well as for his theatrical presentations."

Iptur turned away, not bothering to watch Brown John's grin. Then, bringing himself under control, the old man looked back at the steamy emporium of fleshy delights and his face hardened.

Two naked women, with white towels draped over their shoulders, had come through the door opening on the dressing rooms on the far side of the pool. Doll Harl and Robin Lakehair. They passed through the living gorgets of flesh toweling off there, and stopped at the edge of the pool, facing steps descending into the water. Doll's short, chubby, pink body contrasted starkly with Robin's nut-brown, arrowlike figure.

Here and there about the pool, women and girls stiffened slightly, casting competitive eyes at the young newcomer. Some displayed aloof scorn, but most were sincerely impressed, joyously delighting in Robin's female perfection.

"She's terribly dark," Surim whispered critically. "I'm sure that's not proper for the White Veshta. I'll have to look it up."

"She's filthy, that's all," Dagan whispered with contempt.

"Yes," Iptur said, his whisper so faint it seemed he spoke to himself. "She does need a good scrubbing. But she is special."

Brown shifted nervously, a guilty ache centering in his chest. As Robin's protector, he was duty bound to stop this shameless invasion of her privacy. He slid forward to protest and felt Sergeant Roundell's knee touch his shoulder. He glanced up at the soldier, and the hard man's sober face told him to stay put and stay silent. He did.

A moment passed, then Iptur leaned toward the *bukko*. "This room has proved absolutely essential to our sacred work. The study of women is the priesthood's first duty, and it is here where many of the most profound doctrines and scriptures of our sacred goddess have been formulated. In their most intimate moments, washing and playing, the female reaches the culmination of her loveliness. That is why I wished you to share this moment. We may see something in this lovely child of yours that could aid in her performance, providing she is selected."

The high priest went back to his studies and Brown John did the same.

Robin and Doll set their fluffy white towels on a stone bench and waded into the pool. Doll carried a large yellowish sponge, and a clay vial of soap hung from a rope looped around her sturdy neck. The water seemed to dance away from Robin's legs, then came swirling back, splashing over her muscular thighs, spraying her arms and flat tummy. As if recognizing the water as an old playmate, she laughed warmly and dove into the pool, entering its wet, giving embrace as neatly as a finger slipping into a glove.

As if drawn by the same string, the three priests sat upright on their divans.

Robin surfaced, with only her red-gold hair and brown bottom showing above the frothy water, then jackknifed and plunged deep, leaving a sudsy swirl behind. She did it again and again, like a playful dolphin, as natural as water and air.

"Curious," Iptur muttered. "Each time she disappears, I have this insatiable desire to see her reappear."

Surim nodded agreement, and Dagan's pink face began to excrete fetid beads of sweat, confirming he was of the same mind.

Robin erupted with a splash and Doll caught her elbow, saying something lost amid the chatter of the other women. The older woman led the perky girl across the pool, away from the others, and they mounted an underwater pedestal. Standing on it, the water came to their ankles, with their bodies no more than ten feet from the eyes behind the metallic gauze wall.

Doll uncorked the vial with her teeth and poured thick yellow soap over Robin's head. The girl vigorously rubbed the soap into her hair, raising billowing towers of white suds. The older woman gathered the creamy foam with a sponge,

and began to lather Robin's body, lifting an arm, raising a
knee, turning her around, bending her over.

Brown sat back, his cheeks flushing with shame, but did
not look away. Iptur and Surim sat still, but their heads
bobbed steadily, as if every time Robin moved she pulled
their string. Dagan, being a serious type, stood up and moved
to the wall, did his sweating there.

Doll, growing playful, began to shove and wrestle Robin
about as she lathered her, and Robin fought back, rubbing
her lathered body all over Doll. Doll slapped Robin's bottom
sharply and she yelped, laughed and shoved Doll with both
hands. The older woman went over backward, laughing, and
splashed into the water, sinking out of sight. Doll burst back
to the surface and scampered back onto the pedestal, wearing
a garment of billowy soap bubbles.

Brown John smiled. It was the kind of wardrobe he had
always admired. Suddenly a flash of light swept through the
wall, striking the priests and the *bukko* across the face.

"What was that?" Iptur inquired, shielding his eye with a
hand.

"I'm not sure," Surim replied hesitantly.

They stood and stepped quietly to the wall, as Brown began to sweat with fear.

Robin gathered great handfuls of bubbles and blew them
into Doll's face, as the older woman applied more soap, and
more bubbles gushed forth all over Robin. They slid over
breast and belly, and slipped down a thigh, caromed over a
shoulder and sluiced down her arms to spill between her fingers. The flickering light from the oil lamps played on the
translucent, dancing bubbles, then suddenly thin shafts of
light burst from them. They played across the surface of the
water and over the other women, then bounced off the far
wall, came streaking back across the wet blue depths and
dashed through the tiny holes in the false wall to illuminate
the startled eyes of the secret, spellbound observers.

The priests stepped back, obviously fearing some form of
sorcery, and Brown John sat perfectly still. Petrified. Were
they witnessing some unusual display of reflected light? Or

did the light come from where he thought it did, from the sacred brown body of Robin Lakehair, the White Veshta?

Apparently not noticing the light, Robin heaved an armful of bubbles over Doll's head, and they spilled over her face, drained down her body, pulsating with the same light.

Trembling, Surim pressed his face against the gauze wall, allowing the strange light to repeatedly strike his cheeks and eyes; then it faded. The Great Scribe sighed, turned to Iptur and Dagan with a slightly downcast expression and shook his head, whispering, "It's not what I thought. The light was only an accident of nature. Otherwise my cheeks would have been burnt."

He sat back down and Dagan glared at him. "You fool! You could have been blinded! What if it was her?"

Iptur chuckled at that. "There is no chance of that, Dagan. The stars say clearly she will not rise again until another three hundred years have passed." He looked back at the pool as Doll led Robin out of the water and through the door into the dressing rooms, then added, "But this girl is special, very special."

Iptur nodded at Sergeant Roundell and the soldier closed the curtain, relit the oil lamp. Then they returned to the Vestry. The priests seated themselves, and Iptur, enormously pleased with himself, motioned for Brown John to approach as he spoke.

"Once again, bukko, we are grateful. The girl is as perfect for the part of our goddess as any human being can be."

Elation lifted Brown's cheeks. "She has the part?"

"I believe we are agreed on that?" Iptur replied coolly, glancing at Dagan.

"Quite," the Celestial Clerk said, then addressed Brown. "But she is still too dark. I would like to see her rubbed with white powder, and her nipples painted silver. And it is absolutely essential that an element of pain be introduced into her performance. I suggest thorns or a whip, so we actually see her torment when enslaved by the Master of Darkness."

"Whip her?" Brown asked, aghast. "On stage?"

Ignoring the *bukko*'s outburst, Iptur turned to Surim for his opinion.

"I agree with Dagan, your eminence," the Great Scribe said. "She is as rare a collection of bones and tissue as I have ever seen. But, if you will permit me, I also differ with Lord Dagan. Not with the pain, that is essential, but with the powder and silver. I much prefer her natural state. Except, of course, for the soap bubbles."

"Ah yes," Iptur chimed in, "the soap bubbles were superb." He turned to Brown. "That, sir, is your first task as the castle bukko. You will add a bathing sequence to her performance, so that when she escapes from the underworld she may wash the smell of brimstone from her hair, and clean her flesh of the Lord of Death's repellent kiss."

"A bath?" Brown asked with trepidation. "In public?"

"Of course!" Iptur shrilled. "She must anoint the eyes of her devout worshipers with her most intimate beauty. Without shame or self-consciousness. Hiding nothing. Like a true goddess." He scowled at the *bukko*. "I would think that would be perfectly obvious to anyone." He paused, then leaned forward threateningly. "Yet you hesitate, don't you? Hmmmmm."

"It's . . . well," Brown faltered. "It's just that she is extremely shy."

"Surely you could persuade her?" Brown hesitated again and Iptur sat back. "Ahh, I see."

The door opened and Doll and Robin, their faces pink from the bath, entered, followed by the sergeant. Robin, glancing at the priests nervously, quickly joined Brown and took hold of his hand.

"You've got the part," Brown murmured.

She squeezed his hand excitedly, then frowned. "But how did . . ."

"Don't ask. We're working out the details now. Just be quiet and let me handle it."

She nodded obediently, and Brown turned to find Iptur whispering to the sergeant. The soldier nodded, went back out of the room, and the high priest looked down at Doll.

"Thank you, Dame Harl," Iptur said. "You have once again served us well." He put his reverent, powerful eyes on Robin. "You have a special gift, child, so special that it de-

serves to be nurtured and educated by the most enlightened
instruction available. Therefore, since it is within my power
to grant such favors, I grant them to you. No time or cost
will be withheld in our efforts to attain your enlightenment.''

Trembling, Robin bowed. ''I . . . I am honored.''

''I am sure you are,'' Iptur said, and turned to Dagan.
''Dame Harl and the bukko have served us well, pay them
the full measure.''

Dagan nodded, removed two coin purses from his belt, and
tossed one to Doll, the other to Brown.

Doll, her apple-red cheeks ballooning, caught both purses.
Tucking the heavier one inside her blouse, she bowed, then
handed the other to Brown John, urging him toward the door.
''We're finished, let's go.''

Brown looked at the purse in his hand, then turned to
Robin, reached for her, and Doll knocked his arm down,
whispering harshly, ''Leave her be. She stays.''

''Stays?'' he gasped.

''Shhhh!'' she warned him. ''Don't make a fuss. She'll
have the best of everything. Let's go.''

Hearing this exchange, Robin glanced warily at the leering
priests, then at Brown John, her eyes pleading.

''Don't worry,'' Brown whispered quickly, and boldly
faced the priests. ''I am afraid I cannot allow her to stay
here. She is my ward. I cannot give my responsibility for her
well-being to anyone, no matter how eminent.''

''Holy Zard!'' Doll moaned. ''Do you know what you're
doing?'' He looked at her and she added quickly, ''Just say
thank you. Do you understand, just thank you. And do it
before it's too late.''

Brown, hesitating, looked at Robin and she pleaded,
''Don't let them keep me, Brown. I'm afraid.''

The door opened and Sergeant Roundell marched in, followed by four men-at-arms; hardy, disciplined roughs armed
with sheathed swords, daggers and bare fists big enough to
be hiding bricks. With his eyes on Brown, Roundell moved
to Robin and took her gently by the elbow. Robin's eyes
pleaded with Brown. The *bukko* took a step for her, and a
soldier kicked his feet out from under him. By the time he

got back to his feet, Roundell had pushed Robin out the door
and the men-at-arms were marching out.

Doll gave Brown's sleeve a tug, and whispered anxiously,
"Let's go, friend. Now!"

Brown looked at her angrily, and turned on Iptur, wild-
eyed.

The high priest repressed a smile, and said off-handedly,
"Thank you again, bukko. We will take the matter of your
appointment under consideration, and summon you if we have
any further use for your services."

Sixteen

EMPTY

Brown John sat slumped on the stone guardrail of the castle
bridge, legs dangling over the side. Spring had broken on the
land, and melting snow gorged the river. The current rushed
and churned with the power to tear down trees, drown villages. He stared at the rippling surface. Every wrinkle in his
drawn face said he wished he'd fall in.

Sunshine fell on the world around him, as nature's ritual
dance blossomed. Sprigs of bright green burst through the
brown earth on the valley floor. Bright flowers dappled the
greening foothills. Birds sang in the forested mountains.
Children squealed with delight, skimming smooth rocks on
the turbulent waters.

The *bukko* scowled at all of it, and began to rip off his
black patches, throw them into the river. He continued until
someone pinched his bottom. He flinched, nearly throwing
himself into the river, and turned sharply, scowling more
than ever.

Doll Harl stood on the crowded bridge at his side.

"Damn you!" he growled. "I could have fallen in!"

"It would serve you right," she said behind a grin. Then she rested her bare forearms on the guardrail, using the flat stone to support her spilling breasts, as if it were a serving platter, and added, "Something's got to wash that scowl off your face."

He turned away, ripped another patch off and threw it into the water. "You knew," he said bitterly. "You knew all along what those lecherous bastards were going to do."

"Of course, and so did you," she replied casually. Hauling herself onto the guardrail, she sat with her back to the river so she could face him. She waited until he looked at her, then added, "You were just too damn caught up in your own excitement, in your own glory, to think straight, or you would have seen it coming the day you got here. The bath! Everything."

"You set the bath up?"

"I'm part of the game," she said candidly. "I've played it a hundred times. And the better I play it, the better looking the girl, the more generous they are." She chuckled. "Robin was very profitable."

"You bitch!" he growled.

"Oh, go on, you old rooster," she chided him. "Don't tell me you didn't enjoy it."

He blushed bitterly, tore more patches off, then stared at the current, his tone matching its irresistible plunge. "I haven't quit yet, Doll. That stage is mine."

She laughed at him, enjoying his anger. "I just love an ambitious man. Makes them feisty. Gets their blood up. Makes them act young when a woman needs them young." He spit into the river in reply and ripped off another patch. She watched it land on the water, then asked, "So, what's the plot? How do we get you that stage?"

"Whatever it is," Brown said quietly, "you're not likely to be part of it."

"Oh, stop it!" she said. "I only did what had to be done." She took hold of his chin, turned his face to hers, her eyes suddenly hard. "You said you wanted her to have the part,

and she got it the only way she was going to get it. And
damn you, you should have known it! Don't be blaming me!''
Their eyes held each other's, and he nodded angrily, pulled
away. She asked, ''All right, now what's the hair-raising,
blood-curdling plot?''

He tossed his last patch into the river, watched it bob helplessly on the frothy current, then looked at her with no more
will inside him than the patch had. ''I don't have one.''

She laughed gaily. ''You really are tired, aren't you? How's
the leg?''

''Terrible. It hurts all the way up to you know where.''

''Then don't be coming around my bed, bukko. I don't
need any cripples.''

He smiled, a little. ''We could play this game all day, Doll.
It won't help.''

She thought about that, and compassion showed in her eyes.
''Relax, Brown,'' she said quietly. ''You'll come up with
something. You always do. You've got two whole days before
the festival begins. Let the girl's beauty work on them awhile,
soften them up. They're not dumb. Sooner or later, they'll
see you really do have the eye for what they like best. Hell,
they're showing her off already. They drove her through the
Market Court just a little while ago, had her posing on a
wagon bed heaped with spring flowers, like she was responsible for every bud. And all three of them followed in their
golden coach. Proud, that's what they are, and probably falling in love.''

''Was she all right?''

''What do you think?'' she replied tersely.

''The bastards!''

''Of course. Dangerous bastards. But they're showing
amazing restraint.'' His eyes questioned her and she added,
''They're entertaining themselves with her, don't doubt it.
But they haven't hurt or abused her, not so far. They're just
frightening her, shaming her. You know how aristocrats are.
They like to tease themselves, deliberately put off their pleasures to make them all the more pleasurable. I figure they
won't rape her until after her performance.''

Brown's head dropped. Tears welled in his eyes. ''Damn

me,'' he whispered. ''How could I have listened to them? How could I have believed one word?''

''Because they believe them.''

He laughed at her.

''Don't laugh, friend. That's what makes them dangerous. They actually believe all this nonsense about the goddess. They're sure they're divinely inspired, and that they can't ever be wrong. If you would have gone along with their wishes, they'd have let you do the work for them. But Iptur saw you wouldn't play. He knew you had your own ideas about how things should go.''

He looked at her suspiciously. ''What'd you tell them?''

''Don't look at me like that,'' she snapped. ''I didn't say one word about you being as fanatic as they are.''

''Do they suspect?''

''No. They're not fancy like you. They don't care for dreams and flashy displays of light. Religion is a practical thing to them, and the way they worship depends completely on which girl they take to bed at night.'' She patted his arm. ''Robin won't be one of them, not for a while anyway, so rest easy. They've given her the best room in the Stronghold, and they'll dress her in silver and gold. They're not stupid, Brown, just corrupt.''

He grunted, ''That really helps.''

''Then give Robin some credit,'' Doll persisted. ''She'll survive, believe me. She's not all skin. The best-looking part of her is inside, and she's strong. She'll be full-grown when this is over, a woman.''

He studied her a long beat, then said, ''You've been there, haven't you, Doll?''

''There and back,'' she said lightly.

He gave her a real smile. ''Thanks, Doll.''

''Glad to help, but what about you? You're in trouble yourself.'' His expression tightened and she explained. ''That husband of hers, Jakar, he saw her riding through the Market Court, found out what had happened and went crazy. He tried to rescue her. The castle guards beat him bad. But he still tried to get to her, so they did it again. He's lucky they didn't kill him.''

"How bad is he hurt?"

"Bad. But not so bad he's forgotten who set his wife up. He's looking for you right now." Her face darkened. "He's crazy, Brown. He'll try to kill you." She winked. "You want to hide in my wagon?"

Brown John laughed without humor, looked past her shoulder at a commotion and cursed silently.

Jakar, his angry face streaked with blood, was shouldering his way through the people crossing the bridge, scattering them as he, limping awkwardly, led a small crowd of thrill seekers straight for the *bukko*.

Brown looked around, saw people blocking the bridge in both directions, and dropped onto the bridge. Seeing Jakar, Doll dropped beside him, tugging on his sleeve. "Let's go. You don't want to talk to him now."

Brown thought about it and shook his head. "He won't try to harm me. You'll see."

"You old fool!" she snarled, and he looked into her eyes. "You still don't know what you've done, do you? You may still get to be the bukko, and Robin will survive. But not because of you! You're never going to see her again, Brown! And she won't want you to, can you understand that? Neither you nor her husband will see her again—and the lad knows it."

Struck motionless by her words, Brown John didn't move until Jakar's fist hit him in the side of the head. He bounced off the guardrail, spun and fell face first onto the bridge, passing out halfway through the trip.

When he came to, Doll squatted over him, dabbing his bloody ear with the hem of her black skirt. The crowd had backed off, and three castle guards had Jakar on the ground, keeping him there with their fists, knees and boots. The *bukko* cursed them, but only a sputter of rage left his mouth. He tried to get up, but fell instead. He considered thinking of something else to try, but nothing came to mind.

He was empty.

Seventeen

CAMP FOLLOWERS

Fleka's makeup did not flatter her. Wet mud circled her eyes, giving her the "wild eye" of the Novalldaa, those gone mad from fear of the ice mountains. Rouge brightened each freckle on cheek and breast, like a pox. Her skirt had been tied up high on her left hip, giving an attractive view of her shapely legs, her best feature. But the smeared henna and quail feathers on the inside of her thigh told every curious eye she had the harlot's rash. Nevertheless her appearance pleased her, and she liked her part. Spy.

Walking with her legs spread awkwardly, and a beggar's cup in hand, she had crossed nearly the entire length of the vast tent city spread outside the palisade walls of the Jani war camp. Making side trips, she had followed the scents of burning pork, leather and steel, and explored steaming tent kitchens with hulking cooks and bakers, the wagon houses of tailors repairing leather armor, and the pits of the iron priests who repaired helmet, sword and spear. She had visited the stalls and pens housing wranglers, waterbearers, grass cutters, sweepers and washerwomen, begged at the rear of endless open-air taverns, and run from the stones of orphaned children wearing scraps of fur and armor. She had searched dilligently the face of every camp follower she passed, barber, harlot, tinker and vandal, and each face in the lines of soldiers waiting to spend their silver on sweetmeats and wine. But she had seen no red spot on a forehead, no indication that the ranks of the army were filled with demon spawn, that the war camp was the source of the plague of knives.

Turning down a footpath, she headed for a spread of bright red tents standing on a rise at the upwind end of the camp. The breeze coming from the tents smelled of smoky incense, myrrh and jasmine, mixed with the odor of male sweat. Then the music of tambourines and drums reached her and she hesitated thoughtfully. If entertainers dwelled in the camp, then she, Gath and Billbarr had traveled all this way into the Barma High Country for nothing. Then, catching the vulgar beat and the lyrics of singers, she understood. Every other word was Yang, Chuzz, Bajaz or Sharma, and properly so. The business of the red tents was fornication.

Reaching the tents, she smiled with bitter memory. Lines of big, proud, boasting soldiers stood in front of each tent, talking loudly and guffawing every time they heard a female scream erupt from the shadowed, smoky interiors of the cloth brothels.

Passing along the backs of the lines, her eyes searched every face that turned her way, and the soldiers backed away, warned off by her odious scent, caused by the paste of pitch and dead beetles which Billbarr had concocted just for this purpose. But here her stench attracted the hordes of flies feeding on the men's filth, and they buzzed around her head, tangled in her hair. Then three yapping dogs appeared from nowhere and snapped at her heels. She jumped away from them, forgetting to limp, and the soldiers hooted, rooting for the dogs as the animals chased her.

Dashing down an alley with brown tents on either side, she plunged into a cloud of smoke smelling of burning flesh and strange herbs. The dogs skidded to a stop short of the smoke and yapped at it, then whimpered, tucked their tails between their legs and ran.

Fleka looked around warily, saw a group of men in dark furs squatting in a circle under a large canopy. A fire burned at the middle of the circle, giving off more smoke than flame, and the fumes settled against the underside of the canopy, swirled in place just above their heads. Every so often one of the men stood and breathed deeply of the smoke, teetered, then more fell than sat back down.

She edged closer, the smell of her own fear strong. Suddenly the role she played seemed very real.

Four magicians, wearing violet and pink silk robes, knelt before the fire, holding something in their hands. Huge butterflies, dragons and snakes, skillfully sewn with brilliant colors, decorated their robes. Their heads were shaved, except for topknots tied with black ribbons and fresh orchids. They suddenly stood, in unison, and turned, displaying red-hot pokers in their hands.

Half-naked, dusky girls, of no more than twelve or thirteen, streamed out of a nearby tent in two lines. The first line carried brass platters holding flaming dates, the second, yellow jars of smoking salves. The first group kneeled in front of the row of men forming the inside edge of the circle, and each girl placed a date into an open mouth. Then the second line took their places. These girls trembled with excitation, their smooth faces flashing with startled eyes and jerking smiles.

Holding her breath, Fleka scurried forward, hiding in a cloud of dense smoke trapped in an alcove between two tents. From there she saw the faces of the sitting men and gasped.

Their scarred, dirty flesh stretched tautly over their skulls, their eyes gleamed with fanatic intensity—and on each forehead a red spot glowed.

The girls dipped their little fingers into the jars of salve, removed them, and held them high, the sticky paste smoking on the tips. The four magicians stepped up behind four of the girls, and spoke softly to them. Each of the selected girls leaned forward, kissed the red spot of the man in front of her, then drove her smoking finger into it.

Fleka had to put her fist halfway down her throat to stifle her scream.

The men's bony foreheads did not resist. The red spots gave way, like holes covered with thin tissue. One finger went in up to the second knuckle and the man howled with ecstasy. The other fingers only went in as far as the first knuckle, but with the same result. The girls quickly withdrew their fingers and the magicians stepped forward, took hold of the backs of the men's heads, drove their hot pokers into the holes made by the girls.

Flesh sizzled and smoked. The victims growled and whined, but held still. Their heads swelled slightly, turning red. The magicians pulled the pokers out and moved quickly to another four girls, spoke quietly to them.

Fleka crept through the smoke, intending to get away as fast as she could, and stopped short.

The four victims had stood up, easily and naturally. Now they turned, chatting with each other, and removed coins from their pouches, dropped them in a brass bowl standing on a black tripod. Then they strolled her way. The red dots on their foreheads once more looked like simple tatoos. But now they were the size of lemons. One was even larger, the size of a grapefruit. It spread down onto the bridge of the soldier's nose and through his bushy eyebrows onto his upper eyelids. They were not victims at all. They simply had the marks of their demonic nature enhanced so they could show them off better.

Seeing Fleka within the smoke, they paused, made horrible faces at her, thus putting their unnatural decorations to brilliant use, then laughed riotously and moved off. She followed them at a distance, made the alley and raced past them as they hooted again, delighted by her fear.

On reaching her forest camp, high on a mountain overlooking the hidden valley, she found Gath, Billbarr and the black bear waiting around a small fire. Its wan smoke, like their wagon, Gath's horse and the camp itself, was hidden by the towering pines. She greeted them, then disrobed in silence, quickly bathed from a bucket of water in the same manner, doused herself with her last splash of rosewater, and toweled off, humming the tune she had heard coming from the red tents.

Gath, sitting between his axe and horned helmet, smiled knowingly and said, "Are you going to perform some indecent dance, or tell us what you found?"

"It's a spirited tune, isn't it?" she said brazenly, puffed

up by her success and a sudden sense of belonging. "I understand men are very fond of it."

She laughed at her own humor and Gath joined her. Billbarr frowned. "Would somebody tell me what's so funny."

"When you're grown, Billbarr," she said teasingly, then said it again, eliciting a larger frown. She roughed up his hair, then sobered, sat down facing them, and told them all that she had seen, relating each detail in the sequence as it had occurred, thus putting off the best part for the finish and keeping their attention as long as possible. She knew there was no urgency in her report. They could not move until the army moved, and she had seen no indication that that was imminent.

When she finished, Gath said, "Well done, both the report and the telling of it."

That brought a smile to her face, and she shared it with Billbarr. Then the boy said wisely, "Then we wait, follow the army when it breaks camp?"

"I have no other choice," Gath said.

Fleka and Billbarr shared a nod, then she said, "But even if what you suspect is true, that this black bitch of a queen is behind all this, we still don't know if your friend, the bukko, and, you know, this girl you're looking for are even alive."

"She's alive," Gath said easily. "The fury of the magic in the black dagger could only be aroused by Tiyy's natural enemy, the White Veshta."

"Then she'll use that whole army against her," Billbarr blurted. "What chance will she have?"

"With Robin," Gath told them, "there is always a chance. Somehow she'll find help, from Brown John, his sons, someone, and hold on. She knows I'm coming."

"How?" Billbarr asked.

"I don't know," the Barbarian answered.

"But you can't defeat a whole army," Fleka complained, then quickly changed her tone. "Can you?"

Gath shrugged. "We will see." He nodded in the direction of the valley. "There were entertainers in the camp?"

"Oh yes, lots of them," Fleka said with playful authority, then dropped her punch line, "Whoremasters and whores."

Gath grinned a little and looked from Fleka to Billbarr. "You'll need disguises."

Billbarr nodded, then became thoughtful. "Whoremaster! That's hard. I don't know that part."

Fleka chuckled with bitter irony. "I know mine."

Eighteen

THE TEAR

Sergeant Jarl Roundell sat on a stool, staring at the dying embers in the stone hearth. Within the red-hot glow, he saw battles raging along the ramparts and towers of the castles he had served. Brutal, mean battles fought by young men now grown old. Battles and sieges in which he had earned the right to laugh the raucous laughter of the strong. He smiled a smile born of that laughter, and glanced at the wall.

Its white rock was barely visible in the dim light, but he sensed its strength, felt its breadth and weight around him, and relished the feeling. The walls defended the West Tower of the Stronghold, framed the fifth-story room. At this height, they were fifteen feet thick. Impenetrable, if properly cared for.

He stood, stretched his hardy body, feeling each of his forty-three years, unbuckled his sword belt. Laying it quietly on a stool, he moved to his blankets spread at the side of the fire. His hand idly touched the wall and he paused, wondering at his joy in the feel of the cold stone. A flash of light struck across the wall, turned his hand a blinding white and was gone.

Roundell jumped back, reaching for his sword, and glanced about the room.

The drapes, bed and heavy furniture stood in deep indigo shadows, barely visible except where narrow swaths of moonlight graced them. The cool light drifted through the arrow slits along the staircase, leading to the trapdoor and turret above. No light came from the staircase. The trapdoor remained bolted. There were no windows. The source of the light lay somewhere in the room.

More intrigued than concerned, Roundell set his sword back on the stool. No firefly or bug could emanate such a flash. The only possibility was the girl.

He crossed the room, staying on the thick rugs to muffle his boots, and stood at the side of the bed. As big as a small room, the bed rose to his hips, supported by thick posts carved in circular patterns. A stepladder rested against the sideboard. Tousled, thick quilts covered the girl, except for her beautiful face and head of red-gold hair, nestled among a heap of pillows. She tossed slightly, as if in the middle of a dream, and her hair, strangely luminous in the darkness, tumbled in lovely curls beside her face.

He more felt than saw her cheeks blossom in a smile, their rose color and the scarlet of her lips glowing out of the indigo shadows. Suddenly tiny streaks of light exploded off her cheek, slashing across Roundell's scarred jaw. They reached as far as the bedposts, then faded. He moved closer, placed a supporting hand against the head of the bed, leaned over her.

The light came again, barely a flicker. The source was a tear perched on the crest of her smiling cheek. He extended his little finger to explore it and hesitated, enjoying being so close to her, close to the source of contentment and joy and warmth which made the smile in her cheeks.

To Roundell, she seemed to be a decent lass. Common yet unique, just as he liked to think he was. The priests, afraid that she might try to kill herself, had ordered him to never let her out of his sight. But he was sure they were simply acting like the fools they were, and that there was no need of it. She enjoyed life too much to purposely end it. Reaching

for her cheek again, he touched the tear with a fingertip . . .
and quickly withdrew it, the whites of his eyes large and
startled.

The tear was a jewel, a diamond, and it had not been there
when he had put her to bed.

Gently, he plucked the tiny stone off her cheek with two
fingers, and walked back to the fire. The jewel was warm,
almost hot, against his fingers. Holding it up to the light, it
flashed and glittered like any other diamond. Growing more
curious, he bit it and it was as hard as a diamond should be.
He thumbed it thoughtfully, and glanced back at the bed. The
girl was sitting up, hugging herself.

"It's cold," she said quietly. "Would you mind putting
some wood on the fire?"

"My pleasure, lass," he said, setting the diamond on the
stool. He moved to the stack of logs against the wall and
picked several up. "Sorry about that, I shouldn't have let it
die down."

"Oh, it's not your fault. Normally I can even sleep out-
doors. I love the fresh air. But, well, I guess I'm worn out."

"No wonder," he said, placing a log on the embers.
"Having those old freaks pick at you all day would tire a stud
bull. They must have bathed you a dozen times." She made
no reply and he continued putting logs on the fire. "From
my way of thinking, they're going to a whole lot of trouble,
and making it a whole lot more miserable for you than need
be. They should just poke you and have done with it. But not
them, no. They have to make a big thing out of it, as if
showing you off and letting everyone know what they're going to do to you is more important than doing it. Of course,
if a man isn't willing to lie and cheat and fight for a woman,
then he's got no right to enjoy her in the first place."

He stirred the fire with a poker until the logs flamed, filling
the room with orange light. Then he set the poker down,
turned to the girl, and saw her smile was gone.

"Sorry," he said. "I should have better sense than to talk
about it like that."

She shrugged. "It's not your fault."

"No, it isn't. That's a fact. But for some reason, it seems

I'm always saying I'm sorry to you. I guess it's just my rough way.''

"That's all right. I like your, you know, roughness." Her smile tried to climb back into her cheeks.

"Those are nice words, lass, and I thank you for them." He grinned wickedly. "But don't think you're the first young thing that thought that way, and try to take advantage.''

Her smile got back where it belonged, and she laughed a little. "I bet you are a scoundrel with the women, aren't you . . .''

"Roundell, Sergeant Jarl Roundell.''

"Roundell, that's nice. I'm called Robin. Robin Lake-hair.''

"That's a pretty name, nearly as pretty as yourself." She blushed and he added, "It's a pleasure, lass, guarding you instead of some mean bastard. But you are a confusing thing, that's certain. Almighty confusing.''

"Confusing?''

He nodded, picked up the diamond, holding it with finger and thumb, and held it up to the light so that it flashed.

"What's that?" she asked.

"Looks like a diamond, but I'm not the least bit sure it is." He walked to the bed, dropped the gem on her palm and it glowed, filling her hand with a ball of light. The color left her face, and she looked up at him, startled, afraid.

"You're some kind of sorceress, right, lass?''

She trembled slightly, and the diamond calmed down, began to behave like a normal jewel. "It's not mine," she said. "I . . . I didn't—''

His wise smile stopped her short. "If I were you, girl, I'd give up lying. You're real bad at it." Her expression turned as helpless as anything he'd seen, and he added, "It's yours, lass. Leastways, I found it on your cheek. And those priests checked every inch of you. All you had on was your night-gown when we came up here.''

She nodded weakly. "Then it probably is mine.''

He pulled a chair to the bed, sat down, his hands on his knees. "What are you? Sorceress? Magician? Witch? Do you do other tricks?''

"I'm not sure," she said, lying back among the pillows.
"I . . . I guess I'm not sure of much of anything these days.
It's just that, when I'm really happy or care deeply about
someone, strange things sometimes happen. I don't know
how. But, well—"

"You spit light all over the room?"

She sat up. "Did I do that?"

"Couldn't have been anyone else. You lit up the whole
place." He nodded at the diamond in her fist. "But where'd
that come from?"

She opened her fist and the jewel glittered quietly. "That's
part of it. They just appear sometimes."

"In your eyes?"

She nodded. "Or on the palms of my hands and," she
blushed, "other places."

He grinned, sitting back. "Something tells me, lass, that
that other places trick is something old Jarl Roundell would
like to see."

Her smile scolded him a little. Suddenly she gasped,
"You're not going to tell the priests about this?"

"That's my job, lass."

"I know, but if they find out, they'll try to force me to
make more, and when I can't, there's no telling what they'll
do to me."

"You mean it's not like making a dove fly out of your
mouth?"

"No! It's not a trick."

"You can't control it?"

"No. It just happens, usually when I least expect it to.
Like tonight, when I was dreaming."

He rested his elbows on his knees. "Well now, girl," he
said, smiling slow and easy, "it seems to me that's a poor
kind of magic to try and make a living with."

She put her sober eyes on his twinkling eyes. "You don't
believe me? You're teasing me?"

He laughed warmly. "I'm trying."

"Don't," she pleaded. "It's not funny."

His twinkle sobered a little. "I suppose you're right. If I
were to tell them, they wouldn't be at all likely to believe

me, unless you could do it again. And if you can't, like you say, then it wouldn't be funny at all, for either of us."

A smile lifted the corners of her plush lips. "You're not going to tell them?" He did not reply and she added, "I won't say a thing. I swear it. Here," she handed him the diamond. "Take it, please. So they won't find it." He hesitated, then took the jewel and she smiled. "You're not afraid of magic, are you?"

"Not of yours, lass."

Her smile said she liked that, and his said he liked making her smile. He loosened the tie string on the coin purse dangling from his belt, dropped the diamond inside and pulled the string tight.

"Thank you," she said quietly.

Hauling a quilt around her bare shoulders and arms, she dropped to the floor and walked to the fire. Roundell watched the firelight play in her hair, then asked, "I guess you weren't dreaming about Iptur, Dagan and Surim?"

She shook her head. "No. About an old friend. A man."

"That makes sense," he said, joining her. "Girls your age ought to dream about a man." He pushed the stool behind her, squatting before the hearth as she sat down. "Will he try to save you?"

"I don't know," she said thoughtfully. "Once, long ago, he said he would never let any harm come to me, and I still believe that. But I haven't seen him in years."

"If he's going to try, I hope he's got a very big sword."

"An axe."

"Good enough," he said, raising his hands to the heat of the flames. "An axe can be clumsy, but when a man can handle it, it's a terrible thing to watch work." Her eyes questioned him and he explained, "I was the Master-at-Arms at three fine castles, Foalld, Endemmeer and Splitt, and survived five sieges. No weapon does what anyone would call pretty, but the axe is the worst of the lot. It's a dark weapon made for dark work." He changed the subject. "I came to Whitetree to be Master-at-Arms, seven years ago. But I quit after a year and signed on as a sentry."

"A sentry?"

He nodded and squatted. "I didn't want to be responsible for anything, because of the way they do things here." He pointed at the wall. "That wall's fifteen feet thick, and at the base of the tower, more than thirty. This is the finest castle ever built, but they don't take care of it." He pointed across the room. "See that crack. It looks like nothing. But if you follow it down to the foundation rock, it's probably a foot wide." He turned to her. "But nobody bothers to check, and there are dozens more like it, all along the west wall."

"Is it going to collapse?"

"Not for hundreds of years, unless somebody gives it a shove."

"Oh!" she said, beginning to understand.

"Except for the tower I command, this place is a shambles. There's no pitch in the whole place," he added, surprised at how the girl made him talk so freely, "no wood cut for hoardings, no catapults, nothing! Most of the common soldiers, the men-at-arms, are all right, but there's not near enough of them, and that's not all. The wall walks are full of potholes; the river's eating under the west wall; the moat is full of silt and about a third as deep as it should be; and the river's grown narrower each year. It could be dammed up overnight."

"Are you expecting some kind of trouble?"

"No, but I wish I was." He chuckled derisively. "It would do these pious bastards good. They've become so cocky, they use some of the wall towers as storehouses. They're full of furniture and baggage, all kinds of things, just like this one." He nodded at the room above. "It's full of old bedding."

"Bedding?"

He nodded. "You can hardly get through it to reach the turret, and it's the most important tower in the whole castle. You can see the entire valley from up there, all the way into the mountain passes. But they haven't had a lookout stationed up there since I've been here."

She looked up at the trapdoor. "Could we go up there? Look at the valley?"

She turned to him, the firelight stroking her cheeks and lips, and he said, "I shouldn't do it, lass. But if you smile, I'm just liable to start acting like a silly old man."

She smiled.

Laughing, he stood, took her hand and led her up the stair-case into the upper room. There the dim fire's glow revealed heaps of bedding stacked as high as the ceiling and crammed into recessed loopholes nearly six feet high. They pushed through and crawled over the debris, reached an old rusted door. Roundell unbolted it, put a shoulder to it, and it swung open, revealing the crenellated turret and night outside.

Robin moved to an embrasure, an opening in the top of the wall two feet wide and four high, and looked out at the moonlit valley. Dark and undulating, it spread like the silence to the distant mountains, black and threatening against the indigo sky. She let the quilt drop away from her cool brown shoulders and breathed deeply, reveling in the scents of lilac and heather riding a gentle breeze. Then she let it drop to the floor, and stood in her long harvest-yellow nightshift, as round and lithe and vibrant as all of Jarl Roundell's childhood dreams.

"Aren't you cold?" he asked, picking up the quilt.

"No," she said, "not anymore. It's so wonderful up here. I can see everything." She lifted a bare foot into the embrasure and he stopped her. She smiled over a shoulder. "I won't jump. You know that."

"I know," he said, "but someone might see you."

She nodded, her eyes eager.

He glanced past her at the apparently empty moonlit valley, then at the dark shadows gathered in the foothills. "Is he out there? Waiting for your signal?"

"I hope so . . . but no. He's just in my dreams."

He studied her, his mind and senses suddenly dazzled by her eyelashes and lips and the turn of her small ear. "Who are you?" he asked.

"Does it really matter?" she asked quietly.

He thought about that, his fingers enjoying the firm warmth of her youthful arm, then let go.

Robin climbed into the embrasure and stood at the outside edge, facing the valley. Below her, the side of the Stronghold tower descended in a sheer slope for two hundred feet to the rocky cliff, which descended another hundred feet to the rushing river. Moonlight danced on the turbulent water and its roar was a song.

She stared into the night, enjoying it, then suddenly took a sharp breath, as if seeing something. Pressing her hands against the cold stone crenellations for balance, she leaned forward, staring out across the valley into the darkness of the foothills. There, massive shadows seemed to shift and writhe with power, a violent power like that possessed by Gath of Baal. Was he there? Had he, by some miracle, come to her rescue? It was impossible, but she could no longer accept anything as impossible. Holding her hope with all her might, she looked up into the star-spattered sky and surrendered to her dream.

Darkness rolled and roamed about the endless dark void of the sky, tumbling on itself, gathering, hiding the moon and revealing the stars. Then he appeared, dark and magnificent, riding across the sky on a black stallion. Fire boiled behind the eye slits of his horned helmet and smoke trailed behind him, like banners of his honor. A parade of memories followed him, images of his fight at Wagon Yard and the battles of Chela Kong and Baharra, accompanied by the ballads and marching songs of the Grillards, Dowats, Kavens. Then came images of the blackened thorntree atop Calling Rock, of the wounds in his side and leg, of her hands healing them, of smoking ashes on his burnt cheeks after removing his terrible headpiece. Visions of Upper Small, En Sakalda and Pyram followed, then came the song of her youthful laughter, the cry of the wolf called Sharn who sang a love song, their love song as they shared their first and only kiss. He, Gath of Baal, the Death Dealer, led all the memories, a horde of yesterdays, her yesterdays. Theirs.

Suddenly she gasped, and leapt back down into the turret, crouched behind the parapet. Roundell threw the quilt over her, and peered out into the night. A moment passed, and he crouched beside her. Her eyes were wet and enlarged by fear.

"What is it?" he asked. "What's wrong?"

"I . . . I shouldn't have shown myself," she said, her

breath breaking up her words. "I . . . I've made a horrible mistake."

Nineteen

BLACK KISS

Tiyy's lips parted, and she gasped repeatedly, pleasure coursing through her young body. More than she had ever felt when filled by a man.

She straddled her black and white horse, bare thighs gripping its muscled girth, arms thrust before her, fists knotted in the black mane. The animal stood as motionless as the rock cleft beneath it. All around her the shadowed mountain held as still as the night itself. Only her leopard-skin cloak, a cool yellow in the moonlight, moved, rising and falling as her body heaved. Her hot moist cheeks pulsed, but her eyes held steady, focused on the source of her pleasure.

Far below, the massive castle stood dark and ominous against the moonlit valley floor, except for a few campfires burning in the lower courtyards, and the billowing glow of white light inundating the parapet of the stronghold's tallest tower. A glorious light which only she, the Black Veshta, could see.

The light had only been a surprisingly wan aura around the girl, when she and the soldier first emerged from the door to the turret. Then, when she climbed into the embrasure, she had exploded with blinding balls of whiteness and showered the tower and cliffs below her with cascading streamers of light. Then the glow had suddenly abated, and the girl and soldier quickly reentered the tower.

Now the shafts of white light shot through the loopholes

in the top room, then speared through the arrow slits of the lower room as the girl descended a staircase on the inner side of the wall. The light continued to glow dimly behind the arrow slits, then faded, replaced by the orange glow of a dying fire.

Exhausted, the nymph queen sagged forward, lying on the animal's mane, arms dangling. When her breathing slowed, she sat up, threw her cloak back over her bare shoulders. Her dark supple torso was moist and flushed under her chain mail halter and loincloth, and her legs hot inside her black and silver boots. For a long moment she let the cool night air caress her.

Her pleasure was sublime now, the warm, enervating afterglow of ecstasy and triumph. The White Veshta had arrived at Whitetree, just as the nymph's visions had said she would, and soon now the jewels of the Goddess of Light would again belong to her, the Goddess of Darkness.

Tiyy turned her horse, drove her heels into its flanks and galloped up into the trees. Two mounted bodyguards waited in the shadows, vermilion crossbows in hand. She reined up between them. Their faces, unlike on the previous nights, were hard with excitement. They had been dutifully watching her and knew something had happened.

"She's arrived," Tiyy said. "The Goddess of Light awaits us in the castle."

Malevolent smiles cut into their savage features, and they removed small jars of poison paste from the satchels on their belts, dipped the tips of their crossbow bolts into it, making certain the poison was fresh. Then they put the jars away, cranked their drawstrings tighter and looked at their queen, awaiting her instructions. From the surrounding shadows came the sounds of more crossbows being cranked and nervous horse's hooves stomping the ground as the rest of her bodyguards, concealed by the trees, took the same precautions.

"Good," she said, smiling with brutal approval. "You are wise to be careful. If she is here, then he is nearby." She nodded downtrail. "We must return to the camp, as fast as we can."

One bodyguard promptly turned his mount, kicking it into a gallop, and Tiyy rode after him, the second bodyguard close behind. They dashed through the trees, following a narrow moonlit trail, and the hidden bodyguards rode out of the shadows behind them, following.

They reached the bald crest of the mountain, galloped through a rocky gap, descended a defile to a tree-filled gut between steep cliffs. Sentries stood guard within the shadows of the trees. The lead bodyguard hailed them and rode through the trees with the nymph queen and others close behind. They reined up around a campfire burning in a clearing at the center of the trees, and dismounted, their horses snorting and stomping the earth.

Hide tents surrounded the fire, and several bodyguards stood around it, roasting a pig on a spit. Wakened by the commotion, more bodyguards emerged from tents, wiping the sleep from their eyes. Behind the tents, horses were tethered in a makeshift stall, snorting at the commotion.

Tiyy faced one of the waking men. "Ride to General Ghapp. Tell him the time has come. The army marches tonight."

The soldier grabbed his weapons and cloak, and as a horse was saddled for him, mounted and galloped out of camp.

Tiyy did not watch. She turned to another bodyguard. "Bring the Feyan to my tent." The bodyguard hurried to a tent set apart from the others as Tiyy moved to hers, a slightly larger one of black hides. Standing on the red carpet covering the ground under the awning, she threw off her cloak and stripped.

The old crone, Aillya, stumbled out of the tent and stared with bleary eyes, then bent to pick up the nymph's garments.

"Leave them," Tiyy snapped. "My breechclout and rouge. Quickly!"

The old woman dashed back into the tent. Turning, Tiyy, naked except for the orange lick of the firelight, propped her fists on her hips and faced three Feyan dervishes as they hurried across the camp. Seeing her, they stopped short and gawked.

Heat glowed in the shadows of her quarrelsome breasts and

thighs. War was ripe within her, demanding release; it swelled her hips, colored her cheeks, transformed her. Made her more beautiful, more perverse. A nasty jewel.

The dervishes groveled at her bare feet. Grime matted their long black hair. Tattered tunics and cloaks, rent with rips and holes, only partially covered their unwashed bodies. Their ancestors were desert nomads, shadow people who, when the Kitzakks occupied the sands decades earlier, had cast out their primitive male god and become fanatic worshipers of the Butterfly Goddess. Now they were converts again. Devotees of the Black Veshta.

When they looked up, foam flecked their lips and blood dripped from one's empty eye socket; the results of excessive doses of Hashradda. Their foreheads, hands and ankles showed traces of carmine stain and welts left by whips used in their rituals. They worshiped pain and slept with the tools which would serve their own deaths: long serrated knives shaped like wiggling snakes which showed under their belts, and leather satchels containing jars of carmine stain and pitch.

Their leader, a short, leather-faced man, rose and bowed to his goddess.

"Your associates have entered the castle?" Tiyy asked.

"Yes, O breaker of hearts," he whispered. "Six now hide within the white walls."

"Good," she said.

The crone emerged carrying Tiyy's breechclout, belted knife with the blade of black light, and short, fringed, rawhide boots. Tiyy indicated the knife. The old woman belted it to the nymph's forearm as Tiyy again faced the Feyan leader.

"Tomorrow, we strike. Are you ready?"

The leader bowed. "Always, O beloved flesh."

"Don't snivel," she shrilled. He straightened, pride flashing behind the hard pits of his eyes, and she demanded, "Can you get in the castle? Unseen?"

He nodded once. "There are many ways, few guards."

"Then you will enter tonight. By first light tomorrow, General Ghapp will bring the army within striking distance.

When the castle awakes, you must locate your targets as quickly as possible, then signal me in the agreed manner and strike.''

He bowed in reply.

''If more than two hours of light pass, the chances of surprise will be endangered. If you cannot find your primary targets before that time elapses, you will attack your secondary targets.''

He bowed again.

The crone handed Tiyy the breechclout and she pushed it aside. ''The vial of black wine. Quickly!''

Dropping the breechclout on the carpet, Aillya dashed back into the tent and the nymph stepped closer to the Feyan leader. ''The chosen one, is it you?''

He shook his head and indicated the one-eyed dervish, a young man of no more than seventeen summers, with hard, stringy muscles. ''He is the fastest, the most worthy.''

Tiyy stepped in front of the one-eyed Feyan and looked down at him, smiled over her nakedness. He shifted excitedly and she said, ''Rise, worthy one, and receive my blessing.''

The young man, trembling with a heady mix of humility and erotic expectation, stood uncertainly before his deity. The crone came back with a black leaden vial in her hands, and handed it to Tiyy. The nymph held the vial up before the young man.

''I have specially conjured the Nagraa, so that it will prepare you both for your special sacrifice . . . and your reward.''

Enjoying the raw lust, suddenly bright on his smooth cheeks, she circled the young dervish, her fingers lightly touching his shoulder and neck. The other Feyan and bodyguards quickly backed away, their wary eyes leashed to their goddess. Stopping at the young dervish's side, she allowed her nipples to graze his hard arm. He watched her out of the corners of his eyes, his breath coming hard and fast. She ran a slow hand up over his shoulder and across his chest, then took a step back, pulled the leaden stopper from the vial. A shaft of black light shot out of the tiny mouth, disappeared into the night.

The Feyan and bodyguards cringed.

The one-eyed youth could only shudder, his expectation raw now. Holding the youth captive with her black, sloping, eyes, Tiyy thrust the vial into his fist, and raised it to his mouth. The black light struck his chest and cheek, burning them, but he did not draw back.

"Drink!" she commanded.

He put the vial to his lips, hesitated, and black light singed his hair, sizzled on his nose and forehead, causing smoke to rise off his face. He held his breath, and poured the black wine down his throat, gulping it. Suddenly she ripped the vial away, downed the remainder of the Nagraa herself, and tossed the vial aside. Pressing against him from thigh to breast, she ran her hands up into his dirty hair, then suddenly pulled his face down to hers, stopping it with her parted lips meeting his.

The young man groaned, lost control and gathered her in his arms, lifting her off the ground. Her knee came up, grabbing his hip. Their mouths writhed against each other, and fire erupted inside Tiyy's heaving breasts, spreading quickly to her belly and face.

The Feyan and bodyguards scattered back. Spellbound. Terrified.

The fire darkened behind the nymph's cheeks and her face slowly turned pitch-black, then the blackness bled into the youth's lips. He gasped and pulled away, but her hands did not permit it. They held him to her in a black kiss.

The youth shuddered and shook, threw his head back, his body convulsing, and gasped out his guttural ecstasy. Suddenly his strength drained from his body and he staggered, letting go of his goddess. Tiyy dropped nimbly to the ground and the youth fell to his hands and knees before her. The blackness faded.

She watched him shudder and tremble, then stroked his head and whispered, "Your goddess thanks you, worthy one. Now go and do what must be done."

One of the dervishes helped the one-eyed youth to his feet as the leader fetched a black bow and quiver from their tent, then the trio hurried off into the night.

Tiyy wiped the tangy taste of the youth's sweaty kiss from her lips, then tied on her breechclout, drew on her rawhide boots and moved to the fire. Tearing a piece of meat off a roasting pig, she ate the hot, greasy flesh. Standing in the red light of the flames, she knew she looked her best. Like the savage she was. Made to make men mad with war.

Twenty

PINK FIRE

The tip of the sun, a silver ball of radiating light, appeared above the eastern wall of the castle. The glowing orb painted the empty yard of the Sacred Close with wide stripes of brightness, rushed up the front of the wooden stage, and exploded off the shiny steel straps of a large wooden tub commanding center stage.

The wooden tub, four feet in diameter and three feet deep, rested in a cradle of heavy timbers. A two-sided stepladder rose to a shallow platform on the rim, the other side descending into the tub. A fire blazed under the tub, the flames heating hammered metal plates covering the bottom. Water filled the huge basin and steam rose off the surface, drifting like flimsy pennants up through the streaming sunlight past the huge saurian skull forming the second-story set.

Workers moved about the front of the stage, painting the baseboards, hanging wreaths of yellow, red and blue flowers, and raising bright pennants on the flag poles. Upstage, a bald *bukko* beat out a rhythm with a staff as a line of black-haired dancers, wearing garlands of pink flowers on their young, nude bodies, pranced and whirled.

Two acolytes appeared, mounting the stairs at stage left,

and all movement stopped. A moment passed, and Iptur, with Robin Lakehair on his arm, appeared behind the acolytes, followed by Jarl Roundell, Dagan and Surim.

"Ahhh, splendid," Iptur intoned, seeing the steaming tub. "But the steps must be directly in front. When she mounts them, her back must be to the audience, so that when she emerges, she will face the audience."

The acolytes motioned at the nearest workers and they dropped their hammers, hurried to the stepladder. They placed it in the position the high priest desired, and backed off.

"Yes, that's it," Iptur said, more approving of his decision than their efforts. Facing Robin, he half-circled her, one way, then the other, his eyes measuring her wardrobe.

Her soft leather dress fit as snugly as a glove over her breasts, belly and hips, then fell loosely in a fringe of thick thongs, reaching to the middle of her thighs. Fringe also decorated the low square-cut collar and shoulder straps. Stained a deep nutmeg, it matched her short, fringed boots and blended perfectly with her light brown flesh. Bracelets of silver banded her wrists and upper arms. Silver hoop earrings glistened against the carefully combed waves of her long red-gold hair.

"Yes," Iptur said, "the leather is a good choice. It adds an element of verisimilitude to your illusory beauty." He took Robin's elbow, guiding her to the first step. "Now, precious flower, mount the steps slowly, as if fearful the water will not wash away the Lord of Death's stench. Then, keeping your back to the audience and behaving as if you were quite alone, remove your clothing."

"Again?" Robin moaned.

"Of course," the high priest said sternly. "We must rehearse, this is the most important part of your performance."

"But I just had a bath."

"I am aware of that," he said, smiling benignly. "There is no need to get in the water, not immediately. I only wish to see you remove your clothing."

He half-pushed her onto the first step, and she reluctantly mounted the stepladder, stood on the platform. Hesitating, she glanced over her shoulder at Roundell, her cheeks as bright as embarrassed cherries. Seeing that Jarl's face held no more expression than his belt buckle, she looked down at Iptur and shook her head.

"This isn't going to look the way it should," she said. "The leather is so tight, I'll have to pull it over my head."

"You will push it down over your hips," the high priest insisted, "just as I told you to."

"But it takes forever and looks terrible. I end up with red streaks all over me."

"The longer it takes, my flower, the better. I want you to fight it, to wiggle and squirm as long as possible."

Her lower lip stuck out defiantly, and she reluctantly pushed the shoulder straps down, using both hands.

Iptur flew up the stairs. "No! No! One at a time. Slowly." He lifted her shoulder straps back in place. "And hesitate before you lower each strap. Tease them, child, tease them. Make the audience pant to see every inch of you. Here, I'll demonstrate."

He reached for a strap and hesitated at the sound of a commotion in the yard. They all turned toward it.

Workers were gathering noisily at the far end of the stage, pointing up at the sky above the Close. There a dark arrow streaked up into the empty void, a black streamer unfurling behind it. There were three red circles on it.

"What's that?" the high priest asked, turning to Roundell.

"Somebody's celebrating early," Jarl replied, his eyes on the arrow. "Or signaling someone."

Frowning, Iptur looked back at the arrow, shielding his eyes with his hands. Roundell glanced at Robin. She looked directly at him, her face suddenly void of color, her eyes wide with fear. His instinctive trust in her fear shocked him, and instructed him.

Roundell yanked Robin off the stepladder, shouting at the others, "Take cover!" and hauled her to the side of the stage, covering her retreat with his body.

One of the acolytes shrieked and backed away from the tub, staring wide-eyed at something directly overhead.

A naked man, stained carmine from toe to forehead, stood

at the tip of the ramplike red tongue extending from the shad-owed jaws of the huge saurian skull. He glistened with sticky paste, held a long serrated knife in one hand, a torch in the other. He put the torch against his shins. With a loud gush of air, his body erupted with pink fire, and he leapt forward, hurtled in a blazing streak for the steaming tub.

"Assassins!" Roundell shouted, drawing his sword.

Bodies scattered in all directions, except for Iptur. Still standing on the stepladder, he stared up at the flaming man falling directly at him, and frowned, annoyed that this crea-ture would presume to attack his holy self. Then his piety failed him, and he screamed, turning awkwardly to flee.

The assassin fell short of the stepladder, splashed in the tub, fracturing his leg on the rim and clutching Iptur's flowing robe. He sank into the water, hauling the high priest back-ward, and they both plunged out of sight, slopping water over the sides.

The two acolytes raced back to the tub and up the steplad-der, knives in hand, and Iptur rose halfway out of the tub, wearing the long, serrated knife in his chest. He shuddered, fell back in the water, and the acolytes jumped on the assas-sin, stabbing wildly.

Dagan made it halfway across the stage, heading for the Vestry door, and a trapdoor opened up in front of him. A second blazing assassin rose out of it, and Dagan stumbled into his scorching arms, screaming. The killer, hugging the priest tight, jumped back into the dark hole and the screams stopped short.

Surim, four strides behind Dagan, turned and ran into Jarl Roundell. The mercenary grabbed him and shoved him to floor beside Robin Lakehair. Growling "Stay put!" Jarl faced a third flaming assassin charging out of the false trees form-ing the set, his knife raised and body glowing with pink fire.

Grunting with contempt, Jarl slapped the knife out of kill-er's hand with the flat of his sword blade, at the same time shifting his weight and turning the blade, knowing what the Feyan would do next. The dervish did it, charged and skew-ered himself on the blade. Roundell shifted his weight again,

pulling the blade around so that the assassin's weight helped
him throw the dying man off the blade.

The flaming body hit the floor beside Surim, and the Great
Scribe screamed, bolted toward the Vestry door. Stepping
away from the flaming flesh, Roundell and Robin watched
Surim make the gold door and enter, then glanced around the
yard.

The Sacred Close was empty. Silent. Except for the distant
howls and screams coming from the lower yards. At the far
side of the stage, the black arrow, its streamer fluttering on
a breeze, pinned a dead carpenter to the stage.

Holding Robin by the elbow, Roundell guided her across
the stage. "Stay close," he breathed.

As they passed alongside the wooden tub, a bloody froth
of water sloshed out of it, splashed on the floorboards in front
of them, and they stopped short, staring in disbelief.

Hands appeared, gripping the rim of the tub, then Iptur's
head rose out of the pink water. His flesh appeared partially
cooked, and he gasped for air, blood draining out of the
corners of his mouth.

He said, "It's so hot," then died, sinking back into the
water with a gentle splash.

Twenty-one

REVELATIONS

Roundell put a protective arm around Robin, guided her away
from the tub. "Just stay with me," he said calmly, his eyes
searching each shadow.

Robin nodded, and they stopped beside the dead carpenter.
Letting go of her, Jarl ripped the black streamer off the arrow

in his back, tucked it under his belt, then grabbed Robin's arm, and they raced down the steps, across the empty yard. Climbing an open staircase to the wall walk, they dashed along it. Reaching the door to the Round Tower, at the corner of the castle's western wall and the wall separating the Sacred Close and the Market Court, he opened it and drew her inside, bolting the door behind them as he spoke.

"I'm in command here. You'll be safe."

"Thank you," she said, breathlessly.

He did not reply. They crossed the straw-covered floor of the third-story room, heading for the door to the stairwell. Rough-hewn bunks occupied the area, and a long table littered with pitchers of ale and overturned cups. Weapons and armor hung on hooks set in the stone walls. Hides covered the beds, and the air was thick with the smells of dry sweat, old wine and men.

A man-at-arms, bearing a loaded crossbow, came out the door to the stairwell and shouted, "What's going on? Who are these fanatics?"

"Later," Jarl said, drawing Robin through the stairwell door. "Don't let anyone in who doesn't belong."

They raced up the stairwell, entered the armory on the fourth floor. Except for the thick tangled roots of a lime tree growing up through the center of the stone flooring, the room was neat, clean, ordered. Stacks of wood, precisely cut for hoardings, and piles of slate for their roofs, stood waiting to one side. Boulders rose in a pile beside them, ready to be dropped through the murder holes of the hoardings in case of an attack. Along the portion of the curving wall facing the valley, sunlight streamed through arrow slits. On the opposite side of the circular room, spears, armor, crossbows and quivers of bolts hung on hooks in neat lines, their bodies glistening with fresh oil. Ready.

They climbed the stairs to the open trapdoor, and rose onto the sunlit parapet, listening to the screams, shouts and sounds of running bodies coming from the Market Court.

Four men-at-arms, sturdy men with hard, common faces, stood in the embrasures looking down at the yard. They turned as Roundell and Robin crossed toward them. One started to speak and Roundell cut him off.

"Check the tower, floor by floor! Everything! Closets, latrine galleries, under every damn bed! And be careful! Shadow men have infiltrated the castle." They stared in disbelief and he shouted, "Move!"

They jumped down onto the parapet floor, disappeared through the trapdoor.

Holding Robin by the arm, Jarl helped her up into an embrasure, and they looked down.

Below them, in the lower yards on the southern side of Round Tower, panic-stricken men, women and children fled in all directions through the ruins, the Water Court and the Market Court. They crashed into each other, shoved, screamed, fell and jumped back up to run again. Fires blazed from the roofs of the stables and two house wagons. Men and women beat the fires with blankets and threw buckets of water on them.

At the center of the Market Court, a crowd slowly approached a smaller fire, throwing rocks at it. The blaze consisted of a screaming, thrashing White Archer wearing a red apron, and a naked man covered with pink fire.

"Another one!" Robin gasped.

"Not one," Roundell said, "four." He pointed at a wall walk, then at the top of the gate tower, then at a corner of the Water Court. In each place, a blazing assassin embraced a dead or dying White Archer in a red apron. Robin moaned as he added, "They're killing the commanders of the garrison."

Screaming came from a tent brothel in the Market Court, and two men, a naked assassin and a burly soldier in fancy leather armor, rolled out the door, followed by bellowing women carrying butcher knives and buckets of water. One leg and arm of the assassin flickered with meek flames. The women doused the pair with water, quenching the flames, then proceeded to stab and kick the assassin. The soldier rolled free, wearing a knife in his back. Dead.

"Tedukkk, the Master-at-Arms," Jarl said, and smiled with rare appreciation. "The bastards are good. Damn good."

She looked at him. "They've killed everybody who was in charge and any good at it."

"The Great Scribe's still alive."

He nodded. "Probably. But Surim is no leader." He chuckled sardonically. "If this is the beginning of what I think it is, this castle, without a single leader, is going to eat itself from the inside out." He pointed at the bridge. "There's another one."

Pink flames streaked across the bridge, coming from the back of a thin, muscled young man with a bloody eye. He headed for the outpost fortification. Several pikemen, standing at the center of the bridge, stabbed at him. He danced aside, jumped onto the guardrail, raced along it past the soldiers, and leapt back down. Up ahead of him, three White Archers stood on the ramparts of the outpost, watching. Suddenly, they raised their bows, fired down at the assassin. Two missed. The third put an arrow through his shoulder. The impact spun the young fanatic around, but he plunged on.

Nearing the rear entrance to the outpost, he spread his arms wide, screaming. Sparks shot from the tips of his fingers, then one by one his fingers exploded, and the stumps of his hands broke out in sparking pink flames.

The White Archers on the ramparts lowered their bows and watched in horror.

The young assassin's arms burnt away, amid a flurry of flames and sparks, and the pink fire blazed from his shoulders. Then he vanished into the outpost.

Robin stared open-mouthed. Roundell's wrinkled eyes thinned. "Sorcery," he murmured.

A moment passed, and an explosion shook the outpost, blowing flames and chunks of huge stone out the front entrance, along with door timbers and the twisted steel and wood of the portcullis. With half the rampart flooring blown away, flames shot up through the openings and torched the massive lime tree. Black smoke gushed out the front and back entrances to the outpost, along with half a dozen men-at-arms and several White Archers, coughing and slapping at their flaming tunics. The smoke thickened, billowing out holes blown in the rampart roof, then concealed the entire building except for the flaming branches of the lime tree.

Roundell nodded, "Yes, they're good, all right, and whatever army they're working for is likely to be the same."

"Army?"

He nodded. "I saw shadow men work once before, at Splitt. They soften a castle up for a siege."

"Siege?"

He nodded, looked directly at her. "Yes, siege. This is what you were afraid of last night, isn't it?"

"No!" she cried. "No! I was just afraid."

"Of what? The assassins weren't after you."

"No," she said, "they weren't, but—"

"But you know them."

"Not them," she said, giving up, "their master." She pointed at the black streamer under his belt. "The three red circles on the streamer. That's Tiyy's emblem, the Nymph Queen of Pyram."

He withdrew the streamer, noting the circles, and his eyes thinned. "And?"

"She's the Black Veshta."

"You mean, she thinks she is."

"No, she is."

He grinned. "You believe that kind of stuff, huh? All right, how big is her army?"

"I don't know, I guess as big as she wants it to be."

"That's no help, lass," he said. "How many regiments?"

"I don't know, Jarl. Years ago she had an army and lost it. But she's clever, smart. There's no telling what she's capable of."

"So, the consort of the Master of Darkness, the bitch goddess of all that's rotten and mean, has raised an army, of only the gods know what kind of demons, and is marching here to lay siege to Whitetree? Is that it?"

"Yes," she said with spirit. "If you believe that sort of thing."

He chuckled. "You're all right, lass." Suddenly he sobered. "Forget this hocus-pocus stuff for a minute. Do you know what she's after here in Whitetree?"

"Yes," she said, "but you won't believe it."

"It doesn't happen to be diamonds, does it?"

"That's part of it."

He laughed quietly. "Lass, you were a lot of fun last night, but today, you're a riot." She fumed, and he raised his hands, as if to defend himself. "Don't get mad. That was a compliment. I like this throwing spears and knocking down walls." He glanced over the parapet, and climbed into an embrasure, adding, "And it looks like we're going to have a whole lot of it."

He pulled Robin up beside him, pointed out at the valley. In the distance, a low cloud of dust spread from right to left as far as they could see. Flurries of wind swirled above it.

"That's how a siege begins," he said solemnly. "With frightened birds and a low rolling dust cloud, kind of pretty from here, isn't it? They're burning farms and villages, encircling us. Cutting off all escape. Stopping any messages for help and driving refugees this way, to crowd the castle and add to the panic they've already started."

He pointed down at the lower yards.

Chaos reigned everywhere. People hollered and shrieked and ran about as groups formed, then broke apart, arguing over what exactly had happened, who the assassins had killed and what it meant. Others sought out the White Archers, seeking the same answers. The aristocrats, having no answers, beat them off for their trouble and fled from the lower yards toward the Sacred Close.

There the now leaderless archers gathered in animated groups, arguing the same questions. Others stood on the ramparts of the Stronghold, pointing off at the army on the horizon, and talking excitedly as more archers joined them.

Robin turned to Roundell. "What are we going to do?"

"Nothing," he said. "Everything that needs to be done would take months. All we can do now is wait for those refugees to crowd in here with their sicknesses and stinking bodies, and hope they bring enough food with them to feed all of us for the few days we have left."

"Few days?" Her face was ashen.

"The castle can't last much longer. Not if this queen is

any kind of queen I've known." He grinned at her. "Unless you've got some fancy ideas."

"I do," she said, "and maybe it is fancy to you. But it might help. Remember the man with me at the audition?"

"Brown John."

"Yes, he says that there's a formula someplace here in the castle that will give me control over, you know, my tricks. If you took me to him, and we found the formula, maybe I could make some diamonds, like the one in your pouch."

"And buy this queen off?"

"Perhaps. I don't know just how it all works. But sometimes my tricks stir people up, make them do things most people normally aren't capable of."

He chuckled. "If you show yourself to those White Archers, and convince them this nymph queen wants you and your diamonds, they'll give you to the black bitch just to save their worthless skins."

"They wouldn't!" she blurted. "They serve the goddess."

He laughed again, and crossed to an embrasure overlooking the Sacred Close. "For a goddess, lass, you surely don't know anything about men." He pointed down into the Close as she joined him. "Look at the archers now. They've found out what's going on and don't give a damn about anybody but themselves."

On the floor of the Close, stableboys, their young faces terrified, led strings of saddled horses out of the stables into the yard. Reaching the gathering of archers near the closed gate to the lower yards, the stableboys turned the animals over to them, and the archers threw bulging saddlebags over the horse, mounted up. Nearly three hundred were already mounted. Better than five hundred still needed mounts.

"There won't be enough horses," Roundell said. "They'll have to draw lots to see who gets to run away."

Tears welled in Robin's eyes. "What about your men? The others?"

"They'll stay and fight, unless they panic." He turned to her. "They're like you and me, they don't know any better." She forced a smile, and he asked, "Now, where's this bukko of yours?"

Twenty-two

FLIGHT OF
THE ARCHERS

Robin and Roundell, exhausted and battered after hunting Brown John for over an hour, stood at the edge of the Water Court, their eyes searching the bedlam.

Bodies plunged, bumped, shouted, argued. Mothers searched for lost children, wives for husbands, plunderers for food. Arriving refugees flooded into the castle, feeding the fear and panic and confusion, driving flocks of goats and sheep before them, hauling wagons. They searched for shelter, finding none, and everyone hunted answers to the questions that plagued the castle.

What army attacked them? What did it want? How could it be defeated? By whom? Who would lead them? Were the White Archers really about to desert the castle? Leave everyone to be butchered?

"I don't see him," Robin said breathlessly. "Let's try his wagon again."

Roundell nodded and they pushed through the throng toward the Grillard wagons parked near the well. Reaching them, the surly crowd suddenly parted and the *bukko*'s red wagon teetered, crashed to the ground on its side. Several Grillard men immediately hauled furniture, barrels and baggage into the gap between the red wagon and another wagon already lying on its side.

Doll Harl stood behind the rising barricade, shouting at

them. Seeing Robin and Jarl Roundell arrive, her eyes widened with curiosity, moving over Robin's attire.

"Well, well, child," she said, climbing over the debris. "Look at you, all prettied out in fringe with your hair done, and everyone else getting ready to die."

"There's no time to explain," Robin gasped. "Where's Brown? We've been looking all over for him."

"Have you now?" she said, eyeing Roundell suspiciously. "And just what would Iptur be wanting with him at a time like this."

"Iptur's dead," Roundell said flatly. "So is Dagan, the Master-at-Arms, and the commanders of the White Archers. And the regiment is about to desert. I think you better answer her question."

"So," Doll said quietly, "the rumors are true. The castle is up for grabs."

"That's why I have to find Brown," Robin blurted.

Doll frowned. "Forget your bukko, lass. He thinks this whole mess is his fault, and is no good to anybody anymore."

"Doll," Robin said anxiously, "I must find him. Please. There may be a way he and I can help."

A cruel laugh leapt between Doll's painted lips. "So, you're a fanatic too? I might have known. Well, forget your magic tricks, lass, and help us build this barricade. There's no telling how many spies are coming in with the refugees, and they're bound to try to poison the well."

Roundell turned to Robin. "The old whore makes sense, lass."

"Trust me, Jarl," Robin pleaded. "Please."

He turned to Doll and shrugged. "She wants to see her bukko."

Doll grinned at him. "So, a big brute like you believes in the tart's hocus-pocus? No wonder everything is gone to zatt."

"Right now, woman, I only believe two things. That you know where this Brown John is and that you're going to tell us."

Doll smiled, liking his style, and pointed at the wall behind the Water Court. "He's up there, trying to find out what army's about to eat us."

On the wall, people stood in the embrasures, talking excitedly and pointing out at the valley.

"Thanks, Dame Harl," Roundell said, and hurried Robin toward the wall.

"Don't call me dame, soldierboy," Doll shouted after him. "And don't call me old whore, either. I'm a young one." He grinned back at her and she nodded at the distant mountains. "These hips could ride you over those mountains and back again."

He glanced at her hips, her eyes. "I think that's a trip I'd like to take."

Doll Harl laughed, and Roundell and Robin plunged through the crowd, ran under the lime trees sheltering the well, reached a staircase and rushed up, dodging bodies both coming and going. Making the wall walk, they raced behind the crowded bodies, staring silently out at the valley. Up ahead, Jakar stood in an embrasure and Robin cried out.

"Jakar!"

He turned, saw her rushing toward him, jumped onto the wall walk and gathered her in his arms, hugging her.

"Oh, Jakar," she whimpered. "Don't ever let me leave you again. Not ever."

"I won't," he said softly, then said it again.

They looked into each other's eyes, then kissed as Roundell shifted impatiently beside them.

"I thought you were dead," Jakar said quietly.

"I'm not," she said, looking at him. "But I am a whole lot of trouble, just like you once said, aren't I?"

"Yes, you are, fluff," he said, "and I can't live without it."

"You won't have to," she said, and looked past him. "Is Brown here? I've got to see him." She looked up at Jakar's sudden frown. "Oh, Jakar, don't blame him. Please."

Jakar did not answer. He put his dark wary eyes on Roundell. "Who are you?"

"Oh, I'm sorry," Robin said, turning to Roundell. "This

is Sergeant Roundell. He saved my life. Sergeant, this is my husband, Jakar.''

Roundell nodded and Jakar shook his hand. ''Thank you, sir. I'm deeply indebted to you.''

Screaming erupted on both sides of them, and people leapt out of the embrasures onto the wall walk, fled down the stairs.

Robin, Jakar and Roundell climbed into an embrasure, and looked out at the valley.

In the distance, troops, strung out in undulating lines, marched across the valley floor, closing in on the castle. They wore all variety of armor, tunics, furs, and advanced in loose units, organized by tribes, but with the same measured stride. Relentless. Shields rode their backs, and pikes and spears glittered above them. A dark pennant waved above each unit, signal flags.

Cavalry units rode behind the infantry and filled the gaps between them. Behind them, siege engines, mounted on wheels and drawn by men and animals, lumbered forward over the uneven ground. Catapults, mechanical slings, wicker shields with arrow slits in them, battering rams housed in long, wooden huts with peaked hide-covered roofs. Wagons followed, packed with scaling ladders, siege baskets, buckets of arrows and heaps of spare weapons; bows, pikes, spears and swords. More wagons carried large boulders for the catapults, and piles of cut timber for the construction of palisade walls and countervallations.

Some distance behind the army, a horde of camp followers ambled forward, driving baggage carts and tented wagons for the army's commanders, leading strings of spare war-horses and herding cattle, meat for the troops.

Robin held her breath, transfixed by the sight, and Roundell nudged her, pointed at Brown John, standing in the next embrasure. His tunic was filthy and all his patches gone.

Robin jumped down onto the wall walk, leapt up into the next embrasure and embraced the old man, as Roundell and Jakar followed, waiting on the wall walk below the pair.

Startled, the *bukko* started to push her off, saw who it was and gasped, ''Holy Bled!'' He crushed her against him. ''Are you all right, child? Did they hurt you?''

"I'm all right," she whispered, smiling bravely. "That's all over now. Forgotten."

"Forgive me, Robin, I . . ."

"There's no time for that, Brown," she said, and glanced out the embrasure. "Do you know who's out there?"

"No. Nobody knows. It's a—"

"I do," she said. Roundell handed the *bukko* the black streamer with the three red circles on it as she added, "It's Tiyy!"

Brown stared at the streamer in horror, then at Roundell, as he explained. "The streamer was attached to the signal arrow that started the assassins' attack."

Brown trembled. "Then she knows we're here?"

The sound of thundering drums came out of the valley, and they turned sharply toward it, Roundell and Jakar leaping up into the embrasure with them.

The army stood in swirling dust, about four hundred strides from the castle walls. Standing on wagons lined up behind the ranks, bare-chested brutes pounded huge drums mounted on the wagons. At the rear of the ranks, wagons rattled and bounced toward a ridge commanding the open ground in front of the castle. There, warlords and queens sat their horses, the officers and general of the army on their horses behind them. Above them, a nearly naked nymph sat on an unsaddled black and white pony at the crest of the ridge like a savage deity.

Reaching the base of the ridge, the wagons halted and workers scrambled out, bearing sections of a command deck, and began to assemble it just below the tyrant queen.

Suddenly the drums stopped and the army began a high-pitched screeching, every man holding a dagger.

"The plague of knives," Jakar said gravely.

A string of riders galloped between the ranks, turned and dashed across the front of the castle, long black banners streaming behind them.

Not understanding, Robin turned to Roundell. "They're sending us a message," he explained. "Circling the castle with black banners means they intend to kill everyone inside and destroy the castle."

Robin shuddered and Jakar held her close, as Brown John shook his head slowly back and forth. "I've killed you," he said, then said it again.

"Don't, Brown," Robin said firmly. "There's no time. The White Archers are going to desert the castle any minute."

Brown John looked at her, disbelieving, then at Roundell, who said, "The castle's not fit for a siege," he said, "and the archers know it. So they're deserting. They'll try to run for it, or give themselves up if that's their only choice, and try to barter for their release." He paused, then grinned ironically. "The lass says you know something about a formula, a prayer, something that might help."

The *bukko*'s tangled eyebrows gathered thoughtfully. A glint came into his eyes. "Yes, yes, I do. It's in the castle library. And it will help us, I'm sure of it. Can you take me there?"

"I'll try," Roundell said. "Maybe when the archers leave, those left behind will let us in the Stronghold."

Shouts and the sounds of charging bodies erupted from the Market Court, and they turned toward them.

The rabble in the lower yards, intent on breaking into the Sacred Close to find shelter, was charging up the ramp, attacking the gate. They carried heavy timbers in their arms, and swung them like battering rams, hammering the wood. The gate splintered a little, and White Archers suddenly appeared on the ramparts above the gate, longbows in hand, and fired down at the mob, point-blank.

Men and women dropped in bunches. The flood of bodies kept coming, surged over them, and hammered the timbers of the gate, splintering it again. It did not give. The archers kept firing, taking down swaths of bodies, their arrows splitting necks and chests and legs. Suddenly the rabble broke and fled back the way it came.

Horses whinnied behind the wall of the Close, and the gates swung wide. Mounted archers galloped out, wielding swords, and a long white column of grim-faced men, plunging animals and flashing blades galloped down the ramp.

The rabble split apart in front of it, screaming and dragging children out of the way. Horse's hooves and sharp metal drove the slow ones to the ground, and fountains of blood spurted into the air.

The lead archers reached the main gate, charged through the last few refugees entering the castle, and rode out. The column followed, slowing and jamming up at the sharp turn in the narrow, angled passage leading to the gate. Horses bumped into each other, bucked and got turned around, isolating several archers. Instantly the enraged, blood-mad rabble threw itself at them. Two archers hacked their way free, but hands dragged four out of their saddles, and the crowd ate them with knives.

Suddenly the jam-up cleared. The column of archers surged forward, plunged past their fallen comrades. For a long moment, the moving white column stretched all the way from the Close to the main gate and across the bridge. Then the tail of the column rode out of the Close, and the archers left behind slammed the splintered gate shut, bolting it again. As the tail of the column rode across the Market Court, the crowd edged close, then attacked it with pitchforks and spears and bare hands. Horses stumbled, became separated from the column, and their riders swung their bloody swords wildly as the rabble dragged them out of their saddles and butchered them.

The rest of the rabble watched, panic hard behind their eyes. Suddenly the mob lurched forward, began to rush after the escaping riders, mindlessly seeking to escape.

"Holy Bled!" gasped Brown. "They've lost their heads."

"Stop them!" Robin pleaded, turning to Roundell. "Tiyy will murder them!"

Roundell glanced at the Market Court.

Confused, dazed people and animals milled just inside the gate passage, momentarily blocking those trying to get out.

Jarl turned to Jakar, nodded at Robin. "Take her to the Round Tower at the end of this wall walk." He pointed at it, then spoke to Brown. "Follow me."

Roundell charged along the wall walk toward the looming gate towers forty strides off, with the *bukko* right behind him. They dashed past startled groups of people, made the door to the gate tower, and charged in. The families of the men-at-arms stationed in the gate towers, having fled the lower yards, huddled in the room with their belongings. Roundell and the *bukko* pushed through them, went through a narrow door into the room above the gate passage, and Roundell drew his sword.

Two large winches occupied the room. One stood on the floor, its ropes rising to loops in the ceiling, then descending to the floor. There they were tied to loops in the top of the massive portcullis, hanging in a slot cut in the stone floor. The second winch stood on a landing eight feet above the room, its ropes running through holes in the front wall to the heavy drawbridge outside the gate. The ropes wound tautly around the drums of the winches were nearly seven inches thick. The ends of the ropes were tied to heavy counterweights dangling in deep holes in the stone floor. Dust covered both winches. The ropes were flayed and dry, unused for years.

Throwing an arm at the landing, Roundell shouted at two men-at-arms stationed in the room: "Raise the drawbridge!"

The two soldiers raced up the ramp. Roundell raised his sword, shouting at the *bukko*, "Use your sword! We'll drop the portcullis."

Roundell brought his sword down on the thick rope where it was stretched taught over the drum. Brown did the same. The blades ate into the hemp as squealing, creaking noises came from the landing. There the two soldiers, grunting and straining against the handles at each end of the winch, raised the drawbridge.

Growling, Roundell and the *bukko* kept hacking. Suddenly the rope split apart of its own accord. The drum of the winch spun furiously, screeching, the loose end of rope flaying Brown and Roundell. They ducked away, the scream of metal tearing across stone making them flinch, and the portcullis dropped, landing in the passage below with a heavy thud and sharp scream.

Looking down through the stone slot, Roundell and the *bukko* saw a White Archer under the portcullis, one half outside the castle, one half inside. Shouting grew suddenly loud, and a horde of bodies rushed into view, came to a stop against the portcullis, screaming and reaching through the bars for escape. The sound of the drawbridge slamming shut quieted them a moment, then they screamed louder.

Roundell turned to the two soldiers. "Seal the gate towers! Barricade yourselves in here until I tell you different."

Jarl led the *bukko* back the way they came, with the two soldiers following, and stepped back onto the wall walk as the men-at-arms closed and bolted the door behind them. In front of them, people hurried up the staircase onto the wall walk, eager to see what would happen to the column of White Archers.

Roundell and the *bukko*, breathing harshly, looked out through an embrasure, saw the white-clad riders riding arrogantly toward the black-clad army. A moment passed before Brown spoke.

"Strangely colorless for a battle, isn't it?"

"It won't be for long," Roundell replied.

Twenty-three

THE DIRTMASTER

Tiyy dismounted, dropped her reins, and walked to the edge of the ridge commanding the battlefield. Naked except for breechclout and the weapons strapped on her forearms, she squatted in the dying sunlight, a dark, hot animal glistening with a golden sheen of heady excitement.

At the sides and back of the open ridge, her Jani bodyguards sat their horses, vermilion crossbows in hand. They watched the line of trees, every so often glancing at the activity developing in the valley below.

Her army's line of investment contained Whitetree. Escape was now impossible.

Two hundred yards to the north, the army's main camp rose rapidly. Farther north, General Ghapp's engineers had already completed a raft bridge across the river, and patrols rode across it, guarding against any attempt by the besieged to escape in that direction. A mile south of the castle, a second camp rose. Beside it, engineers constructed a bridge over that end of the river so sentries could maintain contact with the smaller guard camp beyond the bog and marshes on the opposite, the eastern, side of the castle.

When night fell, Ghapp's engineers and the sappers she had conjured for him would advance and begin to close the investment, dig ditches, throw up countervallations to defend against counterattacks, and begin to mine the massive white walls.

Now, directly below the ridge, Ghapp's attack forces, extending out in neat lines out of range of the castle's longbows, faced the western walls of the castle, displaying the Black Veshta's might to the terrified inhabitants. Shouted commands came from the ranks, and the front line of pikemen lowered their long spears, placing the butt end against their boots, ready to greet the column of mounted archers if they charged.

Tiyy's eyes glistened, and she dropped forward onto her fists and knees, like a jackal about to pounce. Both excited and afraid.

The column of White Archers did not charge, but continued to trot across the open ground, their formation loose, seemingly without a leader. None of them wore a horned helmet or carried an axe. The Death Dealer was not among them.

The nymph goddess sat back on her haunches, her malevolent smile in place. The White Veshta and the dark Barbarian remained behind the castle walls, caged in Whitetree.

The archers rode closer to her pikemen, and the nymph rocked in place, suddenly hungry to join the coming action, to fling herself into the center of the blood and screaming

where she belonged. But she held her place, looked down at
the man she had selected to conduct her siege.

General Izzam Ghapp watched the unfolding drama from
his command deck, a tiered wooden platform standing at the
base of the ridge. His shiny black bamboo armor, plated with
silver, glittered. The horsehair crest on his wide-brimmed
helmet moved on the breeze. A flagman waited beside him,
orchid signal flags in hand.

The army's commanders watched the unfolding battle from
the lower deck. The Dirtmaster, a sallow, emotionless man
in charge of prisoners and administering punishment, stood
below the command deck, his eyes on Ghapp. The gray-faced
officer's horse stood untethered beside him.

In the valley, the column of White Archers reined up forty
paces short of the front line of pikemen, and several archers
unfurled white flags of surrender.

Tiyy jumped up, her black almond eyes stabbing at the
cowards, as frustration flushed her orchid cheeks.

Ghapp looked down at his Dirtmaster and nodded. The
dark man mounted his horse, rode down the slope toward the
deserters. Nothing else moved on the battlefield except for
the new grass swaying under the gentle stroke of the cool
breeze.

The Dirtmaster eased his horse between two troops of cavalry, turned through a gap in the ranks of pikemen, rode into
the open. Twenty yards short of the cowards, he halted,
waited silently.

The archers began to argue, shouting, then three riders
advanced, reining up short of the Dirtmaster.

The three archers talked at length. The Dirtmaster listened. He abruptly pointed at the sun, low above the western horizon, obviously giving them an ultimatum. Then he
walked his horse back to the line of pikemen and again
waited.

The three negotiators rode back to their comrades and arguing broke out again, but ended quickly. The column dismounted, removed their bows, quivers and sword belts, and
in groups of three walked up the slope to the Dirtmaster,

tossed their weapons at his feet. As they did, grooms hurried
to their horses and led them away.

Then the Dirtmaster raised an arm and three wagons rumbled through the ranks, stopped beside the weapons. Workmen jumped off, heaped the weapons on the wagon beds and
rode away. The Dirtmaster signaled again, and a small formation of soldiers trotted between the ranks toward the deserters. They wore black hoods, carried black ropes.
Executioners.

The startled White Archers backed away, turned to flee and
two companies of mounted spears galloped across the open
ground, one coming from the north and the other the south,
blocking all retreat.

The archers bunched up, then threw up their arms, and the
executioners moved among them, tying their hands at their
backs. Ten flatbed wagons rolled into position, in a line facing the castle. A huge black-hooded, bare-chested executioner stood on each wagon bed, behind a chopping block.
A large basket waited beneath the block. Stacks of them
waited beside it. Without pause, the executioners roughly
herded the stunned, struggling archers, ten at a time, to the
wagons and forced them to their knees, necks snug in the
grooves of the chopping blocks. The axes swung down, almost in unison. Ten heads fell into the baskets. Another group
promptly followed the same routine.

Stunned silence came from the castle. Then, after twenty
heads fell, scattered shouts, encouraging the executioners,
broke out along the walls, followed by wild cheers.

When a basket filled, pairs of workers ran it to three light
catapults that had been rolled close to the walls, along with
large wicker shields to protect the crews. The loaders dumped
four to five heads into the bowls of their weapons, along with
brittle straw baskets filled with black adders and clay bottles
of quicklime. The firing teams wound the windlasses tight,
then released them with loud, rasping twangs. The counterweights dropped, the heavy bowstrings snapped forward, and
the bowls, positioned at the tip of the firing beams, sprang
forward. The beams banged to a stop against the padded
crossbars, and their elastic ashwood bodies whipped forward,

throwing the contents of the bowls in a high arc toward the castle walls.

Faces along the walls looked up in horror as the terrible ammunition flew over their heads. Some reached for their cheeks, obviously splattered by drops of blood. Others ducked and fled. The heads splattered and bounded across rooftops, baskets of snakes broke apart, bottles of quicklime exploded and screaming erupted from within the castle.

Tiyy watched the bizarre bombardment with rising impatience. It held little amusement for her. It had no thaumaturgy, no dark sanctity, no erotic finale. It consisted purely of the business of war, ordinary terror.

Bored, she watched Ghapp standing stoically on his command deck, totally in control, and remembered when he had behaved in the opposite manner in the underground chambers of the castle, and lost all control. She liked him better that way and, being his goddess, she could have him any way she wanted him.

Tiyy strolled back to her tent, standing at the rear of the ridge, dropped among the deep blue and green pillows heaped on the black rug, and shouted, "Aillya!"

The old woman appeared immediately and kneeled before the young goddess. "Yes, mistress."

"Fetch General Ghapp," Tiyy said, using her queenly tone. "Tell him his goddess is celebrating the advent of a successful siege, and commands him to join her in her tent . . . so that they might worship together."

"Now?" the crone asked, her tone dismayed. "There are still two hours to sundown."

"Now," Tiyy said.

Twenty-four

PANIC

The hairy object flew over the wall of the Sacred Close, hit the roof of the looming stage with a crunch, bounded into the air.

Brown John and Roundell, hurrying across the front of the abandoned stage, stopped short and looked up.

The object hurtled down, hit center stage with a mushy splat, tumbled to a stop at the edge. A human head, bleeding so profusely from nose, mouth and neck that the wet movement made it appear alive.

Roundell stepped back to the head and the *bukko* groaned. Another delay.

The old man had waited patiently as Roundell had quartered Robin, Jakar and himself in Round Tower, then found space for Doll Harl and her harlots after they had been driven out of the Water Court by the rabble. Now, just around the corner of the stage, the gold door to the Vestry waited, and beyond it, deep within the massive Stronghold, in the castle's fabulous library, the sacred formula also waited, the formula with which he, Brown John, *bukko* to the Goddess of Light, would reveal her, not only to the terrified rabble, but to the Black Veshta and her army, and save the world. Providing Jarl Roundell ever got around to showing him the way.

"I think we better keep moving," Brown said, trying to control his impatience.

Roundell nodded, started for the door and again stopped short, as two more heads splat against the white stone on the far side of the Close. Then a basket hit the ground near them, exploded with wiggling black snakes and white dust.

"Snakes," Roundell said flatly. "Adders or asps, and jars of quicklime." He nodded at the wall separating the Close from the Market Court. One of the remaining troops of White Archers guarded it, and screaming, pitiful cries of pain came over it. "They're what's causing all the noise in the lower yards."

Brown nodded fretfully. "I know. Can we please keep moving?"

Roundell looked at him. "You really think this hocus-pocus will do us some good, don't you?"

Brown's eyes thinned angrily. "I don't wish to discuss it. Can we go?"

"Slow down," the mercenary said, moving again. "Getting in there is not going to be as easy as you think. You're going to need your wits about you."

They rounded the corner of the stage and stopped short. The gold door was gone. In its place, heavy stones, set in mortar, filled the entrance opening, blocking all entry.

"Holy Bled!" groaned Brown. "Why did they do that?"

"Same reason they do everything," Roundell muttered. "They're looking out for themselves. They know there's no chance of defending the lower yards, and are getting ready to hole up in the Stronghold."

"And let everyone be slaughtered?" Brown gasped.

"Everyone but themselves," Roundell said bitterly.

"Then we've got to get in," Brown said, suddenly frantic. "Now!"

Roundell shook his head. "Forget about the library, old man."

"Forget?" Brown exclaimed. "What are you saying?"

"I'm saying," Roundell said, nodding up at the jagged face of the massive Curtain Wall, "I'm not going to risk getting trapped in there. Not with them."

"But we must!" Brown protested.

"Not me," Roundell said, heading back for Round Tower.

"Wait!" Brown pleaded, moving after him. "You don't understand. I—"

Shouting and the sound of running men buried his words, and they stopped short, turned toward the noise.

The troop of White Archers was flooding off the wall at the southern side of the Sacred Close. They leapt down the stairways, hit the ground in crowds and raced across it, heading for the ramp rising to the gate of the Stronghold. Acolytes, their robes held above their knees, spilled out of the buildings under the walls and joined the stampede.

Roundell leapt up onto the stage, hollering, "Look out!"

Brown stared at the archers in disbelief, all hope draining out of him, then climbed onto the stage and plunged after Roundell. They slipped behind the half-burnt trees of the set and held still, robed in shadows. The sound of running men came from all sides of the stage. Then one, two, a third archer ran across the front of the stage, leapt off and fled toward the crowd of bodies surging up the ramp.

"We've got to get out of here!" Roundell shouted. "This way!"

Brown dashed after Roundell as he slid through the sets into the wings, and plunged past the great round drums of the wind and thunder machines. The *bukko*'s eyes trailed over the marvelous devices, then they jumped the railing enclosing the backstage area. Roundell landed running, but Brown's bad leg gave slightly on impact. He staggered, then limped hurriedly after Roundell as the soldier leapt up an open staircase leading to the wall walk. The *bukko*'s calf cramped tighter and tighter as he ascended the stairs, then threw him down.

Roundell bounded back down the steps, kneeled beside him. "What's wrong?"

"Bad leg," Brown said, breathlessly. "Give me a hand."

Roundell helped him to his feet, and they paused, staring across the Close.

The last of the archers and acolytes, shoving and pushing, surged through the Curtain Wall gate, then a huge rusted portcullis dropped out of the ceiling of the recessed entryway, hit the ground with a heavy thud, dust billowing away from its long unused body.

Hammering and howls of rage came from the opposite side

of the Close. The gate in the southern wall suddenly fell inward, and the rabble, weapons in hand, flooded in over its splintered body, as others, using ladders, came over the wall. Wild. Exultant. Crazed.

Roundell urged the *bukko* up the last steps. "Come on, you don't want to watch this."

Brown started after him, then hesitated, hearing something in the soldier's tone that chilled him. Screams erupted behind him, and he turned sharply.

Bodies writhed and spun and fell at the front of the plunging rabble, their chests and legs and faces drilled with arrows fired by archers on the ramparts of the Curtain Wall high above. The archers kept firing. The rabble finally fell back, dragging its wounded with them, and the archers lowered their bows. At the bottom of the Curtain Wall, dust billowed through the bars of the portcullis as stones and rubble were heaped up behind it, barricading the gate tunnel.

Brown John turned to Roundell, desperate. "Now how do we get in?"

Roundell stared at him, a mocking grin at play on his face. "Nothing stops you, does it, old man?"

Brown lifted a calming hand, controlling himself more than Jarl, and said, "I know it seems callous, with all those poor creatures dead down there. But it's important. Is there another way?"

"Maybe," Roundell said. "There's a gallery under Round Tower with tunnels leading off of it, one runs under the Close and Stronghold to the Hall of Beds, the women's quarters. The library is directly above. We might reach it that way, but it's risky now. Real risky."

"It's worth it, Roundell, believe me."

A moment passed, and Roundell shook his head. "I don't think so." He turned and leapt back to the wall walk.

The *bukko* stared after him, aghast, then shouted, "It's not tricks I'm after, you fool, can't you see that?"

Roundell did not break stride.

Brown glanced back at the rabble, now spreading out over the Close, plundering and taking refuge in the buildings, tending its wounded, weeping over its dead. Then he looked up at the archers on the looming Curtain Wall, frowned angrily, and limped after the sergeant.

Twenty-five

THE DARK ONE

Roundell led the *bukko* along the wall walk to the door to Round Tower, knocked, giving the signal. It swung open and Roundell and Brown John entered. Scattered, sullen men-at-arms occupied the bunks, stood at the arrow slits of the barracks room. Silent, their uncertain eyes watched Roundell. Taking no unusual notice of them, he crossed the room as if he knew precisely what he was doing and entered the stairwell, the *bukko* following him.

Reaching the crenellated rampart, they found Robin, Jakar and clusters of men-at-arms peering over the embrasures at the enemy in the valley below. They stood silently, despairing, and all along the western wall, both to the north and south of Round Tower, people now stood doing the same thing.

Roundell stepped up behind Robin, touched her shoulder and she turned, startled, then sighed, "Thank the gods, you're all right." She glanced at the *bukko*, back at Roundell. "Did you—"

He shook his head. "The Stronghold's barricaded." Nodding at the valley, making certain his gesture and tone created no alarm, he asked, "What's happening?"

"We're not certain," Robin replied, staring at Brown John's sullen, silent face. Then she looked back at Roundell. "You better look."

Jarl Roundell, finding himself surprisingly flattered by the

girl's confidence in him, and doing his best not to let her see
it, boldly climbed up into an embrasure.

The valley lay empty, except for distantly scattered patrols
and lines of wagons in front of the command tower below
the ridge where a mounted bodyguard surrounded the bitch
queen's tents. Filled with trenching equipment, the wagons
stood ready to advance as soon as the night covered their
movements. The bulk of the besieging army's troops had
marched to their camps to the north and south.

Roundell studied the quiet calm filling the valley, searching
for some sign that would indicate which wall of the castle the
enemy would attack. Then he saw it.

A dirt road had been cleared, rising from the flat ground
opposite the lower yards to the crest of the highest ridge,
vanished. Dust billowed in the depression behind the ridge,
huge billowing clouds. Steadily growing, they came closer, then the heads of bunched men bobbed into view. With
their backs bent and feet set wide, they hauled on ropes,
trailing in crowds back into the cloud of dust. Moments
passed, and a massive, square structure emerged from the
dust, teetering slightly from side to side.

"What is it?" Robin asked, climbing up beside Roundell.

"Siege tower," he replied.

Every eye in the parapet looked at him, stunned. Then
Jakar, jumping up beside Robin, said, "They can't be stupid
enough to attack at this time of day."

"They won't attack, lad," Roundell said. "They just want
us to see it, so no one will sleep tonight." Robin nodded
forlornly and, feeling obliged to keep her from feeling
trapped, he added, "Now would be the time to mount a
counterattack, hit them before they can raise their own
walls."

"Can you do it?" Robin asked, as if Roundell had suddenly been put in charge of the castle's defense.

"Well," he said, knowing he was about to show off and
unable to stop himself, "twenty riders, even ten, would do
it. Just enough to let them know they're in for a fight, and
give the rabble a bit of hope. Let them know we aren't helpless. Once the feeling of being trapped sets in, and it always

does with folks not used to living in castles, the strength goes out of their sword arms.''

''But we don't have any horses,'' Robin said.

Roundell, shamed by his bravado, changed the subject. ''Here it comes.''

The siege tower crested the ridge. Five stories high, it rocked back and forth as it started down. Dark hides covered its front and sides, flapping on the wind. A drawbridge, mounted at the front of the top story, rattled and shook loudly. Tiny figures, looking like ants perched on the rim of a stool, stood in the turret. Solid wooden wheels rolled under it, digging up the road, spewing dust and pebbles. Taut ropes streamed from its body, held by more struggling groups of men at the sides and rear as they tried to steady it.

Starting down the incline, the wooden tower picked up speed. The bunched men at the rear dug in their heels, began to strain at their ropes, giving ground gingerly. The tower continued to gain momentum, dragging them forward. Their heels dug up the earth beneath them as they fought the weighty pull, and it slowed slightly.

Watching it advance, old feelings prowled out of Roundell's blood and bone and mind. His thigh muscles pulsed, hungry for the feel of a war-horse between them. His fingers clenched and unclenched, wanting to grip his longsword. Now was the perfect time to strike, while the tower was totally vulnerable, and he was helpless. The entire castle was helpless.

''Look!'' Robin said, pointing beyond the siege tower.

A lone rider had emerged, crossing an opening in the forest just above the line of trees. Now he vanished.

''It's probably a messenger,'' Roundell said.

''No,'' Robin said, ''I don't think so. There's something—''

She stopped short, suddenly holding her breath. Jakar looked at her, disbelief stretching his face. The *bukko*, suddenly alive, bounded up into the embrasure behind her and held her shoulders, his eyes white and wet.

''It can't be!'' the old man whispered.

Robin Lakehair only stared, unable to speak or move.

At the line of trees, stately pines and dense brush hid all

that dwelled within them. Then the shadowed rider galloped out of the trees, strangely large and threatening, as if he had the will to command the forest to march behind him. He galloped down the shaded, barren foothills and into a golden orange swath of dying sunlight. A black warrior on a black stallion.

A dark chain mail skirt covered his legs, ornate armor his chest. A black cloak billowed behind him. He carried a narrow triangular shield with some kind of design on it, and a huge curved axe. A horned helmet with a pointed crest rose above his massive shoulders. Its mask covered his face. But the stranger's attire was the least of his attractions. He sat his mount as if man and animal were of one body, one mind, one emotion. One creation. The meat and bone of war.

Feeling Robin tremble against his arm, Jarl Roundell looked at her.

Tears spilled over her smiling cheeks. Her eyes held the light of a thousand daybreaks, her body their warmth. Turning her face to his, she put her smile on him, and youth welled up in him. All of a sudden, all around him, all the world was new again.

"He came," he said.

She nodded. "Just like he said he would."

"Does he have a name?"

"Gath," she said. "Gath of Baal."

"The Death Dealer," the *bukko* blurted dramatically. "That's who he is. The Lord of the Forest. The Dark One!"

Robin's husband said nothing, as if something he had dreaded had finally come to pass. The girl hugged his arm, but her eyes held the dark rider.

A patrol of three fur-clad outlaws, carrying red crossbows, slowed as they crossed the valley, and one pointed up at the lone rider, about five hundred paces away. Then they started toward him, but in no hurry, obviously believing he was on their side.

Turning his horse, the Dark One disappeared behind a foothill.

The patrol, the only ones who had noticed his sudden arrival, trotted over the foothills, up the mountain to where they had seen him, and reined up. Standing in their stirrups, they looked from side to side. Suddenly one pointed down at Jade Road, and they turned their horses sharply, started back down the hills in that direction.

A moment passed, and the Dark One, moving at a full gallop, burst over the crest of the ridge, not thirty strides behind the siege tower. Raising his axe, he plunged alongside the men struggling with their ropes at the rear of the tower, then swung the blade in a flat arc over their heads and severed ropes flew in all directions.

The men who had held them fell backward, knocked down men beside them, got tangled up among the legs of those behind. The bunch slowed. The siege tower did not. It pulled the ropes out of half the men's hands, hauled down those that did not release their grip, and dragged them over their fallen comrades. Yelling and struggling, the bunch bounced along the ground, then gave up, let go of their ropes.

The siege tower lurched ahead, suddenly picking up speed. Tipping forward, it leaned toward the men dragging it, and they scattered, dropping their ropes. The men on the sides, trotting now, held on, trying to steady the huge wooden citadel as it bounded down the road.

The dark rider charged them. His axe ate ropes and arms. Men dropped, screaming. Others fled, diving out of the way of the charging black horse and flailing axe.

The rabble on the castle wall, staring in stunned disbelief, suddenly cheered wildly.

The tower lumbered and bounced down the incline.

A squad of infantry on sentry duty moved up the road below the plunging tower, their spears flashing in the sunlight.

The dark rider heedlessly galloped directly at them, plunged among their thrusting weapons. His shield, armor and headpiece caught a dozen spears, and he did not appear to notice. His axe did what axes do, caved in chests and heads, then he was past them.

Half the soldiers lay on the ground; the others ran, except for one. Covering his bleeding face with his hands, he stumbled blindly up the road, heading directly at the rattling, plunging siege tower. He seemed to sense something and hesitated as the shadow of the tower swept over him, then fell where he stood. The huge tower rolled over him, a wheel riding up slightly as it crushed him. The thundering tower veered slightly, rolled off the side of the road, dipped into a gut in the valley floor, tripped and threw itself face forward. A roar went up from the castle walls, and the siege tower crashed loudly, shattering itself into woody fragments, killing its occupants.

The castle cheered and cheered.

"Is that what we needed?" Robin asked Roundell, her big eyes sober.

Roundell nodded, then his eyes suddenly thinned, wary, curious.

Snarls of smoke lifted away from the face of the horned helmet, as the Dark One rode among the wreckage of the siege tower, but there was no fire to cause it. He reined up facing the bulk of the rubble, and turned in his saddle. The smoke came from the helmet. Then fire showed within the smoke, coming from the eye slits as the dark rider stared down at the broken timbers. The fire grew hotter until the face of the masked helmet became a red glow. Then flames shot forth in fiery spears, struck the wreckage. The siege tower burst into flames.

"Demon spawn." Roundell whispered.

"No! No!" Robin explained. "It's the helmet. The metal is alive. But he controls it."

Roundell looked at her skeptically, but she looked back at her champion, obviously feeling she had explained everything.

The dark warrior backed his stallion out of the flames, turned his horse, and looked across the valley at the castle.

Groups of sentries, still far off to the south and north, rode toward him. Others galloped toward the command tower, shouting.

The three sentries who first spotted the stranger, having hesitated on the ridge upon seeing flames erupt from the horned helmet, now charged down the slope. The Dark One, raising his shield, charged them, axe poised. The distance

between them closed rapidly. The sentries suddenly reined
up, raising their vermilion crossbows. They let him come
within fifteen feet, then fired.

The metal bolts streaked through air, catching glints of
sunlight, pinged off his shield, helmet. His stallion plunged
into their horses, bulling them aside. The animals whinnied,
bucked. The Dark One's axe shattered a knee, opened up a
belly, removed an ear. Rocking in their saddles, the bloody
sentries tried to reload. The axe continued to work. A sentry
spilled out of his saddle, screaming, leaving one leg behind
in a stirrup. Another raised his crossbow to defend his face.
The axe splintered it and he fell, wearing scarlet splinters in
his cheeks and forehead.

The third soldier finished loading his crossbow, lifted it.
The axe blade buried itself in his chest up to the haft. The
impact lifted him out of his saddle. He flailed on the end of
the axe, crossbow still in hand, then fell off. He hit the ground
with his back. The crossbow fired, less than a foot from the
Dark One's calf, and the bolt buried itself in his muscle.

The sentry fell back dead. The dark rider looked down at
his wound, reached down, yanked the bolt out, bringing a
spurt of blood with it. Tossing it aside, he watched the distant
groups of sentries gallop toward him, as if he wished they
would hurry. Then he faced the castle.

With the siege tower smoldering behind him, he sat slightly
hunched forward. He held his axe in his right hand, the butt
end resting on the neck of his stallion, his shield in front of
him, the dark design of a falcon clearly visible. Orange fire
boiled behind the thick legs of the horse. Blue smoke filled
the sky, barely hiding a pair of vultures as they floated down,
following the rising scent of carnage.

Robin moved in front of Roundell, waved across the vast
distance.

In reply, fire glowed behind the eye slits of the horned
helmet. Then he lay his axe across his saddle, reached for
his helmet as if intending to remove it. His hands caught the
rim and pushed the helmet up slightly, then stopped. The fire
in his eyes reappeared. He pushed hard, struggling, but the

helmet appeared to resist him, and black smoke snarled from both the eye slits and mouth hole.

"He can't get it off!" Robin groaned. "Tiyy's done something to him."

Gath gave up the effort to remove the helmet, glanced at the distant sentries. They had slowed, and now came forward in a wide arc, cutting him off from the castle. He turned toward the command deck. There, mounted sentries surrounded the ridge, the black bitch standing stark naked in front of them. Suddenly she took one of the red crossbows from a bodyguard, and held it triumphantly over her head with both hands.

"She's poisoned him," Robin whispered. "She's made the helmet strong again."

As if he also understood, the Dark One turned his horse and galloped up the ridge, disappearing over it. He reappeared, riding hard over the foothills, and headed toward the trees. Just short of the forest, he slumped in his saddle and the horse slowed. A moment passed, then he righted himself, heeled the horse and it galloped up into the concealing trees.

The squads of mounted sentries met at Jade Road, started toward the forest together, and the bitch queen's bodyguards joined them, a dozen staying behind to guard her. Reaching the spot where the Dark One had entered the forest, scouts galloped ahead to find his trail, then the troop rode into the trees.

When Roundell turned to Robin, he found her looking at him. "I've got to go to him," she said simply. "Only I can remove the helmet, and if I don't it can kill him, or worse . . . turn him against us."

"She's right," the *bukko* said with a blustery show. "Robin and I must go to him immediately!"

Roundell did not reply. His eyes held Robin's. "Let's say that as soon as it's night there's a way I can get you safely out of the castle and past their patrols, then what? There's no way we'll find him in the dark."

"I'll find him, Jarl," she said quietly. "Trust me."

He studied her long and hard, then said, "All right, I will."

Twenty-six

TREE HARLOT

The troop of bodyguards rode steadily through the forest, bright vermilion crossbows in one hand, reins in the other. They followed a trail of blood spattered on elderberry, thornbush and forest floor. Scouts, riding a hundred strides ahead, led the way.

Two miles into the mountains, the blood appeared more frequently and in larger drops, and formed a small pool at the base of an oak where the demon Death Dealer appeared to have halted. Four hundred strides farther on, where the pines and oaks gave way to ancient lime trees, their trunks as wide as houses and roots as tangled as wads of string, the bodyguards stopped beside a stream. The scouts waited on the other side, their faces grim in the wan light. Beyond the stream, the blood signs had disappeared and they had lost the trail.

The troop split into three sections. One went upstream, one downstream and one continued forward, moving slowly and alertly through the dense shade cast by the lime trees. Time passed and the gray gloom gradually grew dimmer, as day began to turn to night.

Around them, the shadows took on monstrous proportions, and the center troop slowed their advanced, closed ranks. Except for the sound of their horses' hooves crushing dead undergrowth, silence settled over the forest. It seemed to fill the air, as if with a physical presence, a thick coldness intent on drowning them. When they heard a merry whistling up ahead, their superstitious dread eased out of their grizzled faces, and they hurried their pace.

Entering a small clearing, they found a small boy sitting before a fire with his back to them. He blew his happy tune on a set of wooden pipes bound together with thongs. Beyond the fire, the exposed, tangled roots of a giant lime tree seemed to writhe out of the ground, forming a cavelike opening. The boy was obviously using it as shelter. An old mare, harnessed to a small wagon built like a cage, stood beside the tree. The firelight illuminated jars at the edge of the cavelike opening and brightened the corner of a bright yellow blanket spread in the dark interior.

The boy stopped playing, glanced over a thin shoulder. His startled eyes blinked, then widened with delight, as the bodyguards walked their mounts into the fire's glow, reined up. The child, dressed in a dusty tunic and short boots, had a tiny face set in a large head. From it sprouted a pair of oversized ears and spikes of black hair as thick and straight as nails.

The boy played a jaunty fanfare on his windpipes, then suddenly rolled backward, flipped into the air, twisting his body around, and landed facing the bodyguards. He bowed low, spreading his arms, and spoke from that position.

"Welcome, masters, to the tree of fleshly delight. How may I serve thee?"

The leader of the bodyguards, a thickset man with a square face, glanced around suspiciously. "Did you see a rider pass this way? Big man, all in black with a horned helmet?"

"I have seen no one all day," the boy replied with a show of great tragedy on his animated face, "and my bear and I are very hungry." He picked up a small brass cup resting beside the fire and shook it. It made no sound. "See? Empty?" He dashed around the fire, disappeared into the shadow-filled cave, and emerged again with a huge black bear on a leash. "Would you like to see him dance? Only two aves. He can do a jig and the farandango of the mountain tribes, including the somersaults!"

The boy dropped the leash, put his pipes to his lips and the leader growled, "We have no time for dancing bears."

The boy tucked his pipes under his belt and grinned wickedly. "But you have time to chuzz my sister, right? I will sell her cheap. Only five aves."

The leader stared at him, then frowned in disbelief as several bodyguards laughed, one grunting, "Your sister's a tree harlot, is she? Hah!"

"But this is truth!" the little whoremaster persisted. "She is called Firefly, because she is hot as burning pitch and as quick as your arrows." His eyes twinkled with several unsavory meanings.

The leader grunted.

"Four aves then?" the boy begged. Getting no answer, he added, "I'll fetch her." He scurried back to the tree, smiled wickedly over his scrawny shoulder. "Beware, masters, you are about to fall in love."

They laughed unpleasantly. The boy vanished into the tree cave and promptly came back out, leading a frail girl by a thin red string tied around her neck. She held fronds of leaves across her breasts and hips, apparently naked underneath. Her eyes were childish, a sky-gray. Freckles spotted her cheeks and her bare chest, running down to the upper slopes of her small breasts. Her narrow face was slim and angular, boyish and dirty. Leaves and twigs tangled in her long hair, the color of dirty straw.

"See?" the boy said. "My beloved sister is easily worth a hundred aves. But, since she seems to like you, I will make it three aves."

A naughty smirk worked its way across the girl's plain face, as she quickly passed the fronds back and forth from breasts to hips, revealing flashes of what lay beneath.

The bodyguards grinned at each other, and three shifted in their saddles, preparing to dismount.

"I knew you'd love her," the boy said, laughing, and pushed the girl forward.

She stumbled, dropping her fronds, and fell to her hands and knees. Laughing wickedly, she jumped back up, intentionally leaving her fronds behind. Her small breasts were firm and healthy. A thin loincloth dangled over her womanhood, too thin to conceal a large red rash. Spreading from her inner thighs, up under her loincloth and over her belly, it glittered wetly in the firelight.

The bodyguards stayed on their horses.

"We don't have any time for some halfwit tree harlot," the leader grunted, suddenly angry. "Have you heard anything in the past hour, or seen anything that indicated a rider passed this way?"

"Please," the boy begged. "We are hungry. We—"

"Have you?" the leader roared, cutting him off.

The boy backed away and the girl hid behind him. Shuddering, the lad pointed weakly at a path passing between the trees. "There . . . there was some blood beside the creek, over there, and the ground was all torn up. It looked like some raccoons had been fighting, but it could have been a horse."

Without replying, the bodyguards crossed the clearing and rode into the forest, following the narrow trail.

The bear licked Billbarr's intent face as he watched the backs of the soldiers disappear behind the foliage, then lumbered to Fleka and licked her leg. Without looking at the animal, she tied its leash to a metal ring buried in the ground beside the fire, and grinned at the boy.

"How'd I do?"

"Shhhhh!" he said.

"Well, I was good, wasn't I?" she whispered.

Billbarr lifted a finger to his lips and nodded in the direction of the giant lime tree. "Go to him. And put something on. There was no need to undress."

"It fooled them didn't it?" Fleka grinned proudly and stood, deliberately turning her body so the firelight stroked her nudity.

Billbarr blushed and hurried after the riders, hearing her chuckle quietly, then scampering through the foliage.

Reaching a tree at the edge of an open glade, he jumped up, caught hold of a lower limb and vaulted up into the network of branches. He scrambled up through the limbs to a perch overlooking the glen.

The soldiers rode through the darkening shadows on the

far side, then stopped beside the small creek and leaned out of their saddles, investigating the muddy bank. They looked in silence, then started chattering and pointing at the drops of blood Billbarr had spread on the ground. That led them to Gath's shield. One dismounted, picked it up and tied it onto his horse. He remounted as the others lit torches with fire pots, then advanced into a dark glade. Following the trail of blood, the shadows swallowed them.

Billbarr grinned. The trail would lead them to another stream, a considerable way off, then vanish again where he had dismounted and driven the stallion off. Hopefully the horse was miles away by now, still running. He regretted the loss of the animal, and of its saddle and golden armor. But it was a price that had to be paid. He swung down through the branches, jumped off a lower one, did a somersault in midair and landed on the ground, running.

Reaching the clearing, he dashed to his big black bear, hugged it, then plunged into the tree cave. Neither Gath nor Fleka were there.

He dashed out of the cave and into the foliage behind it. Erupting from the bushes, he stopped short, let go of a startled gasp as flames slashed at the ground cover in front of him, singeing the hair on his shins.

The flames retreated and a flurry of smoke floated away, revealing Gath. He now sat where he had fallen over an hour earlier, propped up amid a shadowed tangle of dead logs, which his armored body had crushed into a crude chair. His helmeted head hung low in front of his heaving chest, the eye slits a red glow. One arm circled the half-dressed Fleka, the other hung loosely from his shoulder, his meaty hand gripping his axe. His leg wound had stopped bleeding but was still unwashed. Black, sticky blood covered his knee and shin all the way to his boot. Ants worked the edges where it was still wet and red.

Billbarr took a step forward and the eye slits spat a four-foot length of flame at him.

"Be careful," Fleka blurted. "I don't think he knows who we are."

That shook Billbarr. Not knowing what to do, he squatted

where he was, hugging his knees to his chest. Searching the glowing eyes for some trace of recognition, the boy found nothing. The helmet not only hid Gath's features, but seemed to alter his entire body and manner. Billbarr looked at Fleka. She had cleaned the fake rash off and put on her tunic, and was pretending to be not afraid. But her voice broke as she spoke. "I'm frightened, Billbarr. He's never acted like this with me before. Not once! He's never even looked at me like other men do. I thought I wanted him to, but not now."

"He can hear you," Billbarr blurted, warning her not to offend the Barbarian.

She shook her head. "He hears, but he doesn't understand. I'm sure of it. Oh, Billbarr, what's happened?"

"I don't know," Billbarr said, his eyes on Gath. "I saw him act like this once before, in the Daangall. He was like an animal. But this is different. I think whatever wounded him was poisoned."

As if in reply, the fire died behind Gath's eyes.

"That's what's happened, isn't it, Gath?" Billbarr asked. "It's some kind of sorcery?"

The horned helmet dipped in agreement. "Tiyy." The Barbarian's voice was low and husky, as if spoken from the depths of a chasm in the underworld.

Fleka gasped, "That's the nymph queen."

Billbarr nodded. "The Black Veshta." He crawled forward, facing Gath. "Then the rumors are true? She does lead this army? She's got your . . . the Goddess of Light trapped in that castle?"

The horned helmet nodded and Fleka groaned, sinking forward and hiding her face with her hands.

"Stop it," snapped Billbarr. "Everything's going to be all right."

"All right?" she shrilled, looking up. "Nothing's been all right since I met you two. I've been used as bait for tigers! Been left alone to die in a tree! And now, after we travel all over everywhere looking for this pretty face he's so crazy about, and finally find this army that leads us to her, what happens? This black bitch, the Black Veshta herself, is leading it! And now she's worked her sorcery on him, and you're telling me not to groan about it.''

''The girl is not just another pretty face,'' Billbarr said importantly. ''She's a goddess!''

''I don't care what she is,'' Fleka snarled. ''What good is her magic to us? She's safe inside the castle, and we're out here with this black bitch's whole army looking for us. We haven't a chance.''

''Stop it, Fleka,'' Billbarr said, trying to remain calm. ''We'll be all right once the poison wears off.''

''Who says it's going to wear off? Look at him!'' She glanced cautiously over her brown shoulder at the horned helmet, not inches away. ''He's a demon himself now. There's no telling what he's going to do next.'' She sank, as if losing all strength, and covered her head with her bare arms. ''Ohhh, gods! I must have been doing something terribly wrong my whole life to deserve this.''

Billbarr stared at her until she looked up. ''Are you finished?'' he asked, as if he had seen her act a hundred times before. She frowned in reply, and he stood up.

''Where are you going?'' she asked, suddenly afraid. ''You're not going to leave me with him again?''

''I'm going to douse the fire and destroy all sign of our camp.'' He looked up at the dark sky. ''It'll be dark soon. They can't hunt again until morning, so we'll be safe until then.''

''Oh, that's wonderful,'' she grunted. ''He has a whole night to kill us.''

''Stop being so dramatic. He won't hurt you, and you know it.''

They stared at each other, memories of the past months ranging behind their eyes, of the trails they had shared with Gath of Baal, of mysteries, dangers, joys. Then Fleka nodded, and Billbarr moved back through the foliage.

When he finished destroying all sign of their camp, and hidden the mare and wagon cage, the boy returned to the small clearing with the bear and found Fleka kneeling in front of Gath, cleansing his wound with a soft rag and bowl of water. She looked up, her bold, frisky smile at play once again on her saucy face.

"So, you decided to come back?" she said, her sarcasm artless.

Billbarr grinned. "I couldn't help myself, you being as beautiful as you are." His sarcasm, not being artless, made her frown, so he changed his tone and said what he truly felt. "You really are, you know."

She smiled, her body and expression suddenly loose and warm. "Don't tease me like that, boy, or I'm liable to forget you're a boy."

He chuckled and looked at Gath. "Has he said anything?"

She shook her head. "I think he's getting worse."

Billbarr squatted beside her. "At least he let you get off his lap, that's a good sign."

She shook her head again. "He was just too weak to stop me. He hasn't moved since you left. He just sits there, as if he were using everything he has inside to fight the poison. But if it's sorcery, well, you can't fight it for long." She looked at Billbarr. "You know, now that he's weak like this, we really should run away."

"Desert him?" he asked in shock.

She nodded solemnly, "It's the smart thing to do." Then she winked. "Too bad we're not very bright."

Billbarr, smiling all over, nodded.

Twenty-seven

HOT CHEEKS

In a corner of Round Tower's ground-floor room, Brown John kneeled over his open trunk, digging through assorted costumes. Dressed entirely in black, he looked like a shadow, and made no sound. Thongs bound the handles of his sword and dagger to their scabbards so they would not rattle. Removing a black cloak, he stood, crossed past the two soldiers, a putty-faced youth and an old graybeard built like a tree stump, and stepped around the open trapdoor in the floor.

The light of oil lamps touched the first three steps, descending into the looming darkness below, and fell over the faces of Robin and Jakar, waiting on a bench beside the opening. Jakar wore a black cloth over his dark clothing, with his crossbow slung across his back. A gray cloak with a worn sheen covered Robin. The *bukko* handed her the black cloak.

"Here, use this, it's darker and has no shine."

"Thank you," Robin said. Taking the cloak, she stood, shrugged off the gray cloak, hurriedly threw on the black one. "Isn't it time to go?"

"He'll be back any minute," Brown replied, and looked at Jakar. "I'm sorry, son, I wish you could go with us, but Roundell is making the decisions."

"Don't concern yourself, bukko," Jakar replied sullenly.

Brown gave Robin a consoling look, moved to the other side of the trapdoor as Robin sat close to her husband, her hands holding his. "Are you sure you don't mind?"

"I mind, fluff, but it's all right," Jakar said, and kissed the tip of her nose. "The fewer there are, the more chance you have of getting through their lines. And Roundell knows every pond and gully in the valley. He has to be the one to take you."

She kissed him, whispering, "There's nobody in all the world as understanding as you are." He pushed a lock of hair away from her brow and she smiled. "Let's promise we'll never fight again."

"Never," he said quietly. "Now take care of yourself, and come back with Gath."

"I will," she said. "I'll bring him back."

Embarrassed at himself for listening to the couple, Brown John stepped to an oil lamp. Wiping some soot off, he spread it on his forehead and cheeks.

A rapping sounded on the door opening onto the Sacred Close, and everyone stood. The young soldier slid the locking bar aside, Graybeard pulled the door open, and Jarl Roundell strode in, dressed in black and carrying a torch. As the soldiers closed and bolted the door, he moved directly to Robin and cast torchlight over her. Under the black cloak, she wore a dark chestnut jerkin, black tights and black boots. A black cap covered her light hair.

"Good," Roundell said. "Ready?"

Robin nodded bravely.

Roundell glanced at Brown offhandedly, then addressed the group. "My men-at-arms hold the towers and gate, but the rabble of acrobats and clowns holds the walls, or think they do. There's forty people in charge out there, and all talking at once." He turned to Robin. "If we can find this demon friend of yours, they might listen to him and put up a decent defense. But we have to move fast, get back here before sunrise."

"I'll find him," Robin said, her tone firm.

"Then let's get started."

Jarl Roundell handed Graybeard the torch, and the old man descended through the trapdoor, the others following. A narrow, switchback stairwell led them to a gallery. Five tunnels opened off of it, dug out of the white stone. Rubble half-filled two of them. Graybeard led them through the one passing under the tower to the western cliffs. It descended sharply for several hundred feet, then the white stone walls gave way to dark earth shored up by heavy timbers.

"We're under the cliffs now," Roundell whispered. "Keep your voices down and your steps light. The surface is only about ten feet above. If they've sent spies to examine the ground and walls, the vibrations could tell them there's a tunnel down here."

They nodded and tread lightly through the tunnel. It twisted around the thick, gnarled roots of lime trees growing out of the cliff, then ended in a shallow room. Thick roots grew down through the center of the room. Steps, carved out of the roots, wound up into their center, leading to a ladder that rose through a shaft in the roots. A stack of small wicker rafts rested against the wall.

Brown John, panting slightly, sat down on a root to catch his breath and choked on the torch fumes, coughed. Roundell shot a hard glance at him, then glanced at Graybeard. The old man nodded understanding, set the torch in a wall bracket, and stood behind the *bukko*.

Watching Roundell climb the steps and disappear up the ladder, Brown John shifted warily, glancing at Graybeard. A moment passed, and the faint sounds of a creaking door came from above. The group waited silently, Robin hugging Jakar, then Roundell came back down the ladder.

"There's no one out there," he said quietly, "and no moonlight. We're in luck." He picked up a raft, extended a hand to Robin. "This is it, lass. It's up to you and me now."

Brown, stunned by the fact that the mercenary excluded him, stood in protest. No one acknowledged him. Robin gave Jakar a last kiss and Roundell helped her up the first steps.

"Just a minute, soldierboy," Brown said imperiously, grabbing Roundell's elbow. "Robin isn't going anywhere without me."

Roundell looked at Robin, and waited. She turned to Brown and smiled weakly. "Forgive me, Brown, but . . . well, it's much safer this way. If only two of us go."

The *bukko* glared at Robin and Roundell. "Do you mean you two have discussed this? That you think you've decided who's going and who isn't, without consulting me?"

She nodded. "We had to."

"Had to?" he blurted.

"Yes," she said evenly. "Gath needs me, Brown, and we need him. Desperately. I can't take the chance that you'll—"

"You don't trust me?" he blustered with mawkish disbelief.

"I do, Brown, but—"

"No, you don't!" His tone accused her.

"Shhhh!" She hushed him.

"Don't shush me," he whispered dangerously. "And don't for one minute think, because I made one mistake, that I don't know what I'm doing. Me? The man who found you in the first place. Who made you everything you are. Who sent you to Gath and stole the jewels of light for you."

"Brown, please," she begged quietly.

"Calm down, Brown," Jakar whispered, putting a hand on his shoulder. "Now's not the time."

"Not the time!" Brown snarled, glaring from one to the other. "Here we stand at the threshold of what could easily be the most important scene we've ever played, and you expect me to stay here and play the fool? Me, who's written every part you've played, and told you where to stand, who to kiss and who to love."

"That's not true, Brown," Robin flared. "Stop it!"

"Ha!" Brown John grunted sarcastically. "So, you think you're smart enough to disobey your bukko, is that it? Well, you're wrong. You're dumb. The lot of you. If you go out there, the black bitch will see your aura."

"I told you, Brown," she said firmly, "that my aura is not there anymore." He flushed, and she added, "That's the problem, Brown. You forget things, and you don't see things coming the way you used to. It's not your fault," she added quickly, "you're just older."

The word buried itself in Brown's pride like a dagger. His breath left him in one long gasp, and he half-turned away, staring at nothing.

"There's no time for this," Roundell said, taking Robin by the arm. "Let's go, lass. Now!"

"Don't tell her what to do!" Brown said, turning hard on Roundell. "Don't say one thing."

Roundell took no offense whatsoever. He stepped back onto the ground and looked directly into Brown's eyes, and shook his head, once. Then, as casually as possible so as to give the *bukko* a demonstration of his incapacity, he kicked the old man in his bad calf.

Brown gasped in surprise and grabbed his leg. It did not help. He dropped, face first, eating dirt and writhing in pain.

Robin reached for him and Roundell stopped her, pushed her back up the steps. She reluctantly glanced back at Brown with guilt-filled eyes, then disappeared up the ladder as Roundell, raft in hand, followed.

Brown tried to stand, but fell instead. Snarling, he hauled himself into a sitting position and began to pound his leg, defying the pain. The knot in his calf softened and he stood up, starting for the steps. Graybeard stepped in front of him, blocking him. Brown glared at him, mortified that a man easily five years his senior had the gall to stand in his way, then swung wildly. Graybeard blocked the punch, put the *bukko* back on the ground with one shove, sat on him. Brown growled and twisted, then watched in dismay as Jakar, unseen by Graybeard, disappeared up the hole carrying a raft.

Groaning, Brown struggled wildly but silently under the stronger man, then dizzied with pain, and his head fell to the ground. The dirt was cold against against his hot cheeks.

Twenty-eight

THE SENTRY

Descending another ten feet, Roundell stopped again. Had he heard a noise somewhere up the cliff? Had someone else come out through the hidden tunnel? He could not tell. The pitch-black night blanketed the castle, trees, cliffs and Robin. Groping for the girl, he found her shoulder and patted it reassuringly.

She had remained silent since they emerged from the concealed shaft in the lime tree, a hundred feet back up the cliff. Her touch betrayed nothing of how she was reacting to the danger. He only had a vague notion of where her face was, even though her warmth lingered on his cheeks, her scent caressed his senses.

He turned toward the sound of the river. The murmur and splash of moving water remained faint, placing the river at least another hundred feet away, much farther than he remembered.

He placed Robin's hand on his back. "Hold tight," he whispered, "and keep your body crouched and feet spread."

She tugged on his cloak, once, telling him she understood, and he smiled to himself. The lass even knew the signals of the night. Had she done this kind of thing before? It did not seem possible, yet he was certain she had. She was delicate as blown glass yet made for adventure, a combination he found extraordinarily intoxicating, and one that surprised him.

She was easily the most beautiful and stimulating female he had laid eyes on, but it had not even occurred to him to try and bed her. There were other things he wanted from her, wild things he had never wanted from a woman before. He wanted to ride with her galloping at his side over distant trails, to share the campfire and see the moon, hear the owl. To explore the unseen and share the dread of dying, the joy of living, the raucous laughter of the strong.

They crept past feathery shadows, hearing the faint sounds of shovels and hammers above the song of the river, then spots of light glimmered on the other side of the river, about several hundred paces beyond the opposite shore. Torches lighting the besieging army's work crews, as they drove shovels into the ground and heaved the dirt onto a rising mound behind them.

"Ditches," he whispered, pointing them out. "They're raising their own defensive works, to stop any sorties from the castle. They don't know we don't have any horses." He pointed at fires a little farther north. There three half-finished wickerwork towers stood behind a palisade wall on a completed terrace of dirt and trees. "They'll mount catapults on those towers so they can fire heavy spears and fireballs directly over the walls." He pointed farther north. There pinpoints of many fires glowed. "That's their main camp." He pointed south. "We'll ride downriver, past their works and the gate, then cross to the mountains. They have a smaller camp south of the castle, but it's over a mile off, and there are gullies running from the river to the mountains. We'll have to avoid their patrols, but if this darkness holds we should be all right."

"I think we better hurry then, don't you?"

Her whisper was gentle, nevertheless he heard the reproach in it, and heat rushed into his face. He was showing off his knowledge and experience, trying to impress her again, wasting precious time.

Growling silently at himself, Roundell led her down another twenty feet and his foot sank into deep mud, almost throwing him down. Righting himself and holding her back, he explored the area with a hand. They stood in the small culvert at the base of the cliff he had been heading for but had thought was still far below. Water normally filled it, but now it was strangely, unexpectedly empty. Where was the river?

"Stay close," he whispered, and felt the tug of her reply.

Roundell followed the harder ground on the side of the culvert, and the sounds of the river up ahead grew slightly louder. Another seven feet and he saw the faint glimmer of distant fires on the surface of the flowing water, moving as slow as melting butter. What he suspected was true, and he grunted.

"What's wrong?" Robin whispered.

"The river's dropped five feet since sundown. They're damming it up, probably diverting it into the moat."

"Why?"

"Because this general, whoever he is, knows what he's doing. Somehow he's found out the foundations of the western walls have been undermined by the river. When the water drops, his sappers will move right in, use the tunnels cut by the river and bring the walls down."

"What can we do?" she gasped.

"What we're doing," he replied, and waded into the shallows. He set the small raft on the water, held it steady with one hand and guided Robin with the other. "Here. Climb on and lay flat."

Robin crawled onto the bobbing raft and lay down. Roundell pushed off and jumped aboard, straddling her legs with his knees, holding the handles on the sides of the raft. He glanced back at the culvert. Had a shadow moved within it? It was too late to investigate.

Tilting the raft with his weight, he steered the small craft into the current and it swept them out into the darkness. They bobbed along the western face of the castle high above, approached the bridge and Roundell suddenly lay down, shielding Robin's body, covering her mouth with his hand.

Dark figures moved along the riverbank, carrying bows. Sharpshooters sent to kill anyone fool enough to show himself on the castle walls. More figures moved about the abandoned outworks and on the bridge up ahead.

The raft suddenly slewed sideways, heading for the bank. Roundell threw out a stiff arm. The butt of his hand hit the solid embankment, stopped the raft short with a splash, then propelled it back out into the middle of the river.

The bowmen took no notice of the small noise. Their raised heads studied the walls high above. One fired. A moment passed, then a scream pierced the night, and Roundell felt the girl shudder under him.

They swept under the bridge and down the dark wet channel, the banks looming higher and higher on both sides. The sounds of hammers and digging grew faint, then only the sounds of the water and night accompanied them. Roundell rose to his knees, peering ahead. Blackness hid the landing site he had planned to use. He waited, hoping for a glimmer of star- or moonlight to show him the mouth of the gully and sandy beach. They did not.

Desperate, he tilted the raft. It rushed toward the bank, ran over rocks and came to a sudden stop, throwing them onto the muddy bank with a loud splash. Roundell rolled upright, gathering Robin to him, and dragged her clear of the shallows. The raft spun, then continued on without them.

Robin stared in terror as their only means of recrossing the river swept away from them, then opened her mouth. He covered it with a meaty hand. Her face, illuminated slightly now that they were out of the shadows of the castle walls, looked up at him, and her eyes said she understood.

He removed his hand, helped her to her feet and stared in dismay. The riverbank rose like a wall in front of them, taller than Roundell. They moved along it quietly, feeling their way over rocks and through the shallows, and found a gully splitting the valley floor. Entering it, they moved twenty feet inland. There, the top of the gully rose only a foot above their heads. Climbing the sides, they could see the valley spreading toward the distant mountains, black against a turbulent cloud-filled sky.

Far to their right, the north, the fires of the besieging army were faint spots. To their left, a faint orange glow on the bottom of low clouds indicated the location of the southern camp. Roundell smiled. Despite missing the desired landing spot, he had stopped in the right place. They were approximately halfway between the camps. The valley lay empty before them, like a huge, greenish-black rug laid on the earth for the exclusive use of oversized deities.

Staying low, so that their silhouettes did not rise above the crest of the gully, they hurried toward the distant mountains. A third of the way across the valley, the gully began to grow more shallow, exposing them. The sounds of hoofbeats rose above the melody of new grass playing on a breeze, and they dropped flat. A moment passed, and a mounted patrol rode down the road up ahead. It passed and they dashed forward, crossed the road, moved into a deep gut between the foothills. It took them all the way to the edge of the forest. There they stopped, catching their breath, as Roundell studied the surrounding foothills, then the shadowed defile they had just passed through.

His neck hair itched, a feeling that had, on many an occasion, told him he was being followed. But he did not hear or see anything to indicate that was now the case.

Hurrying along the line of trees, they made the spot where they had seen the Dark One ride into the forest, and stopped. Gasping for breath and moist with sweat, they looked down at the valley.

The campfires of the army were as faint as distant stars, the only light on the land. They turned toward the trees. There was no light, no possible way to distinguish trunk from shrub, or shrub from open passage.

"All right, lass," Roundell said quietly, "from here on you lead."

Robin nodded with resolve. "Just give me a moment."

He waited as she strolled back and forth among the trunks looming like sentries guarding the base of the mountain. She could sense Gath's presence, almost feel his Kaa, his spirit, grazing her throat and cheeks and hands. But it would not enter her, would not center in her heart and instruct her mind, tell her which direction to take. Something refused it entry. Another kind of sentry.

Fear leapt through her mind. Goose bumps rose along her forearms, across the back of her neck. Even before she had possessed the sacred jewels, she had been able to sense Gath's

Kaa on the other side of a door, sometimes even over a distant rise. Her heart had never resisted him. It could not.

She crouched, hugging her knees, holding perfectly still. Closing her eyes, she surrendered to her memories of him, seeing once again the breadth of his muscled chest and his blunt, sober features, then feeling his hard lips on hers. Still he stayed out.

Opening her eyes, she looked fretfully at Roundell. He stood patiently in the shadow of a tree, trusting her. She winced, glanced back across the valley and the clouds parted slightly, allowing faint starlight to glow on the crests and towers of the castle. A knowing ache filled her chest, then it took form and she realized that the sentry who guarded her heart against Gath was at the castle. Jakar.

The realization shook her confidence, then her body, and she hugged herself again. She knew she would have to force Jakar out in order to let Gath in, and the knowing filled her with guilt. She dared not risk it. What if Gath stayed, even though he had no right to stay, and kept Jakar out? What if, even though she held the powers of the goddess, her heart was helpless? What if, as Brown John so often implied, she, being a goddess, did not belong to one man, but to many?

More questions came rushing through her youthful mind. Storming it. Overwhelming it. There was too much she did not understand, and more she did not want to understand. All she wished for was to dance and sing and love and bear children. Openly. Freely. With all the joy of her youthful heart. Instead, she had spent most of her youth sneaking about like a thief in the night, daring demons and death and the Master of Darkness himself. For years she had gone to sleep, not to the lullabies and songs of joy, but to the songs born of screams and weeping. As if cued by her thoughts, a keening wail came from the castle, and grew louder until the stone citadel seemed to cry out with pain.

Robin covered her ears and turned away. But the message had been delivered and it gave her no choice. Those in the castle called out for help and only Gath could deliver it.

She held still, tears welling in her eyes, and released Jakar from the hold her heart had on him. It hurt terribly, leaving

an emptiness. Then the sentry was gone and her heart surrendered to Gath of Baal, to the Death Dealer.

A warmth rose inside her, swelling her breasts and filling
her cheeks with color. Her breath hurried, and she looked up
at the black sky. The clouds swirled and churned, a brightness showing behind them. Then they parted and the full
moon stared down at the forest, drawing the trails and natural
passageways on the earth with the silvery light.

Roundell stared at the spooky phenomenon, shuddered
slightly and stepped beside her. Glancing up at the great white
eye in the sky, he said, "Don't tell me you did that, lass, and
I'll feel a whole lot better."

He smiled at her and she smiled back, then suddenly sobered. "I don't really know, Jarl," she said meekly. "There
is so much I just don't know."

She shrugged, then turned and strode into the forest, her
pace strong and direction sure. He followed her.

They moved up the side of the mountain, reached the crest
and she plucked a long blade of grass out of the ground. A
dark blotch stained the stem. She rubbed a thumb over it.

"It's his," she said matter-of-factly. "His blood."

"How can you tell?" Roundell said, his shadowed expression as filled with mystery as his question.

"I don't know. I sense things. I always have, in leaves,
herbs, blood. That's how I learned to heal when I was still
only seven." She sniffed the dry blood and her smooth brow
wrinkled slightly. "It's his, but it's different now. He . . .
he's changed somehow."

"Changed?"

"Inside someplace, deep inside."

Roundell chuckled. "I find it hard to believe you can tell
that from a few drops of old blood."

"I know," Robin said. "I don't know how or why myself,
but I can." She gave him a slightly playful smile. "That's
why I knew, even though it is not in your nature to help or
trust anyone, that you would help me."

He smiled back. "I think, lass, you better get moving.
Because I can get over it fast."

"I know that too," she said, and moved deeper into the forest, following the trail of blood.

The moon had drifted slightly down the side of the sky when they stopped short at the edge of a small clearing, miles inside the forest. A torch, half-hidden by foliage, approached from the opposite side. Drawing his sword, Roundell pulled Robin behind a tree.

The sound of horses pushing through underbrush rose behind the torch, then a group of riders entered the clearing and reined up. They carried bright vermilion crossbows. Tiyy's bodyguards. The leader cast the light around the clearing, studying a huge lime tree at the far end.

"She's gone," he grunted with annoyance. "The bitch!"

He rode forward and the others followed, their lusty faces snarling and tired. They passed under a shaft of moonlight, and thin cuts made by branches and leaves showed on their cheeks and arms, then they faded into the darkness.

When they could no longer hear the horses, Roundell whispered, "They're still looking for him. That means they haven't found him."

Robin nodded, led Roundell into the center of the clearing and again stopped short.

"He's here," she whispered. "Close. Maybe within a hundred feet."

Roundell glanced sharply from right to left. "Where?"

"I'm not sure. The feeling comes from all sides now." She held still, then waved an arm toward the giant lime tree. "It's strongest that way." Roundell started forward, and she stopped him. "No. Stay back. If the helmet controls him, there's no telling what he might do."

Roundell's expression said he didn't like that, but he did as he was told, moving to the side where shadows concealed him. There he waited, body crouched beneath a low, heavy limb, sword in hand.

Robin advanced cautiously into a spill of moonlight at the foot of the giant lime tree, and hesitated, peering into the blackness filling the root cave. An uneasiness crept across her flesh, a feeling she did not know. She took a step, bent low for a closer look into the cave, and something heavy dropped on her from above. The side of her face hit the ground and a body straddled her, forcing her over onto her back.

A small hand throttled her throat. Behind it, a boy with dark hair sprouting like nails from his skull glared down at her, a knife raised above his head. He brought it down, and it stopped short of her breast. The hate-filled expression on his face suddenly vanished, leaving it empty, except for one emotion. Shock.

"You!" he gasped.

Twenty-nine

GATH OF BAAL

Roundell rushed across the clearing toward the knife-wielding boy. A freckled girl came around the corner of the huge lime tree behind the boy, a loaded bow leveled at Roundell's chest. He stopped short, still twenty feet from the boy's knife hand.

Turning sharply, the boy saw the sword dangling in the mercenary's hand, and sprang backward with the agility of a young leopard, landing on all fours beside the girl. Rising quickly, Robin backed away, breath racing. The boy held still, poised on toes and fingertips, ready to leap again. His eyes darted from Roundell to Robin. "Is he your friend?"

"Yes," Robin said, "but who are you?"

Her startled eyes searched the child's face and strange hair, his animal-like stance, manner.

"Friend," the boy whispered, "I think." His eyes looked from Roundell to Robin and back. "Don't shoot, Fleka."

The freckled girl lowered her bow an inch, gave Roundell

a clumsy wink. "Good," she said. "I hate to kill the ones with dimples."

"Shhhhhh!" the boy said, glancing about the clearing as if he expected the shadows to walk over and take a bite out of his face. The girl scowled, but stayed quiet. Half-crawling, the boy approached Robin, studying her face, and suddenly smiled with impish delight. "It is you!"

"You . . . you know me?" Robin asked, amazed.

"Oh, yes!" the boy said importantly, standing. "You're the one called Robin Lakehair. I saw you. Sleeping beside the campfire beneath the burnt thorntree."

"Burnt thorntree?" she asked, her tone puzzled. Then she gasped with understanding. "But . . . but that was years ago, on Calling Rock. Were you there?"

"No! No!" the boy said. "I saw you in the dream." His smile began to dance. "You are the fire goddess."

"Dream? Fire goddess?"

"Yes, I see what he sees. When the Sign of the Claw possesses him. When he dreams."

"He?"

"Your champion. Gath of Baal." The boy's chest swelled, and he slid his knife back under his belt. "I am his friend, Billbarr, the Odokoro. And this is Fleka. She is also his friend. We share the Barbarian's trail, his fire, his food. Everything."

"Is he here?" The beginning of a smile lifted Robin's cheeks. "Is he all right?"

The boy started to reply, but hesitated as the sounds of something large stomping through underbrush came from the shadows beside the lime tree. The crack of twigs, a rasp of leaves across metal. Then a massive, shadowed bulk loomed behind the moonlit foliage, coming forward. Suddenly it stopped, pushed branches aside and hung motionless, like a piece of the night itself. A man animal.

He took a loose step and his shoulder splintered a low-lying branch, his hip broke off a sapling. Confronted by two birch trees, growing less than a foot apart, he spread the trunks wide with his forearms, as if they were no more than silk curtains, and put one leg between them, hesitated. His head hung low between his wide shoulders, protected by a masked, horned helmet. The Dark One.

Roundell smiled. Even if this brute killed the lot of them, it would be something to see.

Standing between the trees, the Dark One's axe dangled from his hand like an organic growth, but his spread legs swayed, seemingly as intent on throwing him down as holding him up. A spill of moonlight touched the helmet's horns. They writhed away from it, obviously preferring the darkness, and a growl leapt from the masked mouth, fire glowed behind the eye slits.

"Gath!" Robin sobbed, half in joy and half in pity. Getting no reaction, she tried again. "Gath, it's me, Robin."

The helmeted head turned slowly toward her and Robin raced toward him. The brute watched her come as if she were no more than a bite of meat on the end of a fork. Suddenly his helmeted head lurched up and his body came erect, as if lifted by pride. The flames died behind the eye slits. He let go of the trunks, stepped between, and they snapped back. The trunks slammed his thigh from both sides, but he took no notice and stepped clear, his full attention on Robin.

Heedlessly, she threw her small body against his dark bulk, wrapped her arms around his neck. "It's me," she whispered to the helmet. "It's me, Gath. Your Robin is here. Everything's going to be all right now."

Eyes appeared behind the eye slits. Hard gray eyes. They watched the moonlight play in her red-gold hair. He dropped his axe, his hands lifted, his fingers played where the moonlight played. Then he picked her up, his huge hands spanning her waist, and held her before him as easily as if she were a toy. His body appeared suddenly alert and strong again, under control.

For a long moment, he studied the lift and curl of her smile as her hands slid along the corded muscles of his arms and shoulders, then touched the rim of the horned helmet. There, her fingers trembled against the metal, as if it were hot. Alive. Suddenly shafts of light burst forth from her knuckles and nails, and streaked across the clearing, the tips sparking like shooting stars.

Roundell stared, spellbound, as the light swept past his face, between his legs.

The girl called Fleka ducked out of the way of a particularly bright ball, and hid behind the boy called Billbarr, hugging him. Enchantment widened their eyes, then they gasped with awe.

Droplets of light sparkled on Robin's fingers. They slipped down her hands and arms, then cascaded off her elbows in showers of seemingly wet effervescence, splattering on the ground. There they gathered in glowing pools and rivulets of light that drained between the cracks and creases in the earth.

Roundell watched the bright eddies wash between the feet of the boy and girl, and flow over dirt and under leaf to the tips of his boots. They shimmered brightly, then dissolved into a bright glow that floated into the air, momentarily filling the darkness with a blinding white light before they vanished. He looked back at Robin.

Garlands of diamonds draped her arms, clustered in her red-gold hair. A single, tiny gem glistened wetly on the ball of her cheek, in precisely the same place Roundell had found the tearlike jewel now in his satchel. She smiled and the tiny gem burst with shafts of light, illuminating the horned helmet. The horns now behaved as horns were supposed to, and the metal seemed to be nothing more than cold steel. The shafts of light found the eyes within the headpiece and hers met them, held them. Then a low, thick, husky voice spoke from the mouth hole.

"Robin."

"Yes," she sighed, her relief shaking her small frame. "Yes."

He set her down, his hands covered hers and together they lifted the helmet off. Shuddering with relief, she sagged against him and he held her with one arm, the demonic headpiece propped against his hip. After a moment, she looked up and they both seemed content to do nothing more than look at each other.

Sooty fumes rose from his black, knife-cut hair. Flecks of ash streaked the crests of his wide, blunt cheekbones and jaw, the bridge of his flat nose. Ruddy calluses and the traces of old scars, worn away by wind and fire, marked the sun-darkened flesh of his brutally handsome head. The only soft-ness dwelled in his eyes, but Roundell could not tell if it belonged to the man or the face of the girl they reflected.

"You are not hurt?" he whispered.

"No," she said. "But many in the castle are. Tiyy's as-sassins have killed everyone in command, and more than half of the White Archers have deserted. The others have walled themselves in their Stronghold. They're not going to protect anyone but themselves, and everyone's terrified. Helpless! The castle is filled with tribes of traveling players, merchants and refugees, and they don't trust each other. Everyone sus-pects everyone else of some treachery, and they're turning on each other. Men have been murdered, women raped. It's hor-rible!"

Nodding as if she spoke of trifles, he raised his hand to her head, and his fingers touched her cheek. She sighed at his touch and held his palm against her face with both hands, her fingers insignificant scraps of unimportance next to his swollen muscles and the bigness of his arm and wristbones.

"Please, Gath, you've got to help. Tiyy will kill everyone if you don't."

He nodded again, put a hand at the back of her head, brought her face toward his. She resisted slightly, a trace of panic passing behind her eyes, then all strength seemed to drain out of her. His flat, blunt lips gently kissed her eyelids, her cheek, her nose, then met the round softness of her lips and crushed them. She moaned in surrender. Her arms reached for him, but hesitated, floating above his shoulders, momentarily supported by the meager muscle of indecision. Then she cried out weakly and threw her arms around him, kissed him ravenously. Not a girl's kiss. A woman's.

When he released her, her cheeks flamed with a heady mix of love and desire and shame. She quickly hid her face against his chest, gasping in confusion.

The diamonds had vanished, but Roundell had no idea when or how. He stepped forward, standing in the moonlight so that Robin and the Barbarian could see him clearly. He waited until they looked up before he spoke.

"There are only a few hours of darkness left," he said quietly, "and we'll need all of them if you intend to get back in that castle."

Robin nodded and lifted a hand, asking for a moment more. Roundell took a step back. She glanced at the boy and girl, as if slightly flustered, then forced herself to stand erect and face the Dark One. Her voice, when it finally came, trembled with both fear and resolve.

"Gath, there is something I have to tell you. I . . . the year after you left, I . . . I married Jakar." Her confession out, her voice steadied and cooled. "He's in the castle, with Brown John and the others."

The Barbarian reached for her face, his eyes holding hers, and thumbed her plump lower lip, as if recalling something that had passed between them long ago. A sigh escaped her lips and her eyes closed, her head falling against his chest.

"Oh, Gath," she cried softly. "I missed you terribly. You shouldn't have left me."

"I had to."

"I know," she whispered. "I know. But I wish you hadn't."

"I will not leave again," he said.

Her head lifted and her eyes opened. "I know," she said, "I can see that. But . . . but it's too late."

"No," he said. "You cannot change what is written."

She stared at him, obviously more afraid of her own feelings than his, and her cheeks flushed with shame. She turned away and Roundell stepped forward again.

"Gath of Baal?"

The Barbarian looked at Roundell and said, "Yes."

Jarl liked that. It was an answer, nothing more. There was no threat or declaration of pride in his tone. No challenge. The answer of a man who knew the difference between words and action.

"Jarl Roundell," Roundell said, his tone identical. "Former Master-at-Arms at Whitetree. If we're going back into that castle, we'd best do it fast."

"There is a way in?"

Roundell nodded. "I can get you in through a hidden pos-

tern gate. But don't misunderstand me. It's bedlam in there.
And the castle may not hold, even if you manage to organize
a defense.''

"You'll help?" Gath asked.

Roundell nodded.

Gath smiled at that, and understanding passed between
them. The understanding of men who do their best work amid
the clash of arms, the stench of burning flesh and screaming
fountains of blood. The understanding of men who, war mad
and battle hard, have kissed the face of death.

"How do we cross the river?" Gath asked.

"They're damming it, probably at the mill half a mile
north, where the moat joins the river. My guess is they're
diverting the water into the moat. If I'm right, it won't take
them long. The surface was falling fast when the girl and I
crossed. By now, the bed should be drained."

"That means mud," Gath said.

Roundell nodded. "It'll be four or five feet deep, maybe
more. No one has cleared the silt in years." He smiled wryly.
"Let's hope their sappers have already gone to work, laid
down a straw and plank bridge for us to use."

"The chances?"

"Good, I'd say. This general, whoever he is, is good."

"Izzam Ghapp."

"Ahhhh." Roundell's smile faded. "That explains a lot of
things. He was the best the Kitzakks had, before he lost his
spine. Apparently he has it back. Anyway, he's positioned
his troops to attack the western side of the Stronghold, which
means he must know that's the castle's weakest point. The
river has cut caverns and tunnels through the base of the rock
and mined the foundations. All Ghapp's sappers will have to
do is extend and widen some of the tunnels, then set fire to
them and bring down the walls." A sardonic smile had its
way with his face. "This could be the shortest siege in history. You sure you want to go in there?"

Gath did not reply, and Roundell liked him for that.

The Barbarian questioned Robin with his eyes as she turned
to him, face still flushed. She nodded. "You can trust Roundell.''

She turned and smiled thankfully at Roundell, and he shifted uncomfortably.

A noise came from the tree cave, then the huge, furry head of a black bear peered out. It yawned contentedly and waddled to the boy. The lad hugged it, then suddenly sobered and looked at the Barbarian.

Gath shook his head. "Say goodbye."

The boy wilted a little, but did not argue, and hugged the bear again, holding on tight. Gath turned to the freckled girl.

"Leave the wagon, leave everything here, except what you're wearing."

She stiffened, her slight body rising up defiantly. "Oh no, not my tambourine."

"Especially your tambourine."

The girl grumbled, then threw down her bow and arrow, marched into the tree cave. Gath grinned a little and turned back to Robin. "Ready?"

She nodded. "If you tell me everything's going to be all right."

"Everything's going to be all right." He kissed her softly on her hot cheek, and strode into the forest, taking a narrow moonlit path.

Robin followed. The freckled girl, snarling with frustration, came out of the tree cave, throwing a dark cloak over her shoulders. She pulled the boy away from the bear, covered his shoulders with another cloak, then marched him after the Barbarian, glaring at Roundell as if he were responsible for all the trouble she'd had since childhood.

Grinning, Roundell followed them into the forest. Twenty feet into the darkness, he stopped and stood still, listening. Had he heard something? A man, or more likely an animal? Probably the bear. He hurried after the others.

Thirty

MUD

High on the mountain, Gath crouched on the bald precipice overlooking the moonlit valley, the shadowed castle in the distance. Wind sang through the treetops above and below, muting the harsh breathing of his winded companions. His eyes measured the distance, the obstacles.

Four hundred feet below, the moon spread a cool glow over the flat ridge commanding the valley. Tiyy's tent and the command tower had been moved. The tower now stood on an embankment over four hundred strides to the north, at the front of the besieging army's main camp. Tiyy's black tents, surrounded by flickering campfires and the tents of her vassal queens and warlords, occupied the center of the camp. Outside the circle of fires, her army slept in shadows and silence, its tents veiled in smoky drifts.

Below, in the empty shadowed valley, the moonglow illuminated vaporous tails of dust, revealing the movement of mounted patrols riding between the main camp and the countervallations now investing the main gate to Whitetree. The patrols passed to and fro at regular intervals, but shrubs, eruptions of jagged rock, and gullies marked the vast expanse with black shadows. Hiding places that would conceal their crossing to the river, over half a mile away.

The riverbed itself ran like a jagged black ditch along the base of the the castle's western walls. Silent. Without the glitter of moonlight gracing its wet body. Empty. The river had been diverted into the moat as Jarl Roundell had anticipated, somewhere north of the castle rock. Beyond the southern end of the castle, gushing white water spilled from the mouth of the gorged moat, dumping the diverted water back into the natural riverbed.

Roundell emerged from the shadows, crouched beside Gath and pointed at the middle of the castle's western wall, almost directly opposite them. "Just below the Round Tower, in the roots of a lime tree, there's a hidden postern gate."

"Why weren't the trees cut down?" Gath asked. "The ground cleared?"

"Nothing's been done to prepare for a siege, not in a hundred years."

Gath nodded, his eyes still on the black ditch. "The mud," he said thoughtfully, "may be harder to cross than the water would have been."

"Let's hope they've bridged it."

Gath gave a nod. The sound of breaking branches came out of the shadowed trees behind them, and they turned sharply toward it. A moment passed, and the black bear emerged, stood in the moonlight. Gath frowned at Billbarr's shadowed body, hiding with Robin and Fleka nearby.

"Get rid of it."

"I did." Billbarr's face bobbed into a spill of light. "But he won't listen. He wants to come with us."

"Get rid of it," Gath growled softly. "Now! That castle's no place for a dancing bear."

Billbarr dipped back into the shadows, scrambled up the slope to the bear, and Gath looked at Robin.

Her eyes, awash with soft memories and shame and fear, glimmered brightly in the moonlight, studying him as if he were a scroll.

"We go now," he said, and she nodded, not with obedience as she once had, but with force.

Reaching the bottom of the mountain, Gath led them along a shadowed defile, cutting back and forth across the undulating ground. He stopped for a patrol to ride past, twenty paces in front of them, and watched the moonlight glitter on their cold vermilion crossbows. When the patrol rode out of sight, he led them at a trot across the open ground, dashing silently from shrubs to rocks to depressions. Halfway across, they scrambled down into a deep fracture in the soft earth, halted. There Gath assessed their condition. Everyone was breathless and sweating, but able and eager to continue. Except Roundell.

The soldier had sprawled on the ground, was now peering over the rim of the fracture at shadows covering their back trail. Gath dropped beside him, and he whispered, "Somebody's following us. Not fifty paces back."

"How many?"

"Hard to tell."

Gath studied the moving grass and dark, bulky shadows between shrub and rock. "The bear?"

"No. Whoever it is, is trying to hide his sounds."

"We can't hunt him now," Gath whispered. He turned to the worried faces watching him. "We run the rest of the way, and nobody falls or stops."

They nodded. Gath edged past them and started down the fracture, body bent low and axe slightly to the front, so it would be the first to say hello to anyone traveling in the opposite direction. The others followed, pushing hard to match his pace.

Gasping and sweating, they reached the bank of the river without incident. Motioning the others to stay in the wide mouth of the fracture, Gath jumped down onto the empty riverbed, and sank to his shins in soft mud. He motioned at Roundell and the soldier splashed down beside him.

The mud extended across the bed about five feet out, then dropped away into a pitch-black ditch. Roundell drove his sword into the mud a little farther out. The blade went in up to his wrist.

"Four feet here," the soldier whispered. "The bottom of that ditch could be thirty feet down." He pointed upriver with his sword. "If they've thrown up a bridge, it'll be up there, below the Stronghold, where the water has tunneled the rock."

Gath nodded and glanced across the riverbed.

The opposite bank stood less than forty feet away. High above it, the moon-washed walls of Round Tower silhouetted the lime tree with the hidden postern gate waiting for them not two hundred feet up the side of the cliffs.

"Psssst!" The sound came from behind them, and they turned to see Billbarr motioning at their back trail.

"Someone's coming," the boy whispered. He lifted a hand for them to be silent and they all listened. No sound came out of the fracture, and he added, "They stopped."

"We're helpless here," Roundell whispered.

Gath agreed with a nod, took hold of Robin's waist, lifted her down into the mud, and hurried upriver, pulling her behind him. Fleka and Billbarr jumped down and, high stepping through the mud, dashing along stretches of harder ground, they scurried forward under the concealment of the shadowed embankment. Bringing up the rear, Roundell kept an eye on their back trail.

Where the riverbed curved around the protrusion of rock that marked the beginning of the Stronghold, standing on the heights against the moonlit sky, it widened abruptly. The sides of the riverbed became firmer, but the embankment concealing them from the valley dipped sharply, partially exposing their movements.

Pulling Robin behind him, Gath broke into a run. After a hundred feet, he stopped short behind a clump of boulders protruding from the bank. When the others silently dropped beside them, he pointed ahead.

Above the rim of the embankment, not thirty feet away, the vague shapes of two wagons stood on the hard ground of the valley floor. Timbers, cut to lengths used for shoring up mine tunnels, filled their flat beds.

Gath unstrapped his horned helmet from his belt, slipped the headpiece on. Motioning to the others to remain where they were, he picked up his axe, crept forward. After twenty feet, he stopped, his eyes on the castle.

High overhead, specks of fire moved behind the embrasures of the Stronghold's ramparts. One stopped, and an archer in a white tunic appeared in an embrasure, bow in one hand and holding a torch high over his head with the other. He peered down, holding the torch as far out as possible, casting a flood of flickering light down the side of the white walls. The glow reached for about forty feet, then faded quickly, far short of the cliffs. The archer swung the torch around and around, then flung it out over the cliffs.

The flames streaked through the air, then plummeted down, momentarily throwing light over a straw-and-plank bridge crossing the muddy riverbed about twenty feet ahead. The bridge led to a looming hole at the bottom of the riverbed on the opposite bank. The opening of a tunnel cut by the river. The light of the torch grew brighter, then the torch hit the cliffs, exploding in sparks, and darkness returned.

Gath advanced along the bank, came alongside the wagons and peered over the rim of the embankment. No one guarded the wagons. He dropped back down and saw Billbarr scampering along the bank toward him. The boy stopped, sniffed the air, then scurried up beside Gath, and sniffed again. The Barbarian waited. With the horned helmet's ability to sense the presence of danger, he knew the threat of death was close at hand. But he could not tell from which direction it might strike. Danger was everywhere in the night. The boy sniffed the air and the mud, then looked at Gath with troubled eyes.

"Animals," he whispered.

They exchanged a puzzled glance, then descended a plank extending from the embankment to the makeshift bridge. They edged slowly onto the bridge, and the straw-covered mud gurgled under their boots. Three paces across, Billbarr dropped to his hands and knees and, sniffing, crawled forward. Ten feet across the bridge, he stopped short, looked up at Gath.

"Moles," he whispered.

Understanding swept through Gath. He sank in place, knees bent to catapult his weight in any direction, and shortened his grip on his axe. With his eyes moving from side to side, his free hand caught the boy by the shoulder and shoved him toward the bank. "Get back! Quick!"

The startled boy fled up the plank and back down the riverbank. Robin, Fleka and Roundell came around a corner of the embankment, saw him coming, and dropped down into concealing shadows. When Billbarr reached them, Fleka gathered the terrified boy in her trembling arms.

On the bridge, the Barbarian, body crouched and helmet low, turned slowly from side to side. Moonlight stroked the tips of the helmet's horns and they undulated slightly, then bent toward the opposite bank, pointing. Gath's head came around in the same direction, and held still.

A shadowed form emerged from the dark mouth of the tunnel, crossed slowly to the bridge, stepped into the moonlight and stopped short. It stood upright, its short legs protruding from a bulb-shaped body covered with short, muddy fur, and wearing black-leather chest armor, belt and loincloth. Its face, except for fur and a severely pointed snout, was human, but it had no ears, unless they hid within the skull. Its bare feet were webbed and clawed, and its short, thick, furry arms ended in hands consisting of huge, paddle-like talons nearly ten inches long.

Demon spawn. A mole man.

Gath's shoulders rolled. He two-handed his axe. His eyes searched the slick mud on the sides of the bridge, then the dark, wet earth of the riverbank, expecting more subterranean creatures to appear. Wanting them to.

The mole man dropped on all fours, a long tail swishing behind it. A red spot glowed on its horny brow. The mouth opened, revealing a parade of orange, red-tipped teeth capable of chewing through solid rock and castle walls. A sharp, rasping chatter, similar to a squirrel's, passed between its lips. A sound of alarm.

Gath took two steps forward, knowing it recognized him as the enemy. Tiyy's malevolent thaumaturgy had no doubt planted instincts within its corrupted flesh that warned it against the horned helmet.

Wet bubbling sounds came out of the shadows of the tunnel, the splashing of more creatures, sending a surge of battle hunger through the Barbarian. Consuming him. Veins stood up like steel welts along his arms and the backs of his hands. The axe throbbed in his hands as if with its own life. Then the horned helmet tried to ignite itself and explode with flames, intent upon blinding the nocturnal creature at the opposite end of the bridge. But Gath of Baal held the living metal in check, knowing the fire would alert unwanted sentries with vermilion crossbows, and attract arrows and spears from the walls above.

As if sensing the Barbarian's caution, the creature suddenly bounded forward, darting from side to side, teeth bared. Gath strode to meet it. The creature stopped short and broke loose with a wild, excited chattering. Spittle dripped from its mouth. The red spot burned and blood drained over its protruding snout. The Barbarian kept coming.

He passed the midpoint of the bridge and furry arms erupted from the muddy openings between the planks under his feet. The shovel-like talons serving the arms as hands glittered wetly in the moonlight, ripped at his boots and greaves, chewing into metal and tearing away strips of rawhide. Neither the weapons nor the method of attack had originated in the sperm of warriors. They belonged to eaters. Ancient predators.

With a short chop, Gath sliced off an arm at the wrist and stepped on another, crushing the elbow. More talons thrust up out of the mud, clawing at him, and he dashed out of their reach, heading at the mole man. The creature suddenly rose up like a man to strike, and Gath stopped short in front of it, bringing the axe blade up from the ground with the pull of all his weight and muscle. The blade caught the creature in the groin, sliced up through it, ripped through its soft belly, came to a crunching halt against its rib structure, burying itself in tangled bones. Stuck.

Ducking the slashing talons, Gath short-handed his axe, pivoted and whipped it over his head, bringing the demon with it. Planting his feet wide, he slammed the blade into the bridge, splitting the creature apart. Flesh, fur and bones exploded, spewing blood and organs across Gath's legs. Still the blade remained stuck, tangled in a strange, gridlike rib structure now exposed to the air.

He stepped on the bones, crushing them, ripped the axe free, and five creatures erupted from the mud at the side of the bridge, threw themselves at him.

Revolving, Gath swung the axe in a wide arc. The flat of the blade pushed a snout flat against a skull, crushed a shoulder, broke open a chest cavity, drove two bodies back into more mole men emerging from the mud. They tangled with each other, snarling and clawing with fractious fury, then came at him again.

Suddenly a glow of light fell over the bridge, quickly growing brighter. The creatures stopped, blinded by a fireball thrown down from the castle wall.

Using the light, Gath charged the stumbling creatures. Swinging right and left, he carved a path between them, heading back across the bridge toward his companions. The fireball hit the mud beside the bridge, exploding in showers of sparks, then flamed brightly, momentarily illuminating streaking arrows as they stitched the furry creatures and wooden planks.

Darting free of the screeching melee, the Barbarian made the riverbank, leaving a clutter of writhing bodies behind, and dashed along the bank.

More fireballs cascaded down from the walls. Their flaming bodies spun extravagantly against the black night, throwing off sheets of orange sparks. More arrows followed them down, plucking the life from scattering demon spawn. Blindly, the nocturnal mole men plunged back into the mud, writhing and clawing their way under the brown wetness. Many vanished immediately, but arrows followed them, and bubbles of blood rose on the firelit mud where they had disappeared. One by one the fireballs exploded against the mud and bridge, spewing flaming straw over the suddenly empty crossing. The straw burnt brightly, swiftly, and faded to soft glowing balls of orange light, like jewels on the throat of the night.

Stopping fifty feet short of his companions, Gath motioned them to advance, and Robin, Billbarr and Fleka, with Roundell urging them forward, raced out of the darkness. He watched them come, looked back at the empty bridge, then back at Robin and stood abruptly, snarling.

Sixty feet down the embankment, directly behind and above his racing friends, a mounted sentry galloped along the crest of the bank, his vermilion crossbow leveled at Robin's back. Gath charged, yelling.

Robin and the others slowed, heads jerking wildly from

side to side. Seeing the charging horse bear down on her, Robin screamed. The sentry leaned forward in his saddle to fire and a dark figure erupted from the grass not five feet behind him, crossbow in hand. Jakar. As cold and certain as death, he fired.

The bolt took the sentry in the back, drove him facedown onto the mane of his horse. His crossbow jerked up, accidentally tripping the trigger, and the bolt shot forth with a loud twang. It creased the air with a high whistle, missing Robin's ear by inches, drilled the mud five feet short of Gath, and vanished into the wet ground with a sizzling swirl of smoke.

Robin, shuddering, stared in shock at Jakar as he ran toward her. Gath raced from the opposite direction. Reaching her first, the Barbarian hauled Robin off the ground with his free arm, raced back for the bridge, with Fleka, Billbarr and Roundell on his heels. Jakar, still twenty feet down the bank, stopped to reload his crossbow, then followed.

Reaching the bridge, Gath, with Robin under his arm, charged across, leaping over the bloody remnants of mole men. Suddenly the dull glow of the dying fireballs faded, and darkness once more took command of the night. Instantly, muddy figures erupted from the mud at the far end of the bridge, cutting them off from the castle.

The group pounded to a stop.

Flames erupted from the horned helmet, streaked across the bridge, and fires broke out on furry knees and chests. Blinded again, the creatures floundered back into the mud.

Making the bank, Gath set Robin on the ground and pushed her at Roundell. "Go with him. I'll wait for Jakar."

Nodding, she scrambled up the cliffs after Roundell, with Fleka and Billbarr close behind.

Gath watched Jakar race across the bridge and a muddy creature rose out of the mud in front of him. Without breaking stride, the young man lifted his crossbow, fired point-blank at the mole man's face. The bolt ripped through the demon's skull and exploded out the back.

Seeing Gath, Jakar stopped short, still on the bridge, and

smiled bitterly. "Go on," he shouted. "I'll hold them off. She needs you, not me."

Before Gath could reply, furry arms lurched up out of the mud, tore at Jakar's legs, gripped calf and knee and hauled him facedown. Talons slurped out of the muck and grabbed his neck and hips. Furry snouts emerged beneath his belly and face, spitting mud and displaying rows of orange, red-tipped teeth. Thrashing and kicking, Jakar drove them away with hands and elbows, then they pulled him flat against the mud, ate into his belly and leg.

Reaching Jakar, Gath hauled him off the ground and, holding him in his arms and backing up, spewed flames over the bridge, incinerating planks and straw and creatures. He did not stop until the mud bubbled and boiled.

Turning, Gath carried Jakar halfway up the cliffs, then stopped and looked back. Furry creatures floated on the steaming mud, scalded to death. Otherwise there was no sign of the enemy, except for torch-bearing riders galloping across the valley toward the battle site. Too far away to see Gath. He continued up the cliffs.

When the Barbarian came within fifty feet of the lime tree, Jakar stirred in his arms, opened his eyes. Realizing where he was, the young man struggled weakly, his eyes tormented with jealousy and pain and shame. The effort dizzied him and he passed out again. Gath sensed the young man wanted him to let him die, but the Barbarian did not comply, and the best Jakar could do was bleed on the Barbarian's chest and arms.

Thirty-one

THE WOMAN

Reaching the floor of the underground room beneath the hidden postern gate, Gath dropped a knee on the ground and gently lowered Jakar's body from his shoulder, laying him down on the cloak Robin Lakehair had spread before her. Shuddering, Robin looked at Gath, the flickering torchlight slashing across her chalk-white heade, her eyes thanking him. Then she touched Jakar's unconscious head with her fingertips, and his handsome face lolled sideways, blood draining from his mouth over his chin.

Moaning softly, Robin quickly tore her cloak into strips as Fleka and Billbarr, kneeling beside her, did the same. Then they gently, but swiftly and firmly, began to bind his wounds to stop the bleeding.

Gath stood and removed his helmet, glancing about the dirt-walled room.

Swaths of orange light revealed a soldier, an old graybeard, standing in nearby shadows, his hands resting on a wicker raft large enough to serve as a stretcher. A second soldier, a young, puffy-faced man, stood at the opening of a torchlit tunnel. They both nodded at Gath, acknowledging his welcome presence, but their expressions remained matter-of-fact.

Roundell descended the ladder, dropped on the ground beside Gath. "No one saw how we entered," he said quickly. "We can still use it as a sally port if we need it."

Robin groaned, and the two men looked down at the top of her head as she worked on Jakar. Tears fell from her cheeks, splattering her wrists as she dipped her fingers gently into the wound in Jakar's belly. He convulsed slightly, and blood spattered her arms all the way to elbows. She withdrew her fingers, looked up at Gath. The whites of her eyes were enlarged by desperation, but the mind behind them was under control.

"I need hot coals!"

Roundell motioned at Graybeard. "Take him to the tower!"

With strong, sure motions, the two soldiers lay the raft beside Jakar, rolled his body onto it, picked up the raft and started into the tunnel with quick, steady steps.

Robin rose shakily and Gath took hold of her elbow, steadied her as she faced Roundell. When she spoke, her voice was calm and resigned.

"Jakar followed us, didn't he? All the way? To protect me?"

Roundell nodded.

She glanced at Gath. "He vowed he would never let me out of his sight again, and I was stupid enough to believe him when he said he would stay behind." She gave a short, harsh laugh. "What a silly, mean fool I am." She looked into Gath's eyes. "He saw us, saw everything. He knows how I feel about you. He," her voice broke, "he's probably always known, all these years, even when I didn't."

"Do not punish yourself," Gath said. "Not now."

She studied him, sudden resolve filling her eyes, then new strength firmed her slightly parted lips. She had never been so beautiful. She nodded, hurried into the tunnel.

Gath watched her strong, youthful body run through the smoky haze. She was the same Robin Lakehair, the same beauty that dwelled in the theater of his mind, yet she had changed. There was barely a trace of the girl he had left behind three years ago. She had become a woman.

He turned to Billbarr and Fleka. "Stay with her. Help her."

They hurried after Robin, and Gath and Roundell shared a glance. Then the mercenary said, "We were lucky. We should all be dead now."

"Don't be impatient," Gath replied with dark humor, and they shared a short, grim, raucous laugh.

Thirty-two

TIPSY

The sounds of leisurely yawning came from a shadow at a corner of the underground room, and Gath and Roundell stepped aside, allowing the flickering torchlight to fall on Brown John, huddled in a cloak against the wall. With his eyes momentarily blinded by the sudden light, the *bukko* turned his head away, and yawned and stretched again, taking his own good time.

Gath frowned uneasily. There were no patches on the *bukko*'s tunic, only holes and squares of faded cloth where they had been torn away. Three years ago, Brown's pride would never have allowed such an indignity. Something was wrong.

Sighing tiredly and rubbing his eyes with the knuckles of his thumbs, the old man sagged against the dirt wall. His legs were crossed in front of him, cradling a round wine jar large enough to be something to ride rather than drink from. Brown yawned again and stopped short, seeing the Barbarian.

"Gath!" he gasped.

Gath nodded hello. "Brown."

"Are you all right?" Brown sat forward slightly, glancing about the shadowed room. "Did everyone get back safely?"

"Robin is safe, but Jakar is badly wounded."

Brown groaned and sagged back again. "I knew it. I should have gone with them. But they wouldn't let me."

"Are you all right?" Gath advanced behind his words and looked down at the tattered *bukko*. Brown's cheeks were flushed by too much wine, the rims of his eyelids red and wet.

"I'm fine," Brown protested. "Fine! I just have a game leg. Otherwise I would have bounced right up, just like my old self, and given you the hug you certainly do not deserve, having deserted us all these years."

Gath extended his hand to help him.

Brown scoffed at it. He groped at the ground and wall, as if he didn't know which was which, then finally found a perch and tried to get up. The *bukko* made it halfway, then his bandy legs wobbled like water spilling from a pitcher, folded up and dropped him on his side. Grabbing his calf with both hands, he writhed into a ball.

"It's nothing," he blurted. "Nothing! I'm all right." The pain seemed to pass as he massaged his calf with excessive vigor, then sat up against the wall. "It's my right leg," he said lamely, and laughed in a manner Gath did not recognize in him, like a man trying to hide something.

Brown tried to stand again, but his legs again failed to cooperate, and he sat back down beside the wine jar. Pushing his soiled tunic down over his knobby knees, he again laughed his unfunny laugh. "I guess it's hurt worse than I thought."

Gath stared at Brown, and a sudden hot fear spilled through his belly. Unconsciously, without ever thinking about it, the Barbarian had been counting on his old friend to help him organize and command the castle. But now, if he had to choose between the man and the wine jar, he'd have to pick the jar. It looked far more able.

Gath kneeled in front of Brown. "What's happened, old friend? Where are your patches? What's wrong?"

"Everything, Gath! Everything. Or at least it was. Now that we share the same trail again, all that will change."

Gath nodded. "I need your help. To command and organize the garrison."

"And you have it!" Brown extended his hand. "Here, help me up."

Gath made no move to take the *bukko*'s hand, and Brown withdrew it, watching the Barbarian's cool gray eyes. "What's the matter?"

"This castle's under siege, and you're drunk."

"Not drunk, damn it! Just a little tipsy. I've been sitting here all night waiting for you, and the wine was just a little stronger than I thought. But I'm fine now. Actually, superb." His red-lidded eyes twinkled. "I've got the plot that will save this castle."

"Then tell it quickly," Gath said. "There is little time."

"There's time," Brown said slyly. "No need to rush at all. I have it all worked out." Brown winked up at Roundell staring down at him with his cold soldier's face, then looked back at Gath. His tangled white eyebrows arched down over his quick, boyish eyes and his voice lowered to a dramatic whisper. "Old friend, this is the greatest plot you and I will ever share." He leaned closer, lowered his voice another notch. "Right here, Gath of Baal, not a hundred strides from where I sit, is a library, and in that library is a formula, a formula whose words will conjure forth the magic that will finally reveal Robin's true identity."

Gath's eyes narrowed. "No one knows?"

"Only a very few. I dared not tell anyone until she had full control over her powers, for fear of risking her life. And no matter how hard I searched and experimented, I could not find the key to that control. But now it is within my reach. With the formula in hand, she can reveal herself. This very night she can dazzle the rabble of this castle with her radiant beauty and transform them. Show them that she wears the jewels of the Goddess of Light, that she is the resurrected White Veshta. The living goddess who will lead them to victory over the powers of darkness." Gath stared at him, and the old man added, "Don't you see? She'll fill them with hope! Make them fight like demons! Fill them with dreams that demand imitation!"

The Barbarian shook his head. "You're drunk, Brown. Dreams will not defeat Tiyy's army. They are seven thousand strong and led by the Siegemaster, Izzam Ghapp." He stood abruptly. "Sharpen your sword, old man. We will need it."

Gath extended his hand to help the *bukko* up, but Brown John ignored it and pushed himself up the wall, his eyes laden with dramatic warning. "So that's it. You don't trust me either, after all we've been through.'' He glared at Roundell. ''I suppose this mercenary had also told you what's happened here? Is that it? He's told you what I let those heathen archers do to Robin, hasn't he?'' He glared at Roundell, cheeks flushing with shame and anger. ''That's it, isn't it? He's told you everything.''

Gath's face hardened. ''I know only this: to save Robin, we must hold the castle.''

''Of course, but—''

''Enough!'' Gath's harsh voice cut the *bukko* off. ''Clear your head, old friend, if you wish to keep it.'' Gath turned to Roundell. ''You'll serve as Master-at-Arms, organize the garrison, help me plan the defense.''

Roundell dipped his forehead. ''We'll look at the walls and towers first.''

Gath nodded and they strode for the tunnel. Reaching it, Gath stopped and glanced over his shoulder at the *bukko*. ''We'll send someone to help you.''

''Don't bother,'' Brown snarled. ''I'll help myself.''

Gath stared at the old man, the hole in the pit of his belly growing larger, then nodded and Roundell said, ''Douse the torches.''

''I know,'' snapped Brown. The old man turned his back on them and, with a hand braced against the wall, started for the torch, slowly, as if setting forth on a long, arduous trip.

Thirty-three

THE CURTAIN WALL

When the first light of dawn touched the night, a silvery glow beyond Jade Pass in the distance, Gath of Baal and Jarl Roundell climbed into the turret of Moat Tower. It stood opposite Round Tower on the eastern side of the castle, guarding the southeast corner of the Sacred Close. The wall separating the lower yards from the Close, running east and west, linked the two towers. The two men had made a full circuit of the Sacred Close and lower yards, inspecting the walls, towers and gate. Now they stared down at the rabble huddled in the yards.

Traveling players, peasants, itinerant merchants, masons, carpenters and refugees muttered fitfully as they slept on the ground, under lean-tos and in their house wagons, the stables, the buildings. The muffled crying of the women and children sang a tune of terrible fear, and the cool morning breeze strung it out on the flutter and flap of tent and blanket in a soft, haunted melody, like death humming a slow march.

Without looking at the mercenary, Gath said, "You have heard this song before."

"Many times." Roundell chuckled, low in his throat, then added, "And hopefully will again." Gath chuckled with him.

Billbarr's head popped out of the trapdoor in the floor. Standing on the ladder with his hands holding the top rung, he looked up at them, obviously baffled by their laughter. They did not bother to try and explain.

"Jakar?" Gath asked.

"Still alive," Billbarr reported, "but still unconscious. The girl, Robin, she closed his wounds and fed him strange herbs in a hot soup. But he is very weak. I don't think he'll—''

"Don't think," Gath said, cutting him off. "How is Robin?"

"She is a miracle," the boy said, his cheeks swelling into a smile. "She has not slept, but gets stronger instead of weaker."

"She's eaten?"

"Yes, she takes good care of herself. But she's terribly frightened, even though she hides it. And she's full of guilt, you know, because—''

"Never mind," Gath interrupted again. "How does Fleka like living in a castle?"

"She hates it. Every woman she's met is either a harlot or dancing girl, and she can't stand them. She says they're all better looking and more talented than she is. Especially the Grillards. She's sure she'll never be an actress now."

Gath laughed, Roundell joining him, then said, "If that is what she's worried about at a time like this, then you can assure her she is an actress." He waved the boy off. "Stay with Robin."

"What about the Grillard bukko? You promised to introduce us."

"Not now, boy," Gath said quietly, "not now."

Nodding reluctantly, Billbarr slid back down the ladder, and Gath looked across the lower yards at the gate complex, the shadowed covered passageway between the two towers, the bridge beyond, the unseen portcullis and drawbridge.

Following his eyes, Roundell asked, "We destroy the bridge?"

"No, let it stand," Gath said, picking his way through an evolving plan. "We may have to let them in that way." He turned to Roundell. "Have your men in the gate seal themselves in with plenty of provisions, and have them use stone and mortar so the doors can't be burnt down. They may have to hold out for days."

"With their families?"

Gath nodded. "It'll make them fight harder." He looked back at the gate. "Also, set blacksmiths to work covering the portcullis with metal and hides. I want it solid, so it will serve as a second gate. And have masons dig the murder holes above the gate passage wider, and fill the room above it with rubble." He turned back to the mercenary. "If we let them in that way, I want to be able to seal them in. So we'll need signal flags, to tell the gate when to drop the portcullis and dump the rubble through the holes to plug the passageway."

A knowing smile showed on the face of the veteran Master-at-Arms. "Water."

Gath nodded and they crossed to an embrasure overlooking the moat, jumped up into it.

Outside the eastern wall, water now gorged the narrow moat, churning itself white as it rushed down from the heights, spilling over its sides to flood the bogs and marshes defending the eastern approach to Whitetree. In the distance beyond the marshy ground, spires of smoke rose from the besieging army's guard camp, better than a mile off.

"If we start a channel about there," Gath pointed at a section of the moat about a hundred feet north, where the water rushed the fastest, "and angle it down the dirt slope, then through the wall into the Market Court, we should be able to flood it."

"Drown them."

"If the gate tunnel holds."

"And the walls don't cave in."

Gath grinned. "And if they don't find out what we're up to."

Roundell looked across the valley at the guard camp. "They're too far away to see what we're up to." He studied the ground below. "We can get down there with ladders, and dig in both directions. But that dirt isn't deep, we'll probably have to cut through rock. That will take time. But it makes sense. The foundation rock under the Close is solid. Our best chance is to try and hold its walls and towers." He looked at Gath. "But if and when you decide to do this, we'll have to herd everyone inside the Close."

Gath nodded and they recrossed the turret, looked down

at the Close. Night shadows still blanketed it, except where dying fires glowed beside sleeping groups.

"It will be crowded," Gath said, "but when the walls and towers are properly manned, there will be room enough."

"And no time to complain or quarrel," Roundell added.

A moment passed. Then, thinking the same thought, they looked up at the Curtain Wall looming along the northern side of the Close, defending the Stronghold on the heights.

Dawn light graced the wall's sheer, clifflike surface, the first rays of the sunrise stroking the pitched roofs of the massive twin towers rising above the ramparts, seventy feet above the floor of the Close.

"You have any friends behind that wall?" Gath asked.

"Not since they sealed themselves in," Roundell said coldly.

Gath nodded. "If Izzam Ghapp attacks the Stronghold first, as it appears he will, how long can the archers hold out?"

"It will depend on how many of those demon sappers he has, and how fast they dig. Once the western wall collapses, the archers won't last long. They'll be outnumbered five to one, and they've got no stomach for a fight."

"Then they'll retreat, back into the Close, through the gate and Vestry passage."

"Yes," Roundell said, "and this rabble will slaughter them, or die trying." He looked at Gath. "If that happens, we're finished."

A moment passed, and Gath made a cold decision. "We'll seal the archers in the Stronghold. When Tiyy's army pours into it, we'll bring it down, bury it."

"Countermines?" Gath gave a nod, and Roundell grinned. "It just might be possible. The foundations under the Stronghold are honeycombed with tunnels, so most of the work is done. From them, we can tunnel under each wall and tower."

"Is there timber to shore up the mines?"

"I can find enough, and it will be dry. It'll burn like straw." Roundell leaned on the embrasure, staring up at the Curtain Wall's ramparts. "But we won't bury all of them. The survivors will retreat to the top of that wall, and unload their anger on us. We'll all be sitting ducks."

Gath agreed with a nod. "Our only choice is to take the Curtain Wall away from the archers before Ghapp penetrates the Stronghold." He pointed at the base of the Curtain Wall. "Have your masons tear down the ramp and wall up the gate and Vestry door."

"All right," Roundell agreed. "The ramp will provide plenty of stone for that. But how do we reach the ramparts?"

"Siege tower." Roundell chuckled and Gath added, "Ever built one?"

"No. But I've burnt them down. I know how they're made."

"Then you'll build one, on the floor of the Close below the wall."

"Fine. But what with?"

Gath pointed across the Close at the massive wooden stage. "Tear it apart and you'll have more than enough timber."

Roundell chuckled ironically. "Your friend, the bukko, is not going to like that."

Gath made no reply to that. "How fast can you do it?"

"The castle's full of carpenters, the best there are. I'll have a crude but workable tower finished by tomorrow morning." Gath nodded and he added, "The archers will see us, know what we're up to."

Their eyes met and shared a brutal understanding, then Roundell glanced down at the Close, and his tone hardened. "We'll build shields and barricades. We'll be all right."

"The rabble will cooperate?"

"Once they see you," Roundell said, his grin back, "they may even help. This bunch loves hocus-pocus."

Thirty-four

FRECKLES

Round Tower's ground-floor door opened, and Brown John limped out, blinked at the activity in the Close, sleep still in his eyes.

The waking rabble moved about hurriedly, chattering expectantly in small groups, then breaking apart to form new groups and chatter some more. His sons and most of his Grillards did the same, obviously following orders given by someone other than their father and *bukko*. They stood at the front of the stage, as the crowd began to gather behind them, obviously expecting some kind of performance.

The *bukko* limped into the sunlight, blinked again. It was a beautiful day. The sun glowed brilliantly, low in the eastern sky. The coming day's battles and butchery would be handsomely lit, a spectacle of war unlike any the *bukko* had ever seen. But he had no idea where to stand, what to say or who to say it to. He had no stage to manage. No players. No part.

He had a headache. An active headache of size and vigor that seemed intent on being a lifelong companion. He headed for the backstage stairs, taking his headache with him.

The feel of the wooden steps, and the sight of the giant metal drums of the thunder machines standing in the wings lifted his spirits. He went past the clutter of props and costumes hung on wooden pegs, and the smell of rouge, beeswax and white clay brought a little color into his tired cheeks. He passed along the corridor to the upstage entrance, and stopped in the opening. The sight of the scenery at the rear of the central stage and the empty, waiting boards in front of

it made his eyes twinkle. This was where he belonged. Here
he was king and master, as well as fool.

A funny-looking little boy with hair as straight as nails
stood in the shadows nearby, staring with what appeared to
be an almost identical pleasure at the empty stage. A plain
girl, with freckles on the slopes of her small, pert breasts,
sat cross-legged on a stool beside him, sewing yellow patches
on her plain tunic, as if she thought she were a Grillard.

Brown felt obliged to reproach her, but was too tired for
small quarrels. He addressed the boy. "What's happening?
Why is everyone gathering in front of the stage?"

"Just watch!" the boy said with cheery importance, as if
he had stage-managed whatever event was about to occur.

Brown frowned, limped a few feet away from the annoying
pair, and stood in the shadows cast by the forest scenery.
Between the trees, he had a clear view of the open stage and
the audience forming up in front of it. Roundell, Doll Harl,
Graybeard, and his sons, Bone and Dirken, stood promi-
nently among them, and the *bukko* grimaced jealously.

The castle's new Master-at-Arms climbed onto the stage,
faced the crowd, and began to shout, selecting men from the
crowd, and appointing them as wall captains. Then he selected a group of stonecutters and diggers, putting them under the command of Graybeard. He called forth three master
carpenters from the crowd, ordered them to select a hundred
of their best workmen, then dispatched them to make their
selections and return with their tools.

The growing crowd watched with annoyance, showing no
sign of accepting Roundell's choice of commanders. Then the
more surly members began to shout complaints at Roundell's
high-handed manner, and others abused him with curses. Finally, several bullies surged toward the brash mercenary,
brandishing swords and pitchforks. Suddenly they stopped
short, and a hush fell over the crowd.

People gasped with disbelief, seeing something to the side
of the stage. Mouths fell open. In the distance, heads turned
and stared. Those walking toward the stage began to run.

For a moment, the crackle of cook fires and the song of a
mockingbird somewhere were the only sounds gracing the

new day, then heavy footsteps drowned them out. They came in measured beats.

Brown edged forward a few feet. He knew them.

A shadow fell across the stage, then the dark body of Gath of Baal strode onto the boards and marched to center stage. Commanding every eye, he stopped beside Roundell, stood in the beacon of sunlight, letting it illuminate his blunt, handsome head and embellished armor. He held the horned helmet against his left hip, his axe in right hand.

The crowd stood motionless, staring with wide eyes and open mouths. Silent. Awed.

With a short chop, Gath drove the blade of his axe into the boards so that the axe stood beside him and Roundell, as proud and deadly as a third warrior. The thump of metal in wood broke the tension, and the crowd roared with one voice, surged forward. Cheering. Shouting. Crying with joy, as if they were saved already. Hooting. Hugging each other.

Gath stood still. But his armor seemed to swell and his chain mail skirt jangled, as if the force within him was about to burst forth from chest and thighs. Then he lifted the horned helmet above his head and set it in place, where it belonged. On the head of the Death Dealer.

The crowd gasped in terror, and hushed. Awed by its own sense of sudden, soaring hope.

A red glow slowly spread over the faces of the ragged ranks at the front of the crowd. They edged back, mouths agape. Suddenly a blast of flames erupted from the headpiece, streaking through the air above the heads of the crowd, then swirled and twisted into a black cloud of drifting smoke.

High on the ramparts of the Curtain Wall, two White Archers appeared in an embrasure, their manner haughty and amused as they watched.

The rabble gasped breathlessly, eyes watching the fading smoke. A scream of joy leapt from a single female voice, and more women joined it. Then babes were held aloft, their mothers loudly beseeching the Barbarian's protection. Emboldened by the sight of the Death Dealer, men raised weapons and fists, vowing their undying allegiance to the Dark One, and cheering broke out again, quickly becoming a

chant. The bang and jangle of drums and tambourines joined
it, and it grew louder as more and more people surged through
the gate, coming from the lower yards to look upon their
champion. The Deliverer.

Brown John sank back against the scenery, suddenly tired
and old, as if he were a man made for shadows instead of
limelight. He had seen all this before, years earlier at Pinwheel Crossing. Seen Gath appear before the Barbarian
Tribes, and heard them cheer and cry out his name. He had
seen it because he had made it happen. He had assembled
the audience, selected the stage and set Gath upon it. He had
been a true *bukko* then, both of the stage and of life. Now
he was of no more consequence than the headache throbbing
against his wrinkled brow. The ragtag rabble was being transformed, becoming an army, and he had no part in it.

Downstage, Roundell pointed at Graybeard, Bone and Dirken, and the captains, designating their tasks and assigning
them sections of wall.

The captains, most being professional entertainers, saluted
Gath with lavish gestures, and hurried off, collecting eager
men from the crowd as they passed through it.

Roundell moved to the edge of the stage, facing Round
Tower, and waved at it. Ten men-at-arms immediately disgorged from its door, opened the storehouses under the western wall, and began to distribute to the wall captains and their
men the pikes, crossbows, bills and boar spears stored there.

Round Tower's garrison marched out and took a position
in the open yard, acting as a reserve that could rush to the
point of any attack.

Graybeard's stonecutters and miners fetched their tools and
torches, formed up into a loose unit, and the old soldier, obviously a veteran sapper, marched them into Round Tower,
heading for the tunnels in the underground gallery below it.

Bone and Dirken collected another group of workers, headed across the yard toward Moat Tower to begin digging a ditch from the moat into the Market Court so it could
be flooded.

Doll Harl, having been ignored, strode forward and bois-
terously demanded that Roundell put her in charge of a wall,

claiming that there were many strong women, acrobats and dancers and knife throwers among the traveling players, whose physical skills and courage matched any man's.

Roundell and Gath did not mock her. They charged her with assembling such women, then gave her the responsibility of defending Round Tower, the command tower where both Gath and Roundell would be stationed.

Enormously pleased with herself, Doll flirted with Roundell a bit, then went off to gather her Amazons.

Watching all this, the *bukko* grumbled bitterly, then considered insisting on his own command, but turned and faced the boy and freckled girl instead.

Giddy with excitement, the pair hugged each other. Then, seeing Brown glare at them, the boy threw an arm in Gath's direction.

"Wasn't he marvelous? He's my best friend! And hers!" He hugged the nodding girl. "We've been with the Death Dealer for months! We've traveled everywhere together."

"Splendid," Brown said in a tone that denied the word's meaning.

The boy didn't catch it. He swelled up, wearing a smile proud enough for an entire priesthood, and announced, "We're going to become Grillards! We're going to see the whole world! Perform on every stage in every land."

Brown John chuckled mockingly.

"It's true," the girl said, stepping forward. "Gath has promised to present us to their bukko. And he's famous. Real famous!"

"Fleka's a dancing girl," the boy proclaimed. "And I, Billbarr the Odokoro, train dancing bears." Brown nodded skeptically, and the boy quickly added, "I already have the bear. Gath and I caught it together, in a forest called the Shades. It's a huge black bear, the biggest you've ever seen, and I'm teaching it to dance. It's waiting for me, right now, in the mountains." He threw a hand in the direction of the mountains.

"Waiting for you?" Brown laughed. "A bear?"

"But it's true. It told me it would wait."

"Told you?"

"Yes," the boy replied with blithe confidence. "I talk with animals."

Brown John, despite his headache, began to laugh. Suddenly the stage shook and the sounds of hammers and crowbars came from backstage. Brown hurried back along the corridor, strode onto the backstage deck. There the castle's master carpenter had returned with a crew of workmen. With crowbars and hammers, they pried and banged the planks and railings, tearing the stage down.

"What do you think you're doing?" Brown screamed. "Stop that!"

The master carpenter ignored him. The *bukko* charged, tried to grab a hammer out of the master carpenter's hand. The man pushed Brown John off and two other carpenters grabbed him, dragged him down the steps.

"Calm down, old man," one of them said.

"And stay out of the way," the other one added. "We need the lumber. The Dark One wants a siege tower built. Fast!"

They set the *bukko* down on the steps to the wall walk, and he stared dumbly as they hurried back to their work.

Railings already stood in a pile on the ground, and carpenters swarmed over the second story, pulling up the plank roof, exposing the heavy timbers of the frame.

A shadow fell over Brown's face, and he turned.

The boy and freckled girl stood at the base of the staircase, their young faces showing concern. "Are you all right?" the girl asked. "You look terrible."

"I'm all right," Brown mumbled. "Just fine."

They studied him a moment, then moved off five paces, and the boy stopped, looked back over a shoulder. "You haven't seen the Grillard bukko, have you? We're supposed to meet him."

"You know," the girl said behind a sassy grin, "dance for him." She ran her hands down the sides of her narrow, flat hips and snapped them in what she no doubt felt was a devastating display of sensuality.

Brown John shook his head. "No, I haven't seen him."

The pair thanked him with a nod and hurried toward Round

Tower, passing through shafts of golden sunlight that danced on the girl's bare shoulders.

Watching them, the *bukko* laughed to himself. Here he sat in a castle besieged by the demon spawn of the Master of Darkness, in a castle where a rabble had just been transformed into an army, a castle now commanded by Death himself. A castle full of spectacular activity and promising more. Yet he knew the image that would live the longest in the theater of his mind was the girl's face. She had the most marvelous collection of freckles he had ever seen.

Thirty-five

THE DUNG BEETLE

Tiyy galloped behind the lines of her troops standing at attention, their backs to the looming Stronghold. The remnant of her bodyguard rode behind her.

A tassel of scarlet thongs served as her loincloth. Her other garment, a leather string, dressed her trim neck, and the morning sun painted her dark, nude flesh a golden brown. A small turquoise vial dangled from the string.

Reaching the oak tree she had selected, she glared up at the bodyguards who had hunted the Barbarian.

With ropes binding their feet, and their hands tied behind them, they sat on the dirt ridge under the oak's twisted body. Hot, hard cheeks flamed under their startled eyes.

She leapt to the ground, landing barefoot in the new grass at the bottom of the ridge, and her bodyguards reined up behind her, their vermilion crossbows on display and eyes terrified, seeing their former comrades.

Izzam Ghapp and his commanders, mounted and facing

the ridge, flushed with embarrassment. They had not expected her to dismount, and started to get off their horses.

"Stay where you are," the nymph snapped, and scampered halfway up the loose-dirt ridge, like a girl at play. There she turned and surveyed her army, feeling its thousands of eyes on her. Lifting a hand, she shaded her eyes and scanned the walls of Whitetree.

Only an hour earlier, the castle's wild cheering had confirmed what she suspected. The Death Dealer now commanded Whitetree. But now the castle stood silent, with heads peering through its embrasures.

The whites of her eyes enlarged behind the blackened lids, and her eager fingers touched the turquoise vial. The nasty girl showed in her smile. The spitfire, proud of her snappy body, surfaced, and she tossed her violent yellow hair, cocked her hips, spreading her strong legs so every eye in the castle could see her dark perfection silhouetted against the pale earth ridge.

On her orders, soldiers had plucked every strand of new grass out of the dirt, and stripped the leaf cover from the limbs of the oak. Nothing that might diminish the impending spectacle, or keep a single eye from witnessing its vivid lesson, had been overlooked. No detail had been spared. Stimulants, Cordaa and Hashradda, had been generously supplied to the victims, to heighten their sense of pain. Their tongues still remained in their mouths, so they might express that pain in the manner she desired, with prolonged screaming.

The condemned bodyguards had failed to capture the Death Dealer, failed her, the Black Veshta. Now, every member of the army, from General Ghapp down to the last diseased whore among the camp followers, would learn what it meant to fail the goddess who was the favored consort of the Master of Darkness.

Holding the turquoise vial between her fingers, she uncorked it and placed the open mouth against the slope of her right breast. A moment passed, and tiny feelers emerged from the black hole, probing the air. Then the sharp, clawlike jaws of a Dung Beetle appeared, protruding from its hairy head and the thorax which followed. Minute, glassy eyes peered under brushlike orange hair parted by a speckled horn. The body squeezed past the rim of the vial and stood on her warm flesh. Protected by black leathery wings bearing jagged, yellow stripes, it turned one way, then the other, seemingly lost.

Shivering with expectation, the nymph corked the vial and let it dangle between her breasts, her eyes watching the insect as it began to crawl. Her breath came in startled gasps. A red flush surfaced under her orchid cheeks, spread down her throat, over her chest until the ground upon which the beetle strolled was hot and flushed and moist.

Excitation sharpened her senses, filling her with euphoric rapture, transporting her to a state of immaculate perception. Her lips parted, tasting air and tree and earth and man, and she saw an infinitesimal tissue of smoke, fainter than perfumed air, issue from the joints of the beetle's jaws. Startled, she held her breath. The smoke leaked out of the tiny incisions she had made in the mandibles in order to insert the instincts of the Ambrosia bore beetle and the required drops of treated Nagraa. Now, all that remained to complete the insect's demonic transformation was for the beetle to sip the sacred nectar of her body. But its tiny wounds were still open. The surgery had been imperfect, and a rush of fear coursed through her.

The Dung Beetle stood still, contemplating her erect nipple, as if uncertain of its identity. Had the drops of black wine been adequate? Too weak? Too strong? It was impossible to tell with such dabs of life as insects.

She waited, breasts heaving up and down, threatening to throw the beetle off. It staggered sideways, away from its target. Then the rise and fall of the slick, hot ground it traveled seemed to encourage it. Its feelers tickled the air as it crawled around the globe of flesh, circling her nipple. Then, approaching it, the jaws opened wide and grappled with the pinked erection of flesh. Suddenly the jaws snapped, and a drop of blood washed over the face of the beetle, matting its orange hair. The nymph's arms thrust stiffly down at her sides, her fists clenched, her head thrust back, gasping, as the Dung Beetle drank.

Suddenly afraid that, in its ecstasy, it might drown itself

in the intoxicating elixir, she plucked the insect off her breast.
The Dung Beetle wiggled and snapped, angry at being de-
prived of its pleasure. Feeling it grow strong between her
fingers, she smiled with tyrannical delight.

Holding her hand up, she showed the beetle to Ghapp and
his commanders.

Heat showed on the officers' temples. Moisture glistened
under their eyes.

She climbed to the height of the ridge, and strode through
the naked bodies of the victims to the body of the oak. Placing the insect in the yoke of the trunk and a branch, she
stepped back.

The Dung Beetle, scampering like a nimble runner, ran
two feet up the branch, then back to the yoke. Searching. In
a rising fit of feeding frenzy, it circled the trunk twice, and
came to a sudden stop. Its tail pressed against the hard bark,
secreting acid, and the bark sizzled and smoked. The fumes
momentarily enveloped the bug, then drifted away, as if
blown by the gasps of the watching commanders. Driving its
jaws into the softened bark, the beetle quickly burrowed
under it and began to consume the sapwood, infecting and
corrupting the tree with each bite.

Tiyy walked back through the suddenly white-faced victims, scampered down the mound and, in one bound, leapt
onto the bare back of her pony. Drawing her legs up under
her, she sprawled in a languid spill of curves, her opulent
sexuality glistening, as if she were coated with a sheen of
golden honey.

The victims turned their heads one way, then the other,
uncertain whether they should watch the nymph or the tree. A
moment passed, and the tree made the decision for them.

The trunk suddenly ripped up out of the earth, throwing
aside clods of dirt, as, with one lurch, it grew five feet in
height and three in width. Roots erupted from the earthen
crust around it, and raced under the victims, upsetting them.
They shrieked and tried to right themselves, snarling and
kicking clumsily at each other.

Tiyy sat up excitedly and hugged her knees with ornamen-
tal delight.

The oak stretched, as if the tree were yawning, and thrust its branches out as straight as jointed arms.

Gasps of terror ran through the watching army. Here and there a faint-hearted soldier toppled to the ground.

The branches relaxed, retreating to more normal positions, but their bodies were now elongated and rippled with elastic muscle. Bark fell away in chunks from the limbs and trunk. Globs of sap bubbled out of sores, a steady stream of drops falling on the naked bodyguards, sizzling and smoking as they burned through cheeks, backs, feet.

Screaming, the condemned tried to squirm away from the tree, kicking and cursing in terror. The bonds binding one man's ankles loosened and he scrambled to his feet, started to hobble off. A branch raised up above him, then reached down, circled his waist and hauled him, kicking and thrashing, into the air. The limb's smaller branches wound themselves around his ankles, thighs, neck, shoulders, wrists. He screamed. The tightening pressure silenced him.

Tiyy rolled onto her hands and knees, her eyes the source of all dark pleasures.

The man shuddered. Suddenly the smaller branches ripped themselves away from his torso, taking his extremities with them, and he exploded into eleven separate pieces.

The remaining victims, lying perfectly still, stared up with open mouths. Transfixed. They stayed that way as the tree's limbs reached down, plucked body after limp body off the ground and ripped them apart, throwing the remains into the air. Filling it with limbs, hands, heads, feet, all twirling in a swirl of fountaining blood.

The sky above the tree turned red, then the moisture fell, showering Tiyy, General Ghapp and his commanders. The officers covered their heads and rode away. Tiyy stood barefoot on the back of her pony, and raised her arms, opened her mouth to the descending torrent, drinking her fill, until she, the pony and ground beneath her were bright red. Then she turned, and thrust both her red arms at the castle.

The army erupted with cheers, turned and surged forward. Blood mad. Screaming her name.

Thirty-six

SWORDS

The shallow wooden door leading to Round Tower's third story swung open and Gath emerged, strode onto the wall walk. His eyes gave no indication of what he thought or felt about Tiyy's bloody spectacle.

Women, children, carpenters, masons crowded the wall along with the men-at-arms who belonged there. They watched the besieging army roar and rumble toward the Stronghold in silent fear. The distant twang and thump of catapults rose above the din, and barrels of pitch and flaming spears arced through the pale blue sky above the Stronghold, exploding against the roofs of its towers in showers of sparks and flames. Sheets of burning arrows followed, a few strays dropping into the Sacred Close below, where the tools and materials of partially built shields and the torn-up ramp to the Stronghold had been abandoned.

One stray stuck in the frame of Roundell's rising siege tower, now twenty feet high, and ignited it. Roundell, standing at the base of the huge, wheeled structure, shouted at a carpenter, and he quickly climbed up the heavy crossbeams and slapped the flames out with a wet rag.

Another flaming arrow clanked against the ground where the stage had stood, and tumbled under a pile of dismantled scenery. Smoke rose out of the rubble, then tiny flames flickered in its shadows. Not ten feet away, Brown John sat on the ground, his back against a great round barrel, some kind of stage engine. The *bukko* had not bothered to watch Tiyy's dark theatrics, and showed no interest in watching the grandest siege ever staged. Now, the old man condescended to look at the rubble as the flames grew, but did nothing. Finally, he stood, tiredly walked over and stomped them out.

The Barbarian had no time to worry about his old friend. He took a shield and spear from one of the men-at-arms and banged them together loudly. Heads turned sharply, saw his sober face, and the crowd hurriedly headed back to their appointed tasks. Gath returned the shield and spear without words, strode back into Round Tower, closed the door behind him.

The men-at-arms who had stood the nightwatch slept in the barracks room. Doll's harlots, pretty, soft creatures who somehow no longer looked like harlots, attended the soldiers. Their scents of rouge and exotic perfumes had faded, replaced by the smells of men, leather, cooking fats and vegetables. Several large, big-boned women wearing armor, members of what had instantly become known as Doll's Amazons, stood at the loopholes with longbows.

Gath acknowledged the women with a nod, crossed the room quietly and stopped at the door to the stairwell. Smiling back over a metal-clad shoulder at the harlots, he nodded at the sleeping soldiers. "When they wake up, don't wear them out."

Four of the harlots actually blushed behind their grins, the others giggled quietly.

Mounting the stairs, the Barbarian felt strangely pleased with himself. It had never been his way to joke with anyone. His life had been too mean for laughter. The fact that he now waited for the battle to come to him, instead of rushing wildly to join it, also pleased him. Made him smile and filled him with a strange new power, one of control. Command.

Reaching the fourth floor, he opened the door to the armory and his smile fell to the floor.

Just beyond the roots of the lime tree in the center of the room, Billbarr and Fleka stood amid a pile of armor and weapons, buckling sword belts over leather armor three sizes too big for them. Seeing Gath, the boy, with sparkling eyes, drew a sword and made a display of his swashbuckling prow-

ess. The girl, appraising the Barbarian's mood, quickly
stopped him.

Gath walked across the room, knocked the sword out of
Billbarr's hand, then picked him up by the neck and stripped
the leather armor off of him. When he set the boy back down,
Billbarr fell to the floor, holding his throat and choking. His
face was apple-red. Gath glared down at him, then turned on
Fleka as she, hurriedly shedding her armor and belt, dropped
them in a pile at her feet. She gave them a kick, to make
certain he understood she understood, then backed away from
him, hugging her elbows to her slight body.

"We just wanted to help," she said testily.

"I do not want you to help," Gath said, his voice a low
rumble. "I told you to stay with Robin."

"She sent us away," snapped Fleka. "Besides, why can't
we help? Everyone else is."

Billbarr, coughing, nodded, asking the same question.

"Other women are going to fight," Fleka added. "Even
some of the older children. And why not, if we're all going
to die anyway?"

Billbarr, still nodding agreement, got off the floor and
Fleka put an arm around him. Defiance blotted their young
faces.

Gath studied them a moment, calming the rage that had
unexpectedly taken control of him, and said quietly, "You
two will not fight. You will stay in the room below and help
the women."

"Stay with the women?" Billbarr asked, shamefaced. "For
how long?"

"Until I tell you you can leave. There are beds there and
food, wine. You will be safe."

"But why?" blurted the boy.

"Yes!" Fleka demanded. "We're as good as anyone else!"

Gath shook his head. "I do not have to give you a reason."

"But that's not fair," Fleka protested.

"No," replied Gath, "it is not fair. But it is written. You
will stay in the barracks room, stay out of the battle and
grow."

His tone took the fight out of them, and he stepped aside,

allowing them to hurry past him to the stairwell door. There Fleka glanced back at the Barbarian, and whispered, "It's still not fair."

Billbarr tugged at her hand, and they disappeared down the stairs. Gath glanced at his axe, standing upright where he had buried it in a thick root, and touched the handle, wondering why he did not want them to fight when he was so fond of combat. He had no reason. It had been an act of instinct.

Leaving his axe behind, he climbed to the turret and stood in the shade of the looming lime tree. Stepladders now rose to the embrasures and the hoardings were in place, providing a wooden walkway that extended beyond the circling ramparts, with loopholes in the walls and murder holes in the flooring. Because the branches of the tree extended beyond the ramparts, the hoardings had not been roofed. Several of Doll's Amazons occupied the hoardings, peering over the wooden wall at the unfolding battle. He joined them.

To the north, at the base of the cliffs below the Stronghold, three lines of long, rectangular sheds, mounted on wheels and roofed with wet hides, crossed the riverbed, starting at the mouths of tunnels running under the Stronghold and ending in the valley over a hundred strides off. The sheds formed protective galleries through which Ghapp's sappers moved safely. At the far ends, the heaps of dirt and rock that had been removed from the mines stood several feet high. Wheelbarrows heaped with more rock and dirt emerged from the galleries, propelled by half-naked workers. They dumped their debris, then hurried back into the galleries.

To the sides of the galleries, archers worked behind movable wicker shields, firing volleys of arrows up at the White Archers on the Stronghold ramparts. The White Archers fired down in reply, and sheets of streaming arrows flew in both directions across the sky. Dead men, wearing arrows in their necks and chests, lay in clusters beside the wicker shields, proof of the White Archers' skill.

A cry went up from the besiegers as they saw the defenders of the Stronghold throw down grappling hooks attached to long ropes. Several hooks stuck in the roof of a shed at the mouth of a tunnel, and the White Archers pulled hard. The ropes tautened and the shed began to lean over, threatening to fall and expose the sappers underneath.

A group of dark-skinned Tammbal natives dashed from behind the besiegers' wicker shields, advanced forty strides and kneeled in the open, drawing their long yew bows. Arrows from the Stronghold dropped two of them, then the survivors fired at the taut ropes. A strange whistle came from the flying shafts, then one by one the arrows, mounted with crescent-shaped dal heads, severed the ropes and the shed settled back in place. Another Tammbal savage dropped as they retreated, dragging their dead behind them.

Gath walked around the hoardings, looked down at the lower yards. In the northeast corner of the Market Court, the men under the command of Bone and Dirken worked furiously, digging through the wall in an effort to provide the needed inlet, when and if the time came to flood the lower yards. In the opposite corner of the yard, the gate towers stood in the sun, walled up. From within them came the clang of hammers hitting metal as blacksmiths covered the portcullis, transforming it into a dam.

Gath reentered the turret, descended to the armory and sat down beside his axe. He could do nothing but wait. On the floor in front of him, the sword Billbarr had worn lay in a shaft of sunshine. The Barbarian stared at it, then idly kicked it out of sight.

The night of the same day, Doll Harl emerged from Round Tower and crossed the moonlit Close, weaving through the glowing campfires and sleeping bodies. Shields, lean-tos and barricades defended the camp sites, and moans came from those where the wounded tried to sleep. When the archers on the ramparts of the Curtain Wall had seen the siege tower reach forty feet, they had opened fire and many had fallen. Now a thick spire of black smoke rose against the indigo sky in the far corner of the Sacred Close where the dead burned. Since the first attack, the archers had been too occupied with the invaders to harry those in the Close, but every once in a while an arrow came streaking down from the looming wall.

Seeing a shadowed figure move on the ramparts of the Curtain Wall, Doll halted behind a barricade and caught her breath. She had removed her armor, and under her cloak her feminine abundance was once more barely defended by her pink blouse and split skirt, except for her belted sword. Up ahead, she saw the massive, towering shadow of the siege tower, and smiled with admiration at Roundell's ability.

With three hours still left before daylight, the magnificent engine was finished. Over seventy feet high, animal hides covered its wide, thick body, giving it a strange savage appearance. A raised drawbridge sealed off the front of the open turret, forming the top floor. A wide stairwell rose up the center of the structure, providing support for the wall and access to the top.

Doll almost chuckled. Jarl Roundell was not only a handsome beast, but a genius.

She fluffed up her bright red hair, her many rings glittering in the moonlight, pushed her blouse off her shoulders, and passed through stacks of unused timber to the carpenters' camp. There she studied the worn, exhausted faces of the sleeping men. Not seeing Roundell, she addressed the sentry sitting beside the low fire. "The sergeant?"

He looked her up and down, grinned and nodded at the siege tower. "Top floor."

She looked up at the heights of the tower, somewhat daunted, and grumbled, "Men." Then she walked up the wooden ramp rising to the bottom floor of the tower, started up the stairs.

Reaching the top floor, she sat down and gasped for breath, her eyes on Roundell, leaning against the railing of the turret. Was he smiling? She could not tell. Shadows covered him.

"Just because you knew that I'd be coming," she said, "you didn't have to make it so damn hard!"

A chuckle came from the shadow. "If you had waited another three seconds, I'd have been on my way to you."

"Knowing that does me no good now," she replied, "but I surely do like your attitude."

He chuckled, and that brought her back to her feet. She removed her sword belt with deliberate slowness, tossed it aside and removed her cloak, offering her ample bosom to the moonlight. His chuckle warmed, and she added, "Lovely out tonight, isn't it?"

He laughed out loud and she moved right up to him, her eyes roaming over his easy smile.

"Lovely," he whispered.

She pushed a sweaty curl of red hair away from her eye, tilted her round face at a lazy angle. "I came over here, because I felt, since you've been working so hard to get at that wall over there," she nodded at the Curtain Wall, "that tonight you shouldn't have to struggle for anything."

He lifted a skeptical eyebrow. "Is this a business trip, or have you suddenly gone soft?"

She sobered slightly. "I'm not sure."

"I am able to pay, madam," he said, gently shaking the money pouch on his belt. "And I am more than grateful for the opportunity."

She grinned. "I thought as much. You and I, our kind, we understand each other. But, well, when I first set my mind to come over here, business was no part of it. At least, I didn't think it was. But, if I'm going to be absolutely honest, I did have a price, right from the start."

"As I said," he whispered, "it would be my pleasure."

He reached for his coin purse, and she stopped him. Their eyes met a moment, then she leaned over the railing. The turret of the siege tower stood five feet higher than the ramparts of the Curtain Wall not thirty strides away, and she could see the shadows of a sentry on them, the moonlit towers and courtyards beyond. A moment passed before he spoke.

"You don't want my silver?" he asked. She shook her head, and he added, "Then name it."

"Your sword," she whispered, and looked back at him. He smiled lewdly and she chuckled, shook her head. "I don't mean what you're thinking. The sword I refer to hangs from your hip."

He studied her, then asked dubiously, "You want me to kill someone?"

She thought about that and her face became serious, her

voice flattened, quieted. "I guess I do, I just hadn't thought of it that way. But yes, that is exactly what I am asking." She looked back at the Curtain Wall. "Jarl, there are a lot of women behind that wall."

"I know," he said, showing no emotion.

She nodded. "But what you may not know is, I put most of them there." She looked directly at his eyes. "I found them, and either bought them or talked them into coming here. Not all of them, but all the young ones . . . the ones who didn't know any better."

He looked past her at the wall. "You want me to go in there and get them out, is that it?"

"You said there was a tunnel. You told Brown John that it led to the women's quarters and that the library was just above them."

He nodded. "There is a tunnel."

"Then it's possible." He looked at her and she pleaded, "I'll go with you. All the women in my command will go. And we'll fight hard, all of us. You can count on that. We'd do it ourselves if we could, but we don't know the way. I need your sword, Jarl. I need you."

He shook his head. "If we go in there now and cause a commotion, the archers will find out about the hidden tunnel, and that would ruin everything. Endanger everyone."

"You won't do it?"

"I can't."

She stared at the wall. "There must be another way," her voice started to break, but she stopped it. "There must be."

"Not tonight," he said. "Maybe . . . maybe later." She looked at him, suddenly hopeful. "Sometimes, in the confusion, things happen that seem impossible, if you're willing to take the chance. But I'm not making any promises, Doll, not unless I can keep them."

Understanding passed behind her eyes. "All right," she said, "I don't want to jeopardize everyone. But, Jarl, there is a promise you can keep. If the chance comes, promise me you'll take it."

He nodded. "You have it."

Smiling, she pressed against him, spreading her softness

into the creases and valleys of his hard body, and gathered him in her round white arms. She kissed his smile, then his mouth, and heat flared in their bodies. Instantly. Ravenously. Struggling to get each other's clothes off, they fell to the floor, landing painfully on the pommel of Roundell's sword. Wincing, they rolled into each other's arms, and he frowned at her.

"I thought you were going to make this easy."

"I'm trying, soldier," she sighed.

He rose up over her, pushed her down on her back and hesitated. "Are you sure you want to do this on credit?"

"Don't be a stupid ass," she snapped. "I need this as much as you do."

"I don't know about that," he whispered.

"You will," she said, and kissed him roughly.

They stripped off the rest of their clothes, then vigorously argued the point into the night until the moon, tired of watching, slid from the sky.

The next morning, wakened by a jarring clang, Brown John sat up and reached for the hilt of his sword lying on the floor beside his blankets.

The faint gray light of dawn barely slipped through the two slim windows cut in the wall of Round Tower's second-floor room, the grand hall. Coals glowed dimly in the great hearth, casting light only a few feet into the large room. Robin Lake-hair kneeled on the hearth's stoop, holding her arms above her head. Wan orange firelight played in her red-gold hair, held up by her fist as she savagely sheared it off with her knife. Clumps of her locks lay about the stoop, and a pile of them spilled from a metal bowl, turned upside down at her knees. The source of the jarring clang.

Brown wiped his eyes and yawned, then stood, intending to inquire why Robin was divesting herself of her most beautiful theatrical asset. But he kept his mouth shut.

Robin's moist eyes stared at nothing, were devoid of all light. Places of emptiness. Betraying only the rain in her heart.

A chill ran up the *bukko*'s spine. Forcing his head to turn, he looked through the gloom at the bed where Jakar slept. A gray blanket covered the bed, the body and the face. A motionless blanket. The shroud of death. Groaning, Brown sat back down.

He did not move for a long moment, allowing remorse to have its way with him, fill him with the sweet pain of self-pity.

Ignoring him, Robin threw her discarded hair into the fire, and wiped every trace of kohl and rouge from her eyes, cheeks and lips with a soft cloth. Then she stood. Shamelessly stripping off her tunic, she crossed barefoot and naked to her wooden chest in a corner and opened it. Removing a tasseled rawhide tunic with a short skirt, she sat down on the stoop and cut the tassels shorter so they had no bounce or dash. Standing, she wiggled into the tight-fitting garment and returned to the chest. Removing pieces of breast and back armor that had been fitted to her for her role in *The Song of Geddis*, she laced it on. She added a sword belt with a short chain mail girdle, then slipped on a sturdy pair of rawhide boots. She tied the costume's helmet, a simple and effective metal cup with ear and neck guards, to her belt and checked the sharpness of her dagger and sword. The edges glittered sharply in the fire's glow.

Brown cleared his throat and she faced him. Her hard wardrobe did not hide the woman, could not, but revealed the warrior in the woman.

"It's not your fault," she said, "so don't feel sorry for me, or for yourself. It's over, that's all."

"Robin," he said softly, "do not be hard on yourself, and do not be dishonest with me. It is my fault."

"No," she said simply. "I came to Whitetree of my own free will and so did . . . so did Jakar." The last words had no conviction.

Brown shook his tousled white head. "You don't understand, Robin. If I had been more able, if my gift for words had not failed me, none of this would have happened. But I failed, failed to convince the priests, failed to convince Jarl Roundell and failed to convince Jakar. I even failed to convince you and Gath of the overwhelming importance of your resurrection. Everyone has put everything else first, but it is my own fault. I have allowed myself to grow tired and old. My imagination is dead, and all of this, the siege, Jakar's tragic end, is the sad result.'' He looked at the covered body of Jakar. "I loved him, you know, just as you did.''

"I did not love him,'' she said evenly, and he looked at her sharply. "No,'' she added forcefully, "not as he deserved to be loved. I always held back. I didn't know it, but I did.'' She turned to the fire, giving him her back. "Brown,'' she whispered, "I was always, secretly in my heart, waiting for Gath to return.''

"Of course, child,'' he said idly, "you're bound to think that at a time like this, but you are young, you just don't—''

She glared over a shoulder, stopping him short. He looked at the floor for no reason and she faced him, arms trembling at her sides. "Brown, I am telling you the truth, and it's not easy for me. You must listen.''

"Child,'' he crooned, the word reverberating with condescension, "you're just tired and sad. You must—''

"You're not going to listen, are you?'' she snapped. "You're just going to sit there wallowing in your own self-pity and silly ideas. You've done nothing else for months, and you're determined to keep it up, aren't you?''

"Silly?'' he gasped.

"Yes, silly and sad and wrong! And I'm not going to be any part of you or your plot, not this one, not any of them, ever again.''

"Robin, don't say that!'' he exclaimed, rising behind his words.

"It's over, Brown. The jewels are dead. Gone.'' He stared at her dumbly, and she nodded. "They are, Brown, they died with Jakar.''

He stared at her, wanting to argue, but suddenly empty of words. She picked up a dark cloak, threw it around her shoulders. "Where are you going?''

"Where I must,'' she said, "to see that Jakar is properly buried.''

"I'll go with you.''

"No!'' she shrilled, then quieted. "Jakar wouldn't want

that. He wouldn't want to take anyone from their posts, not at a time like this."

"But I have no post."

"You should have, Brown," she said softly, and crossed to the stairwell, disappearing through the door.

He stared after her, empty and angry, then looked back at Jakar and tears welled in his eyes. He forced them back with the heel of his hand, belted on his sword, then watched as two sentries entered. They crossed to the corpse, picked it up and carried it out.

After three cups of wine, the *bukko* ascended to the armory, found Gath there and told him of Jakar's death. Whatever the Barbarian felt, he kept to himself. They mounted the steps to the turret, climbed into the hoardings and looked down at the Close.

The two sentries, carrying Jakar's corpse on a plank, crossed through the barricaded camps, moved past the siege tower and camps of carpenters and soldiers behind it, and headed toward the black plumes of smoke rising out the far corner of the Sacred Close. Robin, looking like a young soldier, followed.

"That's Robin," Brown explained, "the one at the back. She's . . . she's changed."

"I know," Gath said quietly.

"It's not just her hair and clothing," the *bukko* explained. "Oh, no! It's much more than that. Much more."

The Barbarian did not argue. He looked at Brown. "And you, old friend? What about you?"

In reply, Brown John descended to the armory, found the grindstone wheel, placed the blade of his sword against it and began to grind.

Thirty-seven

BLACK FOG

Izzam Ghapp passed through the camp at a glide rather than
a trot, seemingly with no more effort than a shadow. Soldiers
raced toward the nymph queen's compound, shouting and
pointing in panic, but he maintained his pace. Generals did
not run. He moved around the queens of the Azaabii, Umoori
and Corran, huddled just outside the ring formed by their
gaudy tents, and stopped short. The rumor was true.

Beyond the gold, emerald and scarlet tents, a swirling mist
filled the center of the compound, an ensorcelled black fog
that completely hid Tiyy's quarters.

Ghapp silently cursed the nymph's lack of control. She was
forever making a display of her dark arts. He worked his way
along the edge of the fuming vapors, drinking in the stench
of burning stone. A dark figure appeared, emerging from the
sooty center. He stopped and watched it stagger toward him,
arms extended and fingers probing the fumes, as if blind. It
reached the flimsy edge and stumbled, fell to all fours in the
sunlight. Aillya, Tiyy's body servant.

Squatting, Ghapp grabbed her hair, roughly lifted her face
to his, and alarm widened the thin slits of his eyes. Pain
twisted the thousand wrinkles on the old woman's face.
Smoke and blood issued from the empty sockets of her eyes.
The nymph had blinded her.

"What's happened?" Ghapp demanded.

"She's gone mad!" the crone wailed. "Mad!"

Tightening his fist in her hair, he struck her face sharply
with his open hand. She moaned and he let her drop. She

fell onto her hands. Her head sank between her shoulders. Blood spilled in ropy strings from her eye sockets onto the ground.

He looked up at the watching eyes of the queens and soldiers gathering in the gaps between the colorful tents, and spoke to the hag. "Goddesses do not go mad, old woman. Now tell me, calmly, what happened?"

"I . . . I looked upon her, as I always do when I dress her, and she cursed me violently. Then she pushed me down, thrust her hands against my face and darkness steamed from her palms. She burnt out my eyes! She would have killed me, but I got away."

"She wanted your death, because you saw her?"

The old woman nodded. "She's afraid of being seen. That is why she makes the fog. But I saw her, she has become—"

Before she could finish, Ghapp yanked her head back, drew his knife, and slit her throat. He dropped her into the puddle of her own blood and stood slowly, glaring a warning at those watching, then sheathed his knife and glided into the black fog.

Darkness enveloped him. He paused, held his hand to his face and could not see it. He went on, his feet finding the steps to the mound supporting Tiyy's tents, and climbed them. The vein on his bald head throbbed. His cheeks grew hot. Probing with his hands, he found the felt flaps of the nymph's tent, pushed them aside and entered. A shimmering orange ball of light floated on the reeking darkness where the oil lamp hung. Nothing else was visible. He heard the rustle of silks on the far side of the tent, where the queen's bed of pillows was strewn, then she spoke to him.

"Get out! Find the old crone and kill her! Quickly!"

"She is already dead. I silenced her before she could say what she saw."

"But she told you, didn't she?" The voice came closer.

"No. I came to see myself."

"You dare?" she snarled.

"I dare," he said calmly. "Your demonic displays have frightened the camp. There have been desertions."

"Then chase them down and kill them."

"There is no time. I need every man to storm the castle."

Silence passed between them as the black fog thinned and the light of the flaming lamps filled the interior of the tent with an orange-red glow, painting Tiyy's naked body with lavish heat. She stood as erect as a spear driven into the ground, displaying her spicy beauty with her natural lack of all shame. But her arms were folded across her breasts, hiding them, and the storming fear in her eyes stabbed at him.

"What's happened?" he asked quietly. "Why do you hide?"

"I am afraid!" she snapped. "Something has happened in the castle. I can feel it." She shuddered, turning away, then glanced over a brown shoulder. "You are going to fail me, Izzam Ghapp."

He did not react. He pulled a stool into the light, and calmly sat down, studying her. Her cheeks lacked color and red streaks blotched the normally perfect whiteness of her eyes, the results of some great strain. The odors of her liturgical perfumes, storax and myrrh, lingered on the air, mixing with the smell of hot stone. Emptied vials of black wine lay on the floor, the glimmer of black light rimming their open mouths. She obviously had been working all night on some nefarious enchantment, and had severely drained her powers.

"There is no need for fear," he said, his words as weighted as leaden shoes, "and no need for you to weaken yourself in this way." He nodded at the empty vials. "Save the dark wine for the pleasures you so justly deserve. Our only need is for patience, and soon, very soon, we will not need that."

She shook her disordered hair. "No! I can be patient no longer. Something has changed! The fetish has been weakened in some way. I have not seen her aura in two nights. Not since the Dark One arrived." She turned on him. "He must be destroyed! Now!"

He stood slowly and bowed. "If this is your wish, it will be granted. Today. When my troops enter Whitetree."

Her eyes ate at his face. "Your infernal confidence tires me, General. You will not kill him today or any day without my help! You are strong, but only because of me. Do not forget that! And when you enter Whitetree, it will also be because of me.''

"Your holiness," he said, rising and bowing, "I am never, as you know, anxious to debate you, but—''

"Be silent!''

He stiffened, again bowed his head. She moved to an ornate tripod with thin, snakelike legs supporting a black platter. A rectangular object stood on the platter, its identity concealed by a cloth of vermilion silk. Covering her right breast with her left hand, she plucked the silk away. A wicker cage perched on the black platter. Dung Beetles scrambled about inside. Ravenous. Jaws snapping.

Ghapp looked from the beetles to Tiyy and back again. His eyes had the shine of hard lacquer. "You fed them?''

"Yes. And as soon as my strength returns, I will again.''

"But why?''

"For him!'' He looked at her and a lurid smile twitched across her face. "For the Death Dealer. After the next feeding, you will put them in clay jars and throw them into the castle, at the trees.''

"But there is no need. You shouldn't have weakened yourself.''

"You insect,'' she breathed. "Do not preach to me.''

"But the Barbarian may never go near one of the trees!''

"Do you think I didn't think of that?'' she shrilled.

"But there is no need to drain yourself,'' he protested. "Your sacred powers have already done their work.'' He hesitated, turning an ear toward the castle. "Listen!''

A hush fell over the camp outside, as if everyone had suddenly stopped moving and talking. A faint, distant cracking cut the silence and stopped.

"There,'' he said proudly. "Did you hear it?''

She nodded. "What is it?''

"The castle,'' his voice crooned with oily pride. "The walls to the Stronghold have begun to crack.'' Her eyes doubted him and he added, "It is true. Weeks, months are sometimes needed to accomplish such wonders, and we, you and I, have done it in days.''

She stared at him in disbelief and a rending crack broke

open the day. A rumble followed, shaking the ground beneath them, and they rushed to the front of the tent, threw
open the flaps.

The fog had evaporated, and in the distance, dust clouds
billowed up in front of the castle's Stronghold, then wafted
away revealing a jagged, V-shaped hole at the top of the
Stronghold wall. Suddenly, dark cracks jerked their way up
and down the side of the white stone wall, accompanied by
booming rumbles, and a sixty-foot portion of the wall tilted
away from the side of the castle, collapsed on itself, raising
a storm of dust. When it cleared, crowds of Ghapp's troops
streamed in columns up the sides of the cliffs toward the
breach. Volleys of arrows from the defenders stopped them
and they fell back, then they surged forward again, climbing
over their own dead, and thrust, like a living spear, into the
body of Whitetree.

Tiyy shuddered with ecstasy. Heat plumed from her cheeks
and mouth. Torrid reds flushed her cheeks. Her hand fell
away from her breast, revealing a flaccid sack of flesh, and
she pulled Ghapp back into her tent. Her lips writhed sensually. Her eyes smoked.

"Now!" she gasped.

He stared at her empty breast. "But . . . you're too weak."

"Take me," she snarled.

He hesitated. Then her heat swirled over him, stroking his
cheeks and throat and arms. His hands, as if under her command instead of his, took hold of her and threw her down on
her pillows. She writhed, the breath driven out of her, and
he hauled up his tunic, fell on her. Broke into her. She
swooned and arched against him, her power instantaneously
regenerated, coloring her cheeks, swelling her flaccid breast
with budding youth.

Thirty-eight

UPSIDE DOWN

Roundell charged across the Close, shouldering men and women aside as they raced about in terror, and plunged through the open door into Round Tower.

The wall commanders, Dirken and Bone and Doll Harl, stood in loose order on the ground-floor room. Graybeard, the lids of his sleepless eyes red, dirt clods in his hair and beard, his tunic stained and smeared with mud, sat in the opening of the trapdoor. Behind him, Robin Lakehair leaned against the wall, dressed like a soldier. In the opposite corner, Brown John sat on a stool, his sword across his knees.

Roundell glanced at Doll.

"He's coming," she said.

The sound of footsteps echoed out the open door of the stairwell and Gath strode into the room, axe in one hand and horned helmet belted on his hip. His eyes met Roundell's.

"Ghapp's way ahead of schedule," Roundell said with deliberate ease. "Nobody does anything right anymore."

The Barbarian's eyes smiled with rough amusement. "We're going to have to change that."

"The sooner the better," Roundell replied. "It sounded to me like he broke a forty-foot hole in that wall."

"More than sixty," Gath said. "His troops are marching in twenty abreast. In an hour, probably less, those White Archers will be headed our way." Roundell nodded, and Gath added, "Ready?"

"Ready," Roundell replied. "When you want that wall, I'll give it to you."

The Barbarian almost smiled, and looked at Graybeard. "Ready?"

"No," Graybeard said flatly. "The tunnels are dug under the Stronghold wall, and shored up, but it's solid rock under the Stronghold's East Tower. We're not halfway across yet."

"It has to fall."

"Give me three, four hours."

"Three," Gath said. "Just do it right. Everything depends on your mines."

Graybeard nodded, dropped back down through the trapdoor, vanishing.

Gath turned to the wall captains. "The enemy does not know the White Archers are sealed in the Stronghold. So they'll attack the walls of the Close and the lower yards as well. But these attacks will only be feints, to keep us busy, prevent us from helping defend the Stronghold. Tell your men that, so they do not panic and waste their spears and bolts. Make them wait until they are sure of their kills before striking. Now go."

The captains nodded and streamed outside, broke into a run, heading for their posts.

Gath smiled at Roundell. "I think you have picked your commanders well."

"We'll see," Roundell replied matter-of-factly.

The Barbarian turned to Doll and said, "Hold the tower," as if he expected nothing less, then turned toward Robin.

Only shadows remained where she had stood.

Gath looked at Doll, Brown John, Roundell. They shrugged. None had seen where Robin had gone. Gath glanced up at the tower, then at the open trapdoor. He hesitated. Then he hurried out the door into the Close. Roundell and Doll shared a glance, then the mercenary went after the Barbarian.

Crossing the Close, both men put on their helmets as they glanced up at the ramparts of the Curtain Wall.

White Archers stood in the embrasure with their backs to the Close, firing their longbows into the Stronghold at Tiyy's unseen troops as they spilled through the breach.

"Zatt!" Roundell grunted. "They've already retreated to the wall."

The pair dashed through clumps of stunned, terrified refugees, Gath slinging his axe across his back, and both shouting, "Hide! Clear the yard! Get under cover!"

Shrieks erupted from the crowd and it scattered.

In front of the siege tower, lines of men sat on the ground beside heavy ropes. Seeing Roundell and Gath running toward them, they came to their feet, bringing the ropes with them. Reaching the front of the lines, Gath and Roundell took hold of the ropes, shouting, "Pull! Pull!"

The men pulled. The ropes tautened. The siege tower creaked and wobbled, then inched forward.

"Pull!" Gath's voice roared above the din of the battle overhead.

Men grunted in reply. Backs bent. Booted feet strained against the ground. The twisted hemp cut into fingers and palms. The tower lurched forward, then began to roll. Slow. Heavy. Teetering.

White Archers, standing high above in the embrasures, saw the tower coming, and cheered, stupidly thinking it came to their rescue.

Other archers were less optimistic. They dropped their weapons, leapt off the wall and landed on the roofs of the lean-tos at the base, splintering them, then rolled, dazed and bloody, onto the floor of the Close. There they tried to stand, arms and legs broken and smashed. Several fell promptly back to the ground. Half-mad women, seeing the crippled, unarmed traitors limp across the Close, swept out of their hiding places, shrieking with hysterical rage, and cut the cripples down. Then they went to work on those unable to get off the ground.

The siege tower, rocking back and forth, lumbered forward, and a wheel stuck in a crack in the ground, brought it to a jarring stop.

Gath and Roundell raced toward the rear of the tower, shouting, "Heave! Heave! Keep pulling!"

The men kept pulling. Veins stood out on their sweaty faces, down their arms and legs. Grunts became their sole

means of conversation. An arrow took a man in the hip,
another in the throat, killing him instantly. Both dropped.
The others hesitated. The wounded man got up, wearing his
arrow proudly in his side, and continued to pull. The others
did the same, with renewed force.

At the rear of the tower, Gath and Roundell shouted at the
formation of soldiers waiting to mount the tower when it was
in place. The front rank dropped their shields and spears,
joined Gath and Roundell and put their shoulders to the back
of the siege tower, heaving and driving their legs. The tower
lurched forward, jerked free of the crack, and the rear wheels
bumped across it, then rolled forward and the soldiers re-
joined their formation.

On the ramparts of the Curtain Wall, the White Archers
began to panic. Some continued to fire at Ghapp's invading
troops, unseen beyond the wall. Others fired wildly down at
the ragged men pulling the siege towers. Still others tried to
stop them, urging the tower on.

The siege tower lumbered within twenty feet of the towering Curtain Wall, and Gath slipped his axe off his back,
picked up a shield from a waiting stack. Leaping onto the
floor of the siege tower, he charged up the stairs. Roundell
grabbed up a shield, and the soldiers followed. A steady
stream of bodies poured up through the center of the moving
tower.

Reaching the turret, Gath and Roundell stood behind the
raised drawbridge, peering past both sides.

The white expanse of the Curtain Wall spread for hundreds
of feet in both directions, its ramparts crammed with struggling archers. At the far corners, the wall turned and angled
for another two hundred feet toward the West and East Towers of the Stronghold, looming well above the wall. Archers
fired from the turrets and loopholes in both towers, and arrows sliced through the air, heading for Tiyy's invading troops
somewhere in the yards of the Stronghold far below.

Gath and Roundell, their shields held in front of them,
shared a knowing glance, and waited as the siege tower, under the added weight of the soldiers, inched forward. Arrows
flew into the turret, bouncing off the massed shields held by

the soldiers, and the tower rolled on, came within reach of the Curtain Wall's ramparts.

Roundell and Gath cut the restraining ropes. The draw-bridge fell away in front of them, revealing a crowd of archers on the ramparts five feet below. Snarling. Firing their arrows. Sprouting spears and swords.

Led by Gath and Roundell, a wall of shields surged out of the siege tower, and charged down the drawbridge, propelled by battle-hungry bodies. The tattered rabble had been raised above the arrogant aristocrats.

The world was upside down.

Thirty-nine

SCARLET SPLASH

The horned helmet loomed behind Gath's charging shield. Its eye slits burned hotly, then spewed flames.

Tongues of red fire stabbed the faces and tunics of White Archers, swarmed over shoulders and between legs, rushed into nostrils and mouths. Tunics and hair burst into flames. Cheeks blistered. Bowstrings snapped and whipped wildly into the air, flaming like candlewicks. Armor glowed with red heat, roasting the men within, and they screamed, trying to unbuckle themselves, only to scorch their hands.

The wall of shields and spears hit the stunned, flaming bodies with a deafening crunch of meat and bone, and hammered at it. Then the wall surged forward, drove the massed archers against the opposite side of the wall walk, up into the embrasures. There spear and sword did the finishing work, more in the manner of an execution than a battle.

Gath, having turned out of the initial rush, now faced the

horde of archers on the left flank, cutting into them with fire
and axe. A crowd of ragtag men-at-arms followed him, heading for the West Tower of the Stronghold, bristling spears,
sword blades and flames.

On the opposite flank, Roundell led the charge toward the
East Tower, advancing inch by bloody inch.

Behind the two wedges, a multicolored armed mob of former acrobats, carpenters, farmers, beggars and merchants
disgorged from the siege tower and flooded across the drawbridge to join the battle.

In the courtyards of the Stronghold, far below, crowds of
White Archers stood behind wagons and trees, and on the
rooftops of the Vestry and Sacred Bathhouse, firing volley
after volley of arrows into Tiyy's advancing horde.

Screaming and jangling, the outlaw army swept through
the breached wall, a swarm of bodies in black tunics, furs
and glittering armor. Sprouting steel-tipped spears and
swords, like the feelers of some infectious, living plague,
they spilled across the white, polished-stone floors of the
courtyards, corrupting the Stronghold.

Demon spawn led the attack, heedless of the arrows streaking through the air to meet them. Red sashes flailed between
their legs, the uniform of the Zard Death Cult. Scales glistened on their naked bodies. Horns protruded from skulls
slashed with axe and knife, fatal wounds made just prior to
the assault so they would know all retreat was useless. They
were as soldiers already dead. The only honor remaining for
them was to die with the flesh of the enemy between their
teeth.

The White Archers greeted the fanatic onslaught with
crowds of arrows, chewing large chunks out of the face of
the living swarm. But more bodies rushed into the gaps. The
plague of knives kept coming.

Units of human soldiers followed, Azaabii pikemen and
Corran axemen, seeking less reckless routes along garden
walls and through stacks of barrels and walled passageways. Several tribes split off the main movement of the attack, their warlords leading them against White Archers holed
up in the smaller towers at the northernmost end of the castle.

At the smoking breach, Lorraiil and Tammbal archers and Kleyytil crossbowmen spilled through and formed loose formations at the rear of the main attack, firing at will.

Arrows and bolts screamed over the heads of the swarming horde, thumped into the chests and knees and faces of the White Archers. The grouped aristocrats fell to pieces like old crust and fled, retreating to more defensible positions. Others barely had time to draw their swords before the swarm devoured them.

The battle raged hand-to-hand for over an hour, a meaty symphony of screaming lungs and clashing bones and metal. Then a lull fell over the combatants on the ramparts of the Curtain Wall, as the remnants of the White Archers retreated into the West and East Towers, leaving a great scarlet splash behind on the ramparts.

Roundell withdrew his men to a corner of the wall a hundred paces from the East Tower, and ordered a wall of shields raised against the flights of arrows arriving from the looming tower. He then had his men fill the embrasures with dead bodies and stack them on top of the wall, making it higher.

When the wall walk was cleared of bodies, the Master-at-Arms met Gath, who had had his end of the wall also cleared, at the center of the Curtain Wall, where the siege tower's drawbridge rested on the ramparts.

Side by side, they looked down at the still-raging battle in the Stronghold yards. Both wore bloody cuts on their faces, arms and legs. Arrows tangled in the Barbarian's chain mail, and the face of his masked helmet and chest were black with soot. Bits of bloody tunic and what appeared to be a strip of flesh dangled from one horn of his helmet.

Jarl Roundell, grinning at his grim friend, pointed at a troop of the enemy attacking the base of the East Tower. "It will be a while before they can breach the East Tower. Its only entrances are from the wall walk three stories up, and from the bathhouse, which is built into this wall we're standing on. The bathhouse is strong, the archers will probably hold out there the longest." He pointed at the base of the

West Tower. "There's a half dozen ways into the West Tower. It could go anytime."

Gath nodded and they both studied the battle below.

In the north corner of the castle, the enemy flooded into the smaller towers and across the walls to butcher the inhabitants, and to flush individual archers out of trees in the orchards, and out of alcoves, archways and cellars. Those that surrendered, they herded into the open yards and executed with spears.

In the area of the breached wall, smoke and flames spewed up out of huge, shaftlike cracks in the stone ground, cracks leading down to the blazing mines below. More cracks raced across the stone in jagged patterns, and here and there a flutter of smoke escaped. Tiyy's demon sappers had dug their mines well past the walls.

A steady stream of black uniformed troops continued to pour through the breach, and with them came engineers, sappers and slaves, who began to dig entrenchments and construct a palisade wall facing the Curtain Wall.

Roundell and the Barbarian suddenly glanced at the roof of the East Tower. Flames had abruptly soared from its pitched, wooden roof, ignited by flaming arrows. Then shouts of triumph erupted at the base of the West Tower. Pushing a dead body out of the way, Gath and Roundell leaned over the embrasure, looked down.

Screaming Zard fanatics poured into a jagged hole broken in the side of the West Tower. Others swung axes at the doors. Suddenly two doors caved in, and more red-sashed demon spawn surged inside. A metallic racket rose swiftly up through the tower. White Archers jumped from the high windows, falling to their deaths on the cliffs. A loud hammering came from behind the tower door opening on the Curtain Wall, then it burst open, and archers tumbled out amid the broken timbers and furniture they had used to block it. Wild-eyed fanatics followed them out, heedless of the swords being thrust into their bellies, and killed the archers with teeth and long, sharpened fingernails.

Gath and Roundell started toward the West Tower, and screams echoed up out of the East Tower, faint, pained female screams. The two men glanced at each other, then at the flames on the East Tower's roof, and the same thought passed behind their eyes. Gath gave it voice.

"Burn it. I'll hold the wall."

Roundell turned, ran to the east corner of the Curtain Wall, where his men waited behind their wall of shields, and glanced back toward the sounds of guttural shouts and mad hollering on the opposite end of the wall.

There, Gath of Ball stood atop a half-crumbled embrasure, silhouetted against a sky of red flames and black smoke, wearing the hot firelight as if it were his own. It was. The flames boiled up out of carnage born of the horned helmet. The Barbarian had discarded his axe, Roundell could imagine where, and now used a long spear. He thrust the long weapon into a Zard's body and plucked the demon spawn into the air, its heavy weight bending the spear. Scales covered the strange, naked victim. Horns protruded from its skull, and a red sash flailed between its legs. The Barbarian heaved the Zard over the wall like old garbage.

As if finally finding an altar worthy of them, more Zard Death Cult members poured out of the West Tower to feed themselves to the Barbarian. He plucked another demon spawn off the wall with his spear, threw it into the air, and the creature screamed and flailed in futile ecstasy, surrendering to the will of the Death Dealer.

Roundell turned to the soldiers behind him, and hesitated for a brief moment. The *bukko*, Brown John, stood at the head of the pack, his sword and face bloody. The mercenary pointed at the *bukko*, then at two of his men-at-arms, shouting, "Follow me!"

Turning, Roundell pushed between the wall of shields and raced for the East Tower, the others following.

Forty

JASMINE, BRIAR
AND SANDALWOOD

Reaching the door to the East Tower, they found it bolted,
and Brown John, Roundell and the men-at-arms hacked at it
until the middle caved in. Brown heedlessly rammed his
shoulder into the opening. Pain shot down his arm and body
into his anklebones, and the door splintered apart. Roundell
and a soldier kicked the boards in, made a sizable hole.

Roundell, leading with his sword, crawled through, then
the *bukko*, telling himself he felt no pain, and the men-at-
arms followed.

Inside the door, a narrow passageway passed ten feet
through the thickness of the wall, then opened onto a large
abandoned guard room heaped with bunks and broken tables,
chairs, bedding, baskets, pieces of armor. Roundell and
Brown stepped into it.

A stone staircase climbed the wall to an open trapdoor.
Two archers fled up the stairs. Others aimed bows down
through the opening.

Seeing them, Roundell and Brown, hollering a warning,
pushed the men-at-arms back into the passage as an arrow
screamed on the air. It came to a thudding stop in the mercenary's thigh. Grunting with pain, Roundell dropped to the
floor of the passageway, his back against the wall. Two more
arrows clattered harmlessly against the stone floor as the
Master-at-Arms broke the shaft off just short of his flesh, then

the crash of the trapdoor being dropped into place echoed through the room.

As the men-at-arms helped Roundell up, Brown glanced around the corner of the passage. Dust clouds swirled beneath the trapdoor. The room was empty.

"It's clear," Brown said.

The mercenary grunted and limped into the room, glaring up at the trapdoor. "That's it, you bastards, hide up there and roast." He started toward the stairwell and stopped short, looking at the wooden flooring with startled eyes. As if to convince himself of what he saw, he drove the tip of his sword into the floor, chewing up a hunk of dry, brittle wood, and laughed darkly. "Damn! I forgot the interior of this tower was built of wood. Follow me, lads. Let's find some fire."

Moving with a hurried, lurching pace, Roundell cautiously led them down the stairwell. Reaching a landing halfway between the floors, the mercenary paused to study the room below, and blood puddled beneath his boot.

A corridor divided the room. Doors opened off of it onto lavishly appointed rooms, richly furnished with gold and silver urns, furniture inlaid with amber and jade, silk and velvet curtains. They were empty. Silence prevailed, except for the sounds of the battle outside, muffled by the thick stone walls, and a faint weeping of women's voices.

Brown glanced at Roundell. "There are women hiding in those rooms."

Roundell shook his head. "Not here," he whispered. "Farther down. Below the library." He turned to the men-at-arms. "Keep your eyes open, there's no telling where one of the cowards may be hiding."

Roundell led the soldiers down the steps, but the *bukko* remained on the landing, frozen in place by the word "library." Suddenly, after abandoning all hope of ever learning the secret of Robin's powers, he was within reach of the sacred formula. In a position to once again fill Robin's heart with hope, and save her, save the White Veshta. But did he have time? Could the formula be found before Roundell torched the tower?

He dashed down the steps, taking three at a time, stumbled

and hit the floor of the room below, using his heel like a hammer. The blow shot pain up into the meat of his calf and knee. The muscle burned. Cramped. Threatened to throw him down. He refused to let it and limped on, descended the next flight of steps, trying to catch up with Roundell and the others before it was too late.

He passed another abandoned room furnished like a treasure house, then limped down a narrow-walled stairwell. The outside wall was stone, the inside one consisted of wood panels, walnut, cedar, oak, teak, ebony. Delicately carved figures of women, old, young, thin, fat, tall and short decorated the panels, each of them beautiful in their own unique way. Wooden railings extended on either side of the stairs, also carved with the entwined bodies and flowing hair of voluptuous beauties, their nipples and noses and bellies worn down from centuries of fondling by loving hands. Following the sounds of footsteps below, he descended two flights, and the sounds of swords eating into wood replaced the footsteps.

Leaping four steps at a time, the *bukko* joined Roundell and the men-at-arms in a closetlike alcove at the bottom of the steps. It had no exit except for the huge wooden door their swords hacked apart.

Five feet high and wide, the door was perfectly round, except where a bangled female hand gripped the outer edge of the circular wood and another posed above it. Perfectly sculpted, the large wooden hands were a stirring replica of a mountain girl's hands beating on a tambourine.

Roundell's sword-blade chopped off a giant thumb and it rolled against the *bukko*'s boot. Its touch shook him from toe to eyebrow and he took a step back, as if the wooden digit were alive. Sucking in a deep breath and shaking himself, Brown stepped over the thumb and joined the attack, striking again and again at the beautiful door. A crack splintered open. Hot firelight leaked through it.

Feverish and sweating, Brown drove his sword into the crack and wrenched it violently from side to side, ripping away large splinters of wood to make an opening several feet wide. Roundell stepped back and kicked. His heel met the wood with a loud crack, and the door splintered. Chuckling, the *bukko* drove his shoulders through the opening, breaking off more splinters, and fell into the room beyond.

Roundell and the two men-at-arms climbed in behind him and helped the *bukko* to his feet. Brown could barely stand. He suddenly felt old and worn and beaten. Not from the effort, but from the spectacle spread before him.

The library walls rose fifteen feet to a balcony that ran around the room, then another ten feet to a wooden ceiling carved with figures of naked women lounging among clouds. Each wall was built of a different wood, and pigeonholed from floor to ceiling. In each hole resided a parchment scroll. Heaped on the floor were more, along with stacks of clay and wooden tablets. Dusty. Cobwebbed. Still more cluttered reading tables and stands, and at the far end of the room, on a raised floor beyond a wooden arch, ornate cases with tiny pigeonholes held more precious documents beside a large hand-carved desk strewn with parchments and plates of old food.

The room held thousands upon thousands of documents, each containing vital formulas and data pertaining to the rituals, offerings, vestments and liturgical elixirs, perfumes and totems essential to the proper and devout worship of the White Veshta. It could take weeks to find the right formula.

Roundell kicked and threw scrolls into a heap in front of the huge stone hearth. A fire burnt in it. He picked up a musty scroll and thrust it into the flames.

"Noooo!" Brown shouted and charged the Master-at-Arms.

Roundell turned, flaming scroll in hand, and brought up the blade of his sword, stopping the *bukko* short. The mercenary's eyes said clearly that he would gut Brown if the old man so much as offered one more word of protest. Brown shut his mouth. Roundell threw the flaming scroll on the heap and it burst into flames.

A shriek came from the far end of the room, and the door of a small closet rattled, then burst open, spilling Surim, the Great Scribe, onto the rug. The frail man jumped up, and raced for the flaming scrolls, shouting, "Stop! Put it out! Put it out!"

Roundell caught Surim by the collar of his filthy tunic, bringing the scribe to a sudden stop, and forced him to his knees. "I'll torch the whole library," Roundell barked, "and you with it, unless you show me the secret entrance to the women's quarters."

"Put out the flames first," Surim pleaded.

Roundell kicked him in the hip, driving him ten feet across the rug into the wall. "Tell me, damn you. Now!"

The Master-at-Arms cleared a tabletop with his arm, sweeping scrolls and tablets into the blazing flames, and they crackled and roared. The Great Scribe groaned, staring in horror, then jumped up, raced to the arch partitioning off the far end of the room.

A life-size sculpture of a spangled dancing girl beating a tambourine formed the pillar supporting the arch. As Brown and Roundell joined him, the scribe reached into the sculpture's tangled, flowing hair. A loud click sounded and the wooden dancing girl swung forward, bringing the wall panel with her and revealing a narrow hidden doorway. Beyond it waited a secret stairwell.

Whimpering voices and the scents of subtle perfumes drifted up out of the shadowed passage, then a shrill, helpless shriek of terror. Roundell nodded at the men-at-arms. "Get down there and keep them quiet!" The soldiers vanished down the dark passage, and Roundell, smiling with raw satisfaction, turned toward the *bukko*. "Torch it!"

Brown's mouth opened. His jaw trembled.

Roundell, suddenly weak, heaved himself into the narrow stairwell and growled back over a shoulder, "Torch it, damn you! Hurry!"

Brown did not move, could not. Around him, the scents of the perfumes grew stronger in the air, and he knew them. Jasmine, briar and sandlewood. With them came the warmth rising off the bodies of the defenseless women quartered below. The *bukko* shook his head. "If I torch the library, those women will burn."

"You old fool!" growled Roundell, his voice suddenly weak and bitter. "We're rescuing them. There's a tunnel below their quarters, remember? It leads under the Stronghold to the Close. Now torch it, or we're all done for!''

Roundell limped out of sight, and Brown hurried back to the burning scrolls, understanding suddenly hard inside him. If they could burn down the tower, then there would be no need for Graybeard's sappers to finish mining it, and the other mines could be set on fire immediately. He grabbed up a burning scroll, kicked a heap of tablets and scrolls against the wall, throwing chairs and scrolls on top of it, then torched it.

The scrolls crackled with flames, igniting the old furniture, and the flames blazed up the face of the wall, setting the pigeonholed scrolls on fire, then the wall and the balcony above.

Brown stepped back and stared, suddenly filled with remorse. Before him the sacred work of hundreds of years, the words of a million dreams flamed into oblivion, taking with it his only hope for glory.

He threw more scrolls against the opposite wall. Surim, who had been standing in an immobilizing stupor, suddenly charged across the room and threw himself at the *bukko*. ''No!'' he screamed. ''No! Noooo!''

The scribe's body knocked Brown to the floor, and his flimsy torch twirled into the air, fell onto the pile of scrolls. Flames and showers of sparks erupted from them, then Brown and the scribe, their bodies tangled as they flailed at each other, rolled over the flames. Their tunics caught fire, and they rolled away in panic, spreading the fire. The dusty rug flickered brightly, and flame quickly raced through its dry, dusty nap.

Surim, his mind gone from behind his eyes, continued to flail wildly at Brown and scream, ''Stop! Stop!''

The *bukko* finally threw him off and rolled to his feet, slapping out the flames on the hem of his tunic.

The back of Surim's tunic flamed brightly, but the scribe did not appear to notice. On his hands and knees, he beat at the burning rug with the flat of hands, heedlessly scorching his fingers and palms.

"Holy Bled, man!" Brown gasped, trying to rip the flaming cloth off Surim's back. "You're on fire!"

The small man, screaming unintelligibly, scrambled out of the *bukko*'s reach and ran for the far end of the room, his back a sheet of flames. The Great Scribe threw himself on the floor beside the large desk and wildly hunted through a stack of scrolls piled there, throwing them aside. Several of the brittle documents fell against his flaming garment and exploded with a whoosh of air into balls of fire and smoke, hiding the scribe behind a wall of fire.

Gasping in shock, Brown backed slowly toward the hidden stairwell. All around him, the dry, wooden room and parchments flamed. He turned, leapt over a burning strip of carpet, made the door to the hidden staircase. He took a last glance back over his shoulder at the blazing house of dreams, then limped hurriedly down the stairs.

Reaching the floor of the women's quarters, he stared in dumb amazement at its opulent splendor.

The ground-floor room was carved from solid limestone polished to white perfection. Four times the size of the library, it spread in wide undulating halls to curved rooms and sunken caves piled with red, yellow and silver cushions. Beds of white wood, silver and gold occupied cavelike alcoves, and everywhere there were teak tables spread with bronze mirrors, vials of perfumes, combs and tubs of white, perfumed powder. Against the wall stood open closets, filled with diaphanous garments and white furs. Scarlet, pink, and pepper-red rugs covered the stone floor.

Passing through the opulence streamed a line of pampered, powdered white bodies, each one a fleshy, female treasure. Young. Beautiful. Terrified. Sobbing, they clung to each other, the startled glare of furtive hope passing behind their big black-rimmed eyes. One of the men-at-arms herded them toward a dark hole in the white floor. Beside it were a rumpled carpet and large stone slab which had been removed from the floor. The bodies poured down into the darkness below, from which the voice of Roundell, growing fainter, called out to them to hurry.

The *bukko* sat down on the bottom step of the stairwell,

having only the strength to commit each curve, each whimper, each tear to memory. As he did, understanding again slammed a hard truth against the walls of his mind, and he realized that there came times in life when the magic was not in the words, not in the dreams, but in the flesh.

Finally he had done something right.

A rush of heat spilled over his back and he stood abruptly, turning to face the flaming body of Surim, staggering down the steps. The Great Scribe's arm, extending from a flaming shoulder, weaved unsteadily in front of him, the only part of him untouched by fire. Its hand held a small red-leather canister, not nine inches long.

"Save it," Surim whispered. "Please! Save it!"

The *bukko* grasped the canister, and the scribe's hand fell away, its weight dragging his flaming body to the floor. Brown stepped back, staring as flesh bubbled and peeled away from the scribe's dead face.

Backing up to the line of women, Brown tucked the canister inside his tunic, then turned and followed the men-at-arms down into the secret tunnel below.

Forty-one

RESIN, PITCH AND TAR

In the Underground Gallery far below the Curtain Wall, Robin Lakehair kneeled over Jarl Roundell's leg, cutting his hose away from the broken shaft imbedded in his thigh. Smudges of dirt streaked her face and arms. Clods tangled in her short hair, and the sweat of hours of work, helping the miners dig, stained her torn rawhide tunic. The results of that work, loose pebbles and shards of white stone strewn on the tunnel floor, pressed painfully into her knees. She ignored them, continued to cut.

The Master-at-Arms sat silently watching her, his back against the stone wall.

A bowl of resin burned on the ground beside them. The blade of a knife rested on the lips of the bowl, the steel turning red-hot. The small fire's glow lit her work, and threw wavering sheets of light into the openings of four tunnels leading off the gallery. One of the tunnels had been dug recently, and was no more than a crawl hole.

A line of powdered white female bodies passed across the gallery, moving out of one tunnel into the one opposite it. The rescued women held hands so they would not lose their way.

Neither Robin or Roundell looked at them. She ripped his torn hose away from the wound, jerking his leg. Blood bubbled out around the broken end of the imbedded shaft.

"Take it easy!" he snapped.

"Be quiet," she said firmly. "I want it to bleed."

He did as he was told. She probed the underside of the wound, finding the protruding tip of the arrowhead. Raising his leg so that it bent at the knee with his foot flat against the floor, she straddled it with her legs, pressing her upper body against it and holding it fast against the ground. With strong fingers, she pressed the flesh down around the arrowhead until enough of it showed to grip, and took hold of it with her fingertips.

"Don't try it, lass," Roundell said calmly. "You're not strong enough."

She paid no attention. Squeezing the arrowhead tightly, she suddenly pulled hard. The arrowhead rose out of the wound, enough to hold firmly. She gripped it in her fist, ignoring his moan, and pulled the broken shaft through his leg, free of his flesh. Dropping it, she snatched up the knife and placed the red-hot blade across the wound. Flesh sizzled and steamed, raising a stench.

Roundell's cheeks lost all color. His head fell back against the wall.

She removed some herbs from her satchel, packed the

wound with them, then removed a wad of torn strips of cloth. She quickly wrapped them tightly around his leg, binding the wound, and tied them off. Then she fed some of the herbs into Roundell's mouth, and sat back.

"Chew them," she said. "They're bitter, but they'll help it heal." She nodded at the wound. "I want to look at it again tonight."

"Tonight?" He chuckled hoarsely. "Who says there will be a tonight?"

She smiled wryly. "Why else are we doing this," she asked, "if we don't want to see tonight?"

"It's not tonight we're fighting for, lass," he said casually. "It's mid-afternoon." She grinned and he added, "Don't get too eager. We might not even make it to midday from the way things are setting into place."

She sobered. "Do we hold the Curtain Wall? Is . . . is Gath alive?"

He nodded. "He holds the wall, at least he did the last time I looked." He grinned. "He's a lot like you, lass. Optimistic. I think he's even looking forward to tomorrow night."

She laughed quietly and they turned as the last of the women moved past, and Brown John appeared. Seeing them, the old man, bending low and gasping from exertion, limped hurriedly to them and sat down. He nodded at her, turned to Roundell.

"I torched it."

"Are you sure?" Roundell asked. "You actually saw it? If that tower doesn't burn—"

"The walls went up like kindling," Brown said evenly. "The whole library was in flames before I got out of there."

The *bukko* showed him his burnt tunic and Roundell laughed, but quickly sobered. "I'm, sorry, old man. I know you were fond of such trifles. But they did burn well, didn't they?"

"Beautifully," Brown said.

Robin looked at the *bukko* sharply, and their eyes met. Both strangers to each other.

Graybeard emerged from the new crawl hole, faced Roundell. Mud and sweat covered him. His cheeks, bare arms and knuckles were scraped raw, bleeding through the mud. He said, "You sent for me?"

Roundell nodded. "The East Tower is burning, you can forget about mining it. Are the other mines ready?"

"Ready," Graybeard replied, saving his breath.

"Then set your fires."

Graybeard grinned, hunks of mud falling off his cheeks, and nodded, crawled back into the tunnel.

Without a word, Robin dropped onto her hands to follow, and Brown gasped in dismay, "Robin!" She glanced over her shoulder at his disapproving eyes, and the bossy look of the *bukko* quickly left his face, his tone changing. "Be careful," he said.

Nodding, she moved on her hands and knees into the crawl hole and, splashing through a stretch of puddles, hurried around corners, ignoring drops of moisture falling from the low ceiling.

Reaching an intersection with another new tunnel on the right, she stopped. At its far end, fire pots glowed in the gallery that had been dug under the East Tower, silhouetting the hunched shapes of men crawling toward her. Graybeard no doubt led them, having just ordered them to abandon their mines and return to Round Tower. She crawled on, passing into a smaller tunnel dug out of a vein of earth, and reached the Fire Gallery under the center of the Stronghold.

Timbers shored up the walls and ceiling of the gallery, and three tunnels opened off of it, leading to the West Tower and the walls and towers to the north. Thick globs of pitch smeared the timbers. Jars of the same materials waited on the stone floor. Bound bundles of short dry straw stood in them, serving as brushes. Three fire pots stood apart from the inflammables, casting yellow light over the chamber as well as a sapper wiping more pitch on timbers. He stopped working and looked at her, his eyes afraid and full of questions.

"We're going to fire the tunnels," she said.

The sapper smiled with relief. Graybeard entered the gallery on his hands and knees, jumped to his feet. "Where's Aben?" he asked the sapper anxiously.

The man nodded at a tunnel. "At the end of tunnel three."

"Zatt!" Graybeard cursed, and picked up a fire pot, handed it to the sapper. "Fire number three, then get yourself and Aben out of here."

The sapper, bending low, ran into tunnel three and Robin and Graybeard picked up the remaining fire pots. He glanced into her eyes, obviously wishing she was a man instead of a woman, but did not hesitate.

"You take one," he said, and ran into tunnel two as she dashed into number one.

Holding the fire pot gingerly, she trotted the length of the tunnel, nearly two hundred strides. Reaching its end, she pulled up, gasping on the thin air. She stood far below the walls of the West Tower. Here, the stones above the timbers shoring up the walls had been removed, and the openings were stuffed with straw, old bedding and broken baskets, anything that would burn quickly. Heaps of straw and kindling filled the end of the tunnel. But the jars of pitch and tar and resin waiting on the floor of the tunnel had not been dumped on the straw. Without considering the delay, she set her fire pot down, dumped the jars on the straw and splattered their contents across the timbers, inadvertently smearing the stuff on her arms and legs in the process.

Finished, she picked up the fire pot, stepped back and tossed it into the center of the straw. She waited, to make certain the fire came to life, and the straw suddenly exploded with flames, throwing sparks and burning straw at her. The explosion drove her back into the tunnel, upending her. She rolled onto her hands and knees, shook her head until the dizziness faded, and watched as what she thought was fire broke out on her arms. Nearly blinded by the exploding glare, she was not sure. But the pain quickly informed her she was right, and she slapped it out. Jumping to her feet, she trotted gingerly back into the dark tunnel, feeling the growing heat stroke the backs of her bare legs. When her eyes cleared, she broke into a dead run, heading for a glimmer of light at the end of the tunnel.

She reached the gallery at the same moment smoke billowed in out of tunnels two and three and swirled over Graybeard, waiting for her with a fire pot in his hand. He pushed her at the entrance tunnel and she dropped to her hands and knees, crawled in. Graybeard followed her.

"Faster!" he grunted. "Faster!"

She went faster, and fell on her face. She pushed herself back to her knees and Graybeard bumped into her, fell again. Cursing, the old man managed to untangle himself from her legs without spilling the fire pot, and they scampered forward as smoke spewed between their legs and over their bodies, filling the tunnel.

Robin held her breath as long as she could, then sucked in the hot, reeking fumes and coughed all the way to the Underground Gallery beneath the Curtain Wall. There the smoke thinned, clinging to the ceilings, and she and the old man fell facedown on the ground, sucking up deep breaths of clean, cool air.

A loud cracking echoed out of the tunnel behind them, and Graybeard, his eyes startled, jumped up, shouting, "Hurry! Follow me!"

Fire pot in hand, he dashed into one of the tunnels as Robin leapt to her feet. A booming, cracking sound stunned her. The ground shook, and she fell. Wind swept over her, ripping at her hair and clothing. Smoke followed. Then searing flames, seeming to burn up something invisible in the air, swept through the gallery. The flames vanished as fast as they had arrived. She stood in the smoky darkness and stumbled forward, groped at the walls and found the entrance of the tunnel. Keeping her head low and her feet spread wide for balance, she ran blindly into the darkness. She could not see the glow of Graybeard's fire pot up ahead, but heard his footsteps.

Long moments later, she still ran in darkness, slower now and feeling the sides of the walls for guidance. Suddenly the walls were no longer there and she stopped. Listening, she heard the old man's footsteps. They seemed to be coming closer, then faded away, joining with several sets of footsteps coming form different directions. Echoes. A voice, far off, shouted her name several times, then it echoed through the darkness, also coming from different directions.

Cold fear shook her, and she fought it off, searching with her hands until she found the wall. Moving around it slowly, she discovered she stood in a low-ceilinged gallery with six square-cut tunnels opening off of it. The walls of the tunnels, slimy and crusted, told her they were old. The sounds of footsteps faded to silence and the faint beat of dripping water filled the void. She stood still, thinking.

She had entered the wrong tunnel. Her only recourse was to backtrack. Deciding on that course of action, Robin turned . . . and realized she had no idea which of the tunnels was the one she had entered by.

She was lost.

Forty-two

SCREAMING STONES

Gath left his axe standing upright in the chest of the Zard fanatic, and sat down with his back against the rampart of the Curtain Wall. The dead creature sprawled atop stacked bodies, four and five deep, blocking the corner of the wall. More littered the wall walk all the way to the door of the West Tower, where the invaders had momentarily taken refuge.

A lull hung over the battlements. Quiet. Foreboding. The stench of burnt flesh and leather drifted on the air.

The Death Dealer's remaining comrades sprawled around him, many wounded and all exhausted. Their dead had been carried back down the siege tower to the Close. No one moved.

Thin plumes of smoke rose in feral curls out of the stacked
corpses, rising from burnt clothing and decaying demon
spawn. The dark fumes reached thirty feet into the air. There
they joined a cloud of smoke hovering above the Stronghold.
Black fumes spewing out of the windows and loopholes of
the East Tower provided its source, telling the Barbarian that
Roundell had successfully fired the tower, preventing Tiyy's
army from occupying it.

Below, in the courtyards of the Stronghold, the enemy had
withdrawn and hastily raised embankments to prepare for a
final charge.

Gath removed his helmet, set it between his legs. His arms,
sore and bloody from shoulders to fingertips, felt as clumsy
as tree trunks. Every inch of him ached. Broken arrows
lodged in his chain mail. Dents dappled his armor, the large
ones pressing against his ribs and collarbone. He let his head
sink between his shoulders and closed his eyes, granting himself a moment's rest.

Faint whistling lilted out of the sky, gentle, melodic bird
song. He listened to it, letting the music have its way with
him, then looked up.

Swallows fluttered across the sky, and swooped down onto
the rampart and roof of the tower. A mockingbird sang unseen somewhere in the Stronghold. The bird's gentle voice,
clean and clear on the quiet, filled him with unexpected contentment.

A hammering racket sent the birds back into the sky, and
Gath came to his feet, jumped into an embrasure, looked
down at the battlefield.

At the base of the Curtain Wall, bands of besiegers, having
stealthily crossed the open ground, now hammered boards
over the doors and windows of the Vestry and Sacred Bathhouse, sealing the surviving White Archers inside. Three
hundred strides off, Izzam Ghapp's troops, massed behind
shields, emerged from embankments and palisades, and
formed up facing the Curtain Wall. Over a thousand strong,
their front ranks held scaling ladders, followed by a horde
carrying pikes, bills, axes, swords. Mounted on the embankments, archers and crossbowmen knelt behind wicker shields,

ready to drop their missiles onto the ramparts of the Curtain
Wall like metallic rain.

Gath frowned grimly. They intended to bypass the archers,
storm the wall.

A rumble came from the breach in the wall behind the
massed troops, and they parted, making room for something.
A crowd of slaves appeared, straining as they pulled ropes,
and hauled three catapults into view.

Glowering, Gath put his eyes on his troops, intending to
order them into position, and hesitated.

The East Tower was shivering. It stopped, then shook
slightly again. A board in the charred roof tumbled loose,
fell five stories, clattered on the ground. Suddenly flames
filled the interior of the top room. The White Archers holed
up there, shouting in desperation, pressed into the narrow
loopholes and flames shot past them, incinerating them.

Gath dropped onto the wall walk, waited. The Curtain Wall
trembled slightly under his feet, and understanding rose behind his eyes.

Below in the courtyards, officers hurriedly gathered behind
the invader's formations, one officer pointing at the East
Tower. Flames now engulfed the roof. Trumpets sounded
somewhere at the rear of the assault troops. The officers raced
back to their posts, and the front rank rose, charged forward
with their ladders as Tiyy's archers, aiming high, lofted a
cloud of streaking arrows into the sky.

Lowering his helmet over his head, Gath dashed to the
blockade of stacked bodies, ripped his axe out of the dead
meat as his men-at-arms joined him. Raising a roof of shields,
they thrust a wall of pikes over the blockade.

The door of the West Tower burst open, and a stream of
metal-clad soldiers poured down the narrow staircase onto
the wall walk. Not demon spawn, but big men wearing furs
and armor, carrying vermilion crossbows. Red spots and
blotches glowed on their foreheads. Tiyy's bodyguards.

Gath hauled a shield away from a cadaver, thrust his arm
through the grips and mounted the heaping corpses. His men
followed, and spear tips blossomed around the Death Dealer,
eager to greet the bodyguards. A red glow rose behind the

eye slits of the horned helmet, as fire boiled and churned within the headpiece, waiting.

The sound of scaling ladders clattered against the stone wall somewhere below. Whistling came out of the sky, and the rain of arrows fell on the ramparts, hammering raised shields, streaking through the openings between them to drill exposed hips, calves and feet. Men growled with pain, cursed, but held their position.

Suddenly a booming whoosh, like the bowels of the earth releasing its rage, drowned out all other sound, stunning ear and mind.

The charging bodyguards stopped short, still fifty strides short of the blockade, startled by the noise. They glanced about and began to stumble, unable to keep their balance as the wall shook under them.

A fireball, big enough to fill a great hall, boiled into the sky above the burning East Tower. Its roofing, now shards of splintered, flaming wood, spun away from the sides of the ball, fell back through billowing black smoke into the courtyards below. Jagged cracks split the limestone walls of the tower from the ground to the ramparts. Suddenly the tower swayed, the cracks jerking wide, and its walls fell away in large slabs. Huge, heavy, they dropped like thick stone blankets toward the massed troops below. Buried them in crowds.

Rending sounds of rocks grinding and ripping against themselves filled the air with a grating racket. Tremors shook the entire Stronghold. In the courtyards, clumps of invaders suddenly sank into the ground, making holes in their formations that grew wider in rippling circles, like ponds being drained by the earth. Flames shot up out of the ground where they fell, rising from open sores in the stone ground. Fractures breaking open the body of the earth. Gaping orifices of the underworld gulping flesh, vomiting fire.

The ruptures and wounds ripped across the courtyards, spitting flames, swallowing flailing bodies, earthworks and palisade walls. The growing heat burst stones apart, threw them into the air in jagged pieces.

The terrified invaders turned and threw themselves toward the breach, seeking escape. But the earth under them shook itself open, and the rubble at the base of the breach spilled into the castle, throwing them back, burying them.

With a boom, flame-jawed fractures spread their mouths at the base of the West Tower. Cracks made jagged paths up its sides, darting like black tongues. The tower shook, teetered toward the cliffs, then swung back and toppled into the courtyards, ripping away huge portions of the walls adjoining it.

The stunned bodyguards stared in horror as cracks raced through the stone under their feet. Snarling with terror, they fired their bright crossbows at the rabble, defended by the blockade of dead bodies, and charged.

Steel bolts clanked off the face of the horned helmet, stuck in the Barbarian's chain mail and buried themselves in men-at-arms at his side. Their flesh sizzled and fumed under the attack of the poisoned tips, and they sank to the ground, screaming and clawing at the infernal darts to no avail. Their bodies boiled away inside their armor.

The men-at-arms beside Gath backed away, their minds numbed by the sight. Standing alone on the awful heap, Gath ate the charging bodyguards with his axe, as cracking rocks, tremors and the stink of burning stone, tar and flesh consumed the day.

Suddenly the bodyguards lurched backward in a bunch, as if pulled by a giant hand. Screaming, they dropped in front of the Death Dealer, clawing for a perch on the dead bodies. Then they fell away in one piece, as the wall they stood on dropped out from under them.

The blockade of dead bodies lurched and shifted under the Death Dealer, slipping toward the gap. Gath leapt back onto the ramparts of the Curtain Wall, and the dead men tumbled away, leaving behind a jagged edge of stone at the corner.

Gath pushed through his stunned, terrified men-at-arms to the middle of the wall. There he jumped up into an embrasure, looked down at the Stronghold. A moment passed, and deadly calm settled through his body. He slowly removed his helmet, held it against his hip.

His rabble-in-arms watched him, sharing whispers, then climbed into the embrasures, looked down at the battlefield, and silence spread through them.

Beyond a drape of smoke, flaming wounds in the earth spread to the north end of the Stronghold, where guard towers and chunks of wall continued to collapse. The smoky drape thickened quickly, blotting out everything as the sounds of falling boulders, roaring flames and screaming men sang in horrific harmony. A loud crash of rock boomed, then the sounds made by the falling walls stopped, and the roar of flames intensified, whipping and lashing the air, drowning out the screams and cries for help. Moments passed, and the drape of smoke swelled with dim fire, as if the Stronghold were burning. Then the light dimmed. The sounds of whipping flames abated, and a wind carried the smoke away.

The entire Stronghold lay on its broken body, with over half of Tiyy's army and the remnant of White Archers buried beneath it. There was no trace of anything living, except for steady cries rising up out of the openings in the heaped rubble of smoking rock. But not even these pitiful sounds seemed linked to anything human. It appeared that the rocks cried out, that the stones screamed.

Forty-three

BITCH IN HEAT

Tiyy galloped her stallion through the staggering wounded as they fled across the valley toward the camp. She took no notice of them, their missing limbs or crushed bones. A pain in her right hand throbbed all the way up into her shoulder. A sense of loss, as if her insides had been removed, ached in her belly. She held her right fist against her chest, and blood decorated her forearm, like wet, red lace. But her face showed no trace of agony, only the vivid flush and snarl of an animal in heat.

Her glassy black armor glittered from her throat to groin, perfectly molded to her perfect body. A black belt now carried the sheathed dagger of black light and her tiny vermilion crossbow. The fringe of a slate-gray tunic fluttered on her bare shoulders and thighs. Black-leather boots rose to her knees. Her blond hair tossed at the rim of a shiny black skullcap shaped like the head of an adder. Rubies served as its eyes.

The nymph queen's Jani outlaws, gorged with black wine, galloped beside and behind her, the red spots on their foreheads smoking. They hauled a wagon stacked with small cages.

Reaching the swirling dust of what was left of her army, now marching toward the southern end of the castle, Tiyy rode alongside the lines of troops, rumbling catapults and wagons and the Jani threw sacred vials of Nagraa to the soldiers. Hands snatched the small jars out of the air and, recognizing them, cheered and downed the black wine. Hungrily. Mindlessly. Eager to arm themselves in any way against the axe of the Death Dealer.

Black light streaked from the open mouths of the vials, seared hair and tunics and flesh, and smoke mixed with the enveloping dust. The flesh on the soldiers' faces drew tight against their skulls. Red spots appeared on their foreheads and bubbled and fumed, consuming them with erotic hunger, a need to plunge their blades into the white body of the citadel.

The last of the ensorcelled stimulants distributed, the savages shouted to the marching men, declaring that the Black Veshta, the dark goddess herself, would make a gift of her body to the man who brought her the head of the Death Dealer.

Like a harsh wind, infectious lust swept through the troops, guttural and nervous and loud, and the army rushed madly forward and formed up, facing the walls of Whitetree's lower yards.

Tiyy turned her horse, led the Jani up the sloping valley

and reined up below General Izzam Ghapp's command tower, now back in its original position. Ghapp and his commanders, mounted on their horses, turned to her. The Kitzakk's face twitched with frustrated rage.

Tiyy glared at him contemptuously, and glanced across the valley at dust clouds fading into the distance, marking the trail of deserting tribes, merchants and camp followers. Glowering, she looked back up at Ghapp. "I was right, General! Now you will do it my way."

She raised her right arm, spreading her fingers. Her little finger was missing, all that remained was a bloody stump.

They gasped in horror.

"Yes!" she snapped. "The least I deserve is your gasps. This is the second time I have had to give up a finger because of this Barbarian."

"You cut it off yourself?" Ghapp exclaimed.

"Yes. To feed my pets!"

She nodded at a Jani outlaw, and he rode forward with a small cage of ravenous Dung Beetles, held it up to their startled faces.

The insects, now twice their former size, moved slowly, crawling up and down the sides of the cage. Smoke leaked from their joints, issuing the odious smell of burning stone and flesh.

"You see," Tiyy said proudly, "I have made improvements in their character and abilities. Now they have my stealth, my cunning and my pride. They will not fail. When your catapults throw them into the castle, they will hide in the trees and find a way to trap and execute the Dark One. When that happens, General, your army will attack, open the castle, and you and I will ride with it."

"It's too dangerous," Ghapp protested.

"I will decide that!" she snapped. "Strange events occur behind those walls. I can sense them. The goddess is devising some new means of concealing the jewels, and I must strike! Now! Before the jewels vanish."

She waved an arm and the wagon rumbled beside her. Rats scurried about inside the cages stacked on the open bed, poking their noses through the bars and sniffing the air. A hazy glaze coated their bright red eyes. Smoke drifted from tiny wounds in the loose pink flesh under their leg joints.

"You will also see to it, General," Tiyy continued, "that these animals are thrown into the castle. Their senses are linked with mine. They can detect the presence of the White Veshta, find and track her." She looked off at Whitetree. "When I enter the castle, they will lead me to her."

Forty-four
MURDER

In Round Tower's ground-floor room, black smoke billowed up out of the trapdoor leading to the tunnels below, and swirled around Gath's boots. He stood on the lip, drinking in the flatulent stench of pitch from the mines under the Stronghold. The animal inside him prowled behind his eyes, hungry to take command of blood and bone and send him plunging into the odious darkness in search of Robin.

Jarl Roundell, sitting on a stool on the opposite side of the trapdoor, held his wounded thigh in both hands as Doll Harl and Fleka rebandaged it. His eyes studied the Barbarian. When Gath looked at him, the Master-at-Arms shook his head.

"We can't go down there, not until the smoke clears." He nodded at Brown John and Graybeard, sitting on the floor by the open door to the Close. Soot covered their faces, and their open mouths drank in the clean air with deep, heaving gasps. "They looked for her as long as they could, friend. If you go down there now, you'll suffocate."

Gath gave no indication of agreement or disagreement.

"She's got a good chance," Roundell added. "There is a

maze of tunnels down there. If she just keeps crawling away
from the smoke, she could be all right. She's smart, and
brave as any man I ever met. She'll take care of herself.''

Gath did not reply.

A rat emerged from the shadowed corner beyond Doll, and
sniffed the smoky air. Its pointed face turned rapidly from
side to side. They looked at it, too tired to even react to such
a small, ordinary problem, and it dashed past Doll's foot,
leapt off the lip of the trapdoor. It seemed to float on the air,
then dropped, vanishing into the dense smoke with a soft
plop.

Roundell grunted. ''Mad little bugger. Now even the animals are going crazy.''

The others nodded silent agreement, their eyes on Gath as
he moved to the open door, looked out at the Close.

Throughout the yard, smoke rose from a dozen fires started
by flaming spears and barrels of pitch thrown over the wall
by Ghapp's catapults. Most had been smothered by buckets
of sand, but here and there a wagon or building burned hotly.
Other wagons and lean-tos had been crushed by boulders,
and small groups of people knelt beside them, wailing with
grief for relatives and friends crushed under the rubble. The
thud of unseen objects hitting distant roofs and walls maintained a steady rhythm as the barrage continued, and more
barrels of flaming pitch, stones, spears and rot-infested bodies of dead animals flew over the walls.

Without turning, Gath spoke to Roundell. ''There's no
other way into those tunnels?''

''To some of them,'' Roundell replied. Gath looked at him,
and he added, ''Under the ruins, there is another maze of
tunnels, and they go deep into the rock. But I don't know
which ones link up with those under the Stronghold and
Close. No one does.'' He stood carefully and ambled painfully to the door, looked out at the fires, lowering his voice.
''There's no way you can go down there, friend. Not now.
There's no time even if you could. Ghapp will attack any
minute, and if you're not on the walls where everyone can
see you, the whole castle will panic. And that won't do her
or anyone any good.'' He looked at Gath and smiled, mock-

ing himself. "I'm telling you what you already know, aren't I?"

Gath nodded.

The sound of someone bounding down the stairwell made them turn; Billbarr, his face as white as milk, burst in, shouting, "They've been killed. Murdered! All of them!"

Advancing to the terrified boy, Gath took hold of his shoulders, "Calm down. What are you talking about?"

"Up there!" The boy pointed up. "In the armory! They're all dead. Murdered!"

"The women on guard?" Gath asked as the others, their faces startled, gathered around.

"Yes! I saw one of them. She was lying on the floor, and there was blood everywhere."

"You're sure she was dead?" Gath asked.

"She had to be." Billbarr sobbed. "She didn't move and blood was pouring out of her back. It was awful."

Fleka took Billbarr in her arms, comforting him. Her eyes held on Gath as he turned to Roundell.

"Probably a spear from one of their catapults."

"No! No!" Billbarr protested. "If it was a spear, I would have seen it. But there wasn't. Whoever killed her removed his weapon. And the others didn't reply when I called to them. There was . . . there was only the sound of dripping blood." Billbarr shuddered and held on to Fleka. "There's a madman up there, I just know there is. Someone's gone crazy!"

"All right, boy," Gath said softly, patting Billbarr's head. "I'll take care of it. Good work." The Barbarian turned to Roundell and Brown John. "I'll find out what's happened. You start moving everyone into the Close."

"We better go with you," Brown said, the old authority suddenly back in his voice. "It could be a madman, like the boy says. But it also could be more shadow men."

"My thoughts exactly," Roundell said.

Nodding, Gath picked up his axe and led Roundell and Brown into the stairwell. Taking four steps at a time, they reached the barracks room on the fourth floor. It was empty. The women had fled out the doors onto the wall walks. Weapons in hand, the trio moved up the narrow stairs, heading for the armory, made the landing and hesitated.

Up ahead, the door to the armory stood partially open. Below it, a trickle of blood ran over the lip of the top stair, fell in droplets to the one below.

The Barbarian unbuckled his headpiece, put it on. The living metal instantly warmed, sensing danger, and the horns straightened slightly, the sensitive tips pointing up at the room above.

"There's something up there," Gath whispered.

Moving stealthily, they advanced to the partially open door. A rivulet of blood, following a crack in the floorboards of the armory, passed under the door, feeding the steady drip. Gath pushed the door open with his axe.

The dark, gnarled roots of the huge lime tree, growing up through the stone ceiling, filled the center of the silent, shadowed room. The trail of blood followed the crack to a spiderlike puddle at the base of the roots, then circled to the left and vanished under the white arm of a woman lying on her back, her body hidden by the roots. Beyond the arm, a spill of sunlight glimmered brightly on the floor, reflecting light onto the rows of weapons and armor hung on the walls. The distant sounds of thudding missiles and wailing cries haunted the quiet gloom, and the stench of blood turned the hot air sticky.

Gath stepped into the room, indicating for Roundell and Brown to take the right side of the lime tree while he moved to the left. Reaching the woman, Gath stopped short.

Beyond her, a blanket of blood draped the wall below the open trapdoor in the ceiling. Sunlight streamed through the opening, turning the slow-moving blanket a bright scarlet. The helmeted head of one of Doll's Amazons dangled over the lip of the opening, her dead body lying unseen on the floor of the turret above.

There was no sign of a struggle. Everything was in place, except for the dead woman.

Kneeling, Gath inspected the ragged wound in the woman's chest, explored it with his fingers. Nearly four inches in diameter, it made a jagged tear in her leather armor, and penetrated the rib cage, crushing both breast- and backbones. Woody splinters stood in the leather beside the wound, and more cluttered the floor, dark and corrugated, like chips of bark. The woman's fist, locked in death, held something tightly. He pried the fingers apart and bits of crumpled green fell on the floor. Leaves.

Understanding passed behind Gath's eyes. Simultaneously, gasps of horror came from somewhere on the other side of the room, and Gath jumped up, two-handing his axe. A jagged shadow streaked across the spill of sunlight. He pivoted to face its source and his eyes widened within his helmet.

A thick branch of the lime tree, reaching down through the trapdoor, plunged for him. Its thick body scraped against the sides of the opening, shearing off shoots and twigs, stripping away crowds of leaves.

Gath brought up his axe, his muscles cording like ropes of steel along his arms. As if it had eyes, the branch veered past the sharp steel blade, offering it no more than scrapes of bark, and shot under his arm, whipped around his chest. He spread his legs, raised the axe and brought it down, intending to sever the branch from the tree. The massive roots filling the center of the room swelled, ripped through the stone floor in cracking waves, throwing him sideways, and the axe blade clanked against the floor.

He staggered upright, and shoots from the branch wrapped themselves around his arms, wrenching them backward and pulling them sideways. The axe fell from his hands.

He roared, his arms thrashed and flames spewed from the eye slits of the horned helmet, incinerating bark and sapwood. Another shoot wrapped around his neck, yanked his head back. The branches, gripping him tightly, hauled him off his feet, up through the trapdoor, banging him against the door frame as he spewed flames harmlessly against the walls and ceiling.

He caught a glimpse of Roundell and Brown John watching in horror below the stairwell, then the branch thrust him high, and more branches took hold of his ankles and wrists. They spread-eagled him, thrust him into the thick foliage at the top of the tree. Flames spit from the horned helmet, burning away stems, leaves and branches, then shot into the sky, plumes of black smoke rising off the tips of the fiery tongues, like banners of doom.

He heard the enlarging roots rip up through the stone turret below him, splitting it apart, tearing down the ramparts and hoardings. He listened to the rubble bang and clatter against the sides of Round Tower, then thud against the ground far below, as the distant screams of onlookers announced their passage.

He surged higher as the tree continued to erupt with growth, rising and spreading its branches wide. Proud. Triumphant. Displaying its prisoner for all to see.

Wailing grief and horror rose up out of the castle.

In reply, the tree shook and convulsed, as if bent by laughter. Then the branches straightened. The bark tore flesh on his ankles and wrists. The thongs binding his armor burst. The shoulder pieces fell away, and the breastplates followed, bouncing off woody limbs and scattering leaves on the air.

He watched them fall, and drops of his blood joined them, landing on the ground three hundred feet below. Then the tree began to pull him apart.

Forty-five

CHICKEN BROTH

Brown and Roundell scrambled over the roots, now grown down through the stairwell, splitting the walls, filling the stairs with rubble.

Halfway down, Roundell slipped. A foot stuck between two roots and his weight threw him against the jagged bark of a root, ripping his leg wound open. Cursing, he pushed himself to his feet and grabbed his thigh, trying to pull his leg free, and blood welled between his fingers. He tried to pry the root away and blackness invaded his brain. He teetered, felt the *bukko* catch him by the armpits, then passed out.

When he came to, Brown John stood over him, and Doll Harl held him in her arms, feeding him hot chicken broth from a clay cup. They sat on the floor of the barracks room, against a heap of bedding. The roots had stopped growing, but had left the room a mess. At the hearth, Billbarr and Fleka worked by the fire, brewing more soup.

Dust covered everything and most of the bunks lay shattered on the floor, crushed by falling stones. Thin roots now grew down through cracks and holes in the ceiling, their fuzzy tips dangling in the air, while large ones twisted down through the walls, revealing themselves where their huge demonic limbs had cracked open holes in the wall big enough to stand in. The doors to the north and south sections of the western wall, and to the wall linking Round Tower to Moat Tower, all stood open.

Outside, the rabble crowded the walls, stared in silent horror at whatever had happened to Gath, or was happening.

Roundell questioned Brown with his eyes.

"He's still alive," Brown said, pulling up a stool. "The tree's been trying to pull him apart, and he's trying to do the same thing to it. A bunch of us tried to get up there, but the tree sensed us, killed three before we gave it up."

"Arrows? Spears?" Roundell asked.

"The tree is stitched with them, but it doesn't notice any more than a normal tree. We also tried to severe the roots, but that's dangerous. We lost another two that way." Brown looked off at nothing. "I don't know what else to do."

Roundell nodded thoughtfully, then asked, "How long have I been out?"

"Nearly an hour," Doll said, holding the bowl to his lips. "Here, this will get your strength back."

He sipped the soup, relishing the heat as it poured down through his chest into his belly, and frowned playfully at Doll. "I thought I ordered wine."

"You did," she replied in kind, "and three virgins to go with it. But this is what you get."

She fed his grinning face more soup, as he put his eyes on the *bukko*.

The old man held a thin red-leather tube containing a rolled parchment, yellowed and cracked by age. His eyes held Roundell's as he spoke.

"Can you move?" the *bukko* asked.

Roundell tried to sit up and dizziness dropped him back into Doll's arms. He shook his head. "Not yet. You'll have to take command. What's our situation?"

"Ghapp attacked as soon as he saw the tree had him. That's what he was waiting for. Somehow Tiyy corrupted the tree, probably all of them. So the towers have been abandoned, leaving them defenseless. But the attack stopped once they realized the tree hadn't killed him. Now everyone, inside and outside the castle, is just sitting on their hands, watching Gath and the tree. Waiting."

"How long can he hold out?"

"I don't know," Brown said tiredly, his eyes awash with enough tragedy for three wars, then said it again.

"Oh, that helps a lot, bukko," Roundell said bitterly. "Now's exactly the time to get dramatic on me." The *bukko*'s cheeks turned the color of red apples and his flashy, white eyebrows stabbed down over his angry eyes. Roundell grinned. "That's better. Now, think it out. You know him. How long can he and that headpiece last? How can we help him?"

"I do not know him," Brown said levelly. "Not like that. I can't help him."

"The girl can, though, right? I saw her do some pretty fancy tricks in the forest."

The *bukko* nodded. "Robin might be able to help. As soon as the smoke cleared, I sent Graybeard and some of your men into the tunnels to look for her. But they haven't found a trace of her, and we're running out of time. Tiyy's drugged her troops. They'll attack again any moment."

Roundell frowned thoughtfully and glanced at the red-leather tube. "You get that in the library?" Brown John nodded and Jarl asked, "Any help there?"

Brown shook his head. "Surim handed it to me as he died. It, by some miracle of fate, is the formula I was looking for. But all it's told me is that I've been playing the fool better than it's ever been played before."

"Words," Roundell grunted, as if discussing manure. "I never did trust them anyway."

A deafening howl came from outside the castle, followed by the sounds of charging bodies and clattering armor, and they glanced out the doors, as the men-at-arms on the wall walks crouched down behind the crenellations.

"Here they come," Doll said, the color on her cheeks suddenly pale.

Grim-faced, Roundell looked at Brown. "It's up to us, bukko."

Brown smiled dangerously. "What's the plot, or do we have one?"

"Yes. There's a ditch being dug outside the eastern wall, just above the lower yards. Your sons are in charge of it. The ditch leads from the moat into the lower yards. When it's complete, we let Ghapp's army in through the gate, then seal them in and drown the lot. My men in the gate towers have barricaded themselves in. When you're ready, signal them and they'll dam the gate." He nodded at Doll. "Doll has the flag."

"The people in the lower yards will drown."

Doll shook her head as she stood. "Half have already been moved into the Close, and I'll go now and make sure the others do the same."

Brown stood and the two started out, then looked back at Roundell with concerned expressions.

"Go on," he growled. "Get out of here."

They hurried out, and he sat still, gasping for breath. When he had it, he picked up the bowl. It was empty. He sat back. His fingers and legs felt as cold as gloves left in the snow. His cheeks and forehead were hot and wet to the touch. He glanced at Fleka and Billbarr, and the pair hurried to him, bringing a steaming bowl of soup and large spoon.

"Here are the virgins you ordered," Fleka said, smiling.

Roundell chuckled. "You're catching on," he said to the pair of them, then drank the soup.

Forty-six
UP BY LAMPLIGHT

The red glow of the four tiny eyes staring at Robin cast the only light into the darkness. A glimmer that illuminated two furry snouts. The eyes belonged to rats. She knew that because one had crawled over her leg. The rodents perched on something about five feet off, and she was strangely grateful for their threatening presence. They gave her something to look at.

She could not see her knees drawn up against her chest, nor the walls of the tunnel or the ceiling. Blackness surrounded her, only penetrated by tunnels just as black, and she was too worn and cut and terrified to crawl any farther into them. She now wandered through the corridors of her mind. But there she was also lost.

Why, if she were indeed the White Veshta and the source of all light, couldn't she produce a blaze of shooting stars to light her way? Or even an armful of radiating diamonds, as she had done when freeing Gath from the demon powers of the living helmet in the forest? One bright candle would do, even the puny glow of a firefly. But she was empty. Her own soul had become a place of darkness, of fear and guilt and bitter remorse.

She cursed herself, but did a poor job of it. Having had no interest in vulgarities and base epithets, she could only bring to mind colorless condemnations. Simpleton. Idiot. Prunehead! She laughed bitterly at her own inadequacy and the rats, apparently shocked by her outburst, scurried about and vanished a moment, before returning to their places.

A draft of cold air passed between her legs, and she shivered at its touch, sat forward. Then it went away as suddenly as it had arrived, providing no opportunity to search out its source. She tousled her hair for the thousandth time, making sure no spider had decided to use it as a nest, then held still, sniffing the air. A faint odor drifted through the darkness, the scent of something burning. Torches? No. It smelled like candlewax. She dropped onto all fours to chase it, then it too was gone, a musty dankness again filling the air.

She sank back against the stone wall, finding comfort in the fact that the heat of her own body had warmed it slightly. She wondered what Brown John would have to say in such a circumstance. Not the new, glory-seeking Brown John, but her old friend, companion and savior. His endless twaddle had kept her, Gath and Jakar, and even the mysterious Queen of Serpents, going when all seemed lost so long ago. What was it the *bukko* had said when he first met her? That she, Robin Lakehair, with the *bukko* at her side, could take the first step into a new age of adventure, into the childhood of a time made for legends. And what had he said only months later when the Lords of Destruction chased her? That she was now cast in a splendid part, one on which the greatest artists of the stage had made their careers.

Robin grinned bitterly. The wonderful old fool had always had the right words ready to dance on his tongue, words that inevitably cheered her, filled her with hope. But now, if she was going to find a part to play, one that would keep her from losing all control over her fears, she had to find the words herself.

Gathering in a tight ball, she propped her chin on her knees and made her mind chase itself down its empty corridors, searching for a memory, a thought, an image dwelling there. Suddenly the words came to her.

It was a line of dialogue from *Up by Lamplight*, a line she had delivered on countless stages, both for small crowds gathered on street corners and for crowds of hundreds arranged in neat rows in fine arenas. But now, as she said them aloud with only herself for an audience, there was no trace of theatrical aplomb or fiction in the words, no trace of the actress, only testament to a subtle truth.

She said, " 'It is in times of darkness, my lord, that we most often find the way to paradise.' "

She smiled to herself, recalling how, after saying the line on stage, she would casually blow out her candle and place the hand of the actor, playing the philandering lord, on the slope of her breast. The audience inevitably hooted and whistled, wanting more, and that cued the actor playing her cuckolded husband to rush on stage with a flaming torch and sword in his hands.

It was in this kind of vulgar metaphor that Brown John claimed the greatest truths lay hidden. Now, alone and lost in the dark underground world of the castle, which was to have served as the stage for her most brilliant performance, Robin Lakehair finally understood what those few simple, teasing words from *Up by Lamplight* meant. She realized that the darkness referred to was the darkness of the soul, and that paradise was the revelation of dreams hiding deep within the soul, concealed by hard layers of pride and guilt and fear and shame, layers that only the sharp edge of despair could penetrate, as it did now. Without hope, with no one but herself to argue and deal with, she finally understood herself.

She did not want to be a goddess. She did not want to perform miracles and make great displays of glorious light. She did not want to be venerated, adored, praised, glorified and worshiped from afar. She did not want to be eternally young and forever beautiful. She wanted to set her childhood behind her, along with her innocence and naive expectations. She wanted to taste all of life, to smell the manure as well as the rose. She wanted to run free in the wildwood with the wind on her face and hair, and bathe in the waterfall, dry in the sun. She wanted to cry and tear her hair when her heart broke. She wanted to weep for Jakar, then set him on the shelf of memory and drive him from her daily thoughts, start again. She wanted to love Gath with all her heart, openly and freely, to feel his heart beat against hers, to be the woman to his man, be filled by his passion and make his child. She wanted all this and more, to dance to the song of the tambourine and drum, and give life to laughter and tears wherever, whenever and however she could. With a smile, a saucy breast, a crude joke or the songs of the lark and whippoorwill.

This truth was a madness within her, and she knew it was this truth that had dimmed the jewels of the goddess, put them out one by one. She had no regrets. She was being transformed by her own dreams, becoming a woman again with all the weaknesses and struggles, as well as the joys that entailed. She understood she would undoubtedly die where she sat, alone, and be eaten by rats. But that changed nothing. She was resolved to stop reaching for dreams and take hold of the day.

With this settled, she felt unusually relieved and content, and did nothing for a long moment. Then she realized that her day now consisted of a labyrinth of long dark holes and two rats, and that she had to deal with it.

She lay down slowly, facing the rats, and edged toward them, cooing tenderly. She had tamed the wolf, the hummingbird and hawk, so a pair of rats should be easy. The rodents watched her advance until she was within three feet, then scattered about wildly, and again returned to their perch.

Undaunted, Robin inched forward, then paused, as the rats parted slightly. A third set of eyes suddenly appeared between them, larger and brighter. Furry sounds and the faint clatter of tiny claws echoed through the stone tunnel. Then more eyes appeared, the eyes of ten, eleven, then sixteen rats. The red glow illuminated their furry bodies and spilled dim light three feet across the wet ground.

Robin studied the pests thoughtfully, then glanced from side to side, searching for a speck of light or glitter, anything that might be causing the red reflections in the rats' eyes. There was no light, just as she knew there would not be, and a shudder swept through her as she backed away hurriedly.

The red glow came from within the rats, and she knew it for what it was. Raw hatred. Thirty-two feral eyes glowing with the volcanic heat of the Master of Darkness. Demon spawn.

Feeling the rough-hewn walls with her hands, Robin found the opening of a side tunnel, turned on her hands and knees, and fled farther into the darkness. A moment passed, and the crowd of red eyes scurried after her.

Forty-seven

THE MAN STORM

The tree stood above Round Tower like a leafy colossus, its massive roots twisted in a rough embrace, grasping the tower's two top stories. Erect and proud and green, the plant displayed its prisoner, Gath of Baal, to Tiyy's army as it surged over the shallow cliffs to the walls of the lower yards, threw up scaling ladders, filled the air with arrows.

Naked except for helmet and belted loincloth, only Gath's boots and wristguards protected his flesh against the limb's bite. Where they gripped his knees, chest and shoulders, his flesh was bloody pulp. Lacerations decorated his throat, like a gaudy necklace.

The tree had obviously recognized him by the headpiece, and now, for the hundredth time, pulled his helmeted head backward, poked thin stems through the eye slits. The helmet promptly incinerated them and Gath wrenched his head forward, tearing off and splitting young branches.

The tree took little notice. It stretched its limbs and shook its leafy hair in the late-day sun. Then it swayed and posed, allowing a breeze to preen its faceless body. Not like a beast, like a proud beauty. Tiyy had obviously endowed the plant with her own personality, as well as making it a life-taker.

Gath of Baal more sensed these things than considered them. His mind, battered by incessant pain, had lost the faculties of articulate reasoning and speech. His primal animal nature almost possessed him, reducing thought to instinct, as it panted and clawed inside him, seeking total release. But pride held it at bay.

The tree pulled harder. His body stretched, and contracted, each muscle refusing to allow the tree to tear it out of each bony joint, each bone refusing to be ripped out of each restraining socket. His blood ran rampant under his flesh, making it steam and drip, draining him of fluids. His mouth felt like a dry, dirt hole, his lips like desert sand. Aching numbness dwelled in bone and flesh and mind. The wind battered every pore as if it were an open wound, blowing his blood into the air, atomizing it as if it were some savage perfume. He drank of it, tasting himself, and the animal burst free of the man's restraining grip.

Nature's child once again, bone and blood took command, centering his primordial hunger for life, like the eye of a storm.

His fists curled at the extremities of his outstretched arms. His head thrust down. His knees came up, slow and grudging, fighting the thick branches. The bark bit deep and his blood flowed freely down the boughs.

The tree stiffened. Its trunk undulated upward until it was almost erect. The branches slowly inched his limbs back to their original positions, once more holding him like he was meat to be quartered.

The eye slits of the horned helmet rebelled, turning to fire. His body shuddered, showering the air with beads of sweat and blood. Suddenly his head shook like a wild beast, throwing shards of fire in all directions, and the storm within him roared forth from the mouth hole. An animal cry that thundered above the racket of war. The primal song of the Death Dealer born long ago, in the Age of Howling.

The besiegers hesitated halfway up their scaling ladders,

peered over their palisades and embankments, and from behind the frames of their mighty catapults and wicker shields.

The rabble on the walls and in the yards of the castle stared up at the tree, mouths open.

The Barbarian contracted. His fists balled, his knees came up, his arms drew his fists to his chest. The tree shook and strained, trying to restrain him, but could not. His head bent farther forward and his body curled up into a ball, hiding itself within the thicket of leaves and branches. The tree's body creaked and groaned in inarticulate speech.

Branches yanked Gath's head back, pulled an arm free, but the Barbarian gathered again, draining the plant's demonic strength. Moments passed. Suddenly sap burst through seams in the bark of the limbs binding Gath, flowed over his naked flesh, burning him. He ignored the pain, bunched his body tighter.

The tree shuddered, moaned, the sound high-pitched and strangely female.

Tiyy's army let out a gasp, then roared with defiant anger, as if Gath were punishing their queen herself, and the sounds of war again shook the air and earth.

For Gath, the sounds were faint compared to roar of the pain within him. He growled and shot flame from the eye slits of the horned helmet, trying to incinerate the surrounding branches. But only a sputter of sparks and a spew of black smoke came forth.

The tree convulsed, gathering around him, then suddenly straightened. His limbs exploded away from his torso. The pain sang through him, a high-pitched heat. He gasped and flexed his entire frame, stopping the pull of the branches just short of being torn apart. His chest heaved up and down as he filled his empty lungs with long, harsh gasps of air.

The tree stretched again. He held on. It tried once more, but its strength had slackened. It quit after giving him nothing more than a tug. The fire died behind the eye slits, and a hard glitter shone in his gray eyes.

Moments passed, neither plant nor man giving an inch as they struggled. Again sap seeped through the bark, this time from the trunk, smoking and sizzling. Lesions opened on the limbs, and runny pus leaked out. Odd, gnarled growths erupted on the trunk at the yokes of the branches. The trunk twisted violently, and bent itself low, deformed, as if it had been mauled by lightning and a thousand years of violent winds. The bright green leaves grew limp, then yellow spread from their stems to their tips. A brownish red followed, and the leaves turned dry and brittle, began to fall away.

Gath waited, the way the rock waits. A breeze swept across the Barbarian's hot body, and the storm inside him abated slightly. His mind began to order itself and put words to his thoughts. The once resplendent tree had been humbled, now he would shame it. He gathered his strength, then shook himself violently, whipping the branches back and forth, and the dead leaves flew away in droves, floated to the ground, leaving the tree naked.

Gasps and shouts rose out of the rabble standing in the Close. Except for the men-at-arms on the walls of the lower yards, everyone now occupied the Sacred Close, and every face watched him, mouths open and cheering. The men waved swords and spears, and the women bright scarves.

The tree tried to pull at him, but its limbs, now stiff and brittle with sudden age, lacked coordination. Bark on the shoots and sprigs wrapping Gath's wrists peeled off. The wood underneath had the color of driftwood, and cracks seamed its length.

Gath stretched his legs and yanked them up, cracking and splintering the branches, releasing his ankles and knees. The broken limbs fell away, clattering against adjacent branches, then dropped toward the castle below, roars of approval greeting them.

Dangling by both arms, Gath ripped one arm free and sank onto a lower branch. There he tugged on the branch still holding his other arm, and it cracked apart.

Descending the trunk, he reached the roots. The handle of his axe stuck up out of them, pinned by two roots. He took hold of the handle, set his feet on the roots and pulled. The blade ripped up through the emaciated, dry wood as easily as if cutting through rotten flesh.

. The plant shuddered, then branches began to crack and fall
as death set in.

Two-handing his axe, he advanced along the roots to the
rim of the tower, looking down at the crowd jammed in the
Close. Every man, woman and child sang his name.

"Gath! Gath! Gath!"

He held his axe over his head with both hands, acknowledging them, as the tree crumbled to a stump behind him,
and they sang it again.

Forty-eight
THE FLOOD

A harsh, half-mad howling turned the Barbarian toward the
battle.

Tiyy's reserves were charging across the muddy river and
up the cliffs to the support of their comrades already scaling
the castle walls. More troops swarmed through the burnt-
down Outpost and across the bridge, carrying scaling ladders
and battering rams.

In the valley, troops of cavalry, speartips flashing in the
sun, galloped from behind the raised embankments, deploy-
ing to rush the gate when it fell. Tiyy, in black metallic armor, led them.

Hurriedly climbing down through upended stones and
woody roots, Gath reached the barracks room. There Fleka
and Billbarr helped Doll's harlots tend wounded men-at-arms.
Seeing Gath, the young pair smiled with relief, and started
toward him with bandages. He waved them off with an encouraging nod, and they returned to their duties as he stepped
beside Doll Harl and Jarl Roundell.

She stood in a jagged opening in the wall, overlooking the lower yards, signal flag in hand. Roundell, unusually pale and grinning his soldier's grin, sat on the floor, his back against a broken stump of wall. The racket of battle thundered through the hole above his head.

"I'm glad you're finished, friend," Roundell said, as if Gath had been shaving. "Now the fun can begin."

He looked up at Doll, and the sturdy woman waved her signal flag vigorously at several men-at-arms standing on the ramparts of the distant gate tower. They waved their arms in reply, vanished and Doll turned to Roundell and Gath. "They saw it, went to open the gate."

The two men nodded, and the Barbarian squatted, touched Roundell's wounded leg, and the blood dripping from his arm decorated the mercenary's bandage.

"The leg's all right," Roundell said, "but keep bleeding on it like that. It makes me look like a hero."

Creaking wood and the clank of heavy chains rose above the bedlam, and shouts went up outside the walls.

"Here they come," Doll said, hard fear lowering her voice a good two octaves.

Roundell turned and they peered out through the broken opening.

At the bridge, the invaders suddenly surged forward and plunged through the open gate. A moment passed, then they charged into the lower yards, spreading out like spilled wine. Their hot, leering faces, broadened by expectations of plunder, rape, revenge, led them. They obviously believed, as Gath and Roundell had hoped they would, that their own troops had somehow taken the wall and opened the gates.

Outside the walls, the besiegers abandoned their scaling ladders and raced for the bridge and gate. The deployed cavalry, led by Tiyy and Ghapp, drove a wedge between the rushing bodies and galloped across the bridge.

In the Market Court, the invader's front ranks suddenly slowed, wary at not having met any opposition. But their comrades, shoving and hollering behind them, drove them on, the swarming bodies surging toward the Close. A shower of spears soared down from the wall defending the Close, and brought them to a sudden stop. Bodies fell. The front ranks tried to turn. The soldiers packed solid behind them kept coming, as more erupted out of the gate passage. The best the invaders could do was mill and catch spears and arrows in their bodies.

Tiyy and Ghapp galloped into the yard and plowed into the rear of the shouting, reeling melee. Horses trampled legs and backs, rearing and kicking wildly. Men screamed. Tiyy and Ghapp, unable to see what the problem was, drove their mounts through the bodies, their horse bludgeoning them aside, and led her savages toward slightly higher ground, the unoccupied Water Court.

Gath and Roundell shared a nod. Doll waved her flag again, and the men-at-arms on the rampart of the gate tower again waved in reply, vanished.

A moment passed, then the screech of the dropping portcullis rose above the din of battle. The jam of soldiers crossing the bridge suddenly bunched to a stop, and dust boiled out of the gate, smothering them.

"The gate's dammed," Doll said.

"Don't tell me," Roundell said soberly, "tell the men in the Moat Tower."

Doll leaned out of the opening and waved her flag at the distant Moat Tower. The man standing in its turret waved back, then raced to the opposite side of the turret, climbed into embrasures, began to shout down at the unseen workers on the ground outside the east wall.

Doll turned to Roundell and Gath and nodded, once.

Roundell gave her a wink, turned to Gath. "This is it, friend, this will decide it."

"The ditch is ready?"

"It better be. The bukko went to make certain just before you walked in."

Grim-faced, the two men stared across the lower yards at the gaping hole in the east wall of the Market Court. No water showed in it.

"Where's the water?" Gath growled. "Something's wrong."

"Signal them again," Roundell barked.

Doll signaled them again.

The figures in the Moat Tower waved back again.

No water issued from the ditch.

"Zatt!" Roundell snarled.

The mercenary turned to Gath, but the Barbarian was already moving. He crossed the room in four strides, and bounded out the door onto the wall walk linking Round Tower to Moat Tower.

Men-at-arms, firing arrows and throwing spears down at the trapped invaders, blocked his passage. He leapt into an embrasure, rolled onto the crenellated wall and jumped to his feet, already running. Leaping the embrasures, he ran the length of the zigzagging wall, made the Moat Tower, entering the room below the turret. It was empty. He dashed across it and out the door onto the wall walk of the east wall. Ladders descended from the embrasures to the ground outside. He jumped up into an embrasure and growled silently.

A deep ditch twenty feet wide had been dug from the base of the wall at the northeast corner of the lower yards, up the inclined slope to the side of the flooded moat, fifty strides to the north. There, Brown John, Bone, Dirken, and half a dozen men struggled frantically, trying to remove the last section of rock sealing off the moat. A wall of limestone at least five feet wide and no telling how deep, it ran both north and south alongside the moat for better than thirty feet. There was no way around it. The stone had to be removed.

Gath more slid than climbed down a ladder, ran toward the work gang. Using crowbars and hammers, it attacked both ends of the obstruction. Seeing him arrive, their faces blanched with shock, disbelief, but continued to rain blows on the white rock.

"Holy Veshta!" Brown gasped between blows. "We thought you were dead."

Gath made no reply. He strode out onto the shelf of rock, found a crack near the center, straddled it and raised his axe over his head. Muscles corded up his arms and down his legs and he brought the blade down like a stroke of lightning, driving the cutting edge deep into the crack. He glanced at Bone, extending his hands, and the burly redhead tossed him his huge hammer. Once, twice, three times he hammered the thick haft of his axehead, driving it deeper and deeper into the rock. With the fourth blow, he growled like a thundercloud, and the blow cracked the stone apart, splitting it in six directions.

Huge chunks fell away under the Barbarian's feet. He dropped to a knee. More rock crumbled under him, cracking loudly. He jumped back. His foot landed on loose pebbles and he went over backward, dropping his axe, splashing into the moat.

He sank two feet and the current turned him upside down, threw him and its own wet body into the ditch, crushing the remaining wall aside.

Gath saw Brown and the others standing at the side of the ditch, staring down at him in mute horror, then sank deep. He fought to reach the surface, but the water had no interest in his efforts. It carried him deeper, as if he had no more will than an autumn leaf.

Holding his breath, he jabbed with his hands and feet at the rough sides of the ditch, trying to avoid its bite, then lost control and tumbled over and over. A stone ripped open his back. Another ate into his calf. Suddenly the raging torrent of white water swept him to the surface, and he sluiced down the center of the flume, still in no more control of his progress than spittle in a flooded rain gutter.

Up ahead, the huge jagged hole at the base of the eastern wall frothed at the edges as the torrent swept through it, leaving barely a foot of air between its rushing surface and the top of the hole. Gath rolled onto his back, thrust his arms up out of the water, and grabbed at the edge of the hole as he passed into it.

His fingers caught hold of the ragged edge, brought him to a stop and his body tossed wildly on the surface as the thundering wet body of the river roared under him into the lower yards.

Moments passed, then the rock crumbled under his fingers, and he swept into the hole. He grabbed at the ceiling, caught hold of a deep cleft and hung on. Hauling his head and shoulders out of the water, he got an arm in the cleft and jammed the rim of his helmet against it. Hanging in the torrent, he sucked in deep gasps of wet air, filling his lungs. Suddenly the water picked up speed, filling the tunnel, and he turned his masked face away from its rush, held his breath. Waited.

The pressure increased. Apparently a wider opening had been torn in the limestone wall, allowing more water to spill in from the moat. His lungs began to ache, demanding air. A heavy rush of water hammered his body against the ceiling of the hole. The cleft jammed against the rim of the horned helmet, and pushed it up around his cheeks. Then part of the cleft crumbled and the water took him, ripping off the helmet.

He spilled into the water-filled yard, and the rush of the torrent carried him two-thirds of the way across, tumbling him end over end. Suddenly it gentled its hold on him, and swept him down the center of the main spill. On both sides, screaming, thrashing bodies churned up to the surface of the huge, rapidly rising pool. Others simply floated on the surface, their only movement caused by the pull and swirl of the water, already drowned.

At the far edges of the pool, drenched, weaponless soldiers hauled themselves out of the water onto the staircases rising to the eastern wall. They quickly climbed the stairs to the battlements, seeking safety from the arrows and spears streaking from the Sacred Close. But the ramparts facing the yard had been removed from the wall walk, leaving them exposed to the barrage. Catching spears and arrows in their chests, hips and legs, the escapees fell back into the water from which they had fled.

Taking a deep breath, Gath dove deep and swam underwater toward the gate towers. He passed through the limp legs of a dozen drowned men and turned away from a group of thrashing horses. Then the south wall loomed ahead, a greenish white beyond the veil of water, and he surfaced. Here the water calmed, swirling in eddies that gradually gathered in a slow current, ebbing through the narrow passage between the gate towers. The makeshift dam had held, but obviously leaked.

Looking from side to side, Gath saw the remnant of Izzam Ghapp's army making a stand in the Water Court and adjacent ruins below the west wall. Then he floated into the gate passage, and it cut off his vision.

Up ahead, where the water passed under the gate building, a clump of drowned bodies swirled in the shadows, crowding against the top of the lowered portcullis. Splashing and gasping, three soldiers fought off the push of the dead ones, as they clung to the portcullis. Then they tried to climb up through a murder hole. Spears stabbed down out of the hole, killing two and discouraging a third.

Gath swam hard for the side of the passage, reaching it before he was swept under the building covering the middle of the passage. Thrusting an arm into a loophole, he hung on, shouting and waving up at three of Roundell's men-at-arms looking down from the ramparts of the gate.

Instantly recognizing the swarthy Barbarian, they fetched a rope, tied it to an embrasure and threw it down to him. Grasping it, Gath climbed hand-over-hand up to the ramparts and the soldiers helped him into the turret. From there he could see the battle.

In the Water Court, Ghapp's surviving troops were taking a heavy toll of the men-at-arms defending the west wall, gathering to rush it.

In the ruins, Tiyy scrambled among the tangled rubble and trails, as if searching for something, while several of her outlaws guarded her back trail. Suddenly she drew her dagger, dashed down a stairwell leading to the underground tunnels beneath the ruins.

A chill ran up the Barbarian's spine. Somehow the black bitch's magic told her where Robin was. He turned to dash down the stairwell, and a loud rumble filled the castle.

A piece of the southern wall had collapsed and water splashed through the breach, roaring and churning. Thundering cracks of splitting rock joined the noise, and more slabs of wall collapsed under the pressure of the now deep pool of water. Buildings caved in. Geysers erupted, thick with dead bodies. More walls exploded away, seemingly from all quarters of the lower yards, and the pool spilled away in all directions, carrying the drowned army back out of the castle on a gushing flood of white water. Emptying the castle.

Gath dashed down the stairwell into the room above the gate passage. He plucked a sword off a wall rack, lowered himself down through the murder hole, and dropped onto the rubble of corpses heaped in the passage. Leaping free of their entangling limbs, he plunged through the thigh-deep water and splashed back into the Market Court.

On the eastern side of the yard, the rushing water, still being fed by the moat, flowed steadily, following the natural depression in the ground. In the rest of the yard, the level had dropped to no more than two or three feet, and the survivors of Tiyy's army now dashed out of the Water Court, churned through the water, fled out a huge breach in the west wall.

Gath splashed across the yard into the Water Court and slowed, glancing around carefully. Except for the dead, it appeared empty. Then he saw him.

At the opposite end of the yard, Izzam Ghapp stood under the protective branches of one of the huge lime trees clustered around the well. His bald head hung low between his narrow shoulders as he faced the Barbarian, a battleaxe in one hand and the horned helmet in the other.

Forty-nine

THE HORNED HELMET

Gath kept moving, measuring his stride. An expression slightly darker than the dead of night snarled his blunt features. There was no time for more than two or three strokes.

Izzam Ghapp straightened, the red spots on his forehead glowing with immaculate corruption.

Gath bolted forward, threw his sword like a spear.

Startled, Ghapp more staggered than lunged aside, and the blade creased the side of his armor, buried itself in the trunk of the lime tree behind him.

Moving to a tangle of drowned soldiers, Gath squatted over them, came away with a war hammer. The Siegemaster backed around the tree into the sunlight, a huge vein pulsing across his bald head like a shiny worm. He glanced from side to side, found himself alone, and backed up some more.

With the hammer poised in his hands, Gath advanced through the shade of the tree into the sunlight.

Ghapp rested his battleaxe against his hip, raised the horned helmet over his head and held it there. His arms trembled uncertainly. Sweat drained over his frightened face. The three red dots on his forehead flamed, snarled with black smoke. Then he drew up, as imperious and contemptuous as a monument, apparently gorged with a narcotic delirium.

Was he fool enough to put the helmet on? Gath decided to find out. He charged. The Kitzakk pulled the helmet down over his head and grabbed up his battleaxe, his body cocked. Gath slowed, a smile as dark as wet rock gathering behind his eyes.

The shrieks of terrified women lifted Ghapp even more majestically, then his chest heaved like a bellows, suddenly expanding, bending out his chest armor. Its thongs popped at the seams, and the armor fell in pieces to his thighs, clattered on the ground. He stared down at himself in confusion. His legs trembled under him, then lurched with sudden growth and he staggered. His upper body dipped sideways, throwing him off balance. He stumbled two feet in one direction, three feet back the other way, then righted himself. Looking up, Ghapp's eyes widened within the horned helmet as he saw the Barbarian closing on him. He started to raise his battleaxe, but his arms were too busy growing, and he dropped it instead.

Planting his feet, Gath swung the heavy head of his hammer in a short arc. The flat face crushed the Kitzakk's bulging knee with a wet splat, and took it out from under him.

Ghapp hit the ground with a metallic crunch and rolled, out of control. His muscles bunched under his chain mail, splitting and altering it at will. His arms corded. Their bulging veins crawled over them, up into his neck. His hands grabbed the horned helmet, trying to force it off, and the hot metal scorched them, the living horns twisting like snakes.

Ghapp rolled onto his hands and knees and Gath rose up over him, hammered the helmet to the ground with one blow. Ghapp roared with pain, lifted his head, and Gath's hammer met the face of the helmet. The blow stood Ghapp up on his knees. The Kitzakk's huge, muscled arms drifted at his sides, his mind dazed.

Gath hit him again and again, but Ghapp's now huge, muscled body refused to topple. Jagged bolts of fire erupted from the helmet, shot into the air, scorched the stone ground, then caught Gath across the chest and neck. He staggered back, stunned and smoking, and the hammer fell from his hand.

Ghapp, teetering unsteadily, dropped onto his hands and knees. The fire disappeared behind the eye slits, and he stared blankly at the Barbarian, his mind roasted by the helmet's fire.

Suddenly he lurched to his feet and his bashed knee wobbled, tried to throw him down. But it could not. The horned helmet now mastered the man, and he felt no pain. The headpiece raised up demonically, its steel flashing and pulsing with power, bright against the dark foliage of a lime tree not ten feet behind him.

Gath charged recklessly. The thick corded arms of the Kitzakk rose to catch him. Gath turned his shoulder, drove under Ghapp's arms, rammed his hips, driving him backward. The Kitzakk's arms dropped, caught the Barbarian's back and they hit the ground together. Thrashing and kicking, they rolled into the shade cast by the lime tree.

The Kitzakk squeezed the breath from the Barbarian, and Gath felt his ribs about to crack. Then the ground shook under them, rising and falling with undulating swells, like an ocean wave, as the roots of the lime trees suddenly expanded.

The movement loosened the Kitzakk's grip, and Gath squirmed onto his back. Izzam Ghapp reached for the Barbarian's neck, and Gath's arms blocked him. The horned helmet roared, rose up to strike with its horns, and the branches of lime tree dove down out of the shadowy foliage, wrapped themselves around Ghapp's neck and shoulders. The helmet screamed to no avail. Limb after limb thrust down, took hold of the Kitzakk, then pulled him off the Barbarian.

The plant thrust Ghapp high, spread-eagled his body against the sky, and the man howled with rage and pain. Fire spit from the face of the horned helmet. His body shuddered, straining against the pull of the limbs. Suddenly the tree straightened, and Ghapp exploded into the air in pieces, his blood coloring the air. The tree discarded his bloody torso like an apple core, and flailed its limbs in triumph, throwing bloody pieces of the Siegemaster into the air.

Gath did not watch. He grabbed up the Kitzakk's battleaxe, raced into the tunnel leading to the ruins. Erupting from the other end, he leapt over the rubble, bounding from rock to rock, made the opening into the underground labyrinth he had seen Tiyy use. A dark savage in black furs squatted on the steps, guarding the opening and marking her trail. The Barbarian cut him down before the man got halfway to his feet, and leapt into the darkness below, searching for more trail markers.

Rounding a corner, he saw a torch held by a man standing over another dead savage. Jarl Roundell, bloody sword in hand. The mercenary, showing no shock or surprise at Gath's arrival, cast the light over the mouth of a tunnel descending into the ground.

"I've searched that one," Roundell said, his tone steady and even, as if planning a battle instead of standing in the middle of it, then cast the torchlight over a black abysslike hole. "Let's try this one."

They went that way.

Fifty

THE FETISH

Tiyy stood still, the hostile whites of her eyes unnaturally luminous in the pitch-black underworld. The darkness comforted her, as it always did, but she had no idea which way to go. After descending more than four stories through twisting switchback tunnels, the rat had led her to a hole too small for her to pass through. Now she waited for the rat to return with a new route.

A tiny pair of red eyes appeared thirty feet off. She hurried toward them, the unseen irregular floor of the tunnel coming under her feet as naturally as if she ran through a sunlit day. Suddenly the red eyes disappeared, and she stopped. The rodent, too eager to serve her, had raced ahead. She waited. The humbled rat returned, making squeaky apologies, then scampered off at a reasonable pace. Tiyy followed in silence.

They descended a narrow stairwell, the nymph having to turn sideways in order to pass through it, then entered a large, low-ceilinged gallery and stopped. The sounds of dripping water echoed through the chamber, down long tunnels opening off of it. The rat glanced back at Tiyy, then scurried into the darkness and joined a crowd of red eyes, belonging to fourteen or more rats about twenty feet ahead.

The cluster of small red eyes took no notice of the nymph queen's arrival. They continued to stare up at something, or someone, unseen in the nearby darkness.

Tiyy's breathing raced. Holding the dagger of black light in her left hand, she dried the palm of her right on the hem of her short tunic, then gripped the handle tightly in it. She stepped across the floor, neatly avoiding fissures filled with gurgling water in the stone floor, and stopped behind the rats.

Differentiating between the hundred shades of black before her, the dark goddess saw the silhouette of a short-haired girl standing with her back to the rats, not six feet away. A misted haze blurred her shape, but there was no radiating aura of white light identifying her as the possessor of the jewels of the Goddess of Light, the White Veshta.

A twist of fear distorted the nymph's features, and she stepped silently between the motionless rats. The blade of black light trembled in her hand. Either it sensed some unseen danger or was unable to control its anticipation. Holding her breath, Tiyy crept within inches of the girl's back, so close she could smell sunshine in her hair.

The sound of running footsteps, far off in the tunnels, echoed through the room. The girl straightened. The haze about her thickened, blurring the tips of her hair and shoulders, and Tiyy withdrew an inch.

The girl emitted an attracting vitality stronger than any the dark goddess had seen or felt, but not in the manner of the White Veshta. The girl filled the air around her with the radiating strength of her Kaa, rather than glorious light, as if she were dispensing her spirit to whoever looked upon her, rather than dazzling them with shooting stars. The sounds of the footsteps came closer, and the haze thickened again. Tiyy could barely make out the girl's figure, then the scents of nutmeg and rosewood drifted past Tiyy's face. Lovely. Tempting. Airy fragrances floating about the edges of impossible dreams.

Infuriated, the nymph raised the dagger to strike. Her breasts swelled against her armor, their flesh rigid and hot, bursting with the lust with which she had designed the destructive fetish. The jewels waited only a breath away. Tiyy was now certain of it. They had altered in some way, but they were still within the girl, and the girl, Robin Lakehair, stood before her. Like a willing sacrifice, the White Veshta waited to have the nymph cut into her breast, and again steal the ensorcelled gems for her dark master.

Suddenly the girl's head turned sharply, and glowed with

light that washed over Tiyy's face, momentarily blinding her. The girl shrieked, frozen in place with fear, and the nymph's vision cleared enough to see diamonds glimmering in Robin Lakehair's eyes.

Snarling with rage and lust, Tiyy struck at them. Her arm banged painfully against an iron bar. Her wrist collided with another bar, shooting pain up her arm. Her fingers burned with rushing numbness, and the dagger flew free. Gasping with sudden terror, the nymph dropped to her knees, her hands groping for the clattering weapon. Seeing it, she thrust a hand at it, and the weapon rolled over the jagged lip of a fissure splitting the stone floor, splashed into the water filling it, and sank out of sight.

Panic-stricken, the nymph thrust an arm down into the wet gloom, and her fingertips glanced off the blade. She thrust deeper and her shoulder and cheek hit the sides of the narrow fissure, stopping her. A fingertip touched the dagger, but only served to drive it deeper into the depths.

Stunned, the nymph jumped back to her feet, holding her wet, numbed arm against her. Turning on the White Veshta, Tiyy shuddered with horror, took a loose step back.

The girl's aura, bright now, illuminated iron bars sealing off the arched doorway. Robin Lakehair, a woman now, stood precisely where Tiyy had stood when Izzam Ghapp had filled her body with his, driven her to erotic ecstasy. The design of her thaumaturgy had been perfect, too perfect. It had not only included her body, Izzam Ghapp's body and the castle's Kaa, but the bars that had separated them. And the girl's Kaa, the White Veshta's, had blinded the nymph to its fatal perfection.

The approaching footsteps suddenly grew louder, then torchlight spilled into the room beyond the iron-barred doorway, and two men strode in, a limping soldier with a heavily bandaged leg and the Dark One, Gath of Baal.

Robin Lakehair raced into the Barbarian's arms, gasping with relief and joy as a crowd of footsteps echoed out of a stairwell somewhere behind Tiyy.

The nymph backed hurriedly into shadows.

Torchlight spilled out of the stairwell into the room, then

torches appeared, held by the *bukko* of the Grillards, an old graybearded soldier, a red-cheeked mother of harlots, a thin boy with straight stiff hair, and a plain freckled girl. They rushed to the iron-barred doorway, shouting joyous greetings, and the Barbarian shouted in warning, pointing in Tiyy's direction.

Stopping short, the *bukko*'s group pulled away from the dark goddess, their weapons raised. The Barbarian took hold of the barred door, easily ripped its rusty body out of the old stone. He cast it aside, stepped through the opening with the wounded soldier beside him, his arm circling Robin Lakehair.

Seething with audible hate, Tiyy drew the tiny vermilion crossbow from its holster, and fired it at the Barbarian's handsome head. He blocked it easily with his battleaxe, and the nymph queen's feral eyes smoldered with frustration. For a brief moment, she studied the handsome couple, sensing the passion that bound them together, and saw that the nature of the White Veshta's power had been altered. Safe in the Barbarian's arms, the girl emitted no aura of any kind, gave no indication she possessed the sacred jewels. Tiyy did not understand how or why, but every sense in her demonic body told her that stealing the jewels would now be a thousand times more difficult.

The knowledge made her gut snarl, her body wanting to retch, and her voice uttered guttural sounds, frustration rendering her inarticulate. She had scarred her perfect breast and maimed her perfect hand for nothing.

Venting her rage, the nymph lifted her palms and black fog spewed from them into the room, filling it, until their torches were dim, orange glows forming a protective circle around the White Veshta. Every nerve and fiber within Tiyy wanted to throw her body at them and claw out their hearts. But she did not dare. She hurried through the darkness, fled up the stairwell by which the *bukko* had entered, and vanished.

Fifty-one

THE SILENT
TAMBOURINES

Dark night covered the castle when Tiyy emerged from one
of the many smoking fissures, zigzagging through the rubble
of the Stronghold. Soot smeared her face and hair. Burns
scorched her flesh and tunic, now ripped to threads. Her trea-
sured black armor, too hot to wear in the still smoldering
tunnels she had passed through, lay somewhere far below in
Whitetree's underworld. She cupped her right hand in her
left, and blood from the reopened stump of her severed finger
warmed her palm. Pain throbbed up her arm into the joint of
her elbow.

Dark figures moved furtively, silently through the smoking
rubble, searching, carrying bundles on their backs. Looters.
They no doubt came from the victorious rabble as well as
from the camp followers who had traveled with her army.

She glanced up at the looming Curtain Wall that had helped
defeat her, and a satisfied smile crept into her sassy, heart-
shaped face.

A bright, flickering glow, cast by a dozen or more fires,
rose above the dark wall. The rabble, fearing the ensorcelled
lime trees, had no doubt set fire to each of them, as well as
to the natural afterbirth of battle. Thick, twisted plumes of
smoke rose above the wall, black against the orange glow,
and the stench of burning flesh hung heavily on the air. They
burned their dead, and the weeping moans of the bereaved
was the night's only song.

In a significant way, Tiyy had served her lord, the Master of Darkness. Drum and flute no longer sang. The tambourines were silent.

She made her way through the rubble, stole a horse tied up to a bush outside the wall, and rode down the cliffs, across a bridge of straw and planks laid by her sappers. Crossing the valley, she saw no trace of her army except for abandoned embankments, palisade walls and siege engines. Reaching her camp, she found it plundered. Deserted. Her tent lay in a heap, littered with her emptied jewel boxes and trunks.

Dismounting, she hauled the remnant of her tent aside, exposing the dirt underneath. It had been dug up. The metal box, containing her last vials of the sacred Nagraa, had been stolen.

The nymph barely frowned. Her quick, uncompromising mind, tempered by her ageless wisdom, instantly accepted the brutal facts of her situation. She was destitute. She had no priesthood, no demon spawn, no Nagraa to make them with. She was alone in the world, with neither servant, friend or slave, without a single person who would recognize her for who she was. But it was a position she had faced before.

She mounted the horse, and walked it up into the shadowed forest without plan or direction, nor food or silver. With nothing but her slightly flawed perfection and eternal youth.

Fifty-two
THE FORMULA

Billbarr, skipping and dashing nervously, led Gath through the blackened, smoldering lime trees that had shaded the Water Court for hundreds of years. They would no longer hide the sun any more than they now hid the star-spattered night sky. Plumes of smoke rose from their dark stumps and trailed up into the looming darkness, like ghostly dancers moving to the rhythm of the all-encompassing silence.

Shuddering, the boy stopped and waited for the Barbarian. The huge warrior moved slowly, not because of the bandages binding ankles, knees, waist and wrists, but because of a calm that now pervaded him. In the pit of battle, Gath had spoken freely, taken command, even laughed. Now he was once more the private man of sparse words.

As Gath neared him, Billbarr hurried under a spray of skeletal branches, stopped short and pointed up at a black shape dangling from the tip of a burnt-out branch about fifteen feet above the ground.

"There," he whispered, as Gath stopped behind him. "They were afraid to remove it when they set fire to the tree."

Gath kicked the tree and the object fell away amid a flurry of ashes, hit the ground with a large clang, shedding a cluster of dead leaves and a coat of sooty dust. The horned helmet.

"Thank you," the Barbarian said with profound gratitude, and picked the headpiece up.

"I put your axe in the bukko's wagon."

Gath glanced at Brown John's wagon, parked with several

other Grillard wagons at the edge of the courtyard, and smiled
at Billbarr. "Thank you again."

The boy beamed. "I'll go get it."

"That's all right," the Barbarian said quietly. "I don't need
it now."

As if to demonstrate his point, the Barbarian turned the
helmet upside down and dumped the ashes of Izzam Ghapp's
skull on the ground at the boy's feet. Shuddering, Billbarr
took a step back, his eyes on the charred bones as he spoke.

"Weren't you afraid that somebody would steal it, leaving
it here all this time?"

"No," the Barbarian replied, wiping the helmet off on the
tunic Jarl Roundell had given him. "There was much to do,
and after today I was certain no one would touch it."

The boy laughed with nervous agreement. "I sure wasn't
going to touch it! At least not without you telling me to."

The Barbarian studied the boy, as if intending to let him
touch the headpiece. But he did not. He buckled it to his hip
instead, glancing around the empty, silent courtyard. Then
he nodded at the boy, instructing Billbarr to follow him, and
moved around the tree. Reaching the other side, the pair stood
in the moonlight, facing the well about twenty feet off.

Brown John sat tiredly on the lip of the well, watching Doll
Harl come through the gate from the Market Court. The survivors had laid their camps there, some said out of familiarity
and others because it had been the site of their victory, and
the sounds of weeping and pained groans followed Doll. She
carried a bowl of porridge and a knowing smile to the *bukko*,
gave him both, then sat down on a spill of pillows spread
over a faded carpet in front of him. There she watched him
eat.

"Do you know who that man is?" Gath asked.

"Oh, yes," replied Billbarr. "That's the bukko you told
Fleka and me about, Brown John." He hesitated, then added,
"He's not at all what I expected. I didn't even believe it at
first, when the Master-at-Arms told me who he was. But I
like his wagon, even though he doesn't take very good care
of it."

Gath looked down at Billbarr, reappraising the boy with

shadowed eyes. "So, you have become a critic of your elders?"

Billbarr blushed with bright shame. "I didn't mean to criticize," he replied apologetically. "I . . . I know I have a lot to learn."

"Yes," Gath said. "You have a lot to learn. Now go over there, sit at his feet and grow."

"Now? But I'd rather be with you tonight. I don't want to be alone."

"You won't be. Now go. Sit and learn." He smiled. "Tomorrow we will go into the forest and find your black bear."

Beaming with new excitement, Billbarr nodded obediently, and kept on nodding as he strolled shyly toward the well. Casting a glance back over his shoulder, he watched the Barbarian cross the yard and go out the gate, then stopped, facing the well. The old man was frowning at him.

"Do you want something, boy?" the *bukko* demanded, his tangled white eyebrows arcing theatrically over his cold brown eyes.

"Gath . . . your friend," Billbarr said weakly. "He . . ."

"Speak up!" the *bukko* snapped. "Don't mumble."

Billbarr nodded. "Gath of Baal, he said to come over here and, uh, stay with you."

"Then sit down, you handsome little darling," Doll said, patting a pillow, "and listen to this wise old man's marvelous lies. Every hundred years or so, according to the rumors, there are at least five or six words of truth in them worth remembering, providing, of course, that the listener is a child." Standing, she pushed a pillow at Billbarr and winked. "Here, get comfortable. I'll be right back."

She crossed to the faded red wagon, climbed in and came back out with a yellow wooden bowl and spoon. Stepping up to the scowling *bukko*, she plucked the bowl of porridge out of his hands.

"What are you doing?" Brown John growled.

"Little boys need to eat too, old man," she said firmly, pouring half the porridge into the yellow bowl.

"Would you stop calling me that," the old man mumbled at her. "I am through with being old. Finished."

"That," Doll said, handing the yellow bowl and spoon to Billbarr, "is more than welcome news."

Sitting down beside Billbarr, Doll Harl gave the boy another wink. This one was so bright and playful it made her orchid cheeks seem pale, and he stared at her with delight, forgetting to eat. She pushed the bowl at him, and he quickly spooned the hot food into his mouth as she turned to the *bukko*.

"Now, old man, what lie is it you want to tell me? I can't stay long."

"You prefer mercenaries to bukkos now, is that it?"

"I have always preferred them," she said. "Your pride just wouldn't let you admit it. Besides, tonight I have good reason. Now, are you going to tell me or not?"

Brown John wrinkled his nose, set his bowl aside with a great show of contemplation. Then he leaned forward, folding his arms and resting his elbows on his bony knees, and glared directly at Billbarr. "You will not interrupt. Not a word."

Billbarr nodded repeatedly. "Yes. Yes."

"I said, not one word," the *bukko* snapped.

Billbarr nodded again, and went back to his porridge, his eyes on the suddenly frightening old man.

The *bukko*, tilting his head slightly, turned slowly to Doll Harl. He stared at her, like she was a hole in desperate need of filling, then suddenly smiled with such delight that it shocked the boy.

"Well," Doll said, returning the *bukko*'s smile, "I like your opening, anyway."

The old man chuckled and played with his fingers, as if they were a troupe of extraordinary acrobats. Then he looked at Doll Harl. "You still don't believe Robin is the goddess, do you, Doll?"

"I'll believe whatever you want me to believe, Brown," Doll said sarcastically, "but only if you'll get on with it. Why? Did you find that precious formula you were looking for?"

"I did," he answered quietly, and moisture gathered on the lids of his eyes.

"You're serious, aren't you," she whispered.

The old man nodded, and an intimacy of such tenderness passed between them that the boy felt he should look the other way. But he did not. He leaned closer and watched every movement as Doll put her hands on top of the *bukko*'s.

"I'm glad you found it, Brown," she whispered, "if that's what you truly wanted."

"I did," he whispered, "more than anything I've ever wanted before."

"Then it says what you thought it would?"

"No," he said, chuckling at himself. "Not one word."

"Good," Doll said. "It's about time you grew out of this goddess business."

"Don't get ahead of me," he said, scowling again. "She's the goddess, all right! Just like I told you. But, well, I figured everything wrong, her theology, her powers, particularly her resurrection. You won't believe the formula, Doll, you just aren't going to believe it."

"You're right," she said, "so there's no point in listening."

She started to rise and he put a hand on her shoulder. "Slow down, you've got time." He grinned, pausing theatrically, then looked from side to side, as if a host of spies lurked in the shadows, and whispered, "The essential ingredients are—" He stopped short, looking from side to side again and drawing a groan of exasperation from Doll, then added, "*Chums, Up by Lamplight*, and 'The Women of Boo Bah Ben.' "

She looked at him, dumbfounded. "What are you talking about?"

"Magic!" he exclaimed, lifting his hands. "The instruments of sorcery by which Robin Lakehair will display her divinity to the world."

" 'The Women of Boo Bah Ben'?" Doll laughed riotously. "That's nothing but a bawdy song."

"True enough," he agreed. "But it seems that long before it became the song we all know, it was a tale! A history. And within that history lies the secret of the White Veshta. It is all written here, Doll." He tapped a small red-leather tube dangling from his belt. "Every word is written on the scroll I rescued from the library when it burned. No, that's a lie! Surim, the Great Scribe, rescued it, and gave it to me to keep for posterity."

She groaned. "I suppose you're going to read it to me? Is that it? You expect me to sit here and listen to your outrageous twaddle at a time like this?"

"I'll just tell it to you," he said, holding her down with a quick hand.

"Damn you, Brown," she growled. "I—"

"It'll only take a minute."

"All right," she said, surrendering, and gave Billbarr a wink.

The *bukko* looked off at the ruins. "It seems," he said, "that long, long ago, during the ancient days, when all men still wore furs and ate with their hands, that there was, in fact, a village called Boo Bah Ben." He looked back at Doll. "And this village was, in fact, just as the song says, populated by particularly robust, witty and beautiful women of all ages. The scroll says that all the living that wife and harlot, vixen and virgin, and mother, nymph, crone and saint can engage in filled the daily lives of the women of Boo Bah Ben. Neither death, plague, war or nature's wrath could drive their hunger for life from their bountiful breasts."

"Bountiful?" Doll raised an eyebrow.

"I elaborate slightly," he admitted. "In any event, as everyone knows, the ancient days were a time of constant wars, and warlords, outlaw bands and troops of mercenaries pillaged the land almost at will. Consequently, the village of Boo Bah Ben, residing on a road through which the raiders frequently passed, was regularly plundered and ravaged. And during one particularly brutal year, the depredations occurred so frequently that the sons, husbands and fathers of Boo Bah Ben were nearly all killed.

"It was during that year that a recently widowed young woman did a very unusual thing. Seeing another band of raiders approaching her village, and knowing that another massacre was inevitable, she decided that it was up to her save her village and bring back the days of wit and light and flowers so precious to it. So, she tossed off her gowns of mourning black, dressed in her brightest clothing, took her tambourine to the village well, and waited there to greet the raiders. She beseeched the other women to do the same, but the only member of the village who accompanied her was the village fool.

"When the marauders approached the well they were skeptical of the young widow's intentions. But, being weary and wounded from their wars, they quickly found her joyous songs and tantalizing bawdy manner, as well as the fool's humorous behavior, more than a welcome relief. So they postponed their plundering for a day, and partook of the food, songs, laughter and beauty that the young woman so generously offered them."

"Must have been a strong lass," Doll said.

"Both of body and heart," the *bukko* agreed. "In any event, seeing this, the other women of the village realized that the young widow's plot had great merit. So they compelled their surviving men to hide, then put on their festive best, gathered up their tambourines, flutes and drums, and that night took themselves, and their grown daughters as well, to the well and joined this celebration of life."

"And cuckolded their husbands?" Doll interrupted skeptically.

"Some of them, I am sure," Brown John continued. "And laughed, sang and danced, offering the raiders everything that Boo Bah Ben has become famous for."

"I'm glad to hear," Doll muttered, "that at least somebody has written a decent history about harlots."

"Harlots, yes," Brown John declared, "but women first. You see," he lowered his voice, "some of these women, both young and old, being so full of unbounded life, paid a very dear price." He looked off and nodded soberly, as if with great understanding, then looked directly into her eyes. "They fell in love, Doll, and when it came time for the men, who they had given their hearts to, to ride off and leave them behind, their hearts broke. And some of the bandits, being only men, took similar afflictions away with them."

Doll smiled at him. "You are a romantic old fool, aren't you?"

"It's a gift," Brown John replied. "In any event, such a good time was had by all that the raiders forgot all about sacking Boo Bah Ben. And when they departed, a few even remained behind to fill the places of the men other men like them had killed.

"It was in this manner that the tradition, celebrated by the song we all know, began. Every time raiders approached the village, the women went to the well, greeted their male enemies and seduced them with food and flowers, with tambourines and drums and with their bodies and hearts. In this manner they continued to find men to serve Boo Bah Ben in the capacity of fathers, lovers and all other occupations natural to the male, including fools."

"Wonderful," Doll said sarcastically. "So what's all this got to do with the White Veshta?"

"Well," the *bukko* said thoughtfully, "it seems that sometime later, during a period of terrible drought and plague as well as war, Boo Bah Ben suffered more terribly than ever before, and no band of outlaws or any traveler at all passed its way. Therefore, the audacious young widow did something even more extraordinary. She took several fools and a group of the more adventurous women on the road and traveled with them to nearby villages, entertaining their neighbors in the manner they had entertained the marauders, and with like results."

Doll laughed mockingly, but the *bukko* took no offense. Smiling warmly, he shook his head.

"Do not laugh, Doll. That is how the likes of you and me began." She quieted and he nodded. "Yes, those women and the village fools were the first minstrels. The first traveling players. The first to know the travails and joys of serving the open road, the first to tell the tales of the sad songs, the laughing songs, the love songs."

Silence passed between them as Doll studied the old man. Then she asked quietly, "Truly, Brown? This is written?"

"Truly."

"All right," she said forcefully. "I guess it all had to start somewhere. But that still doesn't make your precious Robin Lakehair a goddess! Or anyone else, for that matter!''

"I'm getting to that," the *bukko* murmured. Again he looked off at the ruins, then down at the well. "Look around you, Doll, carefully. See how old these stones are? How ancient?''

"I see," she said belligerently.

"No you don't," he said, looking at her. "You don't see at all, or you would know that this well I sit on is the well where, during those days long, long ago, the audacious young widow first danced and banged her tambourine.''

"Boo Bah Ben!" Billbarr gasped.

Brown John nodded. "Boo Bah Ben. That was the rock's name, before they built the castle and called it Whitetree. And, just as the legend says, the scroll says it is here that the goddess will be reborn. You see, Doll," he said, the teacher in him showing, "it was when the bold, beautiful young widow first went to the well that the unnamed powers who rule all things decided, in their own perverse way, to grant her divine powers, and made her the first White Veshta.''

"A Goddess of Light," Doll scoffed, "with wooden beads for jewels instead of diamonds.''

"Precisely," the *bukko* proclaimed. "That is the formula's secret. The songs and tales, Doll Harl, and the tambourines and drums, and the baubles and bangles of our trade, all these things with which we create dreams and laughter, were not born of the jewels of the goddess as we have believed. It was the other way around. The jewels were born of the songs that broke in that young widow's heart, born of the drum and tambourine.''

"That makes no sense," Doll said. "Where's the magic then? The jewels?''

"They are the hope and beauty and joy in life she chooses to give away. But they only took form when someone surrendered to that joy.''

"I see," Billbarr said excitedly. "When she danced, when she sang.''

"Yes," the *bukko* said gravely, "but sometimes all it took was her smile.''

"A smile?" Doll said, half-laughing. "Wonderful. But what about all these jewels you claimed to have stolen from Pyram? Where are they now? How did the Master of Darkness collect them in the first place? And I thought you said they were inside Robin someplace?" She shook her head. "You don't make sense, Brown."

"It makes perfect sense," the *bukko* snapped, temper coloring his cheeks. "What do you want me to do, solve all the mysteries for you in one tale? I don't know how the Master of Darkness collected them or gave them to Tiyy." He tapped the red tube. "That part's not recorded on this scroll. But I know this: Robin is the goddess, and she's going to be resurrected right here, in Whitetree, in the old village of Boo Bah Ben."

"I hope you'll send me an invitation." Doll said sarcastically.

Brown John grumbled, "I would, but I won't know when it's going to happen. You can't always see it. When the owner of the jewels controls them, the jewels vanish, and only appear when she gives them away."

"Oh, that's a perfect theology, Brown." Doll laughed again. "Sheer genius. Now Robin doesn't have to make a single display of light to prove her deity? And you, being her high priest, don't have to write her prayers, assemble a priesthood, or build her a temple? You don't have to do a thing. Very convenient, Brown, very convenient."

"You won't ever learn, will you, Doll?" he blustered. "Not even when it's blatantly obvious. The open road is her temple! Every clown, acrobat and dancing girl make up her clergy! Every song and joke is a prayer."

"Including the pratfalls, I suppose?"

"Of course," he said indignantly. "Most of all the pratfalls."

"I see. So I suppose your ridiculous behavior, since your arrival here in Whitetree, being a perfect fool's behavior, qualifies as some form of worship."

"That's not the point!" he snarled. "I made a mistake, that's all."

"Not just one, Brown!" she exclaimed, rising. "You made

them in bunches, and you're going to keep on making them if you believe one word of this rot.''

He glared at her, then said it again, "You'll never learn, will you?''

She shook her head, "Never." She turned to Billbarr and added, "Watch yourself, lad, he can be contagious," then winked and went back through the gate into the Market Court.

The *bukko* did not watch her leave. He sat perfectly still, glaring at his hands. Then, without looking at Billbarr, he said, "Are you still here?''

The boy nodded rapidly. "Gath told me to stay with you.''

"And you do what he tells you?'' Billbarr nodded, and Brown John looked at him. "Well, suit yourself. I'm going to bed.''

The old *bukko* stood up, yawned, then crossed to the red wagon and mounted the steps to the door. There he yawned again, making a show of it, opened the door and stepped into the glow of candlelight within. He sighed in the doorway, scratching his back, then moved out of sight, leaving the door open so that the candlelight spilled invitingly on the ground outside.

Billbarr stared at it forlornly and looked at his own hands, having nothing else to do. Suddenly he looked back at the candlelight and, smiling with understanding, jumped up, crossed quickly to the wagon and climbed inside, closing the door behind him.

Fifty-three

THE JEWELS

Gath strolled alongside the mounds of rubble heaped at the eastern side of the Market Court.

Just before sundown, the entire eastern wall of the lower yards and southeast corner of the castle had caved in under the continuing pressure of the rushing water. As a result, the water had again been diverted, and now the river once more flowed outside the castle.

Stopping, the Barbarian listened to the rushing water, strangely moved by its song, then moved on.

Meeting a work crew that Jarl Roundell had sent out to make certain the river would cause no more problems, the Barbarian stopped and chatted with them in the moonlight.

Bone, Dirken and Graybeard were among them. They assured him that the river was safe, that sentries had been posted and that the camp was secure.

Feeling the ease of relaxation enter his tired, mauled body, the first since he, Billbarr and Fleka had set forth from Pinwheel Crossing, Gath returned with the others to the camp on the opposite side of the yard. There they went their separate ways, and Gath passed through small fires glowing in the middle of huddled bodies, heading for the huge bonfire blazing at the center of the camp.

Around it, the rabble camped in the open. They huddled close together for reassurance, many of the women rocking steadily, their badly wounded lovers and husbands cradled in their arms.

Nearing the bonfire, the Barbarian paused, his eyes searching the camps ringing the bonfire.

Jarl Roundell's battle-worn men-at-arms occupied the camp just outside a ring of open ground circling the fire. They shared it with Doll Harl's Amazons, her harlots and many of the beauties rescued from the Stronghold.

Jarl camped with his men, sitting with his back against an old saddle. His face was pale, and his leg inflamed around the large bandage covering his thigh. Doll, cradled between his legs, was filling two mugs from an amphora of wine. Finished, she passed the jar to Robin and Fleka, camped on their left, and Robin filled three cups as Fleka held them. The Grillards occupied blankets laid beside and behind the two women. Finished, Robin passed the jar to the next in line, then set one of the mugs down beside an empty blanket spread over a saddle resting beside her. All this was done in silence, a silence that spread like a pall to the far corners of the castle.

Gath stepped around the bonfire and Robin, seeing him, sighed quietly with relief, her eyes and hands guiding him to the empty blanket at her side. He sprawled on it, his back against the saddle, and took hold of the mug she offered him, so that their hands touched, their eyes met.

"I'm glad you're back," she said, her simple words rent with complex emotions.

His shadowed eyes agreed warmly. "Don't worry," he said with confidence born of experience, "it's over now."

Reassured, she smiled, and he turned to Roundell, lifting his cup. The Master-at-Arms broadened his grin and vigorously clanged his cup against the Barbarian's.

"It's about time you relaxed, friend," Roundell said heartily. They emptied their cups, then shared a knowing smile as he added, "Of course, I'd be out looking for someone to hit myself, if I could stand up."

The Barbarian chuckled and winked at Doll. "The way I see it, you're safer standing up than lying down."

Jarl laughed out loud, the contagious, raucous laughter of the strong, short and hard and heady with life. The Barbarian laughed with him, the knowledge that the fight was finished demanding expression, and the men-at-arms joined in.

Then silence resumed command of the night, and Gath glanced at the bloody wound in the mercenary's leg, looked at Doll.

"His whole leg's hot," Doll said, her tone hiding nothing. "The wound should be bled."

"Don't listen to her," Roundell grumbled. "She doesn't know what she's talking about."

Doll ignored him, her eyes pleading with Gath for help, and the Barbarian turned to Robin.

There was no hope in Robin's eyes. "I've tried everything," she whispered, so Roundell could not hear.

Gath thought about that, nodded reassuringly at Robin, and lay back against the saddle. He sipped from his mug, then glanced casually at Doll.

"Leave it alone for now," he said, his eyes sharing an understanding with Doll's. "If it gets worse, I'll sit on him and you can do whatever you have to."

"That's fine with me," Roundell blustered. "But I decide when it's worse!"

"We'll argue that later," Gath said. "Right now I want to drink."

Gath and Roundell banged their mugs again and drank. Robin put a comforting hand on Doll's knee and the older woman, struggling to hold herself together, smiled with her round apple-red cheeks.

Jarl Roundell, chuckling, set his mug down, reached for Doll with both arms, and she came into them, nestling her head against his chest. Gath watched them, and gently pulled Robin close, held her trembling body against his, hungry to feel the rush of life inside her flow through him. She looked up at him, a little surprised, and he pressed her head against his shoulder.

A moment passed, then she whispered, "I hate it when it's so quiet. It's like we didn't win at all. As if there was no point in fighting, even for our lives."

"You don't believe that," Gath said.

"No," she replied softly, "but it just feels that way."

He ran his fingers through her short curls, touched her cheek and shoulder, and the warmth of her made him shudder, as it drove the chill of death that dwelled so naturally within him away. A moment passed before he spoke.

"Dance for us," he said. "Sing."

"Now?" she asked, her tone incredulous.

"Now," he answered.

Raising her head, Robin looked into his eyes, the trace of a frown creasing her smooth brow. She glanced across the fire at the rocking women and shadowed, moaning bodies they cradled in their arms.

"But everyone's worn out, and hurt," she said, looking back at Gath. "They don't want to watch anyone dance."

"I do," the Barbarian said.

"And so do I," Roundell said behind his pale smile. "I'd even dance with you, if this leg of mine would cooperate."

"Go ahead, lass," Doll said encouragingly. "They've earned at least that." Robin hesitated, and the older woman, smiling with a wisdom a hundred times her age, added, "Go on, the other girls will join in. You'll see."

Robin looked at Fleka. "You'll dance with me?"

"Oh, yes," Fleka said, beaming with anticipation. "But you go first! Show me what to do."

Gath took hold of Robin's elbow and pushed her to her feet. She looked down at him soberly, then shrugged and unbuckled her belt. Dropping it to her feet, she fluffed her hair and stepped across the ring of open ground to the fire. Turning, she looked at the ground thoughtfully, as the sheets of red and yellow flames danced behind her, then looked up at Doll.

"I don't know what to do. A lullaby? Something happy?"

"Something happy," Roundell answered. "And loud."

"All right." Robin looked from Doll to Fleka. "But what? *Chums? Up by Lamplight?*"

"Anything," Fleka said. "Here."

Pulling a tambourine from under her blankets, Fleka tossed it, jangling on the silence, toward Robin. Robin caught it deftly so that it made no sound at all. Then she shook it lightly and smiled, pleased by its gay song, and throughout the camp heads lifted, eyes found her. Suddenly she silenced the bangles with her hand and held perfectly still, listening as a bright whistle came from somewhere at the rear of the camp. A lively, bawdy air.

"That's it," Doll said. "Do that one."

"But," Robin blushed, "but it's so, you know, so—"

"Do it! Do it!" Fleka pleaded, clapping in time with the bawdy whistling.

"All right," Robin said, putting her suddenly brazen eyes on Gath. "Watch out!"

Gath, Roundell, Doll, Fleka and those around them chuckled with anticipation.

Robin cocked a hip, pushed her tunic down over her bare shoulders and pulled up her skirt, holding it in her fist at her hip. With a slow beat, she tapped the instrument against her naked thigh, the rhythmic jangle singing with the whistling.

Instantly faces leaned forward out of the surrounding camps into the firelight. Curious. Expectant.

As if feeling their eyes, Robin doubled the beat, banging the tambourine up her leg. Chuckles and sounds of murmured approval swept out of the camp toward her, and she again quickened the beat, snapping her hip against the drum of the tambourine, faster and faster, and the whistling followed.

With a rush of light, airy laughter, the crowd came alive, and here and there hands began to clap in time. More smiling faces lifted into the light. A drum began to beat somewhere, then another drum and a tambourine.

Robin, controlled by the music, danced a simple little jig, then kicked off her sandals and whirled around the bonfire, every so often grinding her hips to the sudden thump of half a dozen drums.

Men howled with delight. Women rose to their knees, clapping in time, and began to hum the raucous melody.

Robin, whirling, extended her hand to Fleka, and the girl jumped up, joined her, her blouse already shoved low enough for Gath to count every freckle. The young woman and girl linked arms, did a little jig, then whirled and ground their hips together, as drums thundered approval. They whirled again, as throughout the camp tambourines and drums were hurried out of the hiding places, adding their music to the crescendo of joy. Then flutes and whistles joined it and a child, an infant girl, waddled forward to join the dance.

Robin and Fleka picked her up, dancing with her, and children scampered forward from all directions, boys and girls alike. They linked arms with Robin, Fleka and the little girl, forming a steadily expanding circle. Then grown women rose from beside their men, and flowed like joyous birds into the dance, suddenly sporting bits of bright color on their earlobes, around their wrists and waists.

Roundell grinned at Gath. "This is the best idea you've had, friend."

Gath laughed in agreement, and Jarl and Doll joined him.

The circle grew and grew, expanding throughout the camp, as eyes flirted and faces laughed. Sumptuous, wild laughter. Bold, amorous flirtation. And still the circle grew, a wild frenzy of whirling bodies. Ancient. Right. The circle of life.

Doll laughed and clapped. Then she sobered slightly and turned in Roundell's arms, wiped the sweat from his flushed, smiling cheeks with a soft cloth.

"Don't you think you'd better get some sleep?" she asked. "This could get you all stirred up."

"I'm counting on that," he said, winking at her.

She laughed lightly and kissed his moist lips, then looked over a shoulder at Robin as she whirled by. "She is beautiful, isn't she?"

"Yes," he said, "she surely is."

Doll looked into his eyes reproachfully. "I suppose you think she's a goddess too?"

He shook his head. "I don't believe in that hocus-pocus." He looked back at Robin. "But she does have some pretty tricks, and if there really is such a thing as a Goddess of Light, well," he sobered, "that's what she ought to look like."

Doll smiled sardonically, but said nothing. She touched his forehead with her fingertips. His flesh was on fire. To hide her gasp of fear, she bit her lip, hugged him tight. But her tremble of desperation gave her away, and he looked down at her, shook her a little.

"Hey! What's all this about?" he demanded quietly.

She looked up aggressively, hiding her emotion, and mocked him with her eyes. "Men, that's what it's about. You, all of you, you get so worked up about nothing. There are pretty girls all over the world."

"Thank the gods for that," he said, his eyes laughing at her.

Unable to resist his joy, Doll laughed, then kissed him on the nose. "You silly goat. I suppose you really think you saw her jewels too? Saw her just spilling over with diamonds and light?"

"Well," he said matter-of-factly, "I'm no expert, but they looked like diamonds to me."

She shook her head. "You're hopeless." She lay her head gently against his chest, her arms cradling him, her fingers gathered in his hair at the back of his head, holding on to each precious moment, and whispered, "I suppose you see them now?"

He did not answer. Moments passed, and she looked up at him. He stared at the dancing Robin Lakehair with a calm she had never seen in him before, a contentment unlike anything she had ever felt. Then he nodded, and whispered, "They are beautiful, aren't they?"

Hiding her chuckle, Doll glanced back at the whirling circle of dancers. Seeing nothing but a flush of joy and beads of sweat on Robin's face, she muttered sarcastically, "Yes, they're incredible all right. I don't know how she can dance with all those jewels weighing her down."

She couldn't hold back a short mocking laugh, then turned, lifting her eyes to his, and gasped quietly.

Jarl Roundell's eyes were bright, glassy reflections of Robin Lakehair as she danced and whirled before the soaring red flames, her body and limbs laced with a garment of flashing diamonds, shooting stars.

Not noticing her reaction, Roundell suddenly sank back tiredly and sighed, closing his eyes. Then he opened them and looked at Doll.

"Did I tell you," he asked, his voice suddenly hoarse and weak, "that she gave me one? A diamond?"

She shook her head and kissed his cheek, holding him tight. "No, you didn't tell me," she whispered, her voice more sober and honest than it had been since childhood, "but I'm sure she did."

He nodded, once, then stopped and she held on to him tightly, praying he would move again. He did not. His life had drained out of him, escaped into the night.

Gath reached out and touched Doll's sobbing shoulder, and she looked up. Her eyes emptied tears across her bright cheeks, suddenly more vulnerable than he had ever seen them before. But she shook her head firmly. "No. Don't take him. Let me hold him for a while longer."

The Barbarian nodded and stood. A moment passed as he watched Robin continue to lead the dancing, then he made his way through the camp and passed through the gate to the Water Court. Light still glowed in the ground-floor room of Brown John's wagon. He went over to it, glanced past it at the circling dancers, then opened the door and entered.

At the far end of the room, a candle flickered on a night-stand, casting a yellow glow over the arm of Billbarr, dangling from the upper bunk where he slept. Brown John sat with his knees up on the lower bunk, his head poised beside the open window. Through it, Gath could see Robin and the dancers swirling around the flaming bonfire, directly below. The *bukko* was whistling.

Gath pulled up a stool, and sat down, propping his feet on the end of the lower bunk. Brown jiggled slightly at the impact, stopped whistling and put his boyish grin on the Barbarian. They shared that glance of understanding only given to those who share the endless trail of chance and adventure, then the old man resumed whistling his favorite tune.

The Women of Boo Bah Ben.

THE BEST IN FANTASY

THE BEST IN SCIENCE FICTION

THE TOR DOUBLES

Two complete short science fiction novels in one volume!